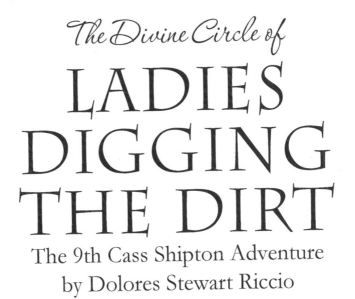

The Divine Circle of

LADIES
DIGGING
THE DIRT

The 9th Cass Shipton Adventure
by Dolores Stewart Riccio

W9-AHP-512

ISBN: 148119321X
ISBN-13:9781481193214

Printed by CreateSpace, An Amazon.com Company,
Charleston, SC.

Also by *Dolores Stewart Riccio*

SPIRIT

CIRCLE OF FIVE

CHARMED CIRCLE

THE DIVINE CIRCLE OF LADIES MAKING MISCHIEF

THE DIVINE CIRCLE OF LADIES COURTING TROUBLE

THE DIVINE CIRCLE OF LADIES PLAYING WITH FIRE

THE DIVINE CIRCLE OF LADIES ROCKING THE BOAT

THE DIVINE CIRCLE OF LADIES TIPPING THE SCALES

THE DIVINE CIRCLE OF LADIES PAINTING THE TOWN

Dedication

To the one whose absence is ever-present…
love forever

Acknowledgements

It's high time I acknowledged the friends and relatives who have unwittingly given me so many great lines of dialogue and philosophy over the years. Possibly you didn't realize that some part of my writer's brain was recording every word, and later those ideas would appear as if by magic in the conversations and beliefs of my fictional ladies. Thanks for the wit, wisdom, and occasional wild ideas.

Heartfelt thanks, too, to my indefatigable proofreaders and technical advisors: Anna Morin, Lucy-Marie Sanel, Joan Bingham, and Don Bingham.

Bright blessings to all friends of the Circle, the readers who inspire me to keep writing with their kind comments and encouragement.

A Note to the Reader

This is a work of fiction. The characters, dialogue, events, businesses, love affairs, and criminal activities are products of my imagination. Although I've researched the traditional meanings and uses of herbs mentioned in the Circle books, their efficacy remains in the realm of folklore. Magic spells and love potions from the Ladies' grimoires, however, have been totally invented by me. (In other words, *do not try this at home.*)

Plymouth, Massachusetts, is a real place, as is Salem, which features largely in this adventure, but many of the streets, locales, businesses, and shops are my creations. The history of Sarah Morse, accused and executed as a witch in the 17th century, is fictional but inspired by actual historical events.

Greenpeace is a true crusading organization which has been involved in some of the issues described, but the Greenpeace ship *Gaia* and its misadventures are fictional.

Recipes for dishes enjoyed by the Circle may have been taken from actual kitchens, probably my own.

In a series, families keep growing, changing, and becoming more complex with time, so that even the author has to keep copious notes. For my ninth *Circle* book, therefore, I'm including a cast of primary characters and their families, to be consulted when confusion reigns. You will find it at the back of this book, along with a few recipes from the Circle.

DSR

Magic is the projection of natural energies to produce needed effects…Contrary to popular belief, magic isn't supernatural. True, it is an occult (hidden) practice steeped in millennia of secrecy, slander and misinformation, but it is a natural practice utilizing genuine powers that haven't yet been discovered or labeled by science.
Scott Cunningham

…no two beings sense the universe in the same way…we all live in different universes. Remember your universe depends upon your senses and how you classify them. ..if you change your metapattern, then you also move to a different universe.
R. E. I. Bonewits, *Real Magic*, "The Law of Infinite Universes."

We've all been deceived. Our perceptions of time and space have led us astray. Much of what we thought we knew about our universe— that the past has already happened and the future is yet to be, that space is just an empty void, that our universe is the only universe that exists—just might be wrong.
Brian Greene in *The Fabric of the Cosmos*, PBS

Believing is seeing.
Fiona MacDonald Ritchie

CHAPTER ONE

What is so rare as a day in June?
Then, if ever, come perfect days…

– James Russell Lowell

When my cell rang that afternoon in June, I was scavenging for kelp and rockweed on the beach. Without my wireless phone, I would have been entirely unreachable.

Which made me wonder: how did women like us keep in touch in the old days? Telepathy, scrying, clairvoyance, and even messenger owls aren't the most reliable forms of communication. I can speak especially to clairvoyance, which is my particular talent (or curse), providing me with tantalizing pieces of a puzzle but rarely the whole picture. A glimpse of danger is, after all, a matter of interpretation; that's the tricky part. And I've had plenty of psychic warnings to interpret since it became my kismet or karma a few years ago to be involved in crime-solving.

So here it was, a dazzling, heart-lifting June day. I'd figured that a tramp on the seashore was just what I needed to calm my nerves which had been repeatedly assaulted by "third eye" images of a shadowy person in a tree aiming a rifle. Only I didn't know *who, where, or when.* It was enough to make me extremely edgy about taking my foraging basket to Jenkins Park as I usually did. Hence, the beach.

Scruffy and his offspring Raffles, my two canine companions, were overjoyed to chase seagulls and cool their paws in the waves. *A good run, that's what we need, Toots. Keeps our muscles strong and our reflexes keen. Gotta guard our place from strangers and package-throwing guys in vans. Way to go—no leashes!* Scruffy made his point with a bold alpha-dog stare and a playful wiggle of his rear end.

No leashes! No leashes! Raffles always echoed his sire. My dogs don't speak aloud, so I'm told, but somehow I always seem to hear them clearly, which can be disconcerting to others.

"Hey, I didn't make the leash laws, guys. Now, quiet down you two. I'm trying to hear."

"Is there someone there with you, or are you talking to your dogs again?" It was Heather Devlin calling from Salem, where she had got herself involved in the archeological excavation at a so-called "witch house." Accused of spectral torture by her niece Patience Blessing, Sarah Morse had been tried, convicted, and executed by hanging during Salem's 17th century witch hunt. The Morse family had owned many acres of fine farmland (which was later auctioned off cheap and scooped up by the Blessings). Recently, evidence of an earlier American Indian village had been unearthed on this historic property. The Peabody Essex Museum and the Massachusetts Archaeology Society had organized a dig at the site, where trained archaeologists worked with eager students to reveal relics of its pre-European past. So far, only broken peace pipes and shards of pottery had been found in the test pits. Nevertheless, work had continued through spring and summer with the persistent enthusiasm and painstaking efficiency of the archaeological ethic.

Heather had been visiting Salem on the North Shore to schmooze with an animal rescue organization when she found her interest drawn into the saga of the Morse homestead's double history. After contributing a hefty donation to the excavation project, she'd wheedled a temporary place with the college crew, equipped herself with a professional archeo-kit, a bush hat, a green rain poncho, and a supply of *Archaeologists Dig It* t-shirts. A romantic at heart, Heather was in her element, lured by the mystery and excitement of discovering clues to the past, however elusive. For a while, all went well. Then...

"We've got a sniper at the site!" Heather announced without preamble.

"Oh, that's it." I was ashamed of the relief that poured over my fevered imaginings like a dipper of cool water. "I've been seeing bits and pieces of this all day. Has anyone been hurt?"

"Yes, Cass! Why do you think I'm calling? One of the young men was working on the dig alone really early this morning when others heard a shot. He was found in the trench, shot through the head. Dead. With his trowel still in his hand. A nice lad named Ernest Huggins. Not too quick on the uptake but very willing."

"It's probably just an isolated incident. Salem law enforcement will investigate, maybe call in the state police. When are you coming home? We need you to celebrate Litha. Especially since we're planning to hold the sabbat at your place."

"I feel that it's cowardly to desert the dig while the team may be in danger. Don't you?"

"No, not a bit of it. But I tell you what. You come home for Litha, and if there's a second sniper attack in Salem, which I doubt, we'll all go up there and track down the shooter."

"I guess." Heather's tone was dubious, but Litha was calling. "Do you promise?"

"Promise." *Beware of the offhand promise*, the inner, wiser voice of Spirit suggested. As usual, I ignored her.

"Oh, and I'm bringing you a rescue. Just your cup of ginger tea," Heather said.

"*Another dog?* With Scruffy and Raffles? No way!" I protested. Heather's life work was rescuing abandoned animals through Animal Lovers, a Plymouth sanctuary she supported with her useful and lavish trust income. From time to time she attempted to foist yet another woebegone waif onto one of us. Thanks to her persuasiveness, our circle was pretty well full up with rescue dogs and cats. It was Heather who'd been responsible for my adopting the redoubtable Scruffy, and truth to tell, he'd been my trusted companion ever since.

"No, Cass. This time it's a *person* in need of rescue. One of the archaeology crew is having a problem with some sort of time-travel thing."

"Well, that's something different," I said dubiously. "Does she disappear and show up in the seventeenth century? Or what?"

"Not exactly. More like unintentional past life regressions. As a result, she's rather a whiz at locating stuff. Like where the midden was, or the privy."

"Very handy. I'd be more interested in her locating an old grimoire or receipt book, but...a privy is better than nothing."

"Don't be cynical, dear. Jordan is a very sweet girl."

"*flowing down the river of time*," I murmured.

"Yes, Rivers. Jordan Rivers."

"Of course," I said. "And what kind of rescue is Jordan in need of?"

"Control, naturally. What always happens to young women with those special paranormal talents? There should be a school…you know, like ballet or something."

"Heather Devlin's School for Time-Travel Gypsies and Wayward Witches?"

"Not as farfetched as you are suggesting. Okay. See you at Litha, then. Perhaps Titania will grace us with her presence this Midsummer Eve."

"We can hope. I'll ask Phil to write a nice invocation to the Faery Queen. Take care."

After the call had ended, I sat on a comfortable glacier-shelf rock for a while and watched Scruffy and Raffles playing Driftwood Keep-away, while I mused on Jordan Rivers zipping in and out of past lives. Where would I go, if I could travel anywhere in time? Just the thought of it made me shudder, suspecting that one of my past lives had come to a fiery end. The wisdom of women healers had been hazardous to their health in darker ages. I reflected on women's inferior status, the persecution of herbalists, barber-surgeons, the application of leeches, brutal dentistry, men owning all property, mandatory church attendance, and outdoor plumbing. So much for the romance of history! *There's no time like the present,* I decided.

∾

We are a circle of five. Our Wiccan adventure began a few years ago when we took a course in women's studies given by the Black Hill branch librarian Fiona Ritchie, whose reputation as a "finder" was legendary. It was at those meetings that I also met Phillipa, a cook and poet with a flair for reading the tarot, Deidre, a young mother who handcrafted poppets and amulets, and Heather, a magical candle-maker and animal activist. In addition to my own penchant for clairvoyance (which I kept under wraps as much as possible), I ran an herbal business out of my home: *Cassandra Shipton, Earthlore Herbal Preparations and Cruelty-Free Cosmetics.* Herbs, books, food, animals, children—it wasn't surprising that we'd felt a natural and immediate affinity that soon deepened into an abiding friendship. It seemed that each of us became stronger in her own unique arts and talents as we connected with one another. Reading our way through Fiona's eclectic book list, we'd become interested in matriarchal societies, ancient times when wise women wielded their natural power in spiritual communities. Learning more about the holy days that predated modern religions led us to the Wiccan Sabbats we celebrated now, holidays aligned to the seasonal cycles of birth, growth, and death.

Litha is the sabbat of deep summer, sensual and bittersweet, presaging as it does a gradual loss as the days inexorably became shorter. July and August would try to fool us with their lush green vistas and sizzling heat, but the sun's power would keep on diminishing just a few minutes a day and we would be aware, down deep, of that inevitable turn of the seasonal wheel.

Midsummer is my most favorite sabbat! I thought. Lolling on one of the Adirondack chairs in my herb garden, with luxurious scents of spicy rosemary, sweet basil, soothing lavender, robust oregano, and energizing sage wafting in on the summer breeze, I was dimly aware that *every* sabbat was my favorite as the cycle of earth turned from one high holiday to another. Hadn't I been just as enraptured with Samhain and Beltane? My Libran desire that all things be beautiful, balanced, and equal, I supposed.

While I sipped my mint-infused iced tea, I contemplated my husband Joe, stripped to the waist and sea-tanned, working in the garden. Although his tightly curled hair was more gray than black now, his Greek profile was as strong as ever, and his bronze muscular back was still compact and agile. "Oh, quit now, honey, and have a glass of tea," I called. I really wanted to lure him near enough to touch, close beside me in the other Adirondack chair.

"Just a minute. There's a few ripe strawberries here."

I closed my eyes and imagined the taste of a sweet, ripe berry dipped in prosecco…perhaps much later tonight, after I got home from the sabbat we'd be celebrating in the stone circle at Heather's place.

As our chief herbalist, I would bring bunches of daisies and roses, a basket of dried mugwort, chamomile, lavender, and yarrow, sage for smudging, and incense of myrrh and lemon, and cinnamon in particular for Jordan Rivers. Heather's woods would contribute the strong scent of pine, and we would burn fallen oak branches, thus completing the midsummer herbal menu.

Jordan Rivers, Heather's new protégé, would be our Litha guest. Even now she was ensconced in one of Heather's lavish Victorian bedrooms, perhaps with a little balcony overlooking the long sweep of streets and houses down to the ocean, visible only from a few of the upstairs rooms and the widow's walk atop the house. I was both intrigued and reluctant to meet Ms. Rivers, wondering what fresh mischief she was bringing into our circle.

༄

It was still light when we gathered to celebrate the longest day of the year. Heather had planted a variety of mints around her secluded stone circle to discourage bugs and beasties that were the bane of outdoor sabbats. The assertive scent of mint vied with the pine woods that surrounded us, and the dried herbs I'd scattered about the circle. Jordan Rivers sat cross-legged in the gathering shadows, watching us with inquisitive brown eyes that missed no detail. A lithe, graceful girl with dark skin and West Indian features, she wore faded jeans, a loose woven shirt of brilliant greens and blues, and deerskin moccasins. Even sitting still, there was an aura of sensuality about Jordan and an energy that positively crackled.

"I'm, like, *so* grateful to you for inviting me to your pow-wow. It's really *awesome*. Because I know it's your own private party." Jordan's voice was a musical contralto. "This thing that keeps happening to me...Well, it's, like, *totally* unsettling. Heather's the first one who really gets me...who doesn't believe that I'm, like, off my meds. She says you all have weird stuff you do."

Phillipa's winged black eyebrows rose as she cast a baleful glance across the circle at Heather. "Well, I wouldn't say *weird*, exactly. Out of the mainstream, perhaps."

"Speak for yourself, Phil." Deidre grinned. With her blonde curls and dimples, she looked more like a teen-ager herself than the mother of four. "I just make dollies."

"Is that, like, voodoo poppets? Aren't you all witches?" Jordan asked.

"That's rather a matter of definition, Jordan. It's true enough that we follow the Wiccan way," Phil admitted. "But not all Wiccans are witches. Although our circle does cast the odd magical spell."

"Which is exactly what I explained to Jordan," Heather said. "Psychic Remedies 'R Us."

"What I need is a *detox* for this thing I do, you know?" Jordan said. "Slipping in and out of some *creepy* past scene. Like, the other day I was at this outdoor table cataloging some stuff we'd found. That's what I do, photograph and catalog artifacts. Boring job, but the team is cool. We all hang out together. *Wicked fun.* So we were *totally* bummed out about what happened to poor Huggins. He was, like, a guy who never got a break Anyway, there I was, shooting away at some moldy pot shards, when suddenly I found myself seeing the homestead the way it must have looked in Sarah Morse's day. Wow, *what a rush!* I looked down at the outfit I was wearing, and it nearly blew my mind, you know? *Heavy* gray bodice and skirt, white apron, and ugly round-toed shoes tied with ribbons. Instead of my Canon, a bucket of clam shells in my hand. I was heading toward the kitchen midden to dump them. *And I knew where the midden was!*"

Although seeing auras isn't one of my talents, at that moment I could sense that Jordan's aura was flaring off in all directions, like the Northern Lights.

"We'd been looking for the midden at the site," Heather said. "When Jordan shook off her trance, she was able to show us the exact location, a mound that was completely hidden by overgrowth. You can learn a great deal about a settlement from its discards. And sometimes the same pit had been used by earlier residents. The Massachusett tribe who lived in this coastal area before the English settlers might also have dumped their refuse there. It could be a rich source of artifacts. But instead of being delighted, the project director, Arnie Dickstein, behaved awkwardly about the incident. As if he were afraid he was being duped. And then, of course, Huggins got shot. Everyone was a mess after that."

Fiona sat down beside Jordan and patted her hand, silver bangles jangling. "Now is the time, dear, and all time is now. Some of us feel that more keenly than others. It's important to be patient with mundane minds and to avoid troublesome incidents. As you certainly have learned while you studied Salem's wretched past. The injustice of those trials. And I think we can help you there."

"To keep a low profile, she means," Phil said. "Something that wise women like us have always had to do. But in our own circle, on a magic night like this…"

"…we can shake out those old brooms and *zoom!*" Deidre finished the thought.

"Let's start then. It's twilight time, faery time, and I have composed an invocation to Titania." Phillipa smiled, that brilliant smile that lights up her otherwise sharp features with classic beauty, and she whirled around in her long gauzy skirt and wrap, both black, her signature color, but with some silvery tracings on the hem.

An orange waxing moon hung low in the sky, and countless stars, both faint and bright, shone above the pines. Crickets and katydids chirped their tunes in perfect concert with the luminous night. The air was still, allowing us to light candles and incense and keep them lit. Heather stepped forward and gave her new chin-length bronze hair a little shake, as if she felt light-headed after years of wearing that long shining braid. She kindled the altar fire and called the quarters, drawing a pentagram with her silver-handled athame toward each of the four directions.   *Spirit of the East, element of air, be with us now. From your wide blue spaces, inspire us with awareness. Spirit of the South, element of fire, be with us now. In your infinite brightness, inspire us to creativity. Spirit of the West, element of water, be with us now. From your deep well-*

being, inspire us in healing. Spirit of the North, element of earth, be with us now. In your vast oneness, inspire us with love.

The circle was now cast, a timeless space for magical workings.

We began with a healing blessing for Jordan, that she might exercise better control over her unusual gift so she wouldn't be sliding into trance states at inopportune moments and having to endure the unwanted attention of mundanes. We smudged her with cinnamon incense for power, healing, and protection, then all of us smudged each other with smoldering sage for purification. Fiona, of course, dusted Jordan with a sprinkle of corn pollen from the medicine bag given to her by a Navajo *hatalii*. But this ceremony would only be the beginning. For the week she'd be spending with Heather, we'd also teach Jordan the disciplines we used to steady ourselves: meditations, breathing exercises, magical gestures, words of power, the art of grounding oneself, and certain efficacious herbal tea blends.

That evening we also blessed Conor O'Donnell, Deidre's new love, who was somewhere in the Costa Rica rainforest photographing tropical birds like the Rainbow-billed Toucan and the Great Kiskadee for the Audubon Society's monthly magazine. Deidre never knew to what exotic place Conor might be sent next, just as I never knew what quixotic adventure would be my husband's next assignment. After years in the merchant marine, Joe now worked as a ship's engineer for Greenpeace, saving the planet from marauders and polluters. The circle had become practiced in protective charms for wandering menfolk. *So good, so far*, as Fiona would say.

As always, we also consigned a few private wishes to the Cosmos, this time in the form of origami birds winging into our altar fire.

As Phillipa swirled forward to recite her invocation, fireflies flickered in the long grass outside the circle, as magical as any faeries.

> *Out of the woods, we call you,*
> *Queen of Midsummer Night,*
> *Show us your glimmering presence*
> *By moon and firelight...*
> *On this night of deepest summer*
> *May our shimmering dreams come true...*
> *Come to us, Queen Titania,*
> *Our hearts believe in you.*

Picking up the last two lines of the chant, we danced with it around the circle, drawing Jordan up to join us, holding hands and moving faster and faster until it was Fiona who stopped, gasped, and bent over to catch her breath. The rest of us threw arms and wishes and blessings out to the starry Cosmos, and then sank down to rest. At that moment, an owl hooted quite close by, and as we all turned toward the haunting sound, a flash of light wove through the pines, like miniature ground lightning.

We all held our breaths.

"Did you hear a little sound of laughter?" Deidre whispered.

A second flash, and a third.

"Will o' the wisp?" murmured Heather.

Fiona held out her hand to the shadows, silver bangles tinkling. A blurred creature, wings beating too fast to be seen clearly, came to her hand for a moment, then sped away.

"Hummingbird," Phillipa declared.

"Perhaps," Fiona said. "We ought to leave an offering, in case." She reached into the old green reticule that was always by her side and took out a slim volume. I barely read the title by firelight: *How to Make Friends with Faeries, Elves, and Gnomes.* She paged though, whistling to herself. "I don't suppose any of you has a wee faery gift? No, I guess not."

"Will this do?" Deidre took a small pink crystal out of her pocket. It glittered prettily in the firelight. "I often keep one of these in my pocket. It's a kind of love charm. But I have others at home."

"That Conor never had a chance," Phillipa whispered.

"I suspect he didn't want one," I replied.

"Perfect," Fiona said. "Let's just leave it on the altar rock as a token."

Deidre plucked a few daisies growing in a clump nearby and surrounded the crystal with a circlet of flowers. She had a crafty touch that made her arrangement look like a sweet offering, a knack I seriously lacked. "Oh, wait a minute. I have these, too. She poked through her woven workbag, pulled out a small ballerina doll with a needle stuck in it, and removed its ballet shoes, just two tiny scraps of felt with sequined toes. "There," she said. "I do feel that's perfect, don't you? I'll make another pair for this dolly tomorrow. Now, Jordan, I see you eyeing this needle. This is not a voodoo spell. I sew these for my shop. "

"Perfect," Phillipa agreed. "I am in awe. Between Fiona's reticule and Dee's workbag, we are prepared for anything."

"I like to keep my workbag nearby, so my hands won't get bored." Deidre added the doll shoes to the crystal and daisies.

"Of course," Phillipa said. "And Fiona doesn't want to be without her library of pamphlets, her essential oils, her lock-picks, and the odd weapon or two."

Fiona said, "I think a round of soft clapping would be in order, don't you?"

Phillipa grinned and tapped out a rhythm, which got us all clapping to a very merry beat in the moonlight, quite reminiscent of a scene from Peter Pan.

Soon afterwards we quenched the candles and altar fire, and Heather opened the circle. We left Deidre's faery gifts on the altar rock. Would they stay there until the next sabbat? Blow away on some brisk windy day? Or mysteriously disappear, leaving behind a tiny faery "I.O.U."?

Enough with this speculation! It was time for "cakes and ale" which on this night would be a champagne punch, petite sandwiches, canapés, and "faery cakes," which are meltingly light sponge cupcakes. Phillipa tasted a lemon butterfly cake with supreme concentration and paused to write a few words in her pocket notebook. Something new to add to her repertoire.

Supper was served by Heather's new butler, the impeccable Maxwell, who spoke what is known as "British stage English" and was as flawlessly correct as Jeeves. (Only Fiona and I knew that the butler and his wife Elsa were really actors on the lam, but we'd decided not to tell Heather, whose bad luck with housekeepers was legendary.)

∽

After Litha, Jordan stayed a few days more at Heather's, learning all the control techniques we could teach her. But she did experience one past-life incident that week. As she herself described it, "I'd climbed up to that little witchy room of Heather's in the widow's walk. *Awesome* view. She'd showed me, like, all about the ladder, so it was okay. Trap doors are *way cool*! But just as I got up there and looked out, I got *wicked* dizzy and had to hang on to the windowsill. For a moment, I *totally* blacked out. When I came to, I saw through the little windows two clipper ships cruising into Plymouth Harbor. And I was, like, practically keeling over, I was so excited, or maybe afraid, you know? My heart was fluttering, can you beat that? Someone was sailing home *to me*. Then I glanced down and saw a lace kerchief around my neck, a blue dress that might have been dimity cotton, and brocade shoes. In my hand, I was holding a small blue silk book. And I totally *knew* that there was something secret in the book that I ought to hide. I tucked the book away into a little space in the wainscoting. Then, *bingo!* Back again to the present, limp as a pricked balloon."

"I wonder if you were tuning in to my great-great-grandmother, Alyce Morgan," Heather mused. "This room has been re-painted more than once since the house was built, and I believe the molding was repaired, but you never can tell, that diary might still be hidden there."

"It would be such a shame to tear the widow's walk apart, wouldn't it?" I said. Heather looked at me uncomprehendingly. Clearly, her mind was set on finding Alyce's book, if it existed. Well, good luck to the carpenter who got the job of climbing through a trap door to dismantle the place.

Before Heather could decide between ordering in a wrecking crew or returning to the Morse dig in Salem, however, a major distraction appeared on the scene in the form of a rabid witch-baiting preacher.

CHAPTER TWO

For modes of faith let graceless zealots fight,
His can't be wrong whose life is in the right.

– Alexander Pope

"It's Deidre! She's under siege at her shop." Clasping my cell phone, I turned away from the bird feeder window to relay the news to my daughter-in-law, Freddie, who was at that moment sitting at my kitchen table. "Willie Hogben is picketing Deidre!"

Deidre was still wailing in my ear. "There'll be TV crews, I know there will. The media feeds on Hogben like pigs on swill."

I assured her that I was on the way. My twin grandchildren, Joanie and Jackie, continued to babble in their private language over milk and Joe Froggers, but Freddie looked up from her mug of coffee with a sparkle of immediate interest. I felt a pang of regret for the punk Freddie of yesteryear who had turned herself into this model young wife and mother... for love. The way women do. Fortunately, the lawless hacker and psychokinetic whiz that Freddie used to be was alive and well somewhere under those suburban togs. No longer sporting five piercings on each ear and a nose ring, at least

Freddie's skirt was still short and her amber eyes as darkly outlined as ever.

"Well, let's get over there, then!" Freddie sprang up, ready for action. "How I'd enjoy zapping that religious rabble!"

"We can't take the little guys with us," I protested. But the little guys had already stuffed the last crumbs of molasses cookies into their mouths and jumped down from their chairs, game for any new adventure, like youngsters the world over. "All those parishioners will be milling about, swinging hateful placards. It's not safe."

"Not one of those crazies will trouble my kids, Cass. Or else," Freddie said firmly. "And besides, this drizzly weather makes it a perfect day for the mall."

Knowing what Freddie could do with her powerful energy, perhaps even better than she did, I thought *maybe* it would be all right. But I punched in Fiona on speed dial, just in case.

"Fiona, Deidre's having a problem with Willie Hogben and his followers over at the mall. They're waving *God Hates Witches* placards and some other nasty stuff. She can't even get out of her shop, and she's afraid of how the media will spin the incident. Can you meet me over there?" Fiona said she could and would, but she'd need to leave her grandniece Laura Belle with her obliging neighbor first.

"You may as well bring her," I said. "Jackie and Joanie are here with Freddie. She says the children will not be bothered. And you know Freddie."

The last person who'd threatened Freddie's children had toppled right over onto the floor with the force of her psychokinetic energy. Although, in truth, the man already had a weak heart. At the time, I'd assured Freddie that she did not have that much power. Especially since the villain died later, and I didn't want her to carry a burden of guilt. Oh well. *The moving finger writes…*

"Still, I'd rather leave Laura Belle next door this time. You know how sensitive she is," Fiona said. "Willie Hogben is not just a run-of-the-mill evangelistic preacher. I believe he's your basic sorcerer. No matter what fundamentalist doctrine he preaches. In spirit, he's as strong as a wild boar. A formidable foe. We'd better call in Phil and Heather, too."

"Sure, but I feel we really need *you,*" I said. Then it occurred to me how Fiona might interpret my plea. "But don't bring anything you shouldn't in that reticule of yours. There's sure to be a police presence."

"Oh really, Cass. When have I ever done that?"

I could have mentioned that incident with her pistol aboard the *Goddess of the Sea,* or the rapier in Rome, but I let the matter go with a small, silent prayer to the Goddess Brigit to protect us all. The main thing now was to rescue Deidre's Faeryland shop from those Bible-toting terrorists.

❧

As Freddie, the grandchildren, and I ran down the Massasoit Mall corridor toward Deidre's doll shop, we could see Willie Hogben waving his arms and babbling loudly, surrounded by the other members of his Church of the Christian Sword and their hateful homemade placards. Theirs was a small congregation, no more than thirty-five families, who met in an abandoned laundromat in Carver, but they made the loudest noise of any church on the South Shore. *The rat who roared,* Fiona called them.

Pastor Hogben was a tall, gangly, sixtyish man with scarecrow shoulders and ferocious dark eyes under wiggling caterpillar eyebrows. His black hair streaked with gray was long and unruly, his beard untrimmed, his mouth wide and furious, his great hands forever gesturing broadly with a Bible in one and a Moses staff in the other. Behind him, like a back-up chorus, his three handmaidens swayed back and forth in ecstasy with his every pronouncement, mouthing the last few words. They wore long-sleeved prairie dresses in pastel shades, braided blonde wigs, face-shading bonnets, and dark glasses.

"Thou shalt not suffer a witch to live," he bellowed, and they sang softly "suffer a witch to live, a witch to live." Between echoing his pronouncements, the handmaidens hummed "Onward, Christian Soldiers."

Freddie immediately elbowed through the throng. I waved to Fiona and Heather, who had come in through another entrance. Fiona stopped for a moment to lean on Heather and catch her breath, then made her own path by waving her Coyote-topped walking stick back and forth. Somehow I got pushed to the rear with Joanie and Jackie, who were hopping up and down trying to see through the jostling onlookers.

"Oh, dear…Oh, dear." The familiar voice I heard beside me belonged to Patty Peacedale, wife of Selwyn Peacedale, pastor of the Garden of Gethsemane Presbyterian Church. She was teetering on tiptoe herself to see what was going on. "I just popped into the mall to pick up some more puce wool for my prayer shawls," she said, raising her voice above its usual gentle tone in order to be heard. "And I found this frightening scene going on. Isn't it terrible! Poor little Deidre, just a hard-working single mother selling dollies to keep a roof over her babies' heads."

Right in front of us, one of the Christian Sword gang waved his placard *Burn, Witch, Burn* around his head, causing us to duck down to protect the children. Instantly I was angry with myself for the folly of bringing the young ones into this arena of hate. I should have followed my own instincts. It's particularly annoying to a clairvoyant not to do so. The placard brandisher, however, suddenly jumped up and away, yelling "Ouch! What was that?"

Glancing over at Patty, I noted that she was putting a steel knitting needle back into her bag of wool. "*The Lord is my defense; I shall not be greatly moved,*" she whispered.

"Rock on, Patty. Can you see what Fiona and Heather are doing?" I still had my arms around the children, so Patty, shorter than I, began bouncing up like Jill-in-the-box to get a better view of the action.

"It appears that Fiona is remonstrating with Pastor Hogben. Heather is trying to pull her away. The pastor is waving his Bible at Fiona, and, *gosh and golly*, she is waving her walking stick right back him. Oh, and there's your daughter-in-law. She's holding her hands straight out toward the pastor. Probably some kind of prayer. Oh, here come the Plymouth Police officers! I think that's your friend Phil with them. *Blessed are the peacemakers...*" Patty clapped her hands.

"Good Goddess, I hope Fiona doesn't get herself arrested. I should be up there..."

"Would you like me to take the little ones for an ice cream while you pray with your friends?" Patty asked.

Joanie took Patty's hand and smiled up at her, that delicate rosebud smile. Jackie tugged away from my grasp, ready to go. *What fun!*

"You just said the magic words. Thanks, Patty," I said. "I'll only be a minute. Meet you at Yum-Yum's, okay?"

Good soul Patty was already coaching the children to hold hands as she set off with her pint-size entourage for the ice cream parlor.

By the time I had reached the front of Deidre's Faeryland doll store, Hogben was arguing his right to free speech with a freckle-faced, red-haired officer who was asking the preacher to step back from the shop's door to an island at the center of the mall. Phillipa had marched right into the shop with a swirl of her black poncho and flung her arms around Deidre.

"Fiona's right. He is a strong-minded devil. I can't seem to make a dent." Freddie herself looked tired, and there were beads of perspiration on her forehead. If her psychokinetic force (which was notable enough to have been occasionally drafted by the CIA for secret projects) couldn't rattle Hogben, what could? But I'd seen his antics before, stirring up the media into a feeding frenzy. He seemed to thrive and grow even tougher on discord.

Not long ago, Hogben and his motley crew had picketed a local Unitarian Universalist Church for displaying the LGBT rainbow banner at the entrance to their circular driveway. In that instance, *"God Hates Homos"* had been the placard of the day.

Patty Peacedale had gone over to the UU church on that occasion to dispute with the picketers and waved her own sign, *God Loves All His Children.* For her good deed, she'd nearly got trampled by the Christian Swords and had to be rescued by the minimal police presence. Hogben had kept on spewing his venom until the local news truck arrived, then he'd cut short his ruckus in time for the press to ferry their "Live at Six" tape to the station news director.

After that incident, my indignant friend Phillipa had demanded that her husband, Plymouth Detective Stone

Stern, check whether Hogben was a bigamist, but Stone had been unable to find any marriage records for the preacher in Massachusetts. Hogben's wife, whether legally or by common law, was Eureka Hogben, a short beefy woman with a wasp nest of gray hair, who guarded the home front while Hogben rallied the Christian Swords. No information was found on the three handmaidens Hogben claimed as nieces.

Pastor Hogben owned a twenty-acre compound in Carver near the laundromat-church, surrounded by an eight-foot fence. He'd been photographed patrolling his property with a gun strapped to his hip and three big nervous-looking mixed-breed dogs. Stone had checked that the weapon was legally registered. Heather thought the animals looked abused and underfed, but she was frustrated by an inability to prove what her instincts told her was true. (This was a wall that all five of us ran into from time to time. The various psychic abilities of our circle tantalized us with pieces of information that rarely made a convincing case.)

When I'd elbowed a path through the gathering crowd of onlookers (my sturdy build makes me a natural for making my way to the front of any mob) I found Fiona, Heather, and Freddie holding hands and humming. One of Fiona's humming spells, I supposed, usually employed to unsettle the misogynist male. As effective as it had been in the past, the spell seemed to bounce right off Hogben in a most disconcerting way.

A surge of anger rose up in me like bile. I wanted to get that hypocrite out of there before the TV cameras arrived to embarrass Deidre on the evening news. So much raging emotion filled me, it was like a hot flash of the spirit, and at that moment I knew something about Hogben I didn't know I knew. I pushed my way forward so that I was standing right in front of him. Then I leaned over and spat my little message right into his ear. No one else heard me but the preacher. For once, he looked struck dumb.

Within a few minutes, Hogben was waving his Moses rod energetically to part the crowd like the Red Sea, and his bemused followers had to run to keep up with him in a disarray of ugly placards. Fiona, Heather, and Freddie watched the unprecedented departure with some surprise, as did the police officers. The tsunami of hatred had receded without harm.

Phillipa popped her head out of the shop, still protectively hovering over Deidre, and demanded, "What just happened here?"

Heather said, "Cass mumbled something to Hogben, up close and personal. Never saw a man wilt so fast. Maybe it was a hex of some kind. What exactly did you say, Cass?"

Everyone looked at me.

"I'm not sure," I confessed. "It just sort of bubbled up in me. I think I said, *I know all about your secret, you creep. And it's going to put you away for a few hundred years.*"

"What secret is that, witch-in-law?" asked Freddie. "Inquiring minds need to know."

"Was it a flash of second sight?" Fiona asked.

"Did you imagine that Hogben is some kind of federal fugitive? Because I'm sure that's already been checked out," Phillipa said.

"Thank the Goddess he left before the paparazzi got here." Deidre sat down wearily on the edge of a large potted plant outside her shop. Her skin color had gone all pale, and even her blonde curls seemed to hang limply around her face. The poor girl was exhausted.

"I have no idea," I confessed. "The words just came out of my mouth without passing through my brain. It's like that with me sometimes."

"But the interesting thing is, you seem to have hit a nerve," Heather said. "Perhaps worth investigating?"

"According to Stone, Plymouth County detectives have gone out of their way to investigate Hogben every time he's mounted another of his odious campaigns against one of his favorite targets," Phillipa said.

Under the banner of free speech, Hogben and his parishioners had picketed liberal churches, out-of-the-closet public officials, military funerals, a mosque in Quincy, Muslim shopkeepers, women's health clinics, fortune tellers, and shops catering to the earth-based religions, like Deidre's, even though most of Deidre's merchandise was delightful and adorable fantasy stuff for children. There was, of course, the issue of her anatomically correct boy and girl dolls, which had caused some customers to complain and demand their money back. *"Rats and snails and puppy dog tails*, that's what they think little boys should be made of," Deidre scoffed.

"We ought to put a spirit tracer on Hogben," Fiona said thoughtfully. "I could go for a double chocolate ice cream cone with chocolate sprinkles, couldn't you?"

"Okay, lay it on me," Freddie said. "What's a spirit tracer?"

Another crisis averted, we made our way to YumYum's to rescue Patty from my grandchildren. Except for Phillipa, who stayed at Faeryland to mind the store and help Deidre to gather her wits.

"You could compare it to a psychic GPS." Like many of Fiona's explanations, we would soon be shaking our heads like swimmers with water in their ears in an effort to follow her logic. "Some ladies use bats, but myself, I prefer owls. And here we are. Oh, look the flavor of the week is Mississippi Mud Pie. Now doesn't that sound restorative!"

"I've had bats hanging around in my Widow's Walk," Heather said. "Very picturesque."

"Bats in the belfry, literally. I think I would prefer owls myself. But how about a good old-fashioned computer search," Freddie said. "I could do that. The Christian Swords have a Web site, do they not? If Hogben has a PC link, I'll hack into it and see what he's hiding under that bellicose Bible of his."

"Shall I call off the owls, then?"

"Save them for back-up, Fiona," Freddie said. "Hello, my darlings. How was Yum Yum's ice cream?"

Joanie, still delicately nibbling at a cone-cup of watermelon sherbet, smiled sweetly. Remnants of a banana split were smeared around Jackie's grin. And Patty was glowing beamishly between the two children, an empty tea cup at her elbow. It appeared that she had enjoyed herself hugely and was in no hurry to be relieved of duty. "Oh, they've been such blessed little angels!" she caroled. "Call on me anytime, Freddie dear, when you need someone to take care of these sweeties while you're praying with Cass and her friends." Her heart-shaped face shone with eagerness and good will.

"Thanks, Patty. I'll keep that in mind," Freddie said.

"I trust that Pastor Hogben has departed and left little Deidre in peace?"

"Yes, Patty, not a whiff of brimstone left behind him, I'm happy to report," I said.

Heather was at the counter ordering scoops of Mississippi Mud and Coffee Bean Ice Cream, declaring that Yum Yum's coffee flavor was unlike any other and not to be missed.

"Cass's sixth sense tells her that the pastor is keeping some kind of evil secret," Fiona said. "And when she taxed him with it, he left in a big hurry with his entire entourage. I wonder if you might have heard anything, Patty?" Fiona laid her many-ringed hand on Patty's, smiled encouragingly, and hummed a little, but Patty could not be swayed by Fiona's wiles

"Oh dear, oh dear…I fear I can never remember church gossip from one friendship hour to the next. My brain is so chock full of knitting patterns, there isn't much room left for calumny and slander. It's Mrs. Chester Pynchon you want to ask. She remembers every slur unto the end of time." Mrs. Pynchon, treasurer of the Garden of Gethsemane Presbyterian Church, was Patty's nemesis. Patty turned away from Fiona's gaze with a diffident request to the counter attendant. "I wonder if I might have a little more hot water, dear. No, no, this teabag will be just fine."

I was pretty sure Patty knew something, though, and I planned to wheedle it out of her later. I had one or two markers I could call in; Patty still owed me for rescuing a couple of her damsels in distress.

After we'd gorged sufficiently at Yum Yum's, Fiona and Heather headed home in her dog-worn-and-drool-splattered Mercedes, and Freddie departed for her home in Hingham with Joanie and Jackie belted into twin child seats in her dashing Porsche Cayenne. Walking back to the Faeryland shop to check on Deidre and catch a ride home with Phillipa, I found them setting up gossamer faery dolls in the shop window.

"My assistant Hal will be coming in shortly, so I'll be able to head home myself and stick pins into my Hogben poppet." Deidre seemed quite herself again. She held up a bearded doll in a black suit holding a miniature red book. "Chairman Hogben's Scriptures" the title read in tiny gilt letters.

"Now, now, Dee...no pins! Let's just concentrate on finding out what ugly crime that false prophet is concealing. I think Patty knows something. Fiona tried to get it out of her, but Patty wouldn't even hint. Sometimes that woman is too good to be true."

"Let's bring her a basket of goodies, then," Phillipa suggested, "and while she's munching, you read her mind."

"I don't read minds, Phil. I have visions, or not. But maybe I can appeal to Patty's sense of justice and fairness. Savories, then. Patty's always full up with social-hour sweet stuff baked by the Ladies League."

"I remember," Phil said. "Don't eat the brownies or drink the Kool-aid, right?"

So we made a plan to stop by the parsonage the next day. But before we could get to Patty's with Phillipa's spanakopita and gougères, a couple of events intervened. Joe got an assignment to sail on the Greenpeace *Gaia* into the freezing waters off Greenland, and Heather, called to announce that there had been another sniper attack at the Salem excavation. Arnie Dickstein had been in touch with her, eager to soften the news-shock to big donors, even before the incident had been reported on TV.

"How I'd like to get my hands on that Son of Sammael!" Her forceful tones assaulted my peaceful morning. "Not a young trainee this time. This victim's name is Fuchsia Woolley, and she's a well-know archaeologist who just happened to be at the site, getting the grand tour from Dickstein. Woolley and Dickstein came out of the old Morse house around dusk. Woolley asked to see the place where the old midden had been discovered, thanks to our new friend Jordan, while it was still light. Woolley was walking ahead, and she turned to say something to Dickstein, which probably saved her life. The bullet penetrated her shoulder. Did a lot of damage to the bone but missed her head. At least I assume the sniper was aiming for her head, because that's where Huggins caught it, poor guy. A funny thing, Huggins wore a distinctive hat, and so does Woolley."

"Distinctive in what way?" A mental image went flitting through my third eye. Well, actually it *was* an eye.

"Huggins wore an egg-yolk yellow hat with an eye of Horus on it. Dickstein described Woolley's bright blue hat as having a Pyramid of Giza motif. Most of the other hats around the dig are sober khaki, like my bush hat. Why? What are you thinking?" Heather asked.

"I'm thinking you should stick with the khaki," I said. "Bright colors make an obvious head target. What kind of weapon is being used, does anyone know? And has the sniper's post been found? It must be a place from where a quick getaway is possible. Maybe crushed leaves, broken branches, or tire tracks in evidence?"

"I don't know if the forensic people have zeroed in on the place where the sniper hid. Or if he used the same spot twice. The weapon was a rifle, a Bushmaster. So I heard from Dickstein. I'd asked him to call on me for support if there was any more trouble. And since he has an exaggerated idea of my 'connections,' he did just that. But when I told him I was on my way and would be asking a psychic friend to look around for clues that may have escaped the police, he was not at all pleased."

"No kidding. Did you tell him you were bringing your whole *psychic friends network*?"

"Well...not exactly. But I only mentioned that *you* seem to have special powers when it comes to detecting."

"Thanks, girlfriend. With all this advance publicity, we'll be lucky if we don't get ourselves strung up on that old gallows tree."

"Oh, don't flatter yourself. You won't be the only psychic on the beach, not in Salem. And remember, you *promised* to take on this mission if there was another shooting."

She had me there.

CHAPTER THREE

Our deeds still travel with us from afar,
and what we have been makes us what we are.

– George Eliot

Joe was always careful to describe each of his assignments as if it were no more dangerous than a sail around some Lake Placid. But a clairvoyant with one foot in reality and the other in possibility is not so easily pacified. Also, I learned a bit more from Googling the Greenland mission. Apparently the Danish navy commandoes were protecting an oil drilling operation that had the capability of spilling oil in the Arctic that might never be cleaned up, according to Greenpeace. *Never* is a long time, but Greenpeace was adamant, and two of their ships (one of them the *Gaia* on which Joe would be ship's engineer) were being dispatched to confront the controversial project. The Scottish oil company's proposal was to drill in Iceberg Alley, where populations of blue whales and polar bears would be assaulted by the toxic chemicals discharged daily from the operating rig. Even without spills, the rig would be deadly to fish, animals, and birds. Also, if this drilling proved successful, Exxon and others were waiting in the wings with their Greenland licenses in hand.

Joe's old duffle stood in the corner near the kitchen door, packed and ready, but we had that last evening together. Another good-bye among so many others. Parting always gave me a little fillip of urgency, not an unpleasant sensation. Shutting the dogs into the kitchen (with the usual canine grumbles), we went to bed, sweetly drunk on red wine, for some mature but lively love-making. What with one thing and another, that rash promise I'd made to Heather (that we'd hunt down the sniper if he struck again) went clear out of my mind.

Even the next morning when Joe departed for Logan Airport in his usual rental, I neglected to mention the new incident, possibly because I am not at my best at 6 a.m. *Oh, well*, I thought, *I'll tell Joe all about it when he calls from the Gaia. If he calls.* Sometimes he's too busy fending off whomever Greenpeace is confronting. *Or I could tell him when he returns in a couple of weeks.*

"Has Joe gone? *Good*," Heather declared when I called her later. "Throw a few things into a bag, and let's get out to the Morse place this afternoon. Dee can't come because she's expecting Conor at any moment, so she sent Mother Ryan off on a Las Vegas junket with her blue-haired cronies, thus cutting herself off from a live-in babysitter. Conor says he bringing Dee a special gift. Let's hope it's an engagement ring."

Looking out my bird-feeder window, I saw a feather floating down on the June breeze. "Maybe it's a tropical bird," I suggested. "What about Fiona?"

"Oh, Fiona is game. Laura Belle is going to stay with Dee. Such a solitary, quiet child. Good for her to be part of that Ryan gang for a few days. And Phil says she'll join us in Salem later so there will be at least two cars to tool around town, 'one of them clean,' as she puts it. I've booked rooms for us at the Crowninshield Inn. You'll love the place. Working fireplaces, and it's reputed to be haunted by a serving wench who fell down the stairs. Cold spot where she landed gives sensitive guests the shivers. Perhaps just as well Dee won't be going, now that she's developed a talent for seeing dead people. By the way, Phil tells me you let her and Stone walk straight into a haunted hotel one Thanksgiving. Without a word of warning. The Bone Rock Inn in Maine."

"Did I? A Thanksgiving pilgrimage to visit Stone's mother, wasn't it? Didn't want to add to her anxieties, I expect. Okay to leave Scruffy and Raffles with your pack?" Scruffy would be bummed out, but the two dogs would have excellent care with Dick the soft-hearted vet and Maxwell the impressive butler. And Elsa, his wife, had a compassionate but no-nonsense way with animals.

"Of course. They need an occasional run with the herd. Looks to me as if Scruffy is getting a mite heavy. Dogs are supposed to show a waist, you know. You've been giving him people food, I'm betting." Heather was winding up for her balanced-diet lecture, but I cut her short.

"Never mind that. Let's talk about the shooting. I'm assuming this is now a matter for the state police. What are they saying?"

"Not much. Two shootings do not a shooting spree make, *they hope*. Especially in Salem where they wouldn't want to panic the summer tourists. That old *Enemy of the People* syndrome. Under different circumstances, this might actually be a fun jaunt, don't you think? And Phil swanning around in her traditional black attire will fit right into the scene."

"Let's see then. Phil in witch's garb, you in amateur archaeologist togs, Fiona in her tartans...I hardly know what to take," I said.

"Oh, you'll be fine in your usual nondescript casual stuff," Heather reassured me. "Come over as soon as you're packed. With Scruffy and Raffles, of course."

"Right. I'll break it to them gently." I closed my cell to end the call. *Nondescript indeed! Some nerve.*

I threw open my closet door and took down my L. L. Bean medium rolling Pullman. Perhaps I should have a duffle like Joe's, ready packed with the necessities for unexpected missions. Searching through pants and shirts, I was deliberately looking for vivid colors, and there wasn't much. How many tan, gray, and navy tops could one woman buy for herself? But I did find a brilliant green silk blouse (gift from Joe), some Greenpeace tees, "You Can't Sink Rainbow" and "Save the Sumatran Tiger" (vivid orange), a blue-pine trail model rain jacket with hood (L.L.Bean), a Scarlet O'Hara hat with a pink hatband and matching pink shirt (gift from Freddie—*didn't I ever buy anything scintillating for myself?*) White skirt, slacks, shorts, well-worn trusty jeans, and my usual Plain Jane underwear completed the selection. To me, it looked pretty colorful spread out on the bed. I added my black commando outfit, a Wiccan travel kit, my butter-soft Italian leather handbag (also a gift from Joe) and, reluctantly, my vision pillow that usually upset me so much, I kept it buried in the linen closet or the freezer. But I had to admit that it had helped to solve some sticky mysteries.

There, that did it!

Going somewhere? Scruffy stood scowling in the bedroom door, with Raffles looking over his shoulder.

Somewhere? Somewhere?

Dogs are always alert for changes involving them, and a suitcase on the bed is an especially bad omen.

"Scruffy, you know you two always have a fun time at the Devlins'. You just hate to admit it. It will only be for a few days."

Yeah, yeah, Toots. I wish I had a Milkbone for every time I've heard that one. This business of dumping us with that mangy herd of strays is getting to be a bad habit. And every one of those mutts is fixed, you know. Makes a canine stud like myself very jumpy.

Jumpy! Jumpy! Having no idea of the issue, Raffles suited action to words and leapt around the bedroom joyously, knocking over a pedestal table and bowl of potpourri next to Grandma's rocker.

"*Okay, that's it!* Scruffy, no one is going to snip your prized possessions. Now *out, out* both of you."

With my cinnamon-soaked besom in hand, I shooed the dogs through the pet door on the porch and out into the yard, where they barked in aggrieved tones that scattered every bird within hearing distance.

This allowed me a respite from canine reproach to peacefully contemplate my wardrobe choices. True it was June, but nights can get chilly in a sea town. I added my green Armani blazer (foisted onto me by Heather in Rome), a butter yellow cotton sweater (gift from Becky), a favorite denim jacket, and a Greenpeace baseball cap with a Rainbow Warrior insignia.

It was now almost impossible to close my Pullman, so I added an *Earthlore Herbal Preparations* tote just for shoes and hats, and my old woven handbag for the vision pillow and toiletries.

⁊

Leaving my grumbling furry friends with Heather's flawless couple, Maxwell and Elsa, Heather, Fiona, and I were

on our way to Salem by early afternoon. I was relieved to see
that their luggage was just as hefty as mine, even if Heather's
bags were Louis Vuitton and Fiona's a Pendleton rolling
duffle in antique MacDonald tartan with matching tote.

"So, you didn't read your own memo about hats that
won't tempt a sniper?" Heather said, glancing into my hat-
and-shoes tote.

"Don't worry about that shooter, dearies. I'm weaving
an impenetrable white light of protection around all of us,"
Fiona said firmly. "We'll be just fine."

Resting comfortably on the head cushion in the back
seat, I said, "Wow, Heather, who cleaned your Mercedes? The
windows back here are spotless."

"Maxwell, of course. He's taken it upon himself to polish
everything in sight, this car included, bemoaning the fact
that our garages are now housing the bigger dogs, thus
allowing all vehicles to be at the mercy of the elements as
well as drooling, muddy-pawed passengers. Maxwell and
Elsa are so perfect in their roles, sometimes I feel as if I've
wandered onto the set of *Upstairs, Downstairs*."

Fiona glanced back at me with a slight shake of her head.
Omertà.

Thus at a loss for reply, I gazed out the window and let my
mind drift, always a mistake with me. Soon I became slightly
dazed with the motion of the car and the lowering sun in
the West. "Actually, I'm seeing two snipers," I murmured
dreamily. "With a van, a dirty blue van. And *another victim.*
Before we even get there!" The vision faded, leaving me
distinctly nauseous. I sure hoped I wouldn't throw up on the
immaculate upholstery.

Fiona immediately fished in her reticule so that she could
wave a small bottle of smelling salts under my nose. I took a

bracing sniff of that old Victorian standby. *Ammonia carbonate.* *Yuck!* Ladies were made of sterner stuff in those days.

The Mercedes was equipped with a hands-free cell phone. Heather was already calling Arnie Dickstein, but the line stayed busy through several tries.

We drove in tense silence for a few minutes. "I wonder who the victim is? or was?" Heather mused. "In a way, I hope it isn't someone I know and like, but on the other hand, I think that's a rather narrow attitude."

"Any man's death diminishes me..." Fiona quoted thoughtfully. "It's a good thing that we've committed ourselves to stop these evil souls, whoever they are."

"I wonder why in Hades they're targeting the Morse excavation crew!" Heather exclaimed angrily. "You don't suppose it's an American Indian protest, do you? Holy Hecate, I hope not. But the project *is* intent on digging up artifacts of an earlier settlement of the Massachusett tribe. Which may include bones of contention, so to speak."

"No," I said vehemently, suddenly realizing that I *had*, after all, seen two faces, two figures. "They are both Caucasians. The older man is quite heavy. The younger, slim and dark-browed. Still, I did see Indian symbols. Strange. I wonder if it would be a good idea to call Tip?"

Tip Thomas, a.k.a. Thunder Pony, a young friend I had once fantasized about adopting, was an expert tracker and a fund of shamanistic knowledge. We'd shared some wild adventures in the past, but now he was a student at the University of Maine, taking advantage of tribal grants to study American Indian music. No doubt he had taken a full-time job for the summer, but it was worth a try. He might be able to wangle a few free days.

"What an outstanding idea!" Heather agreed. "You don't suppose the detectives on the case will be annoyed if we bring in our own tracker and our own clairvoyant, do you?"

I sighed. If only we were in Plymouth where we had Stone to run interference for us with the police. "This is going to be murder," I said.

"Is that what Phil would call an unconscious pun?" Heather said. She was trying Dickstein's cell again. *Still busy.*

"You should talk, with your *bones of contention.*"

Driving into Salem was for me like one of Jordan's trips back in time, although the Salem of today was much more developed for business, enlivened with inviting eateries and occult shops, and crowded with tourists than the North Shore city had been while I was growing up there. My parents had owned a garden shop, Shipton's Perennial Pleasures, and I'd graduated from Salem High School. Later, I'd majored in Plant Science at the University of Rhode Island where I met and married Gary Hauser, father of Becky, Adam, and Cathy. When our marriage had become troubled and abusive, I'd left Gary to return home with my three children. After my parents died, I'd taken over running the business, and eventually the children had gone away to college and new lives. Loneliness, depression, and a bruised spirit had driven me to make a new start in Plymouth, where I'd inherited my little saltbox house by the sea from my father's mother. I was also the heir of the Shipton women's rich herbal lore, recorded in journals and notebooks faithfully preserved throughout the generations. It seemed to be my destiny to replenish Grandma's herb gardens and develop my own business.

Like a drowning person, my whole emotional history scrolled through my thoughts while Heather drove through the familiar streets, leaving me with a sad, uneasy feeling in the pit of my stomach. *Well, if all that bad stuff hadn't happened, I would never have moved to Plymouth and met Joe*, I reasoned with myself.

Our rooms at the Crowninshield were a bit over the top in Colonial chic, but quite comfortable; each had its own little sitting area. Heather and Fiona shared one "suite", me and Phillipa (when she arrived) the other. After we'd settled in, Heather shepherded us back downstairs into the cozy Elizabeth Allen bar. It was there that she had finally connected with Dickstein. He talked for a few minutes while Heather looked increasingly troubled. Finally she closed her phone and sighed deeply.

"The man is totally devastated, and no wonder," she said. "Although I do find it somewhat heartless of him to mention the possible effect of lurid publicity on funding for the Morse project. And this latest tragedy couldn't be more heartbreaking."

"*Who? Who? Who?Who?*" Fiona and I sounded like a pair of doleful owls.

But before Heather could reply, Phillipa swept into the lounge wearing a sleek black pants suit and a black fedora. Her grand entrance did not go unnoticed by the handful of afternoon drinkers, but she ignored them. "I knew I'd find you in the bar!" she exclaimed. "I decided I'd better come early and keep you three out of trouble. In fact, I packed and ran as soon as I heard about the latest incident. It is, of course, the talk of the state police even in Plymouth, and the story's gone viral in just a few hours."

"Heather! Phillipa! Are you going to tell us what happened, or am I expected to tune in psychically?" I complained.

"The victim was pregnant." Phillipa lowered her voice. This wasn't news to be shouted about. "Maybelle Budd. She and her husband William had taken the Haunted Cemeteries tour, but the bus ride was making her queasy. It was at the old Morse family cemetery that she got off and walked away from the others to get a breath of fresh air. The bullet got her right in the stomach. She's still alive, but the child…is not. Do you think that maniac deliberately targeted her belly?"

Now we all felt sick. We took our glasses of wine to a quiet corner, and Fiona ordered a pot of tea to be brought to the table. "They don't have Lapsang souchong, can you imagine?" she complained. "So I told the bartender to be sure to bring a jar of honey with that English Afternoon tea he said could be fetched from the inn's dining room, The Endicott."

"Tea? You're ordering *tea*? What are we, some kind of *sewing society*?" Heather inquired sarcastically. "By Hecate, we need to come up with a serious plan or charm to end this sadistic killing spree. That's why we're here, after all. Cass, you have your herb supplies, right? And I've organized a magic candle kit, travel-size. Just the basic colors, with a bit of appropriate incense and one or two symbols. You have your dowsing pendant, Fiona. Phil…well, Phil has her rhyming spells and the tarot. I'd say we're all set to go."

"The better, the sooner," Fiona said. "But a cup of sweet tea will steady our nerves for strategizing."

"Ah…those candles, Heather," I said cautiously. "Just the rainbow, right? I mean, no black hexing candles?"

Heather gazed out the bar's small-paned window as if she could actually see something through the glazed glass, giving me her patrician profile and Vassar voice. "Dear Cass, the candle complement simply wouldn't be complete without black. Remember that it's not just for hexing, it also banishes negativity."

"Yeah, yeah," Phillipa said. "I think the first thing is to get a line on the killer, and Hazel's book has helped us with that kind of thing in the past. He seems to have kept on the move around the Morse place, constantly one jump ahead of law enforcement. And now he's got away again!"

"Actually, the site is quite well guarded at this point," Heather said. "There are uniforms patrolling day and night and a cruiser standing by. The Morse cemetery, however, happens to be at some distance from the house, separated by the Bishop place and its acreage. Possibly the Bishop property was part of Morse farmland once upon a time, but the bottom line is, the cemetery wasn't being patrolled."

Cass says there are two shooters, Fiona explained to Phillipa. "Caucasians. One is a heavy older man, the other a young fellow. They're traveling in a dirty blue van."

"They may not both be shooters," I said. "The older man could be mentoring the boy. Setting up the locations and choosing the targets." I really didn't know where this supposition was coming from, unless there was something I'd seen in those two faces that didn't register consciously. But I've learned to spill out all ideas as they come to me, there being no sure way of telling whether they were true clairvoyant knowledge, wild intuitions, or plot remnants of some old crime movie.

"Dirty blue van?" Phillipa repeated. "What a pity we can't get the police to follow up on that one. Our usual frustration. *How do we explain what we know?*"

The bartender, looking somewhat disgruntled, carried over a tray with a pot of tea, honey, and cups from the dining room. Fiona smiled her sweetest thanks, and we were all silent until he'd gone back behind the bar out of earshot.

"Dickstein said that most of the young staffers are spooked," Heather took up the narrative again. "No one's willing to dig and sift in the trenches until the sniper is caught. The excavation has screeched to a halt. The place would be deserted if it weren't for persistent reporters trying to find someone to interview. Jordan Rivers is back, though. And some of the other indoor staffers. When Jordan leaves for the day, she's escorted by a tough-looking biker friend. Dickstein thinks he's armed. He lives above a tavern, somewhere near Pickering Wharf. Jordan is staying there with him, Dickstein thinks."

"Who's in charge of the investigation?" Fiona was sipping her honeyed tea with a thoughtful expression.

Phillipa said, "Something like this calls for a multi-jurisdictional task force. Essex Detective Unit, Salem Chief of Police, FBI, all probably vying with each other for control, but my money's on Gallant. Detective Lieutenant Bruce Gallant of the Essex Unit. And before you ask, no, he's not a great friend of Stone's. We were introduced to him and his wife at a North Shore party ages ago. I doubt they would even remember us."

"Do you remember Gallant's wife?" I asked.

"Well, yes, actually I do. We had a long heartfelt chat about the best way to peel a rutabaga. Devilish hard to do without chopping off a finger. Now what was her name? Ah yes, Greta. Greta Gallant, willowy blonde with a discontented mouth."

"Is there any way you could get in touch with her? Maybe offer to read the tarot for her?" Heather asked.

"*Are you out of your mind, Heather?* What do you expect me to say? Most likely she won't remember me from Eve," Phillipa scoffed. "Sweet Isis, ladies, I think I need a real drink." She strode over to the bar and ordered a Jack Daniels on the rocks, specifying two rocks.

"I'll think about it," Phillipa said after she had taken the first swig. "What do you want me to say? *Tell Brucie to look for a dirty blue van?*"

"Just get reacquainted," Fiona suggested. "Tell her you're in Salem for a few days, perhaps researching your next New England cookbook, and you'd like to buy her lunch at Capt's Waterfront Grill."

"Do I have an expense account," Phillipa asked.

"Do any of us?" I asked. "Fiona's right. Make the contact, and then we'll see what develops."

Later that day, I called Tip and told him about our latest mission. "Caucasians, but with Indian symbols, according to my vision. We're hoping there's no kind of American Indian protest involved. I thought you might know if there's any move to stop the excavation of Massachusett artifacts at the Morse homestead."

"No way," Tip said. "The Massachusett tribe was all but wiped out by a European-imported plague in the 1600s. And besides, I'd have heard if a protest was brewing in my own home state. What are you medicine women up to now, Aunt Cass? Is Joe there with you?"

"No, I'm on my own in Salem with the ladies. Joe is cruising through Iceberg Alley trying to discourage a Scottish oil company from drilling in the Arctic. Meanwhile, the circle is having a little pow-wow to bring down the shooters, of course. Like we do. I don't know if there will be any actual tracking involved, but there is that Indian angle. Could you get away for a few days?"

"Sure. I'm back with Uncle John Thomas. He's in Bangor now, working in the construction business, and he'll give me break if I need one. Do you really believe these attacks have something to do with the Massachusett site?"

"It's a motive, however specious," I said.

"Then maybe you should be looking for some Big Chief Wannabe. Those are the kinds of jerks that give Indians a bad name," Tip said scornfully.

"That could be, actually, Tip. And where are we most likely to find bigmouth members of the Wannabe tribe?"

"Local societies, maybe. Local bars, for sure," Tip said.

"Okay, thanks, honey. I'll be in touch if we need a tracker. And even if we don't, I'd love to see you and catch up."

"Me, too. Now you keep your head down, you hear, Aunt Cass?"

"Not to worry, Tip. You know me…"

"I do, and that's why I am worrying."

❦

That evening we had dinner at the *Buona Magia* Restaurant and Lounge on Lafayette Street. The name sounded like our kind of place, but the loud, lively music made it difficult to hold a quiet conversation. Perusing the menu, Phillipa recommended that we try the Atlantic Salmon with French Lentils. We all ignored her and went for the various pastas.

Choosing my words carefully for a public place where you have to shout to be heard, I relayed my conversation with Tip, and we considered the possibility that the shooters were on a bogus crusade.

"It's probably bad karma to say this," Phillipa said.,"but I think we should wait and see what happens next before we go out on the Indian protest limb. I mean, if there's another shooting. Where and when."

"We're here to prevent another incident, not to hang around watching," Heather insisted.

But as it happened, we didn't have to hang around for long. The very next morning, a ten-year-old boy named Simon Stull was targeted while wheeling his grandmother's cart out of Walmart on Highland Ave. Mrs. Stull thought at first that her grandson had simply keeled over in a faint, until she saw the blood seeping out from under his body. A simple soul, she was not savvy enough to fend off the TV reporters who shoved microphones in her face and asked how she felt when she realized that her grandson had been shot and killed.

"Oh, wouldn't you just enjoy hexing that lot!" Heather exclaimed. We were all having the hotel's continental breakfast at a table in the inn's bar so that we could watch the news while we ate cranberry muffins with our juice and coffee.

Cameras took close-ups of every wince and tear while Mrs. Stull explained that Simon had been a good boy who'd attended a special class at Salem Middle School and was always willing to help her around the house. His mother had left home when Simon was seven, and his father was a commercial fisherman out of Gloucester, so Simon was given to Mrs. Stull's care. "What will I tell his father?" Mrs. Stull wailed.

"The snipers are branching out," Phillipa said.

"Maybe the heat's off the Morse project," I said. But I wasn't entirely convinced that there was no connection, at least in the killers' minds. Even if it was only target practice to bring Salem and all its works to a standstill.

The young reporter on the scene continued to say that the shot appeared to have come from the Walmart parking lot, where Simon and his grandmother had been buying supplies for a school pageant, including an Indian headdress which Simon was wearing when shot. A witness who'd been loading purchases into her car claimed to have glimpsed a dirty van wheeling out of the parking lot very fast just before Mrs. Stull started screaming for help.

"There's your van, Cass," Fiona said.

"And your Indian tie-in," Phillipa added.

Heather's cell rang. It was Deidre, who was also watching the morning news. "I don't know what we're going to do," Heather said. "One of the things out of Hazel's book, I suppose. Yes, tonight for sure. Anything going on with Hogben? Did he! Oh, good for Conor, Listen, why don't you come out here as soon as Mother Ryan loses all her quarters and comes home. Yeah. Good. Oh, wait, what did Conor bring you? Really? Okay, talk later. Everyone sends love." She snapped her cell closed while we all waited eagerly for the Deidre news.

"Dee suggests we get down to what we do best, spell-work. She reports that Hogben marched through the mall again yesterday, and his entourage surrounded her shop with 'witch' placards like before. She called Conor, and he rushed over in his Land Rover. When the cops prevented him from assaulting Hogben, Conor began taking close-ups of those girls in weird costumes, you remember the bonnets and the braided blonde wigs? The TV people had more or less ignored them and concentrated on the insulting picket signs and picketers. Conor's interest seemed more disturbing to the mad preacher than any threats of bodily harm, and he soon scurried away with his idiot followers." Heather stopped long enough to pour herself another cup of coffee from the carafe.

"We are all wondering what gift Conor brought back for Dee from the rainforest excursion," Phillipa asked.

"A carved jade ring. Green parrot. Dee says it's an amulet of peace and love because famous paintings by van Eyck and others depict the Holy Mother holding a parrot."

"Peace, love, and virginity?" Phillipa suggested.

"Blessed young motherhood," Fiona decreed.

"And Dee's wearing it on which hand?" I asked.

"She didn't say, and I'm not asking. Dee has decided she'd better join us for the spell-work. She's got Bettikins to stay with the youngsters, and Mother Ryan is on her way. Then we can have a look at that parrot for ourselves. Dee believes we'll need her to complete the circle, and maybe there's something to that," Heather said. "Say, would you all like a shot of Sambuca in that coffee."

"*No!*" we chorused. *Clear heads must prevail.*

The plan was to drop in on Jordan Rivers after breakfast, then spend the afternoon tooling around Salem to take in the sights (*all work and no play* is not in our Wiccan rede.) A quiet dinner along the waterfront. Later, there would be a waning moon, good for banishing, and we had in mind to conjure one of Hazel's "reveal evil" spells in a secluded wooded place, perhaps somewhere on Gallows Hill, if we could get away with it in a recreational park.

But that's not exactly the way the day went down.

CHAPTER FOUR

Time is but the stream I go fishing in...
its thin current slides away, but eternity remains.

– Henry David Thoreau

"Witch City" is a misnomer. The Salem women condemned for being witches in the 17th century were sober, pious matrons denounced by some of the most malicious, mean-spirited teen-agers who ever wanted to throw off the shackles of matronly disapproval and bask in the limelight of masculine attention.

"Real" witches practice an Earth-based religion whose deities are female as well as male. They feel profoundly connected to nature, they affirm that life in all its myriad forms is sacred, and they celebrate the cycle of seasons. Some witches work with unseen energies of the universe to influence the outcome of events, a practice known as *magic*. They may use herbs, incense, chanting and/or dancing to focus their intentions. Their religion predates Christianity and the concept of Satan. Currently, the religion of witches is called Wicca.

The goodwives of Salem who swung and strangled on the Gallows Tree were Calvinist Christians falsely accused of being in league with the devil and working magic on their victims. After these martyrs were dead and the girls had recanted, official pardons were granted and some restitution was made to families forced to pay the costs of keeping their mother or grandmother in jail while awaiting trial and punishment.

It's possible that Sarah Morse had passed down a farmwife's practical wisdom to her young cousin Hazel Morse Eastey (author of *Hazel's Household Remedies*, one of our trusty resources), but Sarah was no witch. She was a respectable church-going wife and mother with considerable skill in healing, using potions and salves of her own making and certain efficacious prayers. Accused by her niece Patience Blessing of spectral torment (everything from screaming fits to visits from lusty imps), Sarah's body was examined and found to have witches' marks (brown moles) and witches' teats (warts), incontrovertible proof of her guilt. She was tried, convicted, imprisoned for months, and finally executed. Her husband Daniel Morse died soon after of a stroke. The Morse property was sold to the Blessings far below its true value. The Morses' only surviving son Benjamin moved to Danvers.

The Morse homestead (purchased back from the Blessings by the Salem Heritage Foundation in recent years and restored to its former title) was a classic saltbox, quite similar to the antique cottage I'd inherited from my grandma, but larger and more austere with clapboard siding rather than silvery shingles. The uncompromising God worshiped by the pilgrims favored structures and clothing that were modest, somber, and unadorned. Their religious ethic took no inspiration from the splendid wild woodland that surrounded their bleak village, although it might have been considered an expression of the Divine Creator's pleasure in beauty.

Three great old oak trees shaded the Morse house and its barn, set among 25 acres of farmland that had originally been a grant of 100 acres. Much of the cleared land was between the house and the main road, so access to the homestead was by way of a long drive lined with tumbling stone walls. Directly behind the homestead were the restored kitchen gardens. Toward the back and to one side was the site where the excavation in search of American Indian artifacts was visible as square-cut trenches that resembled open graves. Back farther, eighty or ninety yards, the Morse property was bounded by a woodland of pine, maple, and oak, crisscrossed by old logging roads.

So we were instructed by the satellite aerial map Fiona brought forth from her reticule as we approached the homestead.

We had to do some fast talking to visit Jordan at the Morse crime scene. A cruiser, two officers, and a yellow tape were guarding the premises and the personnel, those who were still brave enough to work there. In a situation like this, we of course depend on Fiona, the quintessential non-threatening auntie type, to sweet-talk her way inside.

"The dear girl will be so disappointed if we don't say hello." Fiona gazed up at the brawny young officer blocking the doorway to the homestead "She wanted to show us some special artifacts she's photographing for the Archaeology Society. You'll want to ask her, won't you?"

You'll want to ask her, won't you? There was it: the magical voice to which we all aspired. We stood in back of Fiona like children waiting to be taken on tour.

Fiona smiled and hummed and waited until the officer saw the light and decided to go inside to ask the young woman if she had indeed invited visitors, possible relations?

Jordan was intrigued and came out into the sunshine to have a look at her visitors, but she also shielded her eyes with one hand to survey the trees in back of the house.

"Hey, ladies! So here you are in Salem! *Awesome!* But you'd better come on inside where it's safer. We have this wacko running around town. Is that sniper, like, *your mission* here, or are you just doing the tourist trap thing?"

"Maybe a little of both, Jordan," Heather said as we stepped into the cool interior where leaded diamond panes shielded the rooms from the summer morning's rising heat. At one end of the long keeping room, a folding table had been set up for photographing and cataloging the latest finds. We helped ourselves to a stack of folding chairs while Jordan proudly pointed out various prize artifacts. It all looked rather meager to me, but perhaps a trained archaeologist could read whole episodes of American Indian history in those pieces of broken pottery.

"Things seem to have quieted down at last here," Phillipa said. "It appears that the sniper has moved on to other targets."

"That's what Detective Gallant says, but he's keeping a police presence here, *in case.* Gallant is, like, *totally* cool for a cop."

"You're all alone here today? You're feeling more secure, then?" I asked. Actually, I sensed just the opposite. The girl's crackling energy was low and there was a faint crease between her brows.

"Only me and one other cataloger these days. Matt. He's spooked, too. Called in sick today. Like, *sick of work* in the shooting gallery. I still get the jitters, you know what I mean?" Jordan confessed. "My cousin Rafe is a biker. I've been staying at his place, and he's watching out for me. Brings me to work and picks me up after. If I didn't, like, *totally* need the money, I'd be *long gone* out of this freaking town. The job's going to end, anyway, if the field workers don't get back to digging. Don't blame them, though. After what happened to poor Ernie and Fuchsia Woolley. And Mrs. Budd who was only out walking at the cemetery. Then there was that innocent kid at Walmart. Like, that freaking creep is all around us!"

Fiona put her arm around Jordan's thin shoulders and patted her hand. "You'll be fine, dear. You've a strong spirit, and I sense an invisible shield around you, perhaps an ancestral thing."

"Speaking of ancestors, what about those time-travel episodes you were having?" Phillipa asked.

Jordan picked up a pipe stem and looked at it absently. "Handling all these old pieces, it's like, they're drawing me into the past, you know what I mean?" She got up suddenly from the wooden chair at her work table. "Hey, ladies, there's a cooler in back, you know. Sprite? Coke? It's Diet."

We followed Jordan to the back room and selected cans of soda. Leaning against the walls of the small mud room, we sipped our cold drinks blissfully.

There was one wicker chair, where we had seated Fiona, who said, "Do you want to tell us about it, dear?"

"I guess." Although Jordan's tone was unsure, I suspected that she wanted to talk about her latest experience. "I was taking a break, looking out this back door, when everything suddenly went dark, you know what I mean? Like a cloud had aced out the sun. Next thing, I was running across that field out there. Running fast and scared. There were soldiers on horseback, trying to trample me down. I was, like, *totally* freaked out. Racing to a place where I thought I'd be safe. Like a sanctuary, you know? Only it wasn't a church, it was just a big flat rock in the pines." Jordan smiled suddenly. "I'm going to have a look for that rock. Just as soon as they catch this weirdo."

"That rock might turn out to be the most inspired find on this site," I said.

"Yeah, I'm betting there might be, like, some kind of awesome artifacts out there," Jordan said, smiling wanly. "There's a little good in everything bad, like my Mom used to say."

"Well, listen, dear. We're at the Crowninshield Hotel for a few days, so if you need us for anything, anything at all, you give Phil a call. Meanwhile, here's a little Navajo blessing." Fiona stood up, took her medicine bag out of the reticule by her side, and sprinkled a bit of corn pollen over Jordan's head. "Phil, just jot down your BlackBerry number for Jordan, will you, dear? And take Jordan's cell number, so we can keep in touch."

We hugged Jordan good-bye, as we got ready to leave on our Salem sight-seeing tour: lunch at Capt's Waterfront Cafe, then on to the House of Seven Gables and maybe the Witch Museum.

We stepped from the cool mud room into brilliant sunshine and sizzling heat. The officers on duty had taken refuge under the friendly oak trees, where one of them was lighting a cigarette. Heather dashed ahead to open the Mercedes and let some of its hot air escape, Phillipa took Fiona's arm, and they moved sedately, bringing up the rear. I was in the middle and had just removed my Greenpeace rainbow hat to wipe my forehead, when I found myself jumping to the right, impelled by some instinct just below the surface of consciousness.

Then there was a searing pain across my head, above my left ear.

And blackness.

∽

By the time the ambulance came, I found myself sitting up on the back stoop, surrounded by concerned faces, which included Jordan's. The quiet homestead had suddenly become a helter-skelter gathering of cruisers and officers running into the woods and shouting to one another or talking on cell phones.

"I'm all right," I insisted. "Now here's the thing..."

"You're *bleeding*, Cass," Phillipa informed me.

Fiona was dabbing away at my forehead with an actual cotton handkerchief like no one carried anymore, moistened with hydrogen peroxide from a sample-size bottle. "Thank the Goddess for Her protection, although it would have been nicer if..."

"*Now, here's the thing...*" I repeated more strongly. "*No one is to call Joe.* He's probably out of reach, anyway, but wherever he is, there's absolutely no need to worry him about this little scratch. What happened, anyway?"

"You got shot," Jordan said succinctly. "That psycho is back in the woods somewhere. He must have been watching us."

The Salem rescue wagon screeched into the front yard. Two paramedics and a fireman lumbered around back with a carry chair. Over my protests, they insisted on taking me to the NSMC Salem Hospital, to have the bullet graze dressed and to check out if I was concussed.

"I think there was a van way out by the main road," Heather said, walking beside me as I was being trundled away. "I guess I registered it subliminally, glints of metal, but it was parked where trees begin to line the road. Then, after you went down, I heard it take off and yelled. One of the officers chased after the van in his cruiser, but the van had a good head start before these guys got it in gear."

"The shooter must have walked back into the woods with a powerful scope on that rifle. Picked you off, then ran like Hades, caught up with the van before we came out of our shock," Phillipa said. "By the way, I saw you zig-zag to the right just before you collapsed."

"Yeah, that happens to me sometimes," I said as I was lifted into the back of the wagon. "Intuition, perhaps. But I call it a Cosmic Nudge. *Ouch!*" I rather wished the nudge had knocked me a bit farther out of danger. My head was beginning to smart, and I wondered if I was going to have a swath of bare scalp. But Jordan was there, ashen under her golden skin, so I pressed her hand and said, "I'll be all right, honey. You go back inside and don't stir until Rafe shows up to guard you home. I'll talk to you soon."

"That was your sixth sense, Cass," Fiona said just before the paramedic shut the back door of the ambulance. "Or possibly the seventh or eighth. We'll follow you to the hospital, dear," she shouted through the door.

At the hospital, a fresh-faced intern cleaned and bandaged the graze and ruled out any symptoms of concussion. Still he asked my roommate, Phillipa, to wake me up every couple of hours to make sure I was conscious.

With my embarrassing bandaged head, I left the emergency room leaning on Phillipa's arm while Heather shepherded Fiona. *With a flag and a drum, we could have been taken for the Spirit of '76.*

"What happened to our impenetrable white light, Fiona?" Phillipa asked.

"The hand of the Goddess was in that Cosmic Nudge, as Cass calls it. Pushed her out of harm's way," Fiona insisted. "Even the best psychic protection will have a little hole here and there. Just ask Achilles' mother."

As soon as we got up to our rooms, I removed the ridiculous bandage. The graze was so minimal, the air would do it good, I declared over various protests. My main concern was my hair.

"Don't worry. The damage is *barely* noticeable. Possibly you can manage a Donald Trump comb-over," Phillipa consoled me. "As soon as we get home, treat yourself to some kind of deceptive hair-cut at Sophia's Serene Salon. Chances are Joe will never even notice. You know how unconscious men can be. Even detectives."

"I wouldn't count on that, if I were you," I said. "And Joe never misses anything." *Especially on my body*, I was thinking but didn't say.

"Speaking of Joe," Heather said, reading from her BlackBerry. "There's a one-line news item about Greenpeace here. Apparently, some of the activists climbed up on the oil rig *and hung up there in something called 'survival pods'* to prevent drilling. An amazing feat in that frigid climate!"

"I wonder sometimes if I should have joined Greenpeace as a ship's cook or something," Phillipa mused. "Those must be some strapping, well-built guys."

"Oh, Sweet Isis! Phillipa, get out your laptop and see what else you can find out, will you? Like, has any handsome Greek ship's engineer been arrested?"

"Look at it this way," Phillipa reassured me as she booted up. "Joe can hardly complain about *your* putting yourself in danger after this stunt, can he? But don't worry, it must be the younger activists who volunteered to sleep in a pod over the freezing Arctic waters. Joe will be on the ship, cozy and warm, fending off the Danish Navy warship."

"You're such a comfort, Phil."

∽

"I'm fine. I'm really fine," I insisted. "At least we can go out to lunch as we planned. And if I don't faint and fail, maybe we can take in the House of Seven Gables afterward." Phillipa had insisted that I lie down for an hour with a cold cloth on my forehead, but now I was feeling both restive and quite hungry. And so was everyone else; protests were minimal.

I had thought this would be a good time to wear my attractive hat with a pink hatband and matching pink shirt. It was certainly an out-of-character outfit for me, but I was pleased to see that it covered the scabby graze and my weirdly parted hair.

"Hey, Miz Scarlett, I thought you said *no eye-catching hats*," Phillipa complained. She was wearing black straw herself, right in keeping with the Salem motif.

"Yes, Cass," Heather chimed in. "If you hadn't been waving that Greenpeace cap around, you might not have made such a fetching target this morning."

It was late, so the lunch crowd had thinned at Capt.'s Waterfront. We got a scenic table "topside" overlooking a flock of sailboats and the summer-blue ocean. Heather proceeded to study the wine list while the rest of us focused on the food. "I think I'll order a couple of bottles of Kendall-Jackson Chardonnay, if you're all in a fishy mood."

"One will be plenty, if you don't want us to be staggering and giggling through the Seven Gables." I was glad to change the subject from my hat folly. "And I'm definitely in a lobster roll mood."

Heather ignored me and asked for two bottles anyway, and we gave our orders. After the waitress was out of earshot, we began to plan the Gallows Hill ritual we would use to smoke out the snipers.

Fiona had brought a copy of a recipe from *Hazel's Book of Household Recipes* in her reticule, and she laid it out on the table now, pushing aside the bread basket to make room. "Oh, Good Goddess," Phillipa said as she whipped off her hat and held it between the other diners and the object of our attention.

"Nothing we've done before seemed just right for this situation," Fiona said. "But I did find something that might work between *Calf's Foot Jelly* and *Poison Ivy Poultice.*"

I leaned over and read aloud, but softly. *"How to Stop Vermin and Other Unwanted Creatures.* I guess we have a case of Other Unwanted Creatures, all right. Let's see what we'll need. I did bring a fairly complete supply of magical herbs."

"We should wait for Dee," Heather said. "We're always stronger with a circle of five."

"I'll call her right now," Phillipa said. "Maybe she can get away this afternoon. Anything you want her to bring?"

"Yes," I said, still reading. "I'd like to add a couple of poppets to this spell, just to make it perfectly clear to the Cosmos that we're not trying to rid Salem of actual rats. Tell Dee that I've seen one sniper as an older man, a rather heavy fellow, and the other, a slim kid. They're driving a dirty blue van."

"I'm worried about the word *stop*," Phillipa said. "How will that be interpreted by the Cosmos? What we really want is for the law to *catch* them and put them away forever."

"You're quibbling over semantics," Heather complained.

"The precise wording is absolutely vital in magic," Fiona said. "Phil understands because she's a poet, and poets get hung up on that sort of thing. I remember once when my wee Auntie Gracie was saying a few words over a homemade loaf of faery bread…"

Just then a waiter arrived with two bottles of chilled chardonnay, followed by our waitress carrying a heavily laden tray with cups of rich chowder and chunky lobster sandwiches, delectable distractions that lost to us forever the mischief that Auntie Gracie may have loosed upon the Highlands. Phillipa hastily rolled up the Hazel recipe tucked it back into Fiona's reticule, then stepped toward the porch railing to punch in Deidre's number.

"How's the chowder?" she asked when she'd returned to the table. "Real clams, I trust, not chopped elastic bands?"

"What about Dee?" I asked. The wine was going down quite easily, I noted. Fiona reached for the second bottle.

"Dee's going to skip out on Conor and meet us at the Crowninshield at sunset. *Have poppets, will travel*," Phillipa said. "We'd better book a room for her to stay overnight."

"What about the children? Laura Belle is staying at the Ryans, too, and I don't know if Conor…" Fiona worried.

"Betti Kinsey is there and will stay with the kids. You know they all love Bettikins," Phillipa reassured her. "So… Cass, do we have everything we need? Rue? Boneset?"

"Not to worry," I said. "I must have been guided when I packed my herbal travel kit. Hazel also suggests scattering hemp seed in a graveyard, but hemp is *cannabis sativa,* although not the controlled strain of the plant. Still, I think thistle seed around the trees of Gallows Hill will do just as well."

"Hazel seems so real to me now that we've found and visited her own grave site on Burial Hill," Heather said. "Hazel Morse Eastey. Clearly a descendent of Sarah Morse who was hanged as a witch. Hazel even named her own daughter Sarah. I wonder if that wasn't a bit risky."

"By the time Hazel's children were born, the so-called witches had been found innocent and pardoned," I said. "Still, I bet she kept her *Household Recipes* in a secret place."

"Perhaps she had a little space behind the preserves in the cold room," Phillipa suggested.

"Maybe buried in a sack of hops at the brewing shed," Heather said, "or wherever they brewed their ale."

"Not hops. Maize. The Indians taught them to brew ale with maize," Phillipa said. "The only reason the Pilgrims landed in Plymouth in the first place is because they were running out of provisions, especially beer, which was considered nourishment for all ages. I may include a recipe for Pilgrim beer in my next cookbook. Perhaps there's one in Hazel's book."

" Hazel may have foreseen us," Fiona mused. "I hope she did imagine that her book would come into our hands, and that we would put it to such good use. Rousting evil-doers and whatnot. I find that a little fillip of danger adds a welcome zest to the life of a small-town librarian like myself. *Something ventured, something gained*, I always say."

CHAPTER FIVE

A hair perhaps divides the False and True;
Yes; and a single Alif were the clue
Could you but find it..

– Omar Khayyám, FitzGerald translation

The Turner-Ingersoll house is better known as the House of Seven Gables because of Nathaniel Hawthorne's novel of the same name. With its themes of false witness, guilt, retribution, and the supernatural, the book has continued to inspire authors of romantic horror ever since. Hawthorne used the real home of his cousin, Susannah Ingersoll, as the setting for his classic tale. Later the Colonial mansion, beautifully situated right on the ocean, became a historic site and tourist attraction. On the late June day of our visit, Seven Gables was crowded with summer tourists, so that one could hardly feel the spirits of the dwelling. It's much better to visit a historic house on an off-day in an off-season, when with a little luck one might sense the true history of the place. Perhaps, if Deidre had been with us, she would have felt some presence of early inhabitants at the Seven Gables, since she's become so sensitive to the dead.

There was a hint of the past, however, in wedging ourselves through the secret staircase that had been hidden behind paneling in a vertical space beside the fireplace chimney. A tight fit for me, but no problem for Phillipa and Heather. It took the both of them, however, to lift and haul plump, arthritic Fiona up the narrow stairs to the third floor.

Phillipa was much taken by reproductions of the Osgood portrait of Hawthorne as a handsome young man, and declared him to be "hot." She insisted on buying a copy before we left, as well as an authentic Salem cookbook to add to her extensive collection of regional recipes from every place she'd ever visited.

The "cent-shop" operated by the author's fictional character Hepzibah Pyncheon had been recreated as it might have appeared within the house in earlier times. The real gift store, however, was in a separate building, well lit, modern, and thoroughly commercial, with an enormous and resplendent resident cat who glowered at us and put me in mind of Patty Peacedale's regal Loki. For some indefinable reason, this last stop turned out to be the eeriest part of the tour for me. I could hardly wait to get out into the fresh summer air. Having toured the mansion many times in the past, I turned my attention gratefully to my favorite feature, the restoration of the original gardens where fragrant herbs and flowering seaside plants thrived in well-tended beds between brick walks.

"Something strangelet about that shop," Fiona said when she joined me. *Strangelets* were Fiona's name for amorphous evil entities such as we had encountered in Bermuda.

"I believe someone in there was creating a spiritual disturbance," I said. "Maybe I should have zeroed in on the other shoppers, or the young man tending the cash register. Just to find out if it was my imagination."

"It's a relief to know there's something genuinely spooky in this town," Phillipa said. "So much phony witchery."

"Yeah? Let's get out of here." Heather looked around nervously. "It's too late now for the Witch House, but at least we can get things ready for our ritual later."

"Reminds me of Benevento. There's a real spiritual force in Salem existing side by side with all the Witch City promotion," Fiona said. "Remember that Cass grew up in this town, and she's the real deal. And there are other psychics thriving on Salem's powerful vibrations. In fact, I've a friend who has a shop here, a well-known Wiccan priestess, Circe La Femme. We ought to visit her place, if there's time. Don't you find that Salem has a certain mystique, like Plymouth? The pilgrims were drawn to Plymouth for more reasons than running out of ale, Phil."

"I would never argue with you, Fiona, when you're in your oracle mood," Phillipa acquiesced, winking at me. "*Circe La Femme?*"

I glanced back at the shop one more time. A young man ducked out the back door. I realized that I'd seen him earlier, stocking the store's shelves and smirking in a way I found quite distasteful. "See that fellow scurrying down to the waterfront," I said as we got into Phillipa's car. "Would it sound crazy if I suggested that you trail along behind him?"

"No crazier than usual," Phillipa said. "But I think he's just an employee knocking off work. Why him?"

"He gives me a sinister feeling," was the best I could explain.

"Good enough. And besides, this cloak-and-dagger stuff is fun." Phillipa eased out of her parking place and crawled down the street after the figure I'd pointed out. He ducked into a parking lot, and she crept along after him, pulling to one side as we watched to see where he was headed. He got into an old black Dodge van, revved the motor, and quickly zoomed by us onto the street. A bumper sticker on the back of the van read: *The James Younger Gang.*

"It's not blue," I remarked. "But there's something…"

"Do you want me to do the car chase thing?" Phillipa was a little too eager. I got the idea that she wouldn't mind putting her BMW through its paces, similar to the TV ads that warn *Professional driver. Closed course. Do not attempt.*

"No, no. What a silly thing. He's a complete stranger, after all."

"I felt it, too," Fiona remarked. "But let's just wait and see if he turns up in our awareness again. Perhaps he's just a passing aura of unrest. Right now I want to go back to the inn and put up my feet for a while."

"Maybe Dee has arrived," Heather said. "Time to stir up some serious magic."

We drove around to the Crowninshield parking lot and were pleased to see Deidre's Aurora Blue Mazda parked there. We found her at the reception desk; Heather had already booked her a room.

"Got the poppets right here!" she cried across the lobby, waving her workbag aloft. I supposed that her shrill announcement wouldn't seem as off-the-wall as it might have in another town.

We hugged and exchanged "Merry Meet" greetings. It felt good to be together again. Also, it gave us a chance to inspect Deidre's hands surreptitiously; the jade parrot ring was not visible on either of them! Heather and I glanced at each other. Phillipa nudged me. We didn't need telepathy to know that each of us was thinking, *Where in Hades is that ring?*

All our rooms were on the second floor, so we often used the stairs. But at the foot of the curved banister, Deidre shivered and looked around the lobby nervously. "There seems to be an awful cold draft in here," she said.

"It's Salem, Dee," Phillipa said, bundling her into the little gilt elevator usually favored by the elderly and infirm. "City of shivers and specters and such." No need to get our crafty Deidre side-tracked into ghost-whispering.

Later, in Heather and Fiona's room, Deidre studied the page from Hazel's book. *"How to Stop Vermin and Other Unwanted Creatures,"* she read aloud wonderingly. "What a caution that Hazel was! 'Scattering hemp seeds in the cemetery at midnight,' indeed! Rather an untraditional method of getting rid of rats and mice, I'd say. More likely it was Hazel's way of putting interfering busybodies out of business. How do you propose to use my poppets?" She drew them out of her workbag triumphantly, and they were just what the sorcerer ordered.

"This spell is based on herbal magic, but I figured a little sympathetic magic wouldn't hurt," I explained. "And what could be more sympathetic than actual poppets?"

"How about this!" Deidre dimpled and reached into her workbag again. This time the jade ring swung forward from beneath her yellow linen shirt; she was wearing it on a gold chain. She said, "I can just feel all you witches fixing on this ring, right? Well, the answers are, *I haven't decided yet* and *it's too big for my finger right now anyway.*"

After we had admired the intricate carving of its stone, a tiny green parrot, she tucked the ring back inside her shirt and held up a toy van which she had painted a medium blue and smudged with dirt. It was perfect!

Which is what I told her. "*It's perfect*, Dee. You've done it again. Now here's the thing, we sprinkle the poppets with salt water using sprigs of boneset and rue as sprinklers. Boneset to ward off malevolent vibes and rue to ricochet back to the sender all evil intentions. Then we take a leap of faith that scattering thistle around Gallows Hill will be as effective as hemp seed in a cemetery. In arcane herb lore, both seeds break through the shadows masking the lair of *Unwanted Creatures*, as Hazel so cleverly put it. We'll need to chant appropriate words of power, of course. I'm leaving that to Phil."

Phillipa was sitting on Fiona's bed, writing on her laptop. "I'm working on it," she muttered. "What rhymes with *sniper?*"

"*Diaper*," Deidre said, grinning. "Now there's a challenge. Or maybe *windshield wiper*, can you do anything with that?"

"*Pay the piper*," Fiona suggested. "But rhyme isn't strictly necessary, dear.

"*Viper*," Heather added. "And here's good news, ladies. I have just the candles for this spell. Remember those purplish-black ones I used to expose the dog-fighting ring? I wrapped a couple of them up and brought them with me, just in case."

I remembered their heady fragrance very well. Powerful stuff. And Heather had embedded tiny symbols of discovery in the wax: a doll's glass eye, a tiny magnifying glass, a charm-size silver telescope, a little dowsing pendant, crystals for scrying, and even a miniature tarot card, The Star, to enhance psychic insight.

"I've never been to Gallows Hill," Deidre said with a small shudder. "I hope I won't see any*body* there!"

"I grew up in Salem, so these places are not at all evocative to me" I said. "No one really knows the location of the actual gallows tree, except that it was customary to perform executions across the town line. My money's on Danvers. Still, the site of the hangings *might* have been on Gallows Hill, which is a recreational park now."

"How bizarre! I'd just as soon make a recreational park out of Ravensbrück," Phillipa said from behind her laptop. "Where I lost two grand-aunts, by the way. Just as Hazel lost her relative Sarah to the witch hunt. Aunt, cousin, whatever. Have you noticed how often the reformer's zeal for purification conceals another motive, the seizing of valuable property?"

"*Evil is the root of all money*," Fiona declared. "Would that Salem had celebrated its Colonial and shipping heritage, instead, but I must admit, witches are good business."

"Speaking of *The Craft*, it's getting on toward the twilight." Heather was looking out of the window. "Waning moon up there somewhere. Let's pack up our stuff and get going."

"Say, do you think we can go out for pizza afterward?" Fiona asked. "In lieu of cakes and ale. I always get so peckish after spell-work."

"In lieu of dinner, actually." Phillipa closed her laptop and smiled like the Cheshire Cat. Apparently the wording of the chant had been resolved.

We changed into "work clothes": jeans and t-shirts, or in Heather's case, a safari suit from Nordstrom's, and Fiona wore a tartan jumper, the MacDonald muted hunter plaid. Packing up our spell gear, we drove to Gallows Hill in Heather's Mercedes. Phillipa didn't fancy messing up her BMW with magical paraphernalia that might leak, spill, or stain her upholstery.

Gallows Hill Park consisted of a parking lot, a playground, assorted boulders, and a rather high hill with steep paths. We were cheered to see that the hill was well sheltered by trees that would afford us privacy. Looming over the parking lot was a water tower with the town's signature witch painted on it. At the entrance we encounter a warning sign: *No Parking After Sunset.*

"Not to worry, ladies," Heather said. "I'll drop you off here and park the car down one of those side streets. I can jog back here in a jiffy."

Better her than me, I thought. "We'd better be very quiet, though. Police probably patrol the place looking for teen-age witch parties."

"An invisibility glamour, perhaps," Fiona said thoughtfully.

"But that only works for you," Phillipa complained.

Four of us got out of the Mercedes and headed for the trees. Deidre, and I carried the baskets and sachels. Fiona leaned on Phillipa's arm and on her coyote walking stick. True to her word, Heather showed up a few minutes later, *not even winded.*

There were no actual picnic tables where we could unpack herbs, salt water, dolls, incense, and candles, so we laid a blanket on the ground in a small clearing between trees near the top of the hill and unfolded a camp chair for Fiona. A blessed breeze from the west and my natural herbal bug-off kept us comfortable. Crickets played their insistent concert in the trees, and a galaxy of fireflies danced away in the grass. It was all just the ticket for magical working.

Our only problem was that several bikers and their girlfriends were ensconced on the other side of the hill, actually on the street just beyond the confines of the park, with a giant cooler filled with cans of beer. A boom box was playing rap music, spitting out angry words. We conferred while Deidre swiftly set up our altar and laid out our herbal supplies and poppets.

Fiona said, "If curiosity brings them over here, I will handle it. Right now, let me draw the quarters." She stepped up to the top of the hill, and with one graceful movement, drew out the rapier from the sheath of her cane and pointed it dramatically to the east. We could see a glamour coming over her in the last light of the day. Swiftly, she drew a pentagram in the air and called the powers of the east to assist us in our work, then the south, the west, and the north. Phillipa purified the circle with sea salt. Heather lit incense, cinnamon for spirituality and protection, and set up her triptych of Hecate, Goddess of the Night, *She from whom nothing may be hidden.* I used my Italian *strega* scissors to cut sprigs of dried boneset and rue. Deidre rang a small silver bell to increase spiritual power and disperse negative vibrations.

"The circle is cast," she murmured.

"So must it be," we echoed.

On the other side of the hill, the bikers paused in their guzzling and partying to gaze up at Fiona silhouetted against twilit sky with her raised rapier; they were spellbound, so to speak. A brawny fellow lumbered across the hill in our direction.

"*What rough beast…slouches towards us…*Why can't Fiona use an athame like any other witch," Phillipa muttered, her hand on the sheathed ceremonial dagger at her waist.

Heather was oblivious, occupied with fixing her candles with blobs of melted wax to a handy boulder. Deidre and I exchanged nervous glances, but Fiona cut a hole in the magic circle with her rapier and stepped out to meet the muscular emissary. Humming a little, in full glamour now, she was looking quite like a mature Queen Titania. One almost sensed a crown of moonflowers and evening primrose.

Fiona and the biker exchanged a few words, during which the biker leader demanded to know *what the fuck you old broads are up to*, and Fiona explained that we were *astronomers on a field trip and that she'd been pointing out various constellations to the other members of the company. Look, see that orange star? that's the Aldebaran, the "eye" of Taurus, the bull. And over there, Cygnus, the Swan.* Her voice took on a low, soothing magical tone. Suitably mollified by Fiona's charm, the biker relaxed and introduced himself as Rafe.

In further conversation we discovered that this was the same Rafe who had offered protection to his cousin Jordan so that she could continue to work at the Morse excavation. Heather chimed in that we were dear, dear friends of Jordan's, *small world* and all that.

Rafe, speaking for the other beer-swigging, rap-loving bikers, agreed that we would give each other some space for the evening's festivities, and that was that. Détente established.

"Don't we suppose that Jordan will expose your *working astronomers* myth?" Phillipa pointed out.

"Astronomers. Astrologers. Astro-travelers. Same difference," Fiona said airily.

Rafe swaggered back to his buddies (who were now standing on their bikes, the better to have a look at the armed astronomers), Fiona re-consecrated our circle, and we began our ritual with the poppets, the herbs, the salt water, and the chant that Phillipa had created to invoke our spell.

By the waning of the moon,
evil will be banished soon...
By the poppets in our spell,
killers will reveal themselves...

We danced around our discovery candles chanting the words, faster and faster, until Fiona raised her rapier to the sky (jumping around in a rather sprightly fashion for an arthritic lady who walked with a cane) and gave an eerie call that sounded something like *way hey hey way hey hey.*

After we'd open the circle, we scattered thistle seed among the trees and bushes, chanting,

Thistle sown on Gallows Hill
Salem spirits aid our spell!
Thistle reveals hidden places,
Thistle unmasks hidden faces…

Would we reap what we had sown? Or would the spell spin off in unexpected ways, as spells so often do.

CHAPTER SIX

I am as free as Nature first made man,
Ere the base laws of servitude began,
When wild in woods the noble savage ran.

– John Dryden

Later, over *"due grandi pizze* with everything, except no anchovies on one of them" at Frank & Chuck's Pizzeria, Fiona explained that *way hey hey* was a Navajo war song, and she only wished she'd thought to bring along her drum.

"What, and spook those bikers even more? Wasn't the rapier enough?" Phillipa held her slice up in the air to peer at its bottom crust. "Very nice, crispy yet flavorful."

"It's not the bikers we have to worry about. They'll be on our side, if push comes to shove." Heather filled glasses all around from one of the bottles of Chianti Classico she had ordered. "What we have to worry about is where those sociopathic shooters will strike next."

Dee, who had been dreamily admiring the Blue Grotto décor of the pizzeria, sighed heavily. "I suppose you're all going to have a high old time chasing down these psycho murderers while I have to go home tomorrow, because I promised Conor I would. Then there's that cursed 'Planning for the Fourth' meeting sponsored by the PTA. *Bummer.*"

Fiona looked off in space for a moment. "There's always a way to have your own way Dee," she said thoughtfully. "Suppose you convince Conor that there's an intriguing opportunity for a photographic essay right here in Salem, how the real spiritual power of the place is overlaid with a commercial veneer."

"Yeah, and a pox on the PTA," Phillipa added.

"*Tempting*, Phil. But we don't do poxes and hexes, not even when we are snubbed by the mundane," Deidre said. "But perhaps Conor *would* be interested in Fiona's Salem. Could be a saleable Halloween feature different from the run-of-the-mill haunted house stuff. And Mother Ryan might be willing to stand in for me at the PTA. She's always wanted to suggest a casino night fund-raiser. I'll drive home tomorrow and see what I can do."

"Good for you, Dee," Phillipa cheered. "We *need* you to complete our circle. I'm convinced those poppets you made will prove to be the *coup de grâce* for our snipers. Okay then, we've conjured up Hazel's vermin-ridding spell. What's next?"

"Let's hang around Salem for another few days at least, to see what comes of our spell-work," I said. "I'm thinking that I'll call Tip again, to see if he'll come down here for the weekend and look into the Indian angle, He has a theory about the snipers. Maybe he'd like to have a look at the excavation and meet Jordan as well. Tip knows a lot about the history of his people. He might even be able to verify Jordan's last time-travel incident."

"Oh, well then. If we're going to stay awhile, I might as well get in touch with Greta Gallant and see if I can pump her about the investigation," Phillipa said. "Stone will be wild if I don't come straight home, of course. He does worry so when we go off on one of Cass's crusades."

"Sure, blame it on me," I whined.

"Now, now, ladies…the truth is, wild unicorns wouldn't keep any of us away from a good cause like this," Fiona said. "And I believe it was actually Heather who called for a posse this time. Quite right, too. These snipers are targeting innocent people for some twisted reason of their own. And after all, Salem is Cass's hometown. We can't allow this reign of terror to intimidate America's so-called Witch City, even if that is something of a commercial fiction invented to draw in the credulous tourist. "

"Amen, sister, amen," Phillipa said.

○∾०

The Salem sniper had become national news, and the town was now crawling with more reporters than tourists. Bruce Gallant had evidently drawn the short straw; he'd become the official spokesperson for the multi-jurisdictional task force trying to apprehend the shooter. Residents and visitors were warned not to linger outdoors lest they become targets. The Morse homestead was closed to all but a few intrepid members of the archeological project's team who worked mostly indoors, like Jordan. Tourists packed up and scurried out of harm's way; day-trippers tripped elsewhere; Salem merchants wept.

Phillipa did take a chance on calling Greta Gallant, who remembered her and the rutabaga conference quite well. Phillipa explained that she was in town for a few days, sightseeing with her mythic studies circle, and wouldn't it be fun to get together and talk *detectives' wives woes* and swap recipes. She would bring Greta a copy of her latest cookbook, *Native Foods of New England Revisited*, with the intriguing recipes for Moose and Fiddlehead Shepherds' Pie, Venison Mincemeat, and Bison Cassoulet. Greta was thrilled and promptly invited Phillipa to lunch at the Grille Room of the Kernwood Country Club. Indoors. These days, no one was dining al fresco in Salem.

"Oh, well, if I must, I must," Phillipa said smugly. "I understand that there are very pretty water views, a tolerable vodka martini, and a decent grilled burger. We'll see."

"Holy Hecate!" Heather exclaimed. "Never mind the Gray Goose juice and mad cow meat! Concentrate on finding out everything the investigation has turned up. Pick her brains like escargot, of which you are so fond."

"Thank the Goddess the golf links have been abandoned. As long as I don't have to play a round of golf with the woman, I'm game for anything," Phillipa said. "Perhaps her husband Bruce will drop in and say 'Hi'. As I recall, he was rather a hunk, and quite personable for a cop."

"Jordan called him 'cool'," I reminded her. "And you're married to a very personable cop yourself."

"Yes, so I am. Well, *ours but to do and die...*" Phillipa said. "A small sacrifice for a good cause."

ᘐ

While we were waiting for Deidre to cut loose from Plymouth, Phillipa to wine and dine with Greta, and Tip to motorcycle down from Bangor, Heather, Fiona, and I decided to take in the touristy sights, beginning with the Salem Witch Museum and the Peabody-Essex Museum.

The Witch Museum was still the horror show I remembered from my early years in Salem, although some attempt had been made recently to revisit the witch stereotype and educate the public about the "new" Wiccan tradition. In the 17th century retrospective, Sarah Morse was among those good women sentenced to be executed by Judge Hathorne. (The W was added later to author Hawthorne's family name. No wonder he wrote about the curse of a false accusation passed down to descendents in *The House of Seven Gables.* The witch trials had haunted his own family.)

Judging by Sarah's young relative Hazel Morse, who grew up to marry Phineas Eastey and write our treasured book of *Household Recipes*, it was possible that Sarah had dabbled in herb-craft or certain rituals to encourage an abundant harvest, a suitable marriage, or an easy childbirth. Women, even some of the most piously Christian, had often worked a kind of hearth magic in the privacy of their own kitchens. Their intentions were to help and heal; none of them had deserved to be hung.

The Peabody-Essex experience, on the other hand, was thoroughly edifying. Heather, descendent of China Trade sea captains, particularly reveled in maritime art and seafarers' logbooks. Fiona, herself a librarian, was riveted by the library's original records of the Court of Oyer and Terminer that had heard the 1692 Salem witchcraft trials. And I, anticipating Tip's visit, was pleased to study *Shapeshifting*, transitional art of the American Indian.

Tip called that night just as I was collapsing in my room after the rigors of touring Salem followed by another raucous, noisy supper at *Buona Magia*. He said he'd be staying for a few days with a Cherokee friend, Sky Boy Mitchell, who had rooms near the waterfront and local contacts. He and Sky would tour the bars and meeting places where Indians hung out in Salem, to check out the local gossip. We agreed to get together on Sunday to share whatever leads we'd been able to come up with. We'd also visit the Morse place. I would call Jordan and ask her to meet us there to give Tip a tour of the Massachusett settlement artifacts found beneath the Morse tenancy of the land.

"At first I thought I was the only one who had wondered about an Indian connection," I said to Tip, "but Phil had lunch with the lead detective's wife, and she mentioned that notion had come up in her husband Bruce's meetings with the FBI, who favor the idea that some drunk Indian is shooting up Salem."

"Figures! It bugs me that Indians could be suspected of taking pot shots at pregnant women and kids," Tip said indignantly. "If the sniper's intention is to disrupt the Morse project because it might disturb some old Indian bones, it will probably turn out to be some big-talking white arsehole, like I said. We'll scout out AIM, too. Sky says there are a couple of Lakota Sioux up here from South Dakota who are involved in the American Indian Movement. We'll check if any whites have been hanging around local AIM meetings."

"Good plan," I said. "But there's something I should tell you about Jordan Rivers whom you'll meet at the Morse homestead. So you won't be surprised. Sometimes the girl slips out of the present and visits another time, you know. Working on the Indian project, she's had at least one flashback to a past raid on the village."

"Don't worry, Aunt Cass. I've gotten used to the weirding ways of you medicine women," Tip said. "You're still walking on the wild side, right?"

"I wouldn't put it that way, dear. And, by the way, Fiona says what happened to Jordan is not real time travel. The girl is tuning in to someone else's past life energy. It only seems as if she's living the scene herself."

"We Indians are no strangers to visioning, with or without peyote," Tip said.

CHAPTER SEVEN

O death rock me asleep, bring me to quiet rest,
Let pass my weary guiltless ghost out of my careful breast.

– Anne Boleyn

On Friday morning, Conor and Deidre drove in and booked a room at the Crowninshield. As before, Deidre felt an immediate chill in the lobby at the foot of the stairs, the spot reputed to be haunted by a maid who had fallen to her death (or was pushed?) in the 19th century. But Conor jollied Deidre along to the elevator with a warm arm around her shoulders and the assurance that it was all in her imagination.

Conor had decided, after all, that Salem offered possibilities as a Halloween feature, and he didn't give a damn that there was a sniper (or two) on the loose. He was, after all, no stranger to danger. He'd been on location in many places all over the world where there had been threats from wild animals and wild people, and he'd thrived on the excitement. Admittedly, the Rome adventure had been totally terrifying, but he'd survived and triumphed. If anything, Salem would be a dullish subject unless approached from an original angle, and he thought he might have a line on that: *Salem, True and False.*

When he spun this idea to us while waiting for the desk clerk to clear his credit card, glances were exchanged, wondering if we had planted in Conor's mind our own notion of Salem's Janus face by some unexpected telepathic connection.

"It's one of the thirteen powers," Fiona commented. "Remember?"

"Splendid idea, Conor!" Heather said, if only to change the subject. No matter. Telepathic prompting or not, the dichotomy of Salem had worked to bring Deidre back into our circle, and that was what counted.

Soon after Conor had dropped their bags in the quaintly Colonial double room (just the sort of ambiance that Deidre loved most!), he took off in his Range Rover to scout out the subjects he would photograph. He promised to be careful about his own exposure, and Deidre promised to stay indoors at all times. This reminded me of the false promises Joe and I often made to one another.

Early though it was, the cozy Elizabeth Allen bar (*The Liz,* as Phillipa had taken to calling it) was open, and beautifully empty. Again it proved to be just the place to gather for our continental breakfast and a conference. Deidre unpacked and joined us. "I feel so at home here!" she enthused. "Apart from the ghostly front stairs, that is."

Heather commandeered a large pot of coffee and poured it in cups all around; we declined her offer to find the bartender Buzz and order a "sweetener" of Sambuca.

"What's with the cold spot in the lobby?" Deidre demanded. We told her that the innkeepers were promoting a ghost on the premises; it was good for business, especially in Salem.

"Ah, the specter of housemaids past! Well, leave it to you guys to book yourselves into a haunted inn. Personally, I have no wish to encounter the poor waif. Although, perhaps I could work up a sideline as a ghost consultant. *Certificate of ghost authenticity verified by that well-known ghost hunter D. Ryan,"* Deidre said. She grabbed an embroidered pillow out of her workbag, *Home-keeping Hearts Are Happiest,* and stabbed it with a tiny needle trailing red silk thread.

Just then, my cell phone rang its tinny little tune *On a Clear Day You Can See Forever.* I moved away to an empty table in the bar, thinking it might be Joe with news that he'd been arrested or worse on his latest Greenpeace assignment, helping to protest drilling for oil in the Arctic. I just hoped he had stayed aboard tending the *Gaia* and not joined the activists hanging in survival pods from the oil rig over freezing waters.

But the call was from Tip. He and Sky had spent last evening touring the North Shore bars favored by commercial fishermen, where his friend and other Indians often hung out. So far they'd heard rumors about a couple of possible, "whitey" troublemakers who fit the profile Tip had drawn, and they planned to continue their canvassing this evening, hoping to run into the guys and size them up.

"Just the kind of loudmouths I had in mind," Tip said. "Got a guy goes by the name of Gus Standing Bear comes into the White Shark Pub in Gloucester pretty regular, wears an *AIM—Remember Wounded Knee* patch on his jacket, claims he's a Sioux member of AIM, but the Lakota Sioux up here from South Dakota say he's full of crap. Excuse me, Aunt Cass. I mean, he's one of those posers who talks big when he's drunk about purity of blood and taking revenge against oppressors of the native people. The real AIM members never heard of him. Bartender says his real name is Gustav Baer."

"The two guys aren't together?" I asked.

"No. Two different bars, two different blowhards. Why? Is that important?"

"Might be. I've been seeing those two snipers together, one older and bigger, one young and skinny. But go on... who else?"

"Well, there's also this sport who calls himself Big Chief Flying Eagle. Used to be married to a Kiowa girl, Linda Blue Moth Brillhart. Divorced now, but still passing himself off as a 'redman.' Tattoos of eagles all over his fat body. Much drunk talk about taking back what belongs to his 'Indian brothers'. I haven't met up with the wannabe myself yet, but we hear he's a regular at the Wharf Street Tavern here in Salem. Sky and I are going to keep an eye on the White Shark and Wharf Street until we can get a look at these two arseholes ourselves."

"Oh, Tip...I don't know if I'm happy being responsible for you spending your evenings drinking at some seedy bar on account of one of my crusades. What about your job? Surely you need to earn all you can before college begins in the fall."

"It's okay, Aunt Cass. I've cleared the time with Uncle John. Said I needed a vacation to straighten out a personal matter. He said okay, no questions asked. It's our way. And I don't do a lot of drinking. Mostly I play pool. And that can be a source of income, too, if you're good at it."

"And you are?"

Tip chuckled, that dry deep laugh of his that was almost a cough."Yeah, you might say so. But listen, Aunt Cass, what if this badass guy really is the sniper? Remember you said that the FBI would like to nab some Indian for this shooting spree at the excavation? Well, I happen to think they're dead wrong about that, and I'd like to help to prove it."

"Okay, Tip. I agree, that would be a good thing. And it's really fine detective work, finding two Salem big talkers who fit your personal sniper profile, but not exactly a guarantee that either of them is our guy. Of course, if I could meet them, and maybe shake hands or something, we might be able to narrow down our search."

"You mean, catch his soul in your spider-woman web?" he said, chuckling again.

"It's something very like that, smart boy. Anyway, let's meet at the Morse place tomorrow morning, and I'll introduce you to Jordan. She and her co-workers, if any of them has been foolhardy enough to show up for work, may have some ideas, too, and I think you'll like her."

Even as I said that, something flashed across my inner eye. *Yes, Tip will like Jordan all right.* I don't know if I was experiencing a true clairvoyant insight or just my *feminine intuition*, that overworked phrase for emotional sensibilities. Sometimes it's not easy to tell the difference.

"Why don't I give you a ride?" Tip suggested.

"Ah…I don't have a helmet," I stalled.

"No problem, Aunt Cass. I have an extra. Bet you've never ridden on a Harley, have you? Bought this one from J.T. My Uncle John Thomas, you know. Think how impressed the other medicine women will be when we splatter the gravel in the Crowninshield Inn driveway."

"Well, okay. If you promise to go easy on my ancient bones. No fancy, scary stuff."

"Hey, Aunt Cass, your bones don't appear to be that ancient, and besides…no way would I take a chance on spider-woman payback. And this will be one more thing to cross off your bucket list."

"*My* bucket list? My bucket list specifies items like lunch at the Savoy in London, a tour of the Arthurian sites in Cornwall, viewing Paris from the Eiffel Tower, a gondola ride in Venice. Although that one has already been crossed off. Absolutely no daredevil stuff like hang gliding or bungee jumping. Mine is a ladylike, dignified kind of bucket list."

"Don't worry, Aunt Cass. You'll be just fine. Will ten be too early to pick you up?"

"Okay...I guess." Already I was wondering how I could get the others to watch when I took off in a cloud of dust.

Although I was ready to be admired for my bravery the next morning, Fiona was doing a vision quest thing in her room, Deidre refused to go anywhere near the "ghost" in the lobby ("wisps of ectoplasm, ugh!" she'd complained) but Heather and Phillipa ambled out of the Elizabeth Allen bar to watch my departure. Phillipa took a picture of me.

Awesome!

CHAPTER EIGHT

Whoever loved,
that loved not at first sight.

– Christopher Marlowe

When we tooled up to the Morse homestead on the Harley, I immediately took off my Darth Vader helmet, trying to walk with dignity and not to wobble, so the officer on guard at the door would remember me as a personal friend of Jordan's and not as the gal who got grazed by a sniper bullet. He eyed Tip suspiciously, scowled at us, and called Jordan on his cell phone. After briefly checking with her, he granted us access to the cool interior of the keeping room. Another officer at the excavation was scanning the trees and keeping an eye on the one lone college kid sieving through dirt in an excavation pit.

There's a phrase in Italian, *colpo di fulmine*, literally "lightening blow" or "thunderbolt," which could be translated idiomatically as "love at first sight." I prefer the "thunderbolt," however, because to anyone who has experienced that instant connection, it's not exactly a dart from cute little Cupid's child-size bow but more like a mighty zinger straight out of the Cosmos that pierces one's heart. *No kidding.* I know, because that's what had happened to me the afternoon I met Joe at Heather's hastily organized protest to save the eagles nesting in Jenkins' woods. Once the thunderbolt strikes, there's no way back. That bridge is already burned. And I wouldn't have it any other way.

So I didn't have to be a clairvoyant to see that Tip Thomas was felled by *colpo di fulmine*, suddenly and without warning, when I introduced him to Jordan Rivers. I'd known Tip since he was a scrawny teen looking for work and keeping house for an alcoholic father. Now he was a deeply tanned nineteen-year-old, still slim, medium height but wiry and muscular under his navy tee. His slightly Asian eyes were the same penetrating gray, his hair straight black with surprising red glints, long now and tied back with a leather thong. His face had matured into the fine-boned aquiline features of the Northeast American Indian that would only grow more distinctive with age. We'd shared some scary adventures, but I'd never seen him struck dumb with a fatal attraction as he was that June day. A feverish flush suffused the bronze skin of his face as he drank in the girl's presence. *Love and a cough cannot be hid*, as the proverb goes.

Jordan had been at work photographing some recently unearthed pottery shards. Her cloud of dark hair was caught up in a careless knot. She wore a loosely woven top in earth tones, slipping off one of her brown shoulders, faded denim shorts, and deerskin moccasins. Wiping the dust off her hands, she stood up, hugged me hard, smiled brilliantly at Tip, and offered him her hand. Her aura was as sizzling and sensual as I remembered.

After Jordan had disengaged her hand from his, Tip stood as still as a drugstore Indian, still blushing furiously, while I caught her up on our activities in Salem, including Phillipa's lunch with Greta Gallant (but omitting our spell-work on Gallows Hill). "Tip has a theory about your sniper," I said, and waited for him to hold forth. When it appeared that he was still speechless, I added, "Tip believes the excavation has been targeted by some misguided white man who thinks he's championing the Indian cause by protecting the buried settlement from excavation."

"Why not a regular Indian, then?" Jordan asked. "Wouldn't he have, like, a real gripe?"

Coming to life finally, Tip said quietly, "It's not our style to terrorize the community because of some fancied sacrilege. We'd be proud to have one of our early villages discovered and displayed in the Peabody. If shutting down the excavation is the motive, it's the work of some stupid wannabe."

"Well, that might explain why this gun-crazy degenerate branched out to Walmart and murdered some young kid right in front of his poor grandma. I think the boy was wearing, like, one of those fake cardboard war bonnets. That was, like, so *totally* vicious! Maybe you should share your theory with the cops, Tip," Jordan said. She closed her camera and shuffled various papers together on the sturdy folding table where she'd been working.

"Maybe," Tip said. "I think I've got a line on what kind of man this bastard is, but I'd like to have something more to go on than my own hunch."

"I know the feeling," I said.

"I need to take an up-close look at these sports," Tip continued as if I hadn't spoken. Perhaps he'd forgotten that I was in the room. "I've got a buddy in town, Sky Boy Mitchell, who's got my back."

"Tip and Sky have been scouting places on Pickering Wharf and some others in Gloucester for big talkers," I said.

Jordan's direct look was challenging. "So, if I have this right, you and your friend Sky Boy are just hanging around the local bars, waiting for some likely loudmouth to turn up? That is *so* film noir gum-shoe!"

Tip chuckled, his particular deep-throated chuckle, tearing his attention away from the girl's face for a moment and studying his shoes, which were also moccasins. "No, I think our bar-hopping phase is over. We've narrowed our list of candidates down to two jerks. Now we only have to stake out their haunts." He described Big Chief Flying Eagle (whose real name was Ward Creech) and Gus Standing Bear to Jordan.

"The White Shark Pub in Gloucester, too? Are you planning to be in two places at once? Is that, like, some special power you have? *Wicked!*" she teased.

Tip's face seemed to have taken on a permanent blush under his dark skin. A small smile played across Jordan's lips, the Mona Lisa mystique. I thought she must be completely aware of her effect on him and perhaps slightly amused. He was, after all, a younger man, but not by much.

"If you actually track down your prime jerk, my cousin Rafe would be *charmed* to give you a hand bringing him down, you know what I mean? And Rafe has friends who would help, too."

"Local bikers. Great guys," I said. "Rafe's been looking out for Jordan since this whole mess began."

"And the Wharf Street Tavern is right here in Salem. It just so happens, I know the place. I could stop by there myself, you know," Jordan said.

"No!" Tip said in a voice suddenly strong with alarm. "That's no place for a girl like you!"

I'd have to have a word with Tip about how we women react to that sort of statement, I thought, noting Jordan's enigmatic smile as she winked at me.

"Would you like to see the Indian stuff we've dug up, Tip? All except the most recent finds are in the museum's cellar, under lock and key. Arnie Dickstein is, like, *major* paranoid, as if this whole sniper thing is aimed at *his* project. But I *could* show you my photographs."

Jordan was deftly changing the subject. Possibly the circle would have to keep an eye on those two nightspots ourselves, if only to keep Jordan out of trouble. Meanwhile, Tip was looking as if he'd just been granted an interview with the Goddess Herself…in her maiden incarnation, of course. He fell back to gazing at Jordan as if she, too, were some newly discovered, precious artifact.

Jordan's photographs were cataloged and filed in case boxes. She took out one set after another, explaining the significance of each item. Her enthusiasm made it apparent that she'd developed a deep interest in archaeology in the course of this summer's work, but when I asked her about her future plans, she declared her intention to switch her major to anthropology. She'd had been late in starting college and was only a sophomore this year, at the University of Massachusetts in Amherst. Dickstein, the project director, was encouraging her, although he would have preferred her to choose archaeology.

"But it's the *culture* of peoples that *totally* turns me on, you know what I mean?" she explained. "Especially since I've experienced a glimpse now and then." Jordan paused and glanced at Tip, as if considering whether it would be wise to reveal more of her psychic flashes. And quite right, too. Only she didn't have to be wary of Tip, who would have been just as pleased if she admitted to being a whirling dervish.

Tip was majoring in anthropology, too, with a minor in American Indian music, so they were soon chattering away like old friends. But whenever Jordan paused and turned away long enough to return one set of photos and take out another, Tip's expression as he watched her was one of pure adoration. I sure hoped Jordan wouldn't break his heart. Although she was only a couple of years older than he, there was something infinitely more sophisticated about Jordan.

When she'd finished her photographic tour, she took us out to the little back room where we drank Cokes and looked out at the excavations. "It's not exactly safe to walk around out there as long as that sniper may be lurking in the trees," Jordan said. "But you can see how the pits are situated from this window. They look like graves, don't they? Except the midden dig that I found is hidden back among those trees. No one dares work the midden just yet. Bummer! That head you see bobbing around in the pits nearest the house belongs to crazy Bill Cody who persists in sifting sand despite the weirdo taking potshots at us. We call him Buffalo Bill, of course. His pa is supposed to be some far away descendent of William Cody, so maybe that explains his foolishness. I've warned him not to wear, like, some stupid eye-catching hat. As you see, he's sticking to a dirt-colored headband. That cop out there is assigned to watch him."

Tip was in no hurry to leave, but it was time for me to get back to the Crowninshield to have lunch with the others, and Jordan expected her escort, Rafe, to arrive soon, as she was only working a half day. "Come back sometime, if you're still here, Tip," Jordan said carelessly, and turned back into the keeping room.

As we had been gracefully dismissed, we roared away down the long driveway and onto the main road on Tip's Harley. It occurred to me then that we were sitting targets, albeit quickly moving ones, riding in the open like that. I was grateful for our speed in getting back to town.

"So…what did you think of Jordan Rivers," I asked him when we'd careened to a stop in front of the inn. *As if I didn't know.*

"She was okay," Tip said.

"Maybe you two can get together again. Talk about the dig and all." I handed him my borrowed helmet.

"Cut it out, Aunt Cass. She's way out of my league." He was looking off down the road.

Not in the Universe of Infinite Possibilities, I thought. I invited Tip to lunch with us, but he simply muttered that he'd arranged to meet Sky Boy and took off.

It would probably be better if I didn't mess with Tip's love life anyway.

CHAPTER NINE

A faithful friend is a strong defense:
and he that hath found such a one hath found a treasure.

– Ecclesiasticus 6:14

We met for lunch in The Liz bar, at the same round table in the back of the room where we'd been having our continental breakfasts. Wherever we went, we seemed always to stake out our sacred space. I could almost feel the vibrations of light surrounding us.

"What's next?" Phillipa demanded as she studied the bar's luncheon menu. "Not much inspiration here!"

"Just order whatever we all like, Phil. That nice bartender will send out to the dining room kitchen. Chowder and salad will be perfectly adequate," Fiona said. "I hope you found Jordan faring well, Cass. Brave girl. It's rather like working at ground zero. But she's a sensible soul, as well. Apart from those occasional trips through time, that is. But that's merely one of the several dimensions. Are we following up on Tip's suspects?"

"He hasn't even sized them up himself yet. He'll be on the prowl tonight, along with Sky Boy Mitchell," I said. "So I thought we might split into two groups this evening and

spend some time at the Wharf Street Tavern or the White
Shark Pub until Tip's prospects show their faces. From
their descriptions, they'll be easy enough to recognize. Faux
Indians."

Deidre clapped her hands. "Oh, goodie! I hope Conor
will be tooling around in his Range Rover looking for
picturesque night scenes. Maybe the moon will rise over
Gallows Hill. He'd like that. Oh, I think he mentioned
a séance he wanted to attend. Madame Circe La Femme.
One of those commercial things that's probably entirely
phony, he says. Fits his theme, in the False column. But
Conor knows better than to ask me to go along. What if
a real ghost showed up and I freaked out?"

"Conor may be in for a surprise," Fiona said mildly. "I
happen to know Circe's a true channeler. Maybe a bit over-
the-top, but hey, this is Salem. The place has its own unique
genius loci."

Phillipa winked at me and murmured "*caveat emptor,*" then
went to the bar to order our chowders, a platter of lightly fried
clams with banana peppers, cole slaw, and sour dough rolls on
the side. The bartender, Buzz, a red-faced ex-wrestler type, gave
us the long-suffering gaze and resigned shrug that often greeted
our off-the-bar-menu orders. Nevertheless, he was getting used
to our taking over the corner table for our frequent conferences.
At least we were ordering something this time.

"And a bottle of Pouilly Fuisse," Heather called after
Phillipa. "Or two."

"I'd like to go to Gloucester," Fiona said. "With Cass, in case."

"In case of what?" asked Heather.

"In case she intuits a suspect and needs help. You are
going to try to contact them physically, aren't you, Cass?
Touch of truth," Fiona said.

"That would be one way," I admitted. "But let's not forget that there's someone else involved. If my vision was accurate. A younger man with the older. And I don't really know which of them is the shooter."

"Of course your vision is accurate, girlfriend. When has it not led us directly into danger?" Heather said. "Oh, very well, then. Phil and I will hoist a few at the Wharf Street Tavern."

"Hoist a few what?" Phillipa asked, having returned from overseeing our lunch order.

"Glasses, of course. Cass and Fiona are going to Gloucester looking for trouble, so why don't we see what turns up here in Salem?" Heather suggested.

"What about me?" Deidre demanded. "I want to go to Gloucester, too."

"Are you sure Conor will be otherwise occupied?" I asked.

"Pretty sure. Anyway, if he's not photographing Salem's spooky night life, can't he come with us?" Deidre suggested.

It might have been better if Conor had been with us in Gloucester that evening, but he did indeed decide to attend the séance. I saw the photos later. The angles and lighting he chose were slanted to suggest a certain sleaziness. But Conor himself had doubts about his own preconceived opinions.

"I have to admit that something weird happened," he'd said later, his tone somewhat chagrined. "When Madame slumped over in what the others told me was a deep trance, she claimed to have a message for me from my great-aunt Bridey Quinn. Unfortunately, the message was in Gaelic, and I am not fluent. But when Madame came out of her stupor, she said it felt like a warning to *watch out for a loved one tonight*. A bunch of Blarney, I thought at the time. Little did I know what caves of calumny you'd lead my darlin' into."

"Your darlin' has a mind of her own," I said.

But Conor was absorbed in reviewing his own work. "I'd like to shoot a séance with a real ghostly presence, if there is such a thing," he said.

"Just keep Dee in your camera sights," I advised.

❦

While Conor was having his séance experience, we were on our way to stake out the White Shark Pub. It was almost nine o'clock when we arrived. We figured that any loud braggarts would makes themselves known later rather than earlier.

The place, not to put too fine a point on it, was a dive. But it had a certain picturesque quality, like the set for a movie that might be called *Sailors' Saloon.* Dimly lit with dark wooden walls, it was decorated with cobwebby harpoons, rusty anchors, ragged fishnets, tarnished ship's lanterns, and garish ceramic lighthouses. On a large flat-screen TV looming over the scarred bar, a baseball game competed with noisy patrons. Lining the opposite wall was a haphazard arrangement of what an auctioneer would call "distressed" tavern tables of oak so blackened by age it could have been teak, and behind those, two ominous-looking booths, perfect for criminal conferences. We could hear the sounds of pool players arguing in the back room. Through the door I could see some younger men shooting darts at a target amid shouts and curses. From all I could gather with a quick uneasy glance around, the patrons were mostly males, ranging from the stringy to the beefy, many of them heavily tattooed, in various stages of beer-induced stupor. The bartender, however, was a woman, with a tough, ravaged face, long blonde hair (two-inch black roots), and a whiskey laugh. The tattoo of a rose snaked up her arm. I rather thought that was her name. *Rose.* With plenty of thorns.

"Holy Mother!" Deidre exclaimed gleefully. "Isn't this *wicked?*"

Fiona, Deidre, and I found ourselves a little table near the back where we could see everyone at the bar but not attract too much attention ourselves. Well, that was the theory, but, of course, our threesome did include Fiona, wearing a full dress MacDonald tartan jumper, carrying her coyote walking stick and the inevitable moss green reticule. And Deidre with her mop of golden curls and excited smile with adorable dimples; wearing well-fitted jeans and a *Salem Witches* t-shirt, looked more like a cheer leader than the mother of four. As a number of rough-looking fishermen types looked us over curiously, I scowled warningly at them, feeling myself slipping into the role of spoilsport duenna.

Fiona ordered a Glenfiddich single malt scotch. I thought this didn't look like a Glenfiddich kind of place. But the bartender found a bottle, which she dusted off for the occasion. Deidre asked for a double Bushmills Irish whiskey. I settled for a glass of the house white wine, predictably sour, the easiest to nurse for however long we were going to hang around the place. Phillipa had loaned me her BMW so I probably wouldn't even finish that one glass. Rose (or whatever her name was) brought over our drinks, and Fiona insisted on paying for them, drawing an old-fashioned purse stuffed with bills out of her reticule without even looking. It always amazed me how she could unerringly find whatever she wanted in those mysterious depths. I could only wonder what else might be lurking at the bottom.

Later, I would find out.

There was a bowl of dry-looking peanuts on the table, which Fiona decided should be dowsed before pronouncing them harmless but unappetizing. By leaning forward across the table and flapping my black shawl (also borrowed from Phillipa), I did my best to screen the crystal pendant she was waving about with a tinkle of silver bangles.

We had hardly taken a few sips of our drinks when Gus Standing Bear arrived. I spotted him by the *AIM— Remember Wounded Knee* patch on his sleeveless jacket, and inclined my head in his direction to alert Fiona and Deidre.

"Is that one of *them?*" Deidre asked in a stage whisper.

Her question was answered by Gus's (or Gustav's) rowdy voice as soon as he had his bottle of beer in hand. He addressed himself to Rose and anyone else who would listen that he'd be heading for San Francisco this fall for the American Indian Movement's 43rd Anniversary conference. *Land, Sovereignty and Self-determination* would be the theme, and he, Gus Standing Bear, would be ready and able to kick some whitey butt to bring justice to his people. His long dark, frizzy hair and heavy beard shadow gave him a sinister appearance. If I saw him walking toward me on a deserted street, I'd want to cross over to the other side.

A young man with a long blond braid and a vivid blue headband, who'd been playing darts in the back room, quietly walked down the length of the bar to stand beside Gus. After he'd ordered a Miller Lite, we watched him engage Gus in conversation, but we couldn't make out what he said.

We had no trouble hearing Gus's reply, however.

"You're fucking right I'm a member!" he shouted, pointing to the AIM patch on his jacket and holding a signature fist in midair. "Local director of the Leonard Peltier Defense Fund."

The young man said something to Rose, shook his head, and indicated the contribution jar on the bar.

"Hey, you creep," Gus bellowed. "You don't look like no fucking Indian to me, either, blondie. That there jar is for folks to contribute a few bucks to free our brother falsely imprisoned by the Feds."

Rose picked up the jar, scowled, and said in her gravelly voice "Where'd you say these contributions go, Gus?"

"That money goes directly to the Grand Governing Council in Minneapolis!" Gus pounded his bottle on the bar. Then he thrust out his shadowed jaw and moved a step closer to the young man. "Who the fuck do you think you're calling a faker? I'm gonna break both your legs, whitey."

A heavy-set, red-bearded fellow stepped up at Gus's back, while several other men milled about, some behind Gus and others siding with the young man. A brawl was definitely on the boil. I could see that Rose was moving two ceramic lighthouses out of harm's way. She opened her cell phone and spoke rapidly to someone.

"I wonder if that isn't Sky Boy Mitchell," I said. "With the blue headband."

"The slender blond guy? He sure doesn't look like an Indian," Deidre said.

"You'd be surprised, then, to meet Tip's Uncle John, a blue-eyed blond who's as much Indian as Tip," I said absently, because I was busy trying to size up the vibes. It appeared that the young man had his own group of friends who'd been in the back room playing darts. They were younger but less brawny than the regulars at the bar. One of them was wearing a *Custer Died for Your Sins* t-shirt.

"It's not that unusual for American Indians to have blue eyes or even blond hair. In the early 1700s, a number of canny Scots traders sought to improve relations with the natives by marrying Indian girls," Fiona said. "My great, great-uncle Cuthbert…"

A chair at a table near the front door crashed to the floor as a grizzled bear of a man sprang to his feet and strode toward the Gus side of the crowd.

"Oh, there *is* going to be a fight! How cool is that!" Deidre interrupted in an urgent whisper. "Ought we to get out of here, do you think?"

"No one will harm us, dear, but I, too, sense it's time to depart," Fiona said, casting her arms around hither and yon to surround us with white light. "Protective charms are all very well, I always think, but discretion is the better part of wizardry." She reached into her reticule, took something out, and palmed it. I was relieved to note that it wasn't big enough to be an illegal can of mace, or worse, a pistol.

"Yes, Dee, you're so right. Let's see if we can get out the door before all Hades breaks loose." I agreed, pointing my little fingers toward the incipient melee to ward off trouble.

We didn't make it.

An instant later, we were on our feet, looking for the safest route out any door, front or back, although I couldn't really see where the back door *was*. I just assumed there would have to be another exit, possibly from the pool hall.

Fiona downed the rest of her Glenfiddich and thrust her reticule at me. "Carry this for me, dear, would you?" The green suede bag was surprisingly lightweight for being a hold-all of so many surprising goods.

I couldn't be sure, but I thought it was Gus who threw the first punch, aimed at the young man with blue-banded hair. He ducked nimbly and jumped behind a table. Gus's backers came barreling forward roaring rude threats that drowned out the TV. Rose screamed, grabbed a red-bearded ruffian by his collar, and banged his head on the bar. The young man and his friends danced around the punches that were thrown their way, and one of them actually laughed with a high pitched cackle. Someone else, I couldn't see who, was uttering a series of curses in a bass voice.

I was taking all this in subliminally as we pushed through, having no choice but to make for the front door because Fiona had already forged ahead of us, swinging the coyote end of her walking stick from side to side to clear our path.

Deidre tripped over a fallen ship's lantern and screamed a little-girl scream. I hauled her to her feet and propelled her forward. There was a cut over her eye. Muttering something that sounded mighty like the Hail Mary, she rubbed at it, smearing her forehead with blood.

Fiona marched onward, still swinging her stick amid flying punches. Suddenly Gus loomed up ahead of her, his eyes blazing red with rage in his dark-visaged face. Didn't realize he was threatening a defenseless older woman and not another rowdy drunk? Oblivious as a berserker, he raised his fist and pulled it back to deliver a knockout, but before he could deck Fiona, it appeared that she punched him in the jaw. Gus fell over a tipped-up chair, and I fell on top of him, tangled hopelessly in my shawl but still holding Deidre's hand.

A series of sensations traveled through me when Gus grabbed my other wrist. It was like falling down a dark cave into that man's consciousness. An ugly experience, and my arm felt on fire. I'd be lucky if it didn't break.

Suddenly the silver coyote flashed forth and struck his hand with its little pointed snout, breaking his grip. At the same time, little Deidre hauled me to my feet with surprising strength.

"Let her go, you scumbag!" Deidre ordered in a voice that would have quelled a classroom of unruly middle-schoolers.

Gus was groaning and rubbing his hand. We made our escape, in the midst of a terrifying cacophony of crashing glasses and bashing heads.

Once on the street, but not out of trouble, I could hear distant sirens getting louder. That's all we needed, to be arrested in a bar brawl!

I grabbed Fiona and Deidre and pushed them into a shop doorway with a deep entry. The door to a tattoo parlor was on one side and a tarot and palm reader on the other.

"I wonder if I should get a tiny shamrock tattooed on my shoulder," Deidre said.

"'Tarot requires a particular sensitivity to symbolism," Fiona said. "Phil, for instance…"

"Be quiet, you two! In fact, *be invisible*," I whispered urgently. A moment later, I could feel Fiona doing her invisibility thing, swirling like smoke. That was all very well for her, but Deidre and I were not as talented in the glamourous arts. I pulled Deidre back into the darkest corner.

Two patrol cars skidded to a stop in front of the pub. Three officers rushed into the pub and another ran around to the back alley.

Now! I grabbed Fiona and Deidre by the hand and made a dash to Phillipa's BMW, which I had parked in a public Witch City Parking lot around the corner.

Fiona was huffing and puffing, but Deidre giggled the whole way. Actually, she sounded a bit hysterical as she jumped in the back of the BMW while I helped Fiona into the passenger seat, tucking her reticule in beside her feet.

"Did you see the punch that Fiona landed on the big Indian's jaw?" Deidre said happily.

I glanced sideways at Fiona. She was unclenching her right hand from a roll of quarters, which she dropped into her reticule, now that it was back in her grasp. "A little tip I picked up at a Senior Self-Defense Seminar for adding power to the punch," she said. "The best offense is a good defense. Also, you always have spare change for a parking meter."

I shook my head to clear the confusion. Was a roll of quarters just as effective if you'd used a couple of them in a parking meter? Fiona's advice routinely zapped my brain.

Fiona dug out a gauze pad and a small bottle of hydrogen peroxide from her reticule which she handed back to Deidre along with an old fashioned mirror compact. "You won't want to alarm Conor with that cut, dear," she said, squirting a mist of refreshing sage over all of us. "Leaping Lords of the Wildwood, that was a close one! I think that protective light I cast around us saved the night, don't you?"

I peeked into the rear view mirror as I raced to Route 128 South to Salem. The cut on Deidre's forehead didn't appear as scary now that she was cleaning it up a bit. But an ugly red lump was rising under the wound.

"So, Cass, you were practically on top of that big guy," Deidre said. "Flesh on flesh. Did you get any sniper vibes? Tell me this wasn't all for nothing, except an awesome good time."

"Gus Whatever-his-name is a con man and a false Indian, that's for sure," I said. "I'm glad Sky Boy, if it was Sky Boy, exposed Gus's little game to Rose. A boisterous con man on the surface but underneath, a dark, hollow soul, quite sad, really."

"Rose?" said Deidre. "The bartender?"

"I call her Rose because of the tattoo," I explained.

"A new dharma is manifesting in our circle, have you noticed?" Fiona mused

"Oh, never mind that," Deidre demanded, leaning over my shoulder, "Cass! *Was that man the sniper...or not?*"

'*Not*," I said.

"We are obligated by dharma to restore the natural order of justice." Fiona continued undeterred." And lately, our dharma has been all about the true versus the false. This Indian imposter business, and Salem itself, the paradox of its spiritual values, sleeze and substance. Obviously, Conor has been under the influence of our dharma as well and has turned it into a subject for his feature. But our quest goes back farther. Even before we came here, it was the same in Plymouth, that devilish *Man of God* who picketed Dee's shop. *Verily, that which is Dharma is truth,* so it's written in the Upanishad."

"Yeah, yeah," Deidre said, peering into the compact mirror. "I think I'm raising a bump on my forehead. I need ice, and I need it now."

Fiona took a bottle of beer out of her reticule and handed it back to Deidre. "Here, dear. Hold it against the bump. It's still nice and cold."

Where our dharma led us next that evening was to an uncomfortable confrontation with Conor, waiting in the lobby for Deidre when we returned to the Crowninshield. He'd begun to get anxious when it got past eleven and we still hadn't returned to the inn.

"Mother of God, Dee darling, what happened to you?" he cried when he saw Deidre's lumpy head and generally disheveled appearance. For that matter, all of us were pretty untidy. He looked at Fiona and me with narrowed eyes. No more *Mr. Nice Irish Lad*. "And it's a fine mess you are, ladies. What have you got Dee into this time? It looks as if you've been in a bar fight."

No kidding.

"We just wanted to experience a little local color, honey," Deidre said soothingly. "So Cass took us to this White Shark Pub in Gloucester. Cass grew up on the North Shore, but she says it was much different in her day. The pub used to be a respectable place for ladies to visit and sip a little Harvey's Bristol Cream. Tonight, though, there was a bit of a brawl. But, as Cass often quotes, *Nobody expects the Spanish Inquisition.*"

Conor cast a menacing glance my way, and no wonder. *Everyone blames me.* I felt a flush of sorry-for-myself.

Fiona leaned over and whispered to me reassuringly, "Danger is not your dharma, dear. It's your karma."

I was saved from making a sharp retort by the appearance of Heather and Phillipa wafting in on a breeze of alcohol fumes and chuckles. Obviously, there were stories to exchange. "The Liz is still open," Phillipa said, so we headed for the Elizabeth Allen bar, where she demanded a fresh pot of coffee for our table.

Conor sighed heavily and went off to another table to review the night's work in his camera, and Deidre winked at me. "Sorry," she said, sitting down with us. "He's getting a tad over-protective. But it's rather sweet, really."

After we'd regaled Phillipa and Heather with the White Shark brawl, Fiona's knockout punch, and what I had divined about Gus Standing Bear, Phillipa smiled her Cheshire cat smile. "We found our quarry, too, Cass. I ran into Tip at the tavern, watching that dreadful Flying Eagle person, with tattoos all over his flabby arms and hairy chest. But Eagle kept a low profile tonight, just drank steadily and quietly at the darkest corner of the bar. So we are no wiser. Oh, and Jordan stopped in with her cousin Rafe. Tip didn't appear to be best pleased and said a few words to Rafe. They both bristled a bit but then started talking motorcycles like old friends. Jordan fumed, of course, even though Tip's eyes turned to molten honey every time he looked at that girl. The boy obviously has a lot to learn, and you ought to have a word with him on how not to piss off a lady by telling her when and where she may not go. Anyway…no big excitement at the Tavern tonight, not like you three. Thank the Good Goddess that Fiona stuck to her ladylike roll of quarters and didn't skewer any of the brawlers with her stick or shoot up the joint. Meanwhile, as ten o'clock rolled around, with Heather ordering liqueurs, I started to get a buzz on. But about ten-thirty, some kid came in and dragged Fat Bird away, home to fall on his bed, I assume, so we left, too."

I'd been starting to feel a bit draggy, but at the mention of kid, I perked right up. *"Kid?* What kind of kid? How old? Did they exchange any words that you could hear?" I demanded.

"I'd say he's about twenty," Heather said. "Do you know who he looked a little like? Do you remember that young man you made us follow at the House of Seven Gables shop? Maybe him or a similar type."

"Sweet Isis," I exclaimed. "I'm going to have to chase those two down. We might be on to something here."

"Well, not tonight," Deidre said, yawning prettily. "I'm knackered."

"And not ever, Dee darling." Conor may have been intent on his camera, but he'd been listening to every word. "At least, not without me going along to keep you out of harm's way."

Although Conor would be classified a light-weight as a fighter, he was wiry and quick and would be a match for any casual ruffian, I had no doubt, but our snipers were cold-hearted psychopaths who killed from a safe distance. A frisson of fear ran from my neck to my first chakra. What was I getting us into?

CHAPTER TEN

As sure as I've the gift of sight,
We shall be meeting ghosts to-night!"

– William Wordsworth

Getting Deidre upstairs to her room was always a treat. She was still shrinking away from the cold spot at the bottom of the front stairs, reputed to be haunted by the maid who had fallen to her doom. And we all believed something had certainly happened there, judging from Deidre's shudders, shivers, and shakes. Sometimes we tried to bustle her into the lobby elevator, a miniature gilt affair, but apparently that was still too close to the chills and thrills, so other times we went through the kitchen and up the back stairs. Tonight we had Conor, however, who believed in the straightforward approach. He simply swept Deidre into his arms and carried her right up the stairs like Rhett Butler.

Heather sighed. "No one has been able to carry me upstairs since third grade."

"I bet Dee doesn't weigh more than a hundred pounds," Phillipa said crossly. "I wonder if I should give up fois gras. And clotted cream."

"That Conor's really stronger than he looks," I said. "Did you hear that Mother Ryan calls him her 'dear little leprechaun'?" We were all somewhat surprised that the mother of Deidre's deceased husband Will doted on Conor, who was clearly in line to be Will's replacement. A tribute to Conor's fey Irish charm. "Deidre may be small but she's sturdy herself. She hauled me up off the floor of the pub tonight without breaking a sweat."

"*And yet a Spirit still, and bright, With something of an angel light,*" Fiona quoted Wordsworth. "What we ought to do, ladies, instead of trying to guess Dee's weight, is to exorcise that cold spot at the bottom of the main staircase. That way we might prevent Dee's vapors and a possible hernia for Conor. I don't think anyone would mind, do you, if we kept it down to a couple of candles and a little chanting?"

"How about we look into the history of the Crowninshield first?" I suggested. "You could use Phillipa's laptop, unless you happen to have one in your reticule, *ha ha*. Find out if there really was a maid who fell or threw herself down the stairs. I mean, we don't even know her name. How can we demand that she *begone*, if we don't know what to call her?" Such a search would be right up Fiona's street, our quintessential finder, and might buy us a little time before we had to embarrass ourselves with a séance in the lobby. And besides, in my experience, a good ghost can be an asset to the inn which she is reputed to haunt. Especially in Salem.

"No need to trouble Phillipa," Fiona said. "I have a smart phone in my reticule. I can research our fallen maiden on that.

Phillipa smirked and rolled her eyes. "Maybe it's time for the rest of us to upgrade, ladies. A laptop can be so cumbersome."

I hadn't even learned how to use all the features on my cell phone yet. Well, I'd think about that tomorrow. Right then, all I wanted was to retire and sooth away the day's *slings and arrows of misfortune.*

⤳

I was just drifting off to sleep when my cell phone rang. It was Joe!

"Hi, sweetheart. Are you all right?"

"Oh, honey, are *you?* I've been so worried that you'd do something foolish, like climb up on that drilling platform. You're not in jail are you?"

"Not exactly."

I sat up in bed, my heart beating wildly. "What in Hades does 'not exactly' mean? That's like saying you're a little bit pregnant."

He chuckled. "*Not exactly* means that I'm being detained for questioning due to a little altercation with a Danish navy commando."

"You're hurt, aren't you?" I demanded to know. "Where? How badly? It's not another leg thing, is it?"

"Nothing vital, sweetheart, I promise. I can walk, and that's not all I can do. Now how about you answer *my* question? I caught a report on CNN that a sniper has been active in Salem around some historical site. Several victims, killed or injured, including a rather famous archeologist, Fuchsia Woolley. And that people are being warned to stay indoors. Wasn't Heather in Salem digging up Indian artifacts when I left Plymouth? You're not in Salem, are you?"

I thought for a moment before deciding that outright lying might not be a good thing for our relationship.

Especially since Joe would surely find out the truth as soon as he came home.

"Well, actually...after Heather got involved in the Morse homestead archeological dig that's been the center of the shootings, and it appeared not to be an isolated instance, she asked us to come up and help, you know, just try to figure out what's going on, *not to get involved or anything*. We're leaving that to the cops. There's a multi-jurisdictional task force investigating the shootings, so they hardly need a bunch of middle-aged soothsayers hanging around the crime scenes. So we're all just staying at a place called the Crowninshield Inn to keep an eye on Heather. Perfectly pleasant and safe. Seeing the sights, actually. It's my hometown, don't forget, honey, and it's been rather fun to revisit the old haunts. But never mind that...*tell me what happened to you!*"

"A black eye and a few facial bruises. Not just a pretty face anymore. I look as if I'd gone a few rounds with Mike Tyson. I'd like to say, *you should see the other guy*, but the other guy looks fine. Those commandos are fast and tough. See, what happened was, one of those activists is a girl, Jean McKenna. Treated her roughly, even though she made no protest. I couldn't just stand by and watch."

"Yes you could, you idiot. Weren't there any young men there to jump in to the rescue?"

"Ouch. Now that hurt, Cass. I'm not too old to defend a damsel in distress. And that includes you, sweetheart."

True enough. Joe had rescued me from my own folly more than once. The last time I'd been backed against a cellar wall armed only with a few cans of tomatoes to defend myself from a knife-wielding maniac. "You've always been my hero, you know that, honey. When you're here."

"The *Gaia* is on its way home. So tell me, what's the gang of five up to? Can you please stay out of trouble just until I get home?"

The Antarctic siege was over, Joe explained. It had ended predictably with the arrest of the two activists who had hung off the drilling platform in survival pods over freezing waters. Danish navy commandos had broken into the pods and removed the two young people, Paul Dickey and Jean McKenna, who were now in jail but would probably be deported soon. Greenpeace rejoiced that they had prevented the drilling if only for a few days. Might not seem like much, but the protest also brought the world's attention to this new danger threatening a fragile environment.

"Not only my hero, but also a Greenpeace hero. I'm proud of you, Joe. Now don't you worry about me. Honest, honey, we're just doing the tourist thing and keeping an eye on Heather. We'll probably be back in Plymouth by the time you dock in New York."

"Amsterdam," he said. "I'll be flying home from Amsterdam."

"I've missed you these long hot summer nights," I murmured, glancing over to make sure my roommate Phillipa was still asleep. She turned over with a complaining grunt but apparently didn't wake.

Well, at least she couldn't hear Joe's reply. His husky-voiced suggestions of how we could celebrate his homecoming gave me an involuntary throb between my legs and quite melted my resolve to concentrate on crime.

Phone sex is better than no sex at all.

ᘐ

"We've got to catch these guys!" I exclaimed at breakfast the next morning, in the bar as usual. "Joe's coming home, and I need to get back to Plymouth."

"Yeah, so what's your plan?" Phillipa was waving her croissant in the air with a displeased expression. "Would you just look at how limp this thing is?"

"My plan is that we stake out the Tavern tonight and let me get a look at Flying Eagle."

"You mean *a feel*, don't you?" Deidre said. Conor had whisked her down the back stairs through the kitchen, deposited her in the bar, and, seeing that the light was perfection, had taken off to shoot the harbor and the House of Seven Gables, which he said had once been real but was now tarnished with commercialism.

"*Feel* doesn't sound ladylike. If I *see*, in the psychic sense, that he's the one, however, we'll follow Flying Eagle and his young friend to wherever they're holed up. Check if there's a blue van. Have a good look. Maybe they have their guns locked up in there."

"We'd need to break into the van," Heather said.

We all looked at Fiona who smiled modestly. "I can manage that, dears. I've a Slim Jim lock-out kit in my reticule."

"Hold on, Fiona! Breaking into a car that's not your own is a felony!" Phillipa protested. "The thing to do is just to follow the bastards. See where they go, what they're up to. They won't be expecting us. We could take turns. Most of the sniper attacks have taken place in the late morning or early afternoon. Cass and I will wait for them to get into the van, if there is a van, and slink along behind them. Heather and Dee will spell us later. With Fiona, of course."

"You'd better take me along on the first run," Fiona said. "Remember who got you, sound and safe, out of that pub, Cass."

"Sure Fiona. And do bring your quarters," I said.

Deidre giggled. She had smudges under her eyes this morning and a self-satisfied little smile that was reminiscent of Vivian Leigh after the stairway incident.

"Sounds like a plan, albeit a crazy one," Phillipa said. "The tavern tonight. But what about today?"

"I'm going over to the Morse place to speak with Arnie Dickstein. With all the shooting that's been happening over there, money for the project is drying up," Heather said.

"So you're discussing a donation?" Phillipa said. "Good. We'll all go with you. I'd like to see what you've dug up over there, Heather. Snipers be damned. And anyway, I've been in touch with Greta Gallant. According to her hubby, Detective Lieutenant Brucie the Hunk, the whole place is crawling with cops, so we should all be as safe as houses."

Famous last words.

Phillipa, who never forgets that people get hungry, went into the kitchen to supervise a picnic basket for our excursion, and we were on our way by ten, which is fairly early for women who drift through life on Wiccan time. Except Deidre, that is, who was always spot on schedule. As the mother of four youngsters and the owner of a full-time faery business, she should have been stretched out pretty thin, but in fact, she rarely was late or appeared rushed. As she has explained, she operates on the theory that time can be expanded to fit one's needs. If we would only get rid of our watches and alarm clocks and stop obsessing about *tempus fugit*, she insists, we could do the same. I haven't been able to kick the habit myself. My Timex takes a licking and keeps me ticking, and Heather is pretty closely wed to her black Sea-dweller Rolex as well.

It was an overcast, humid, dismal day. But weather forecasters had promised disappointed vacationers that afternoon would bring clearing skies, cooling breezes, and a perfect June temperature of 80 degrees. We traveled in Heather's Mercedes, which was roomier than the BMW. Fiona sat in front, her reticule in her lap, humming *Amazing Grace* and checking her smart phone.

After a few minutes, she said, "Here it is. The girl's name was Fenella Tupper. Last night, I accessed an interview that James Woolgar and Derek Witt, the inn's owners, gave to a reporter from *The Salem News* a few years ago. A Halloween feature, naturally. According to Woolgar, there's a Crowninshield legend that a chamber maid named Fenella Tupper had fallen to her death down the front staircase at midnight in the summer of 1882. Subsequently, a number of guests at the inn have complained of an odd draft in the same spot where her body landed. During the investigation of Fenella's death, another chambermaid, Abby Dunlap, testified that a male guest, Byrd Page, had seized and raped Fenella while she was turning down his bed. Abby had heard the screams and accusations, and, peeking out into the hall, had witnessed Fenella running out of Page's room and threatening to expose his lechery. He raced after her and, before Fenella could get away from him, pushed her down the stairs. However it happened, her neck was broken and she died instantly. Abby later retracted her story and the case against Page was dismissed. Possibly a pay-off."

"The same old story," Phillipa said. "What would we have to do to convince Fenella to leave the premises?"

"I *so* don't need to get into this," Deidre said.

"You wouldn't want the poor girl to be roaming around the Crowninshield lobby for eternity, would you?" Fiona said. "I think if we simply contact Fenella and explain that she's dead and so is Byrd Page, she would feel free to spiritualize onto a higher plane."

"With Page's death, justice would have been served," I said.

"Except that Byrd Page's heirs have inherited a fortune from one of the largest mines ever discovered in the good old days of the Gold Rush," Heather said. "I went to Vassar with Bernie Byrd Page. She wore gold nugget heart-shaped earrings. Talk about kitsch."

"Let's think about what Fenella would like from the Byrd fortune," Deidre said. "If there were, like, a heavenly civil court. Do you suppose she has descendants?"

"Table that one for now," Phillipa said as Heather drove down the long road to the Morse homestead. She'd been right about the police presence. The last time I'd visited, with Tip, there had been only two officers under the shade tree, but now there were two cruisers and four men, three under the shade tree and one at the front door drinking a Red Bull. Heather parked, and we all got out. The officer with the Red Bull hurried over to intercept us. Heather showed him her Morse Archeological Site work permit and exchanged a few words. He nodded and went back to leaning in the doorway.

"Arnie is probably in his office in the parlor," she said. "I'll go and say hi while you gals find Jordan. See if she'll give us a tour."

Jordan was at her post in the keeping room, arranging pottery shards for a photo. She smiled warmly, but when Deidre mentioned a tour of the grounds, a shadow passed over Jordan's face. "It's better if we don't go out there," she said. "The woods in back are too good a cover for those crazy snipers. Especially on a gray day like today."

Just then Heather came into the keeping room with Dickstein, who was introduced to the rest of us. He was a plump little man with rosy cheeks who appeared to be walking on his toes in an excess of enthusiasm. "Mrs. Devlin and her friends would like to see the trenches," he said to Jordan. Heather's offer of another donation, and no doubt a generous one, seemed to have put Arnie into a hospitable mood.

Jordan draped a cloth over the shards and sighed. "Are you sure it's safe now, Arnie?" she asked.

"Ask one of the officers to accompany you," Dickstein suggested. "I've been assured that the team protecting us will be a reliable deterrent."

The cop with the Red Bull. Officer Wayne Wedge, a short, square guy with a pale blond buzz-cut, was drafted to guard us, and we all trooped outdoors. Jordan and I seemed to be the only ones glancing around fearfully. Nevertheless, she managed to explain the archeological process, with the help of Heather and the intrepid Bill Cody, who was still working in the field. He was a well-built young man with a cocky gleam in his eye and a dirt-colored headband holding back wild, shoulder-length brown hair. Not much would faze him, I thought. A large area beside the homestead had been marked off into a kind of grid. Bill was working on a trial trench, one of several. The dirt was loosened with two tools, mattock and trowel. When a larger artifact was dug up, it would be cleaned on location with a soft brush. The rest of the dirt was carted by wheelbarrow to the barn where it was sieved to reveal smaller objects. The trench revealed the land's history in reverse time. First a layer of the 17th century Morse leavings was excavated, and below that, a layer of earth that contained artifacts of the American Indians who had lived here earlier. Several such trial trenches were proving that the area was well worth excavating.

In addition to photographing smaller broken artifacts, Jordan also photographed important objects *in situ*, cataloging the particular strata in which each was found.

"Okay, okay," I said. "Most interesting! Shall we return to the homestead now?" I was having the jittery experience known as *someone walking across my grave*. Or maybe my nervous system had its own memory of my being creased on the noggin by a bullet on a previous visit.

The sun came out for the first time that morning just as Fiona was gazing at the woods behind the Morse house. She tapped on Officer Wedge's shoulder and stage-whispered, "Sir, I believe I saw a gleam of metal between those oak saplings. You may wish to investigate."

Officer Wedge did not appear eager to dash blindly into the woods. Putting his hand on his sidearm, he peered at the trees to which Fiona had drawn his attention and took a step in that direction.

A shot rang out, pinging off the wheelbarrow beside Bill Cody's trench.

CHAPTER ELEVEN

The mind gathers its grain in all fields...
then suddenly it bursts into awareness
which men call inspiration or second sight...

– Louis L'Amour

Instantly, the bucolic homestead scene erupted into pandemonium. The officers lounging under the shade tree galvanized into action and began running about, shouting at one another and at us to *get down! get down!* and radioing for back-up.

I knew it, I knew it, I thought: the clairvoyant's lament. We didn't need to be told twice to duck. Heather eased Fiona around the trenches and behind the nearest cover, which was a stonewall well. Deidre raced around the back of a cruiser. Phillipa and I crawled on our elbows toward the building. Jordan jumped into the trench with Bill, where they both crouched down.

A second shot took out the window of the cruiser where Deidre was hiding. "Holy Mother of God!" she screamed. "Whose idea *was* this?"

"They swore we would be safe," Phillipa hollered back. "Just stay where you are."

Arnie Dickstein came running out the front door. The project director's naturally ruddy complexion had paled to ghastly white. "Heather! Heather, are you all right? Is everyone else unhurt? God Almighty, officers, you were supposed to prevent another incident like this from..."

All the while, the officers were shouting at him to get back into the house. In the distance I could hear several sirens. Police back-up was on its way.

Too late! One last shot felled Arnie, who crashed onto the front walk. Deidre screamed. Fiona shook off Heather, crawled over to the wounded man, and peered at the gunshot, which was in his thigh. She pulled a gauze pad out of her reticule and applied pressure to stop the bleeding.

The cruisers screeched up the driveway. It looked as if about twenty cops jumped out and erupted into the woods with weapons drawn. One officer was accompanied by a police dog to track the shooter. Shortly after, an ambulance arrived; paramedics hurried to stabilize Arnie and rush him off to the emergency room. The rest of us cautiously got ourselves into the house to regroup and recover. We huddled in the keeping room, shaken and disorganized. Bill Cody unfolded enough chairs for all of us.

"Well, then," Phillipa said brightly. "Who wants a sandwich?

There were several groans.

Phillipa ignored all protests. "I have roast turkey and brie on whole grain bread and egg salad with olives on sour dough rolls. Hot Earl Grey tea in the thermos and for dessert..."

I could hardly follow the menu, so rattled was my brain from the extraordinary events of the last few minutes. But somehow my hand automatically reached out when the egg salad was offered. I'm very fond of egg salad. "How do you suppose those snipers have the nerve to attack a police-guarded property?"

Soon everyone had a sandwich in hand, except Heather, who was calling the hospital on her cell to check on Dickstein. "Nice little man, didn't deserve this. Haven't you got anything stronger than Earl Grey, Phil?"

Deidre took a slim silver flask out of the little green shoulder bag that matched her green sundress, now wrinkled and muddy. "Try a drop of the Irish. I carry this for Conor."

"Sure you do." Heather accepted the offer with a grin. The grin faded as she listened to a reply from someone at Salem Hospital. "Arnie's lost a lot of blood," she told us when the call had ended. "But he's in stable condition."

Phillipa sighed and unwrapped a package of lemon tarts, handing it to Bill Cody to pass around. "I turned down brownies in deference to you, Cass. I know you've lost your taste for chocolate since the hemlock incident."

"Listen, I have an idea for you, Phil," Heather said. "Here we are with psychic flashes about these snipers that no mundane would credit. And we'll know more when Cass checks out Flying Eagle tonight. Then *you* should have a word with your pal Greta Gallant before these guys wound or kill anyone else. If necessary, confess that you have intuitive, sensitive friends."

"If you're going to the tavern tonight, Cass, I'm going with you," Jordan said.

Fiona patted her hand. "If you promise not to alert this Eagle person, dear."

"Greta has heard of us, I fear," Phillipa said. "She pestered me for a tarot reading, which I begged off with some murmurings about having low psychic energy that day. But what she really wants, she told me, is to consult a genuine medium regarding some lost family jewelry. What if Dee did the medium thing and some of the snipers' victims came forth to name their assailant? Wouldn't Greta then have word with her husband?"

I helped myself to a lemon tart and considered. "Can't hurt, might help," I said.

"Oh, sure. And what if I encounter a real spirit while I'm doing that *medium thing*?" Deidre complained, sweetening her cup of tea a second time and capping the flask. "It's enough to drive a girl to drink."

"The missing jewelry was her grand-aunt Ella Boole's stash," Phillipa continued. "Just make up something Aunt Ella might say, and if all else fails, teach her the finding charm: *nothing is lost in spirit*, et cetera."

"You mustn't ask Dee to fake it, Phil," Fiona said. "A true medium has a responsibility to *tell it like it was*."

"There's something else going on out there," Bill Cody said, looking out the window. "The cops are hanging over one of the car radios. I'll go find out what's up. Thanks for lunch, Ms. Stern. You don't think you're going to be hungry after a scare, but you are."

A few minutes later he was back. We all seemed to be waiting for his report, but in no hurry to rush outdoors ourselves.

"There's been another shooting," Cody announced. "It was just coming over the police radio. Some guy riding his bicycle along the road a couple of miles from here. He's dead."

"Do you mean the snipers got away from all those cops, and the canine, too, and *hit someone else?*" Heather demanded.

"Back in those woods, there's a crisscross of old logging roads. If someone knew those roads well enough, he could drive in and out pretty fast, all right," Cody said.

By the time we got back to the Crowninshield, the breaking news coverage of more shootings at the Morse homestead and the deadly assault on the cyclist that followed was broadcasting on the bar's television; a number of employees as well as guests had gathered to watch. As it turned out, the murder victim was a young female (unnamed, pending notification of her family) wearing biking gear and a helmet, not a male as was first reported. It appeared that she'd been shot from a vehicle traveling in the opposite direction, away from the Morse place. The Morse Homestead's project director Dickstein, wounded earlier during the shooting spree, was in Salem Hospital, expected to recover fully.

Predictably, Conor came zooming back to the inn in his Range Rover to find out that, yes, indeed, Deidre had been at the homestead with the Circle when the morning's shootings had occurred, but she was fine, just fine. Conor vowed to cut short his Salem project and stick closer to Deidre than Crazy Glue for the remainder of our Salem sojourn. "It's the curse of the banshee," Conor groaned. "Last night I heard her keening in my dream."

"I think we're going to wrap up the shooting thing tonight," Fiona reassured Conor. "After that, there's just a couple of little séances, and we're home free to Plymouth."

"Séances? Maybe I'll take a few shots of those," Conor said, recovering from his whim-whams instantly.

"Oh, no, you won't," Deidre declared. "Spirits don't like to be trapped in film."

"And just how do you know that, darling Dee?"

"Because…because I've seen what I've seen."

"Ah…*an dara sealladh*. You're having the Second Sight and all?" Conor questioned with a gleam in his eye.

"Don't use that tone with me, sweetie. It's Cass who has the Sight. I just visit with dead people," Deidre said sharply.

They went off to their room, still arguing.

"I hope we won't be the cause of breaking up that romance," I said after they had disappeared into the kitchen to take the back stairs.

"No way," Phillipa said. "After our Italian adventure, Conor owes us all, big time."

Later bulletins that day gave the murder victim's name as Rochelle Owens, a Salem State University student who'd been training for the Boston Mayor's Cup race in September. By that time, we were back at The Liz having a pre-dinner drink.

Detective Lieutenant Bruce Gallant of the Essex Unit gave a press interview at six o'clock on the steps of City Hall in which he made absolutely no comment on anything. I wondered why they bothered to send him out to face that avid horde of reporters. Perhaps because Gallant looked as if he'd been sent down from Central Casting to play the quintessential lawman: Salem's answer to Hugh Jackman.

Gallant's interview was followed by a statement from the mayor. A slim stylish woman with a politically correct blonde helmet that looked shellacked, Mayor Deborah Rose deplored the wave of shootings that had been terrorizing Salem and warned that, if the culprit was not caught within a day or two, the Fourth of July celebration and concert on the waterfront would have to be cancelled in the interest of public safety. A chorus of groans could be heard rising from the crowd that had gathered to hear these announcements.

The general air of disappointment was echoed by somber reflections from the two TV anchors on what a great financial loss this would be for the city. Next came the irony of a perky weather reporter promising near-perfect weather for the Fourth. The televised local news concluded with film footage from a news helicopter buzzing FBI and local law enforcement teams who were swarming through the Morse woods looking for clues to the shooter and his vehicle.

Long gone.

❧

Fiona and I borrowed Phillipa's BMW and took off for the Wharf Street Tavern at seven. Early, but we planned to have dinner there before the Chief arrived, if indeed he was going to show. The others decided on a quiet dinner in the inn's dining room. Heather and Phillipa had already spent an evening stalking Flying Eagle. We feared their second appearance might spook him off. And Conor insisted that Deidre stay close to him and out of trouble. So I called Tip and told him our plan. He might want to join us and bring Sky Boy.

The Tavern had a pleasant view and a spruced-up nautical décor, hoping to attract tourists as well as the locals with whom it was a favorite nightspot. Seated in the restaurant at a small table overlooking Salem Harbor, we ordered a Greek pizza, which came laden with feta cheese, Kalamata olives, sliced onions, and fresh tomatoes, just the way Joe made it. He would be home within a day or two, and I dearly wanted to meet him in Plymouth. How I missed him! I pictured his jaunty Greek cap and neat gray beard, tried to imagine the black eye and couldn't. Joe's eyes were a perfect Aegean blue, and I liked them that way. Time to wrap up this sniper business. He would definitely not approve and might actually interfere if he suspected I was in danger.

When we'd finished our pizza and paid the bill, I suggested we should stake out a place in the adjacent bar.

I spotted Tip and Sky Boy at the far end of the bar (he *was* the same young man who had caused such a rumpus in the White Shark Pub!) and I just nodded slightly in their direction. Better if we didn't appear to be a posse.

The live music consisted of a three-man group called The Boys from Gloucester, featuring classic rock and new country. We settled at a little round table some distance away. Fiona ordered a Drambuie, and I ordered a Chartreuse, which is a kind of green liqueur that tastes so medicinal you can't possibly drink it fast. The Boys were playing on a tiny stage, no more than a step up, and the loud music was deafening. It was impossible to talk over the din, so we simply sipped our liqueurs and watched the clientele. And watched. And watched.

It was about nine o'clock when the unmistakable Big Chief Flying Eagle swaggered in, as gross as he'd been described, in an armless vest that put his eagle tattoos on display as well as too much of his hairy middle. He draped himself over a bar stool and ordered a boilermaker. I couldn't imagine that a man who had shot up Salem earlier in the same day wouldn't want to keep a very low profile, but soon he engaged others seated nearby in conversation so booming as to rise above the Boys' clamor. I nudged Fiona lightly under the table.

"I see him, and a sight he is," Fiona said quietly. "What are you going to do?"

"I'm thinking." I mouthed the words without sound.

Just then I saw Tip rise in his chair and look past my shoulder, with an intensity that could only mean—yes, it *was* Jordan Rivers who had just come into the bar, bringing her own captivating aura of energy and excitement. She was wearing an off-the-shoulder turquoise blouse, chunky silver earrings, slim jeans, and sparkly ballet flats. Giving a slight wave in Tip's direction, she pulled up a chair to our table.

"I thought I'd find you ladies here," Jordan said. "If you're zeroing in on the freak who's been shooting at us, I want to have a look at him, too, you know what I mean? Is it that big ugly guy you've got your evil eye on? *Awesome!* Can't you, like, hex him on the spot? Only what makes you so sure it's *him?* Your witchy ways, I'm guessing."

"Jordan, we don't do hexes, and we don't know anything yet," I whispered. "This is just a scouting expedition, based on an idea of Tip's. It's important not to get ourselves noticed."

"Hey, Cass! I'll be, like, invisible as a spider in its web," she assured us. *As if.* Already a couple of guys on their own were eyeing her with interest. I didn't even dare to glance at Tip.

Jordan ordered a rum and Coke. The Boys took a break, and in the welcome silence that followed, Flying Eagle could be heard holding forth on the protection of the sacred earth from all who would despoil and disturb her. He ranted on, lambasting the Federal Government in general and the FBI in particular. I was getting bored with his diatribe, and I was sure others at the bar must feel the same. A couple seated beside him got up and left.

"He's too stupid to be dangerous," Jordan said, watching us watching him.

"It's never or now," Fiona said.

"Now," I replied. Fiona held Jordan's hand to prevent her following. I got up and headed for one of the now empty bar stools, conscious that Tip was keeping his eye on me and shaking his head warningly. I ignored him. Making as if to hop up beside the Chief, I swung my hand across his beer and knocked it over onto the bar. People jumped out of the way and cursed. The bartender rushed over to mop up the mess.

Apologizing profusely, I grabbed a bunch of cocktail napkins, swabbing at dripping liquid, and while I was at it, at a few drops of beer that had fallen on Big Chief's bare arm.

Then, like an idiot, I fainted.

CHAPTER TWELVE

Not the quarry, but the chase.
Not the trophy, but the race.

– Proverb

It wasn't a pretend faint, it was the real thing. The last thing I remembered was touching the Chief's skin. A black cloud of turbulent emotions had instantly enveloped me, and then...*nothing*.

The next thing I knew was the noxious odor of smelling salts under my nose and the soft tinkle of Fiona's silver bangles. I was lying flat on the barroom floor. Above me loomed a circle of concerned faces, including the Boys from Gloucester, who had just come back from their break, reeking of something that wasn't nicotine. Tip knelt beside me, still frowning with disapproval. Jordan was putting a folded jacket under my head.

"What happened to you? What the fuck just happened?" Jordan was obviously very upset.

"You shouldn't have come here at all," Tip said sternly to me. "You know how you are!"

"I'm all right. Help me up, for Goddess' sake," I whispered faintly. "Has he gone?"

"Yes. When you keeled over, he called someone on his cell and took off out the back door. But that's okay. Sky Boy followed him," Tip said, his cell phone in hand, waiting to hear from his friend.

Two of the Boys from Gloucester hauled me to my feet and sat me down at the table that Fiona and I had been sharing. The bartender brought me a cup of rank burnt coffee and a sour expression that suggested that he'd seen his share of lady drunks.

"Well, Cass, my dear," Fiona said, "that was a serious reaction, but what did it mean?"

"I feel that Flying Eagle is involved in the shootings." I could hear myself speaking strangely, as if the Delphic oracle had just taken over my tongue.

Tip's cell rang. He listened, and we all listened, too. "I'm on my way."

"You're on your way *where?*" I demanded.

"Sky says a van just raced into the parking lot and picked up Fat Eagle. Looked like a young guy at the wheel. I'm going after them," Tip said. He dashed out the back way, and Jordan followed, her sparkly shoes flashing down the dark hall. Fiona grabbed me when I tried to follow them.

"You're still too weak, dear. I saw how that vision took you down. Just stay still for a moment and let the evil aura pass."

The Boys from Gloucester got started on some rollicking country music. When the spotlight of attention moved away from me as people returned to their drinks, I breathed with relief. And kept breathing deeply. *What exactly had I sensed in Flying Eagle?*

"He may not be the shooter, but he's the instigator," I said finally. "The marksman must be the other guy, the young one whom we haven't even seen yet."

After a few minutes (me inhaling and exhaling deeply, Fiona patting my hand) Tip and Jordan reappeared, too out of breath to speak at first. Jordan leaned over with her head down and her hands propped on her legs. Finally, she recovered her voice and said, "they were all gone by the time we got there. The van and Tip's friend, as well. We think Sky followed them on his motorcycle. But he doesn't have his cell. We found his cell smashed in the parking lot. It must have happened soon after he called us."

"Surely Sky will find some way to keep in touch. We'd better wait to hear from him," I said.

"Sky's rooms are right down the street from here, over the Wicked Good Gift Shoppe," Tip said. "That's where he'll expect to meet me. I'm going back there to wait for him."

"We're going, too!" Jordan announced. "That's okay, isn't it? Can you make, like, real coffee?"

Tip's face blazed with pleasure. "Indian coffee. Black and strong.

With Jordan and Tip in the lead in all their youthful energy, Fiona and I followed, leaning on one another. I wasn't any too steady yet, and predictably nauseous. I wasn't sure I could stomach Tip's coffee, which as I remembered it, could hold a spoon upright.

"The Wicked Good is Circe's shop," Fiona said to me, still patting my hand from time to time. "It's late, so probably closed now. A force of nature, that Circe. I hope there's time for you to meet her before we go home to Plymouth. I feel this troublesome situation will all be resolved soon, don't you?"

"Yes. Or we'll see her in Plymouth," I said, with no notion where I got *that* idea.

"Sky's rooms" were really one spacious room with two blanket-covered cots, sofas by day, backed by *Souvenir of Salem* pillows. A tavern table under windows overlooked the wharf, with three straight chairs grouped around it. There were pegs on the wall for clothes, a kitchenette with an under-the-counter refrigerator, and, I assumed, a bathroom behind the one closed door. The walls were decorated with reproductions of Southwestern Indian art. A few shelves held a radio, some books and Tip's flute. There was a drum propped in the corner. The pine-plank floor was worn and bare except for a Navajo rug of stylized birds. Tip set about making coffee in a battered old percolator, and heated up water in a tea kettle as well.

"I've got some tea bags if you'd rather, Aunt Cass."

I must have looked as rattled as I felt.

Fiona took out a small plastic bag out of her reticule. "Here, Tip, use these, dear. It will settle Cass's stomach." It was, of course, peppermint tea, just what the herb doctor ordered.

Less than an hour later, Sky Boy ran lightly up the stairs and found his apartment fairly crowded with the four of us. Tip and Jordan were at the table playing Crazy Eights and drinking coffee. A fat yellow candle stuck in a large flat pottery dish was flickering as they swapped cards. Fiona was curled up on one of the cots, and I on the other, both of us sipping peppermint tea from mugs.

"You're probably wondering why I called this meeting," Sky grinned, helping himself to a mug of coffee. Shyly, Tip introduced each of us to his friend.

"We've been hanging out here to find out what happened," Jordan said, casting the rest of her cards onto the heap on the table, the game taking second place to the real chase.

"We found your phone," Tip said. "Crashed."

"I called you when the big guy jumped into a black van. From what I could see of the driver, he looked lean and tough.

Had a cap on and his jacket collar turned up. They saw me come after them, and the kid at the wheel tried to back over me and my bike. That's when I dropped my cell. I chased them about three miles, then I lost them. They were heading south out of town on Route 114." Sky's mouth quirked into what may have been a slight smile. He took a tobacco pouch out of his pocket and dropped a pinch of it onto the fat candle's flame. An offering. Sky must have a close call with that van trying to run him over in the parking lot.

"Oh dearie me," Fiona said. "I was so hoping we could wrap this up tonight."

"You and me, both," I said.

"Wait," Tip said. "There's more. Sky?"

"I took a chance that they were headed for Route 129, so I went on parallel roads and got there first. Waited at a side street in East Lynn, and sure enough, they came racing past. Lucky again, I saw them hit the brakes before they got out of sight. I figured they've got a place down there, either Stephen Lane or Ruby Road, so I'd better not follow too close on the bike and spook them. I got their license number, anyway. 94F-6881"

"*Awesome!*" Jordan breathed, her eyes shining. "Can we tell the cops?"

"Tell them what?" Tip said. "That these medicine women identified the shooters in a vision?"

"I'm not, like, *totally* dumb, you know," Jordan said hotly. This was not going well for Tip.

Fiona said, "Phil is a friend of Lieutenant Detective Gallant's wife. We were thinking we'd find some way to let Greta Gallant know about Flying Eagle, and maybe she would tell her husband."

"You know, Fiona, that scheme is beginning to sound awfully tenuous to me. Talk Dee into holding a séance with fake ghosts? An idea that's bound to come back to haunt us, so to speak," I said.

Fiona sighed. "A blot on the escutcheon that could follow us through lifetimes to come," she admitted.

Jordan looked from one to the other of us in dismay. "I'm not following you, witch ladies. What's an escutcheon?"

"It's a kind of heraldic shield, dear," Fiona said. "Although, medically speaking, it refers to a triangle of pubic ha..."

"Oh, never mind all that, Fiona," I interrupted hastily. "It simply means a black mark against one's honor, Jordan. In Wicca, as in scientific research, faking results is a very bad idea."

"Oh, yeah? Do all the storefront witches in town know that they're blotting their whattiz when they go into their acts?" Jordan was scornful of commercial Salem, but there was true power here as well. It had nourished me while I was growing up with my uncomfortable flashes of vision.

"Karma will get 'em, don't you worry, dear," Fiona said. "But we have to do *something*, Cass. It's our psychic duty."

"Later, Fiona, later," I said. Sky was looking at us with a curious expression and a raised eyebrow.

A vague idea was dawning. What I had in mind now was a kind of "field trip" to smoke the snipers out of hiding. It was a scheme that I didn't dare share with these enthusiastic young people who would rush in where witches tread with care.

I'd need a daring (possibly foolhardy) partner. Phillipa would worry about the illegalities, of course. And Deidre would worry about Conor worrying about her. Fiona would be all for taking action, but she tended to be a bit of a loose cannon. Literally. But Heather would do it! Crazy covert scenarios didn't faze her a bit. I remembered how she'd got us into a well-hidden arena when we had been chasing down an organized dog fighting ring a while back.

Okay, okay, I told my wiser self. *I admit it's a bit dangerous.* But I was after the quickest results. What I wanted to do was go down to where those two had last been seen by Sky, between Stephen Lane and Ruby Road, find the snipers, and let them know we were on to them. Then they would come after us and give themselves away.

Sounds like a plan, I said to myself. *Simple, but effective.*

❧

Wearily, I drove Fiona back to the Crowninshield, but there was no falling into bed just yet. Phillipa, Heather, and Deidre were eagerly waiting for a report on the evening's sleuthing at "our" table in The Liz. Conor was hanging around, too, nursing a whiskey at the bar and trying his best to watch the soccer game on TV rather than to show an interest in activities of which he disapproved. I doubted he missed much, though.

I was thankful that Fiona took up the gauntlet and gave her own pixilated version of events, gesturing dramatically with tinkling bangles. Especially the part where I'd "swooned dead away." But when she got to my vision of Big Chief Flying Eagle, she insisted I take over the recitation.

So I said that touching the fat man's flesh was a descent into his psycho psyche that was truly terrifying. But before I'd fainted with fear, my sixth sense had told me that Flying Eagle was part of a murderous team, but perhaps not the shooter. Actually, I was having a problem sorting out exactly what my vision *was* telling me about their relationship. I could see the two of them struggling in an aura of darkness, like two crows fighting over carrion. But I thought the younger man, the one who had been driving the van, was gesturing with a wooden arm that looked like a rifle. Visions can be as symbolic as dreams, and the right interpretation was vital. "Anyway, that's my best guess," I concluded.

"I'll take your best guess over a police report any day," Phillipa said.

But there was much more to tell. I related how Sky Boy had valiantly attempted to chase the van on his bike had partially succeeded. And best of all, that we did have the van's license number.

"But what are we going to do?" Deidre cried. "We have to do something. Would you like Phil to call Greta Gallant right now?"

"You're kidding, Dee. Do you know what time it is? She'll think I'm drunk," Phillipa complained.

"I'm zonked," I said. "I need to sleep now. Then we'll see what we can do. I thought maybe Heather and I..."

"Oh, bollocks!" Deidre said. "Am I going to miss out on all the fun *again*?"

Heather grinned and shook her head affirmatively, her new shoulder-length hair loose and gleaming. "Just say when, where, and what," she said.

"Early, before the van vanishes. The place where Sky last saw it. Canvass the streets until we see that license number," I said.

"Won't the van be hidden in a garage?" Deidre said. "Come to think of it, didn't you say that the killer's van was blue?"

"Maybe there are two vans," Fiona said.

"I'll talk to Stone," Phillipa offered, somewhat reluctantly. "In the interests of having me home someday soon, perhaps he'll run that license plate. There should be an address, and the owner may have an arrest record."

Conor, who had indeed been listening to every word, said: "Perhaps it's time that you and I went home, Dee. I'm just about finished with the Salem shoot anyway."

"But Conor, you're not really finished yet," Dee said. "You don't want to miss some of the witch-and-famous characters everyone talks about, the ones who feud with each other over who is the 'official' witch of Salem. I'm betting the commercial witches would just love to be in your Halloween feature."

Conor hesitated. "Dee, darlin', I'm a wee bit suspicious that you're giving me a load of Marlarkey here, just so that you can keep on chasing around Salem like a banshee."

"Conor, darlin', I just want you to expose the real undercurrents here. Anyone can do the superficial Salem stuff."

They smiled at each other, neither one fooled. But I'd have bet my best rowan wand that Deidre was going to stay around for a while, no matter what Conor "decided." Cute and dimpled she might be, but underneath there was a whim of iron in Deidre's character.

Before we dragged our weary selves up to our rooms that night, Fiona insisted on waving us through a purification and protection spell. Fortunately, the bar was nearly empty as we white lighted and sage-smudged and shuffled around the table. Buzz the bartender looked on incredulously.

"Don't trouble yourself, Buzz. The girls are right as rain," Conor assured the bartender. "It's just an old sorority thing of theirs." He grinned and hopped off his bar stool.

Putting an arm around Deidre, Conor escorted her through the kitchen to the service stairs. Phil accompanied a weary Fiona into the little gilt elevator, and Heather and I braved the cold spot in the lobby. Amazing how the temperature plummeted just there on such a soft summer night. I rubbed the chill out of my arms as we walked upstairs.

"What time do you want to get going?" Heather asked as we trudged along the landing to our rooms.

"Six. Can you make it?" I wondered if I could make it myself. Perhaps the old adrenaline rush would kick in. And a very large cup of Dunkin's coffee we would pick up on the way. "In case that shooter goes out to work someplace, we'll get there before he leaves. We need to scout those streets before he takes the van away."

"Won't they see us lurking about?"

"That's the idea," I whispered. "I want him to follow us. Spook him out into the open."

"*Hecate, preserve us*...what a splendid idea!"

CHAPTER THIRTEEN

I see the right, and I approve it too,
Condemn the wrong, and yet the wrong pursue.

– Sir Samuel Garth from Ovid

When we met in the morning, both of us ten minutes early, Heather was wearing a brilliant orange Witch City t-shirt, black cargo pants, a law enforcement duty belt with cell phone and flashlight attached, and oversized Jackie O sunglasses with a pair of binoculars hanging around her neck "Well, you said you wanted us to be noticed, didn't you?" she said.

I was in my plain serviceable black commando outfit, with a black scarf tied around my hair, pirate-style. I'd taken the precaution of picking a few sprigs of large-leaf periwinkle, a ground cover growing under trees at the Crowninshield. An excellent magical plant for banishing evil influences. Now I tucked one sprig in Heather's pocket and another in mine.

We sped away out of the parking lot in Heather's Mercedes while she hummed Jimmy Buffet's *Burn that bridge...*

The sun was struggling to give us another brilliant summer day, but the clouds won out. The sky was completely overcast by the time we found the Dunkin' in downtown Salem. We cheered ourselves with two *grande* coffees and four chocolate donuts, proper fuel for sleep-deprived ladies on their way to bait the local killers. By six-thirty we'd arrived at the place on Route 129 where Sky had last seen the black van, license number 94F-6881. Sky thought the van had turned in either at Ruby Road or Stephen Lane, streets that ran parallel to one another. It was an older neighborhood: small clapboard ranch houses, raised or split level, pastel colors, interposed with the occasional shingled bungalow, gray or tan. A few garages among the ranch houses, but most vehicles were parked in open driveways. Navy or red seemed to be the most popular van colors. We spotted only two black vans, neither with the right license number.

"Maybe in one of those garages?" Heather said.

"Maybe. Let's try some of these other streets, though."

We continued to cruise, Harold Street, George Street, Perry Street. Now the houses were even older, unpretentious cottages of the 40s and 50s, and farmhouses perhaps dating back to the 30s, and their yards were less tidy.

Heather drove, and I bumped along as passenger, deliberately letting my mind go blank (easy enough after a glut of chocolate donuts). I got my first real psychic hit on Perry Street. One long rutted road led to a small rundown farmhouse in back of others, surrounded by trees in a rough woodland area between Perry and George Streets.

I put a hand on Heather's arm and pointed. "I'm getting a pinch from that place in back of the trees. Can we drive in there?"

"Sure, but I don't know how we'll get out again," Heather said, yet she was already easing the Mercedes down the overgrown road. There was a decrepit barn on one side, no van in sight.

Heather honked her horn.

"Oh, for Goddess' sake! Are you crazy? Turn around, and let's get out of here," I exclaimed.

"Wait a minute, Cass. You said we should catch their attention." Heather was studying the little house through her binoculars. Nothing stirred. "It's number 39. I assume Perry Street, since it's facing this way."

She backed up and turned around where the ruts in the yard suggested was the best place to do so. A dog barked inside the house. Heather stopped and turned the key off in the ignition.

"Why don't I just go and knock on the door?" she suggested. "I mean, you got that twinge, right? And for all we know, there may be a dog in danger in that house. Hungry, crated, maybe deserted…"

"Oh, come on, Heather. He sounds like any dog in any house. *I wouldn't go in there, if I were you.*"

"Famous warning words ignored by all proper gothic heroines," Heather said. Jumping out of the car, she marched up to the house and knocked assertively at the door. No one answered.

"Hey, you in there! *Ding-a-ling! Avon calling.* Is anyone home?"

Still no answer. Heather turned to me and shrugged. Then she strode over to the barn and peered in a side window. Unhooking the sleek flashlight from her belt, she shone it through the dirty glass.

The dog barked again. The sound seemed to be coming from the second floor. Using her binoculars, Heather looked up at the windows.

I opened the car door, prepared to rescue my idiot friend if necessary.

I saw a shade flicker in one upstairs window. *Uh oh.* Was there a glint of metal? Surely no one would hazard a shot where he could be trapped by the police in his own residence. My imagination was running riot again.

"Heather, *come on!*" I got out and waved her over. Surprisingly, she came right away, we both got in, and she started the car. But she stayed in Park.

"Let's go, then," I urged her. "This doesn't feel safe to me."

"I want to give him time to read our license plate," Heather said. "We're in just the right place for him to see it from the second floor. Also, I pasted a Crowninshield Inn sticker on my rear window. You do want him to find us, don't you?"

"I thought you just wanted to be in position for a quick getaway."

"That, too. Don't you want to know what I saw in the barn?" At last she moved the automatic shift into Drive and moved along the impossible dirt road at a dignified Queen Mum pace.

"Could you really see anything?"

"*Two* vans, Cass. Couldn't be sure of the colors. Couldn't read the license numbers. But there were definitely two vans."

"Jumping Juno! I think we've got them! That's *wicked*, Heather!"

"Yeah. But now what?"

"Now we wait for them to find us," I said. Actually, that part of our investigation wasn't crystal clear in my mind yet. *Let go and let the Goddess.*

∾

It was still so early when we got back to the inn, everyone was still at our table in The Liz, lingering over breakfast.

There was regretful talk of not celebrating the fourth in Plymouth, and whether City Hall would indeed cancel the Salem gathering on the Common and fireworks on the Wharf. We made compensatory plans for when we got home: a moonlight picnic and bonfire on my private beach, maybe celebrating an esbat under the July moon variously named Thunder Moon, Buck Moon, Hay Moon. *If only we could get a bead on those snipers and wrap it up in Salem.*

Fueled with more coffee and a cranberry Danish from the tray requisitioned by Phillipa, I related the details of our scouting expedition and our hope that the snipers would be lured to the Crowninshield.

Then Phillipa broke in. "I think we're onto something here. I talked to Stone last night. This morning he called me back with a rundown on that license plate. It's a 1995 Ford E-series Van belonging to a man named Gregor Sokol. Twenty-two years old. No priors unless it's some juvenile thing that got expunged."

"Well, that's no help," Heather said. "We've got him at 39 Perry Street, and he ought to have priors. But the house probably belongs to the other guy, Flying Turkey, or whatever his name is."

"Eagle," Fiona said. "Interestingly enough, Ben Franklin wanted the turkey to be our national bird, which would have fit right in with our economy, gobble, gobble, gobble. But the eagle won out."

"Yes, yes, but what about Sokol?" Heather asked impatiently.

"If Sokol is a rifle enthusiast, he might belong to one of the North Shore gun clubs," Fiona said. "Might even have won a prize. Let me see if I can find him online, now that we have his name." She took the smart phone out of her reticule.

"*Rifle enthusiast?* Is that some kind of euphemism for *sniper?*" Phillipa raised her expressive black eyebrows.

My cell rang its tinny tune, which was as good an ending as any to the discussion. I took it to another table and said hello.

"I'm home, sweetheart. No pineapple of welcome, no homecoming kisses," Joe said. "So I'm wondering, *where's my wife?* Still in Salem? What's going on there, anyway? And where are the boys?"

"Oh, honey, how wonderful! Scruffy and Raffles are with Dick Devlin, having a sporting time at the Morgan manse, sort of like a spa vacation. They're better off there this week, away from all the fireworks displays on the shore," I rationalized. "And we're still pulling things together up here in Salem. That dig at the Morse homestead that Heather's involved with has been in a spot of trouble, and I can't just run out on her."

"*Spot of trouble?* Oh, yes. You think I haven't been watching the news? Salem residents being warned to stay the hell indoors because there's a crazed sniper on the loose. Targeting personnel at the Morse place but that's not all. Took out a gal on bicycle just for practice. The mayor is threatening to cancel Salem's Fourth of July celebration, for God's sake! And some of the townspeople have sworn to party down on the wharf anyway. So, sweetheart, exactly what things are you pulling together?"

Caught! So I gave Joe a carefully edited version of events, omitting our tracking Gregor Sokol to his lair. But Joe would probably see right through the camouflage, as usual. "We're not without our resources, honey" I added. "Tip is here, staying with his friend Sky Boy Mitchell. And Jordan Rivers has a cousin Rafe who rides with a bunch of bikers."

"*What have you done?* You're up to something else. I can hear it in your voice. I'll be there in about two hours," he said firmly, in his brook-no-opposition voice. "Can you book me a room? Preferably, with you in it, sweetheart."

"As it happens, I can probably book us a lovely room overlooking Salem Harbor in this marvelous old inn, the Crowninshield." In fact, I knew that most of the guests were leaving or had left already. Who wanted to vacation in a town where the police warned you to stay indoors at all time, and the Fourth of July is celebrated *not with a bang but a whimper?* "It will be like another honeymoon."

"Every time we're together," he said in that low sexy voice that went right to my inner goddess, the one who has no reservations about enjoying sensual delights. Even while a crazy shooter is on the loose.

"Okay, then. Two hours. I'll be waiting."

"It was Joe," I said to the assembled curious faces at our table. "He'll be here in two hours."

"Well, that's good, isn't it?" Phillipa said.

"Before we foil those snipers and go home, I hope to exorcise the inn of Fenella's restless spirit," Fiona said.

"I do admire your optimism," Phillipa said.

"Believing is seeing," Fiona reminded us.

Just then Conor joined us carrying a mug of strong tea he'd made at the breakfast buffet in the dining room. A camera was slung over his shoulder. "I can always depend on finding you colleens in the bar," he said, putting his arm around Deidre, who smiled up at him impishly.

"Haven't you always told me it's the best place to have a conversation? We've been discussing whether we should have a séance here before we leave Salem. You know, to rid this place of the spectral maiden."

"Glory be to God!" Conor exclaimed. "Isn't that better left to the priests?"

"Same difference, darlin'," Deidre said. "Better check with the inn owners, Fiona. I did. James Woolgar and Derek Witt are Brits, and Brits love ghosts. They've been delighted that Fenella appears to be lingering on the premises. They feel that it's only natural that a Salem inn as old as theirs should be haunted by a wronged woman. Rumors about Fenella attract tourists. Or will, when the sniper crisis is over. When I mentioned that I'm sensitive to ghosts and so needed to use the back stairs to avoid Fenella's chill, and that I myself had seen the misty outline of the fallen girl on the lobby floor, they offered us a discount on our room if I would provide them with a certificate of authenticity. It has occurred to me lately that ghost hunting might be a profitable sideline to the doll business. I should just let the word get around Plymouth, discreetly, of course, that *I see dead people*." She winked, and for a moment the old carefree Deidre was in mischievous evidence.

Conor groaned and clasped his head dramatically.

But a moment later, Deidre looked worried again. She was finding this new sensitivity rather oppressive, especially since she was temporarily lodged in an actual haunted inn. Clearly it would be a relief to her when we all went home.

Fiona dug into her reticule and came up with a small brass bell in the shape of the Greek goddess Cybele. "Here, Dee… ring this if you feel yourself getting worried and depressed. The sound of a bell purifies negative vibrations and lifts the spirits. I often wear a little bell on my ankle when I'm going into uncertain territory."

"Hence the expression, *I'll be there with bells on*," Phillipa said.

"I thought that was for court jesters," I said.

"Don't you worry, ladies. I'll be keeping Dee smiling," Conor grinned, the very image of a jester himself.

"Thanks, Fiona. I love it!" After a couple of experimental rings, Deidre tucked the bell into the pocket of her sundress. With a wan little wave, she hurried upstairs with Conor by their usual kitchen route, while I went to Reception to snag an empty room for Joe and me. Without thinking, I walked through the cold spot at the foot of the main stairway. It felt as if someone had opened a door to January. I hurried past; the girl at the front desk promised that the "room with a harbor view" I'd requested would be ready for its new occupants by two that afternoon.

Joe and I in another hotel room: a breath of sensual indiscretion for married folks—how hot is that!

CHAPTER FOURTEEN

Rich and rare were the gems she wore,
And a bright gold ring on her wand she bore.

– Thomas Moore

"Here's the thing," Heather was explaining to Phillipa and Fiona when I returned from the front desk. "I've arranged it so that this Sokol person could and probably did identify my car, so I've parked the Mercedes in a prominent place in front of the inn, not in the parking lot. We figure this guy is going to cruise by and see it. And probably come calling. If that happens, we can report him and *his* license number to the police as a suspect. All we need, really, is an excuse to tell all. Well, maybe not tell *all*, but at least reveal certain important clues."

Phillipa looked askance, and even Fiona seemed doubtful, but she said, "Well, we've probably got some time before Heather's car draws attention. Let's rev up that Stop Vermin spell that we did in Gallows Hill Park. Cass, you still have some sprigs of dried boneset and rue?"

"Ah yes. How wonderfully actual danger concentrates the mind," Phillipa said. *"By the waning of the moon, evil will be banished soon…and if danger threatens me, impervious to harm I'll be…"* She refreshed her rhyme

"Right. Boneset to ward off villains and rue to boomerang their deadly intentions back to them," I said "I'll go get my Wiccan travel kit…but where?"

Fiona took charge. "Yes, please, Cass, you fetch the herbs. There's a nice little rose garden on the west side of the inn. And, listen up, ladies, I think we ought to use our wands this time. *Everyone bring her wand.* Mine is right here." She removed a green velvet case from her reticule. I wished I'd had the foresight to bring my rowan wand with the quartz tip, perfect to deflect evil, but I'd only brought the fold-up traveling hazel wood wand. Common old hazel, really too nicey-nice to zap the bad guys.

"We'll meet outside in ten minutes." Fiona's voice penetrated my reflections.

"Ah, Fiona. Won't we look a bit outlandish, waving our wands and sprinkling salt water from herb sprigs onto the soggy roses?" Phillipa complained. "And besides, I didn't bring my wand."

"We'll use the wands to direct our energy against evil. Actually, I would have preferred besoms to sweep it away, but I never travel with a broom. I think it makes a woman needlessly conspicuous, especially if she has to call a cab," Fiona said.

"Yes," Phillipa agreed. "Mundanes expect Wiccans to ride the damn things. I'd sooner wear a wooden thong."

Fiona ignored that flight of fancy. "There's a fine mist outdoors to veil us. And I'll try to obscure our circle even more with a glamour."

"I hope it works," I said. "I'm expecting Joe any minute, and I'd rather he didn't find me in the middle of Scene I of *Macbeth*."

But as it turned out, Joe got stuck in summer traffic and didn't arrive until almost two-thirty. That, in itself, was problematic.

Back in my old room, the one I'd been sharing with Phillipa, I found my travel kit and only then noticed that I'd tucked my detested herbal vision pillow underneath it. There wasn't much point invoking a vision now. Our own investigations had already practically solved the mystery of the Salem sniper. I put the pillow back in my suitcase.

I hurried downstairs, and out to the mist-shrouded garden we went, wands and herbs at the ready. Fiona's wand was hawthorn for psychic protection and faery magic, and the hand that held it bore rings set with magic stones: agate for strength and courage, jade for wisdom, and some others. Heather's was serviceable ash; sacred to Norse power; it promotes wise action and good communication, especially with animals. I clutched my hazel wood.

Being wandless, Phillipa pointed forth with her index finger instead. "This serves in a pinch," she declared. "It's been known to quiet unruly children or even quell a growling dog. Used with the magical voice, of course. So let's to work. *By this wood and water spell, those we seek will be revealed.*"

"Oh good," Deidre said. "I didn't bring a wand either. How would I have explained that to Conor? He notices everything. So, I'll just use my pointy finger, too. Actually, I think I *have* used it just the way Phil said, when the kids got into a wilding mode."

Before she cast a quick circle, Fiona waved her arms around us in hopes of sharing her own invisibility glamour. She herself was fading into one of those unremarkable older women who are rarely noticed by waiters, salespersons, or security personnel. Already she quite looked quite wispy and faded.

There's something so timeless about spell-working "between the worlds," that I hardly knew how many minutes, or hours, had passed before we released our intentions into the Cosmos and Fiona opened the circle. Except that my stomach was growling. It had been a long while since those chocolate donuts.

"We ought to take turns keeping an eye on the Mercedes," Heather said. "I'll go first while you ladies have lunch. There's a glider on the front porch."

"I'll just run upstairs and see if Conor wants to join us for lunch," Deidre said.

So we gathered in The Liz again, which had just opened for bar business. Fiona imperiously requested Buzz to order a pitcher of iced tea and lobster rolls from the kitchen.

"Where's the little blonde?" Buzz- asked. "And the tall gal who always orders the wine?"

"Deidre will be along shortly, and Heather's testing out the glider on the front porch," Phillipa said. "You'll be rid of us all fairly soon, I think."

His face got redder, and I got the notion that he would actually miss us but would never say so. I wondered what kind of aura we had brought to our dark corner of the bar, what energies and vibrations we gave forth when we were in full force. Not entirely negative, apparently.

Deidre ran down the back stairs and through the kitchen to join us. Conor had sped off, she said, to interview one of the high profile witches of Salem, Tabitha Wisen. The lunch came with a satisfyingly large basket of French fries. We munched and whispered; by and by Heather appeared. "Not a sign," she said. "Are you finished, Cass? Do you want to take a turn?"

I was, and I did. The glider was comfortably cushioned, and I was comfortably full, even drowsy. Rather than burning off, the mist seemed to have grown even thicker. *Time to call it a fog*, I thought. *I wonder if this is what it's like in London.* Right then, I had a kind of *flash forward*, seeing myself and Joe walking over Westminster Bridge on a foggy morning, heading for Big Ben and the Houses of Parliament. I had to shake my head several times to clear the vision and get back to here and now, *Salem in summer.* Staying on point is not easy for the clairvoyant to whom, at some deeper level, all time is one.

After a half hour or so, Phillipa came out and took my place, keeping an eye on the traffic and the Mercedes, which was parked directly in front of the inn, causing anyone arriving or leaving to detour around it to a less convenient place for unloading luggage. Heather and Fiona were still in the bar, sipping iced tea. I joined them and helped myself to a glass.

Fiona took out her crystal pendant from underneath the gray shirt she was wearing (no tartans when working on the invisibility glamour) to dowse goddess-knows-what. Before she could ask her first question, however, Phil came running back, looking both excited and alarmed.

"A van slowed down near the Mercedes, then went down to the corner, turned around, and came back on the other side of the street. It's parked there now. I can't quite see who's at the wheel, it's so misty," she said urgently.

"A black van?" Heather asked.

"No. Hard to tell, but I think it was a darkish blue," Phillipa said.

"Uh oh," I said. "You didn't happen to get the plate number, did you? In the mist, and all."

She raised that expressive eyebrow. "Of course. I'm married to a detective, so it's second nature. The plate was easier to see than the driver, who *I think* was wearing a cap and dark glasses."

"Let's go, then." Heather pushed back her chair decisively.

I loaded the dishes on a tray, brought it over to the bar, and followed the others to the front porch. On the way, I heard a *crack* sound, like an early firecracker. "What in Hades is that?"

The van was no longer parked across the street, but Heather's windshield had been shattered by a rifle shot. She screamed and tried to rush to the Mercedes, but Deidre and I held her back. Fiona seemed to be waving her arms, or her wand. The blue van appeared from around the corner and slowly cruised down the street toward us.

"Good." Phillipa began to punch in 911 on her cell. "We'll get the bastards now."

"For Goddess' sake, get down," I said to the others urgently. "He may be going to take another potshot."

Deidre screeched and scurried into the inn. Heather got Fiona in back of the open front door. Phillipa and I crouched behind the glider. Then, when I peeked out from behind the glider, my heart practically stopped beating.

Joe was sauntering toward me from the parking lot, his Greek cap set at a jaunty angle!

I jumped up, ran toward him, and pushed him against the side of the porch hard. His knees buckled and I fell down to the ground with him. "Stay down, stay down" I yelled in his ear. "There's a rifle. In that van."

The van speeded up and another shot rang out, striking the glider. I couldn't see the others, so I screamed. Hurtling around the corner, the van disappeared.

We waited in our crouched positions until two squad cars arrived. By then my middle-aged knees would hardly unbend, but Joe helped me to my feet.

"What the hell was *that!*" he shouted in my ear. "I thought for a minute that we were still in Rome. Can't we *ever* say hello to each other without being greeted by a hail of bullets?"

"Déjà vu?" Sometimes, and at the worst times, I can't seem to keep myself from making some smart remark.

"Déjà vu, my ass. The only déjà vu is you and your friends getting yourselves in danger again." Joe was understandably angry and upset, maybe even afraid, but he hugged me hard. I did love the feel of his strong, comforting arms. *It will be all right,* said my heart. *Are you crazy?* demanded my mind.

Obviously, I would have to explain the situation more fully to Joe, but right then it was the officers who had responded to Phillipa's call who were asking the questions. One of them was Officer Wayne Wedge whom we'd last met guarding the Morse homestead. The other was a round-faced African-American who introduced himself as Officer Ossie Burdock.

Phillipa did not waste time getting to our prime objective. "The guy had a rifle and shot out my friend's windshield. Then he shot at us. It's the Salem sniper," she declared. "In a blue van with the license plate SA9-682. He headed out that way," She pointed in the direction the sniper had gone.

Viewing the shattered Mercedes, Officer Burdock sent out an immediate APB to stop the vehicle as described, which was heading south on Route 114 when last seen. While we waited for whatever was going to happen next, we answered more questions. No, we didn't get a good look at the driver. No, we didn't know why we had been targeted. Perhaps for no reason. A few of the sniper's victims had seemed to be chosen at random, although many had been connected with the Morse homestead. No, we hadn't recognized the van.

"But wait," Heather said. I could see from her expression that a nifty idea had just dawned on her. I waited with trepidation. "The other day when Cass and I got lost down on Route 129, we drove into this dirt driveway, where I *may have* seen a van like that one. You know, blue and mud-splashed. And I *just happened* to notice that the house address was 39 Perry Street. Do you suppose...?"

Officer Wedge ran his hand over his blond buzz cut in puzzlement. "M'am, are you saying that you may know *where the Salem sniper lives?*"

"You ladies know about the reward, I guess," Officer Burdock said with a broad knowing smile.

"Oh, damn the reward," Phillipa said.

"Why don't you guys just call in the lady's information and see if your superior doesn't want to send a squad car to that address." Joe had stepped forward, matching macho stance to macho stance, in case the cops were going to give us a hard time. It's one of the nice things that men do.

"Detective Lieutenant Gallant," Phillipa piped up. "He knows me. We met at a party once. I was there with my husband, Detective Stone Stern of the Plymouth Police."

The two officers looked at each other. Burdock shrugged. Wedge reached for his phone.

CHAPTER FIFTEEN

Home is the sailor, home from the sea
And the hunter home from the hill.

– Robert Louis Stevenson

What with the excitements of the morning, we were all quite ready for an afternoon siesta. Phillipa brought us a tray of cappuccinos which we drank leaning around in the lobby where we'd grouped after the interview. Fiona was depending heavily on her coyote walking stick. And I was hanging on Joe's shoulder.

Phillipa said. "I feel we're getting somewhere at last, don't you? I'm even closing my eyes to your extraordinary fabrication about having seen the blue van at 39 Perry Street, Heather."

"Well, I did, sort of. There were two vans in that barn. The point is to get the police into that place, possibly to apprehend the snipers. Then, Goddess willing, we can all go home. Dick is getting lonesome."

"Misses your home cooking?" Phillipa smirked.

"I have other attractions. And that wonderful Kitchener couple to do the rest. I swear they must have stepped out of a dream," Heather said.

Fiona and I glanced at each other. She shook her head ever so slightly.

Whisking Deidre through the cold spot, we limped upstairs to our various rooms, Joe and I to the new accommodations I'd arranged. It was Colonial modish, gold and green, and had a distant but pleasant view of the Salem waterfront from the window. The kind chamber maid had moved my belongings, as I'd requested. Joe, of course, had his whole wardrobe in his duffle bag, which in its own way, was as remarkable as Fiona's reticule.

Joe locked the door, closed the drapes, and took me in his arms. His wiry beard brushed my cheek, a tingling caress. His familiar scent, like herbs on a sunny hillside, surrounded me. He kissed me. Truth to tell, I had kissed a few men in my fifty-something years, but not one of them had kissed me with a mouth as sensual and satisfying as Joe's. And I think I'm being perfectly objective here.

We fell on the bed together. Not exactly restful but certainly stress-reducing. Finally we drifted at the edge of sleep, as in fact, we were both exhausted already, he from travel and I from terror. He murmured that he loved me.

I thought about the sheer chaos into which he been plunged at his arrival. All my fault, I supposed. "But *why* do you love me?" It was an annoying, greedy, female kind of question, but I asked it anyway.

"That's hard to explain," Joe said, coming fully awake at once.

"Try."

" Because I knew from the moment we met that you were the one I'd been searching for and hardly believed I would find. It was as if I *recognized* you."

"Is that like…a soul mate?"

"If I thought in those terms, yes. The woman I could be fully alive and wholly myself with. When I looked at you, I felt as if I were falling into your eyes. As if I'd come home. Is that crazy?"

I sighed. "That's the way I felt, too. About you."

But he continued. "If I'd happened to sail into Salem Harbor when we were younger, I would most certainly have wanted you then, only you."

"I was separated from Gary, running my parents' garden shop when I was a young woman in Salem. And I had three children."

"I was probably still married, depending on the year."

Joe seldom talked about his first marriage, but I was not above pushing for a little more detail. "Did you feel the same about Irene?"

"No, not the same. Not *inevitable* like with us."

"So what would have you done…I mean, back in Salem"

"Run away with you, if you were willing."

"What about this?" I touched the gold cross he wore, which was the only thing he was wearing at the moment."

"Ah, my cross. Keeping in mind that all seamen are superstitious, I feel that it's my 'amazing grace.' It's what I was brought up to believe, but now it's more of a cultural thing than religious." I could feel him smiling in the shaded room. "Else, how could I have married a witch?"

"Yes, how could you?"

"It's that word that gets in the way of what you really are, which is something much deeper. So…would you have run away with me, sweetheart? Back in Salem? I was in the merchant marine then. Young and vigorous, no gray hair, but both of us still married."

"And been the cause of some Homeric war? Still…how could I have ever resisted you? Yes, I would, and always will, no matter where and when we meet in all our lives. Of course, I would have taken the children along. Takes some of the gloss off the mythic adventure, I guess."

"A family circle in tow?" he mumbled sleepily. "Wouldn't have deterred me any more than your present circle."

And that was true. Joe was too strong and centered ever to be put off-balance by the energy of women like us. Maybe it was something he got from all those years of sailing the seas, his love affair with the oceans of the world. Just thinking about lying in the arms of the water, I floated off into blissful oblivion.

My cell phone woke us. First I had to find wherever I had dropped my slacks, but that's the good thing about cell phones; they announce their whereabouts. It was Phillipa. "Guess what! Officer Burdock called. Gregor Sokol is down at the station helping the Salem police with their inquiries. Apparently the blue van, license plate SA9-682, *was* found on the 39 Perry Street premises. No gun though. And the black van was gone. Also no Big Chief Flying Turkey."

"This worries me, Phil," I said. "Unless Sokol gives up his pal, the cops won't know about Flying Eagle, and we can't tell them."

"Keep the faith. I talked to Stone about it, and he thinks Sokol will rat on his accomplice when the going gets rough. But can you imagine? Apprehending the Salem Sniper. What a coup for Gallant!" she said. "Meanwhile, I'm making a dinner reservation for us here at the inn, the Endicott Room. They do a decent Cedar Planked Salmon with Honey Balsamic Glaze."

"Sure, that sounds great."

It was not to be, however. Because Tip called shortly after five, while I was taking a shower. Wrapped in a hotel terry robe, I heard his news with growing alarm. Rafe had showed up at the homestead at four-thirty, as usual, to escort Jordan to his apartment. But she had disappeared and no one knew where she was. The two police officers guarding the homestead had been sitting under the big beech tree listening to a Red Sox game going into extra innings. They'd observed Jordan walking down the long driveway to meet Rafe. They didn't notice, however, if any of the passing cars on the main road had stopped near the girl. When Rafe arrived, Jordan was nowhere to be seen. To say that Tip was upset would be something of an understatement, although he was holding himself together in his usual "strong, silent Indian" fashion. But I could sense the panicked emotions under his stoic calm.

More police and detective units were on the way. Safe to say, the original two cops supposedly guarding the Morse dig and its personnel were in big trouble.

"We're on our way," I assured Tip, not knowing really what help we could be.

I explained this new emergency to Joe, and we dressed hastily. Then I called the others. While I was talking to Heather, I suddenly felt faint and had to sit down. Seeing my ashen face, Joe got me a drink of water, but I waved it away. A glimmer of knowing had passed through my agitated brain.

"What is it, Cass? You sound funny," Heather asked.

"I think Sokol's buddy has taken Jordan. Don't ask me how I know. I just do."

For some unreasonable reason, before we hurried downstairs, I grabbed my vision pillow out of the bottom of my suitcase. Its carrying case was my old woven handbag with the Libran scales. I slung it over my shoulder next to the Italian leather I'd been carrying.

The five of us and Joe piled into Phillipa's BMW (the Mercedes was roomier, but temporarily out of action) and raced over to the homestead. On the way, Heather told everyone that I thought Flying Eagle was responsible for Jordan's disappearance. I was still numb and silent with overwhelming anxiety, for Jordan and for Tip.

"It absolutely makes sense," Phillipa declared. "That disgusting slob has taken the girl as a hostage, blast him to Hades." It wasn't often that I got such a quick vote of confidence from Phillipa.

Deidre wished Conor could have gone with us but he'd rushed off again to trail around after Tabitha Wisen with his camera. "He's enraptured with her fluttering black outfits like something out of Edgar Allan Poe and the white rat she carries with her everywhere in a glass cage, name of Scabies."

Crowded as she was already, Phillipa griped, "Yes, too bad Conor couldn't make it. We could have put the two of you in the trunk. And there's nothing inherently spooky about black outfits."

Heather winked at me. "Occasionally, Phil, you might want to switch to deep purple. Makes a change."

"French women, who are recognized the world over for their fashion sense, wear black in preference to any other color," Phillipa said as she gunned the motor.

Fiona said. "Black repels negativity, so some witches believe. But give me a good tartan any day."

"It must be something to do with their scarves," Deidre said. "French women are very clever with their scarves."

We screeched to a halt at a wooden barrier across the Morse driveway. Of course we were not allowed even to enter the driveway. I could see two motorcycles near the front of the house; Rafe and Tip, I assumed. Tip did not answer his cell, however, so no help there. We got out of the car and stood around in various attitudes of frustration. Except Fiona, who sat on a soft bank of grass and hummed to herself. After a while she said, "Phil dear, why don't you call your friend from the Kernwood Country Club?"

Phillipa shrugged and called Greta Gallant from her cell phone, asking her to persuade her husband that we should be allowed onto the premises to talk to the detectives in charge. Greta asked why she should do that, and Phillipa explained that we had information that Sokol was not working alone, we'd seen him with this big Indian trouble-maker at the Wharf Street Tavern. We believed that Jordan Rivers' disappearance might have something to do with the Morse sniping incidents. Sokol was in police custody but his buddy, Chief Flying Eagle, was out and about.

Greta said that Bruce got really irritated when she suggested stuff like that.

Phillipa said that it was terribly important, and if Greta would help, she was sure that Bruce would thank her later.

Greta said that Phillipa didn't know Bruce who never credited her with having a smart idea about anything, certainly not his cases.

So Phillipa said that she would read Greta's tarot before she went home to Plymouth because she sensed that there were going to be some fascinating developments in her future life. Meanwhile, she needed Greta to do her this one little favor.

Greta said okay.

About fifteen minutes later, one of the officers guarding the driveway got a call, after which we were cleared to drive up to the homestead and park near the motorcycles. We found Rafe and Tip inside the keeping room, their young faces grim and angry, arguing with the two detectives. I could see they hadn't been making much headway with whatever theory they were proposing. Arnie Dickstein was also there, clumping back and forth on crutches, muttering, "Worse and worse and worser..." He barely acknowledged us before resuming his vigil.

With our arrival, the long room suddenly seemed crowded, but Phillipa pushed her way through to get the officers' attention.

Detectives Tom Bentley and Jake Irving were less than pleased to hear another version of the very theory that Tip had been proposing before we got there. Apparently, we all had the same idea about what had happened to Jordan. An accomplice of Sokol's had taken the girl.

Heather chimed in to describe the shooting spree at the Crowninshield Inn, how the shooter had been identified and was in custody only thanks to us. This did not exactly endear us to Bentley and Irving, who knew all about this development already, but they were listening. "We think there are actually two guys responsible for the Salem shootings. Sokol and his Indian pal. He calls himself Big Chief Flying Eagle. His real name is Wade Creech. That's the Indian angle that the FBI is so infatuated with," Heather explained.

"Only he's not an Indian," Tip said. "He's a wannabe who gives us Indians a bad name."

"Listen, guys," Rafe said in a furious tone. "My cousin didn't just disappear in puff of smoke. Those two jackasses you got guarding this place saw her walk down the driveway to meet me. A few minutes later, I'm here but Jordan is gone. She wouldn't ever have skipped out on me like that. Some asshole snatched her, and my buddy Tip here thinks he knows who. That blowhard friend of Sokol's."

"What's the motive, do you think?" Joe asked Tip. "It seems a real crazy thing to do."

Tip wiped his face with one hand. He looked like he wanted to cry. "I don't know. I don't know."

"Maybe he wants to make a deal," I said. "I'm going back to the car for a minute."

"No, m'am, you're staying here," Bentley said. "Detective Lieutenant Gallant is on his way, and he wants to talk to you."

"The lady said she'll be right back," Joe said. He leaned forward, tensing his body, and looked Bentley in the eye in a way was borderline challenging. "She'll talk to Gallant when she's good and ready."

I put my hand on his arm. "It's okay, Joe." No wonder this guy ended up in so many foreign jails.

"Let's go," he said. "You want to go to the car, you're going to the car." He swung me around and marched me out the door.

"Hey, honey, are you trying to get us arrested?" I said when we were out of earshot.

"On what charge?" he said, teeth gritted. Probably he was used to such confrontations working with Greenpeace, I thought. "Now what the hell are we doing?" he asked in a milder tone.

"It's my vision pillow. I brought it, just in case."

"But you hate that thing!"

"You wait outside the car. I just want to get into the back seat and lay my head against it. You know, sometimes, I see things."

"Yeah, I know. You want to find Jordan before something happens. I can understand that. God, I wish I still smoked. Right now…" He didn't finish.

I got into the car, grabbed my vision pillow and curled up with it. I concentrated on Jordan really hard.

But nothing happened.

I sighed. Wasn't the damn thing working anymore?

" Phillipa may have a cigarette in her bag," I said. "She sneaks a smoke now and then."

I smiled thinking of Phil trying to keep a secret from me. But her clandestine vice was handy, in a way. She always had a match or a lighter when one was needed. For that matter, I couldn't keep much from her, either. Between her laser-sharp reasoning and my intuition, not too much got by either of us. I remembered amusing incidents…and scary ones. My thoughts floated away, and I relaxed.

CHAPTER SIXTEEN

Danger gleams
Like sunshine to a brave man's eyes.

– Euripides

Suddenly I felt that familiar whooshing, like Alice down the rabbit hole. The back seat of the car, the Morse homestead, and even Joe simply melted into smoky mist. I was in the woods, what woods I couldn't say. I looked in the window of a black van and saw Jordan, tied up and gagged with duct tape. Big Chief Flying Eagle was outside, leaning on the fender, talking on a cell phone. I could smell him, he was disgusting. Sweat, liquor, nicotine, and some revolting hair gel. I forced my attention to look around for clues to his location. Nothing, nothing. Except...the vague outlines of a water tower. Which immediately got vaguer, as I whooshed back to the present and the back seat of the BMW.

"Let's go back now," I said. As usual, I felt nauseous and wobbly, so I leaned on Joe's arm as we returned to the homestead. He was used to these after-effects and pulled me protectively close. In lieu of Fiona's smelling salts, his nearness acted like an instant restorative.

Just as we reached the front step, Gallant drove in and parked beside the BMW with a squeal of brakes. He stopped me at the door. "Are you Cass Shipton? Where's Phil Stern? What's going on here?"

"Yes, I'm Cass. Phil is inside. We don't mean to be intrusive, but we think we have information about the Salem sniper. Snipers, actually." I pushed forward with Joe to join the others inside. The lieutenant followed us impatiently

"Well, Phil," Bruce Gallant said, leaning over her, almost but not quite smiling. Tall, slim, and rugged. I could see why Phillipa found him so attractive, and why she was responding right that moment with a slight flush of her cheeks and lowered eyelids. "What's this Greta has been telling me? That you and your circle of wacko women have some vital information about our sniper? Which you had accessed by *supernatural* means?"

"I understand you're not a believer," Phil said in a low soothing tone. "But this once, you need to have faith in us."

Was she using her magical voice? Phil was the only one of us (besides Fiona, of course) who sometimes could manage that hypnotic trick.

Gallant was not so suggestible. "You know, if our task force needed a psychic to do our job, we could find dozens of them right here in Salem. We wouldn't need to import them from the South Shore."

"Just remember it was our tip that got you to Sokol. Now, not only are we convinced that Sokol has an accomplice," Phillipa continued with calm authority, "but that his accomplice is a fake Indian confidence man who has kidnapped Arnie Dickstein's photographer, Jordan Rivers. She was taken only a little more than an hour ago, as you know. We believe the kidnapper was driving a black van. 94F-6881. I don't think there's a lot of time to waste here, do you?"

Fiona was sitting in one of the folding chairs, laying a map of Salem on the table. *Good Goddess, if she started dowsing now, we all end up in the loony bin.*

I cleared my throat. And cleared it again. It took a few times to get Gallant's attention away from my luminous friend. Probably awash with pheromones "Here's something that maybe you'll find equally hard to believe, Lieutenant, but I think you'll find that van parked in woods from which a water tower is just visible above the trees."

Bruce Gallant chuckled dismissively.

From the corner of my eye, I saw Tip look at Rafe, and Rafe nodded. They moved toward the door and sidled out.

"Hey, you two," Irving yelled.

"Let them go," Gallant said. "We have enough theorists cluttering up the scene."

A moment later I heard the roar of the two motorcycles. *Okay. Rafe will know just where that water tower is, and he has friends. Maybe Tip will call Sky as well. Dear Goddess, I hope they will be careful not to drive Creech into doing anything rash.*

Gallant was answering his cell phone. "Jesus Christ! Okay...okay...we'll need a negotiator. Yes. Okay, I'll meet you there. In the meantime, if he calls again, stall him. You know what to say. What? Oh, shit." He closed the phone and looked at us, hanging on his words with complete concentration.

"Yeah. Well, girls, we just had a call from this other guy, the one you call Big Chief Whatever. Real name, Wade Creech. A few priors, assaults and swindles, mostly. Nothing involving guns, though. He says if we release Sokol, we can have the girl back. Like, does he really expect that to happen?

Don't bother to trace his location, he said, because he was tossing his cell into a dumpster. He'll call later on another phone. That sonofabitch is not entirely brainless."

"Isn't that water tower near Gallows Hill?" Heather asked. "The one with the Salem witch logo painted on it?"

Fiona put the map away and picked up her reticule. "Let's go, ladies. I think we've done our best here. Detective Lieutenant Gallant is now convinced that Sokol has not been acting alone."

"Maybe he was clever with the cell phone, but that Big Chief Flying Bullshit is still basically an idiot," Phillipa said to Gallant. "Dangerous, though. Most criminals make stupid mistakes, so Stone has often told me. Of course, you can't let Sokol go. Well, ladies, shall we be off now?" She jangled her car keys, "Water tower, hmmm? See you later, Bruce."

I thought Gallant might try to delay us, but he actually looked relieved, and no wonder. Information overload from a bunch of psychics, who needs that? He turned abruptly to Arnie Dickstein and began to question him about Jordan Rivers and the rest of the Morse homestead staff. Although he seemed to pay little attention to our departure as we trooped out as full of purpose as we'd come in, he did take the card Phillipa handed him and put it into his pocket. "Keep in touch," she said.

As we headed for the BMW, Joe followed us but didn't look happy about it. "Now what are you up to?" he demanded.

Deidre answered for me. "We're going to assist in rescuing Jordan, of course. And take down that evil person who's abducted her, the poor girl."

"Hey, wait a minute," Joe said. "You've already told Gallant about the black van 94F-6881 and the water tower. So now you've got to leave it to him. Didn't you hear that the task force is negotiating with the guy? Aren't you afraid that your interference will jeopardize Jordan"

"Bruce thinks we're a bunch of kooks," Phillipa said. "I'm not convinced that he'll follow up on Cass's vision of the water tower, And besides, Rafe and Tip will be there by now."

We got into the car, and Joe had no recourse but to wedge in beside me. I patted his hand reassuringly. Phillipa was already gunning the motor, and soon we were peeling out of the Homestead parking space.

"This is crazy…" Joe protested.

"It will be all right, honey. It's a wee bit against our principles, but I think we're going to hex the Chief. Sort of," I said.

Joe laughed. "Oh, okay. Turn him into a toad, you mean?"

"That's just an old witches' tale," Fiona said. "No one knows how to do the toad thing anymore. Lost in antiquity, I guess. Pity…" She sighed regretfully.

"The thing is, Joe," Heather said, "we know pretty much where that van might be found, and the way the boys shot out of there, Rafe and Tip know, too. They'll surround it quietly, and we'll give them some psychic back-up while they rescue Jordan."

"So, then, just where are we headed now?" Joe asked in a tone of resigned patience.

"We have to make a quick trip to the Crowninshield and get our stuff," Heather said.

Fiona said, "Cass, I think toadflax and squill will work, don't you?"

"*Urginea scilla. Linatia vulgaris*," I said. "Got 'em."

"See, I knew it had something to do with toads," Joe said, now grinning. "How did I ever get mixed up in this?"

"You married me," I said. "From the hotel we're going to Gallows Hill, Joe. But you don't have to come with us, honey. I believe there's an interesting Nova program on this evening. 'Fabric of the Cosmos,' or some such. You could watch that in our room, and then we'll all have dinner together later."

"You're kidding, right? I wouldn't miss this for the world." Joe's arm tightened around me. *Oh, well...*

When we got to the inn, Heather and I hurried upstairs to gather supplies, running right through Fenella's cold breeze with barely a shiver. The others waited in the car.

When we got back, breathless, Fiona was passing out butterscotch candies from her reticule. Obviously, dinner would be late, *if ever*, and a little burst of sugar boosts energy for the work.

"Conor called Dee, and he sounded pretty P.O.'d," Phillipa told us. "I guess there's been something on the news."

"He was probably listening to his police scanner," Deidre said.

"Oh, Good Goddess, how troublesome. What did you tell him, Dee?" I asked

"I told him that Jordan, the young woman who joined our Litha celebration, has been kidnapped by this big ugly thug, but we were not getting involved. We were simply standing by to comfort Jordan's cousin Rafe while we waited for her rescue. And I promised him that, if he was ready to wrap things in Salem, we could head for home tomorrow," Deidre said.

"Tomorrow? *How could you say that?*" Heather demanded. "Jordan must be rescued from that Neanderthal and this sniper thing dealt with before I personally will pack up my wand and candles. I'm committed to the Morse homestead dig, you know. I can't leave while my fellow archaeologists are being picked off like crows."

"I just felt *in my bones* that everything will be resolved tonight." Deidre smiled a bit in the dark car. It wasn't very often that she played the "in my bones" card that each of us held up her sleeve as a trump.

"Ladies, ladies…trust in the divine spirit of the universe to sort out all dilemmas," Fiona said. "A dilemma, by the way, may be described classically as being impaled on the twin horns of a bull."

"*Bull?* I'll say," Heather said.

Happily, Joe interrupted the discussion before it could get testy, eyeing the candle Heather was clutching in her hand. "What the devil's that horrible smell? Rotting garlic? Is that thing black? I thought Cass told me that black candles weren't kosher for Wiccans."

"Asafetida. I say this color is a very, very dark purple," Heather said.

"Pungent, isn't it? Some people call that scent Devil's Dung," Fiona said. "Would you like a mint mask, Joe? I think I have one here somewhere."

"No, no mint mask, Fiona, thanks anyway. But I wouldn't mind if Phil opened a window."

"You're in the Wiccan big leagues now, Joe." Phillipa laughed but did as she was asked. "Believe it or not, asafetida is very popular in Indic cuisine. It's said to lose its disgusting odor when cooked. Personally, I wouldn't know. Devoted though I may be to experimentation, a cook has to draw the line somewhere."

We lapsed into silence for the rest of the ride, except for Fiona humming and Phillipa whispering an appropriate rhyme which she was composing as we drove along, like Cyrano in the midst of a sword fight. This being our first honest-to-goddess hex, we all needed a bit of quiet reflection.

"Just a reminder, ladies. Karma's a bitch," Phillipa said finally as we drove into the parking lot at Gallow's Hill.

CHAPTER SEVENTEEN

Out of the earth to rest or range
Perpetual in perpetual change,
The unknown passing through the strange.

– John Masefield

There were no other cars parked in the Gallows Hill lot, and the night was eerily, unnaturally quiet. No sign of motorcycles either. If my vision was true, where was the black van? The water tower was there all right, with the black crone riding her broom barely visible. Creech's van must be hidden elsewhere, but not far away, in sight of the tower.

It was almost July fourth, only a short while since we had celebrated Litha on the shores of Plymouth: long days and short nights. The sun had only just set, but there was an early moonrise. Lady Moon was still low, three-quarters full, and she looked on our doings with a worried expression, and no wonder.

"What do you think?" Heather said to all of us in general.

"I think we should get the hell out of here before the police arrive," Joe said.

"Let's do our little spell first." Fiona was unperturbed as ever. "I spy a nice flat rock over there near the bench. Joe, why don't you stand guard here by Phil's car and let us know if we ought to skedaddle."

"I can let you know that right now," Joe said. "The sign says no parking after sunset."

"Just give us a few minutes, honey," I said. "It's not quite dark yet."

"*Entre le chien et le loup,*" Fiona said. " 'Between dog and wolf,' that's what the French call this time of evening. Between the known world and the wild unknown. I suppose we'd better finish before the wolf arrives."

Spontaneous magic is a strange thing. We cast our circle and carried out our spell without any plan or consultation, and now I can hardly remember exactly what we did. Just as well, as it was never to be repeated (so far). Heather lit the candle (the smell of the thing, mercifully, has faded in memory) and it burned with a queer dark blue flame. I scattered the herbs around our circle. They were rare ones, there being little call for toadflax and squill in the grimoires we consulted, so my kit contained only a pinch of each. The rhyme was spoken in a bare whisper by Phillipa. That, too, was quickly forgotten, but I think there was something about *faint and fail* or maybe it was *fall…abomination and damnation…*or something like that. Clouds scudded over the moon. Deidre had brought a little gargoyle that she propped in the crook of the tree. I couldn't see it very well except for its red eyes. Fiona drew a small brass bell out of her reticule and rang it once at the beginning and again at the end when we opened the circle. We never spoke of that spell again.

Walking back to the car slowly, we were reflective and silent. Joe was leaning against the fender, arms crossed, only a dark doubtful shadow of him now that the moon was hidden. Fiona, thankfully, had brought a small flask of what turned out to be Drambuie. Still the park was silent as a cemetery, except for the tinkle of Fiona's bangles as she passed around her flask.

"What's that?" Phillipa said suddenly.

"What?"

"*That!*"

Then we all heard it. The revving of motorcycles in the distance. Not very near here, where we waited under the water tower.

"Holy Hecate," Heather said. "Are we not to know what's going on? What shall we do now?"

"Go back to the Crowninshield, wait in the bar, and order sandwiches. I'm starved," Phillipa said. "Where the guys are and what's happening, we have no way of knowing. But we do know that Tip will call Cass as soon as there is something to tell."

Good advice, and we took it.

"The most sensible idea I've heard all evening," Joe declared. "Come on, Cass." He more or less pushed me into the back seat of Phillipa's car. Heather got in beside us and Fiona in front with Deidre. A tight squeeze all around. Heather's "very, very dark purple" candle had been the fast burning variety. She wrapped the stump in foil so we didn't have to endure the odor of asafetida on the way back to the inn.

Finally, around nine, Tip called us. He had just left the Salem Police Station, and he had a tale to tell.

∽

Rafe, who was born and brought up in Salem, had been certain that the Big Chief's van was not in plain view at the Gallows Hill Park, which would have been a dim-witted idea, even for him. No, the van was hidden at another wooded location, he insisted, probably in adjacent Highland Park.

That witchy water tower was visible from many places. Perhaps Tip's medicine woman had got things mixed up in her vision quest.

They could not, of course, investigate with loud motorcycles, so those were parked and left at a friend's house on Swampscott Road. (Noisy indeed; we'd heard them all the way from Swampscott Road to Gallows Hill.) They'd walked in (Rafe, a biker buddy named Spider, Tip, and Sky) to Highland Park, spread out and moving "silent as Injuns," at Rafe's instructions.

What they didn't know, as they entered Highland Park from several directions, was that Jordan (*brave and quick as a mountain cat*, Tip called her in a tone of fervent admiration) had already got loose from the rope tying her hands together, untied her feet as well, but left the duct tape in place on her mouth in case Creech got back into the van to check the status of his captive. While she was worming her way free, the big man was outside, chain smoking cigarettes and waiting to call the promised negotiator on his second cell phone. A Bushmaster rifle was by his side, and every once in a while he would sight with it at whatever rustled in the dark woods surrounding him.

Spider was the first one to spot the secluded clearing where the van was hidden off-road amid some convenient small pines and bushes. He studied the area through a cover of trees, then crept forward as quietly as his namesake, giving a low owl hoot, their prearranged signal. But Ward Creech had nothing much to do but listen hard, and that didn't sound like any owl to him. He picked up his Bushmaster, released the bolt, and aimed it in the direction of Spider.

He might have shot Spider, too, at the risk of revealing his location, but by then Jordan had peeked out the van's tinted back window and seen his silhouette, with rifle raised to his shoulder. She ripped the duct tape off her mouth, and with a wild cry, threw open the van door which knocked the Bushmaster right out of Creech's hands. Before he could land the punch he was aiming at her face, she kicked the rifle out of his reach. The punch kept coming, though. She ducked, but his fist caught her on the cheek and sent her flying into the brush.

Spider gave a long whoop and leaped out from the cover of trees. Tip came out beside him with his own war cry. Creech was a big man, but Tip landed a nose-breaking blow that doubled him up. Spider aimed a kick at Creech's crotch, but he caught Spider's foot and pulled him down. Before Tip could deliver another punishing blow, Creech, although bleeding profusely from his nose, had managed to grab his rifle and jumped back to where he could aim it at his assailants. He swiped away the blood with one hand and adjusted the rifle against his shoulder. Tip and Spider froze on the spot.

Hearing the noise of a fight, Sky and Rafe emerged to find Creech holding the others at bay with his rifle and themselves at the wrong side of it. Creech laughed. "Your rescuers are here," he taunted Jordan as she crawled out of the bush where she had landed. "All lined up like a fucking duck shoot. Which one should I pick off first?"

The rifle wavered from Sky to Tip to Rafe and Spider. "He can't shoot us all," Sky said. "Let's rush the bastard."

Creech turned the rifle toward Sky and laughed again. "I don't know," he said, "I'm pretty fucking fast."

Tip said he felt like a prize fool to be taken so easily by this big blowhard, and he'd figured that one of them, maybe two, would get shot before they could take Creech down. But he knew they'd have to try or they'd all be dead, and what would happen to Jordan?

Then a funny thing happened, Tip said.

"What? What?" I screamed into my cell phone.

Suddenly Creech gave a cry of pain and clutched his gut, still hanging on to the rifle that was now pointed at the ground. He tried and failed to bring it up again before Tip and Spider tackled him. Creech fell under a flurry of blows, still screaming, his arms pressed against his beer belly as if fearful it would explode. It was an easy matter now for Rafe to snatch the rifle away and hold it on Creech. Jordan hopped into the van and grabbed the ragged ropes with which she had been tied earlier. Sky secured the man as well as he could while he moaned and retched. Rafe held the rifle aimed at Creech's head.

"It was like Creech had been kicked by an invisible mule," Tip said.

With Creech no longer a danger, Jordan began to tremble violently with the after-effects of the adrenaline rush that had brought her out of the van at top speed. Her cousin Rafe wrapped his arms around her while Tip called the cops and did his best to describe the location. The van had a searchlight, and they turned that on to guide the cruisers.

Gallant was in the first car at the scene, pleased to have Creech in custody but a little embarrassed at being out-done by a rag-tag gang of bikers. Never mind. It was going to be a dynamite interview once the TV crew caught up with him. Two suspects had been apprehended and two vans were being examined in the case of the Salem Sniper.

The lieutenant wanted a full report from the young men, but Rafe insisted that Jordan be taken home immediately to rest after her ordeal. "You go with her, Tip." He tossed his apartment keys to Tip. Gallant decided wisely that it was best not to intervene. He had the others at hand to fill in the details.

With Jordan riding behind him, Tip had zoomed away on the Harley without a backward glance. At Rafe's apartment, Tip made a pot of coffee while Jordan took a hot bath to sooth her various bruises and cuts. That's when Tip called us. By the time he'd told me about Gallant's arrival to take charge, Jordan emerged, wrapped in a blanket, her cheek black and blue and one eye puffy. Tip said a hasty good-bye, the better to offer sympathy and an ice pack, and to bask in the aura of her admiration and gratitude.

"I'll see you tomorrow before we leave, then," I replied and closed my cell.

"Those boys could have been killed," Joe said. "I wish I'd known what they were up to. I'd have gone with them. I wonder what hit Big Chief in the gut. Good thing, though. Nick of time."

Fiona said, "That was all right then."

"Personally, I put it down to my asafetida," Heather said.

"I wouldn't take any credit for Big Flying Asshole's collapse, if I were you." Phillipa admonished. "Maybe he got seized by a hernia from all that scuffling around. Appendix, ulcer, kidney stones, gallstones. Could have been anything. So let's just close the book on this incident and hope the threefold thing will ease up for once."

"The Cosmos works in mysterious ways," I said. But I had a twinge of discomfort. Something told me that this was not the end of the sniper story, although it certainly seemed to be with the two suspects in custody until they could be arraigned after the holiday in Salem District Court. "Thank the Goddess they're both locked up now. Looks as if Salem will be able to have its celebration after all. Gives a whole new meaning to the phrase 'Have a Safe Fourth'."

"Let them have it. I'm in no mood for any more fireworks. Let's go home first thing tomorrow," Joe said. "I've had enough of the romance of strange berths for the time being. And you're going to have a lot of explaining to do with Scruffy, Cass."

"Scruffy and Raffles are just fine, enjoying the pack life with our gang, as all dogs prefer to do," Heather said crisply. "Really, you need to stop treating those two like little people in fur coats."

Joe and I looked at each other, and he raised his eyebrows. I shrugged. "I'll try explaining that to Scruffy," I said.

❧

Tip stopped by in the morning, reluctantly returning to his job in Bangor. He looked exhausted and lovelorn. I wanted to reassure him, but in all honesty, I didn't think his attraction to Jordan had much of a chance to be returned. Maybe that's just a part of the exultation and despair of growing up, I thought, as I hugged him good-bye, noticing that his shoulders were no longer scrawny, and he was even a bit taller than Joe. A young man now, mature enough to suffer from the angst of unrequited passion. I probably shouldn't interfere. Still, I didn't want to lose touch with Jordan myself, so maybe something would occur to me.

Before we checked out of the Crowninshield, Fiona insisted that we hold an impromptu exorcism for Fenella Tupper, to explain that she was dead and it was time to spiritualize onto a higher plane. After all, Byrd Page, her ravager, was dead, too. So while Joe and Conor were sent to reclaim Heather's Mercedes from the repair shop where a new windshield had been installed, we five got together and held hands in a circle at the foot of the main staircase. Deidre shivered and complained that she could see a wispy filament of Fenella where she had fallen, and what about the certificate of authenticity that she had promised to provide for the inn's owners, James Woolgar and Derek Witt, which they planned to have framed and hung in the lobby? Fiona said, not to worry, all old inns were haunted, and there would always be enough spooky elements to entertain the guests. But at least Fenella would be able to rest in peace.

Heather said, "Let's research the Tupper family tree and see if any of Fenella's descendants are in need, in which case I'll see if I can shake a donation out of Miss Gold Nuggets, Bernie Page. We are, after all, both Vassar alumnae, so used to being canvassed for cash."

Fiona hummed and talked in a low voice to the frigid air about the beauty of the spiritual plane to which Fenella could now ascend, the demise of Byrd Page, and the hope that some of the Page money would find its way to needy Tuppers. While she was murmuring, a newly arrived family started up the stairs with a few strange backward glances.

"Our little prayer ritual for safe travel," Phillipa explained to the curious guests. Uneasy as people usually are when they feel they've intruded on others' religious practices, they hurried on their way. Fiona opened our circle with a flash of her traveling athame just as Joe and Conor strode into the lobby.

"Having a go at the unseen enemies?" Conor inquired. "Come on, Dee darlin', I'm getting you out of here before anything or anyone else spooks you."

We gathered our baggage and trooped out, leaving the lobby a slightly warmer place than it had been before. Deidre sighed and smiled and took Conor's arm gratefully.

"We never got to visit Circe's shop," Fiona complained. "You'd have loved it, Dee! She has some unusually potent poppets, some of them are actually made with shrunken heads."

"No shit," Phillipa said. "All major credit cards accepted?"

"Naturally, dear. And we should have met with Tabitha, too. Tabitha Wisen has a knack with magical potions that you would have found quite fascinating, Cass. Although Tabitha and Circe don't always get along too well. Professional jealousy, you know."

"Ah, potions," Phillipa said. *"The flagon with the dragon holds the brew that is true?"*

"Knock it off, Phil. We'll come another time," I said. My words were meant to reassure Fiona, but I also had the nagging feeling that we hadn't seen the last of her Salem friends.

"Home to the peace and quiet of Plymouth," Joe said. "At least, that's what I'm dreaming of, sweetheart. No more wild shootings, other than shooting stars and crazed fireworks enthusiasts."

I wasn't so sure but we clairvoyants know when to keep quiet. Maybe I'd be wrong this time.

CHAPTER EIGHTEEN

'Tis sweet to hear the watch-dog's honest bark
Bay deep-mouth'd welcome as we draw near home,
'Tis sweet to know there is an eye will mark
Our coming, and look brighter when we come.

– George Gordon, Lord Byron

Say, Toots…is this the thanks we get for being loyal canine companions? Abandoned for weeks *to a pack of vagrant mutts? Wasting away on lousy dry chow, losing all our squirrel-chasing muscle tone, probably picking up a serious case of kennel cough. Ack! Ack! Ack! Do you realize that all the mutts at this refugee camp have been fixed, the poor bastards? Had to be on guard night and day in case the big guy suddenly decided to* snip, snip, *watching out for the kid as well. He hasn't much sense, you know. Just give him a pat and a biscuit, and he'll roll right on his back. Don't think you're going to win me over just because you're cooking something that smells pretty good. Suppose it's not for us anyway. You're probably gonna give us some so-called dog food. Alpo on sale, ugh! Nice picture on the can, ground-up chicken bones inside. But, say…if you really want to make up for deserting us, you could slop a little of that stew stuff into our dinner bowls.*

"Stop kvetching, Scruffy. I promise you're in for a treat."

My superior nose detects the scent of…lamb? Is that lamb for us? Scruffy stopped complaining long enough to sniff the air over the stew pot simmering on the stove.

Lamb for us…lamb for us. Raffles galloped around the kitchen, ecstatically checking out his faux sheepskin bed and bedraggled toys as if fearing they'd been lost to him forever.

"Yes, Scruffy. Free range New Zealand lamb. I'm making a special stew just for you guys. I know I've been away from home a long time, and you've missed me. I've really missed you, too."

All right then, if that's for us, you can give me a hug.

A hug! A hug! Raffles wasn't a great talker.

While I fixed my furry friends a people-food dinner to appease the guilt that dogs so easily instill in us, Joe was outdoors setting sprinklers to water the herb and vegetable beds. I'd paid a neighbor kid to tend the gardens while we were gone, but they still looked weary, neglected, and accusatory, sort of like Scruffy. Basil is especially touchy if it gets no attention; dill simply withers up and faints dead away.

July was gearing up for that one searing heat wave the South Shore produces every year. Like many New Englanders, we got by with a couple of window air conditioners. Heather's place, of course, had central air conditioning, even the kennels. Still, Scruffy was overjoyed to be home, although he didn't let that interfere with his grumbling. He'd already taught Raffles how to dig out a shallow place under the porch where he could chill his belly on the damp earth. Now they were resting on the cool kitchen floor, leaving splotches of dirt wherever they lay. I've always thought, though, that a person has to make a choice between clean floors and canines. There's no having both.

It was now the day after the noisy Fourth. Joe and I had been truly exhausted by the time we got home yesterday and made the easy decision not to retrieve our canine companions until the next day. At least Heather's home wasn't right on the water. Scruffy and Raffles would only have been miserable with the world-war ambiance of our place. On the Fourth, the entire shore was one long continuous display of fireworks. We sat out on the beach for a while watching the exploding stars in the midst of the real stars, twinkling steadily to remind us of eternal mysteries beyond our little histories.

The great patriot party was over. The gathering we had planned for the annual incendiary event, a traditional clambake, had been postponed. We decided to hold it anyway on the coming weekend, which meteorologists had promised would be as clear, hot, and beautiful as July is supposed to be.

Tip decided to take yet another few days off from his job in Bangor to supervise so that the feast would have that original Indian flair, since, after all, clambakes were a native invention. Joe's totem pole would preside from the top of the beach stairs. Eagle, Bear, and Salmon (air, earth, and water), the carving was a gift from a grateful West Coast tribe whose woodlands Greenpeace had helped to save from loggers.

Joe didn't complain about hard work, ever, but I think he was secretly glad to turn over digging the pit and gathering the rockweed (*Ascophyllum nodosum*) to a younger man. As a reward for Tip's labor, I'd invited Jordan Rivers to join us, with any of her biker friends who might care to accompany her. Not knowing if a family clambake was the kind of event she and they enjoyed, I decided not to mention this to Tip ahead of time so he wouldn't be disappointed if she didn't show up. He was still mooning around over Jordan, but possibly he was not brave enough to pursue a girl who seemed, to him, infinitely more sophisticated, as well as older than he. At their age, a few years one way or another took on a greater significance.

The rockweed was soaking in a bucket of seawater, the stones were lining the pit, the firewood had been gathered, and the lobsters were on order when Deidre came over to help me sew and stuff the cheesecloth bags that would hold potatoes, onions, corn in its husks, sausages, steamers, and so forth for the clambake. While we worked, she filled me in about a local mystery, the disappearance of thirteen-year-old Molly Larsson, an older school friend of her daughter Jenny.

"Molly spent last week at a Plymouth girls' camp, Camp Pocahontas, but when Mrs. Larsson arrived to bring her home yesterday morning, she was nowhere to be found. Counselors, cops, firemen, and everyone else are out searching the woods; Conor, too. It's over 140 acres. And then there's the lake to worry about. Jenny has been absolutely traumatized by Molly's disappearance. They weren't buddies at school, but Molly was more tolerant than most of her friends are of the younger girls." Deidre wielded her scissors to cut additional lengths of cheesecloth. "So Jenny is heartsick and fearful. She seems to think Molly isn't lost but stolen. Kidnapped. I don't know where she gets these ideas. She's almost as fey as you, Cass."

"I'm too big to be fey," I said, always conscious of being rather zaftig compared to the typical ethereal faery person. Fortunately, Joe claimed to prefer the Rubenesque form. "Do you think Jenny is having a second sight?"

"I rather hoped Jenny would be spared all that, but I've noticed a few signs. Maybe it's in the DNA, who knows? She asked me for a cross to wear to save her from being snatched away by some depraved soul. Apparently, at Sunday School, Sister Fermina suggested to the class that piety would be the salvation of all good girls, but girls who stray from the path of righteousness and prayer may suffer an evil fate."

"I hope you found Jenny a cross to wear." I laid down the big stitching needle (at which I was not too adept) to put on the kettle for tea. My Wise Woman blend (sage, nettle, lemon balm, dried orange zest and whatever else I was inspired to add that day) would be an excellent pick-me-up. I would offer Deidre some whiskey to make the taste more to her liking. I ducked into the living room to rummage in the parson's cupboard.

"Oh, good idea," Deidre said when I came back with the bottle. "Certainly, I did, Cass. The cross is a very powerful amulet. I gave Jenny a small gold one that had belonged to my grandmother. Mother Ryan was delighted."

"And?" I spooned herbs into the pot and added nearly boiling water.

"And a lovely little jade Tara to keep in her pocket. Green Tara, goddess of peace and protection, originated in the Hindu tradition. She overcomes all obstacles to save us from physical and spiritual danger."

"Sounds like an amulet all of us could use." I began filling the bags we'd made with potatoes, onions, and sausages. Whatever early corn we could find would be bought in the morning. The clams on the porch in a bucket of ice water laced with cornmeal (to filter out salt and grit).

She ignored the hint and went on: "You know I did ask Fiona to dowse for Molly, but the results were disappointing and inconclusive. The crystal pendant just kept circling and circling. Fiona feels there's a powerful spell blocking her attempt to find the girl."

I knew what was coming next.

"So, I'm wondering, Cass, if you'd work with that vision pillow thing of yours on Molly's behalf. The one you used when Jordan was taken. Remember how you kinda saw what Jordan's situation was, and then we put the double-whammy on that Creech character?" She sipped her whiskey-laced tea.

What else could I do but say yes?

"Let's not talk about the whammy, Dee. Ever. But, I will give the vision pillow a try. Although, if Fiona is stymied, I wouldn't get my hopes up too high."

"Okay, but do it tonight, will you? Tomorrow you'll be busy with the clambake and the company."

So late that evening, when everything had been prepared for the feast, I found the damn vision pillow where I had left it, in my suitcase under the eaves upstairs. In the rose bedroom, I lay down on the bed with the pillow under my cheek. Scruffy and Raffles bolted up the stairs to see what I was doing, in case it might be fun, and I shut the two of them into the blue bedroom so I could concentrate. Tip was staying with us, and a bag of his stuff was stashed in there, something interesting for them to scent. After a few minutes of woeful barking and scratching at the door, they settled down for a comfy snooze on the twin beds. All the windows upstairs were open. White ruffled curtains lifted and fell to the rhythms of a pleasant evening breeze off the Atlantic. I let my mind drift with their soothing motion, imagining that they were ghosts or angels.

Nothing, nothing, and nothing.

Fiona was right. There was a force blocking my inner sight, and it was formidable. I would have to push myself farther than ever into limbo. With my eyes closed, I deliberately visualized myself approaching a closed room, putting my hand on the doorknob, opening the door.

There was a blinding flash of light, and at the same time, I registered the sound of thunder in the distance. Was there a real storm gathering? Or was this part of the vision? Then I heard music, a chorus singing, girls' voices. The song sounded faintly familiar, but still it eluded me. A moment later, the door slammed shut in my face.

Well, something was better than nothing. At least now I knew I could cross whatever barrier had been erected between me and the missing child. I would think about this, sleep on it...*Perchance to dream.*

Finally I raised my head from the pillow and stood up in zombie mode. Feeling slightly ill, I let Scruffy and Raffles out of the other bedroom. Scruffy always knows when I'm woozy, and without the usual backtalk, offered me his back to hold onto as we walked downstairs. His dam had been a purebred French briard, so he was built for human burdens of all kinds. I clung to his shaggy fur on one side and the railing on the other. Original stairways in saltbox Cape Cod cottages like mine are narrow and steep.

Joe was in the living room, watching a Nova rerun, *Saving the Kyoto Protocols,* when I joined him, still leaning on Scruffy. Raffles immediately jumped up on the window-seat post usually occupied by his sire and scanned the grounds for strangers in time-honored canine fashion. I collapsed into one of the wing chairs and gave Scruffy a big hug, pushing the hair out of his eyes. "Time to trim this mop again," I said.

Briards prefer to be brushed. Scissors are not to be trusted, Toots.

"You want to be able to see, don't you?"

Do the kid. He won't mind.

"Pull it together, Scruffy. It's either me or Grace Hulke, the groomer over at Animal Lovers sanctuary. And she'll want to clip your dewclaws as well."

This is the thanks I get for herding you downstairs? Scruffy shook his big head, bangs flying, and stalked into the kitchen to flop on his bed. Raffles hopped off the window-seat and followed.

"You really hear what he says, don't you?" Joe looked at me with that wondering expression I see from time to time.

"Sort of. Good Goddess, I'm exhausted"

"Let's go to bed, then," Joe suggested. "Tomorrow will be busy. A good time, but busy. Tip and I have to start that fire really early." Then he took a closer look at my face and Scruffy's attentive stance. "You look as if you've seen a ghost, sweetheart. What was going on upstairs?"

I told him. He knew how much I avoided using the vision pillow, so this was serious business. "I'll put the kettle on," he volunteered. "No, don't you move. Which tea do you use for the whim-whams?"

"Ginger, kava, and chamomile. It's the strangest thing, Joe," I said, but he'd shut off the TV and was already in the kitchen opening cabinets. "Look above the cups for a blue jar labeled Serenity." I followed him and stood in the doorway. "I felt as if there was a fiery light guarding the truth. Shut down my visioning with a bang."

"Maybe it's a fire-breathing dragon," Joe said, spooning tea leaves into the two-person Brown Betty teapot.

"And there was this chorus of girls, singing."

"Sacrificial virgins," he said with an annoying smirk. "Did you recognize the song? Might be a clue."

"Not yet," I said. I thought that Joe had hit upon the key there. I needed to locate that song. "It wasn't a pop tune. There was something old-fashioned about it. Possibly a folk song or a hymn."

"If you can hum it, maybe Patty can play it for you on the parsonage piano. See if that rings a bell. I wonder what the Peacedales are doing tomorrow." He poured boiling water into the pot and put it on a tray with two tea cups. I liked watching Joe moving around the kitchen; it was a warm night, and he was wearing a v-necked white t-shirt, the gold cross gleaming on his chest. I hoped it was as powerful an amulet as Deidre believe it to be. At least he wouldn't be attacked by vampires. On the other hand, that bronzed, muscular hunk might have to fend me off before the night was over.

"Okay, pups, last run of the evening." Joe opened the kitchen door, and the dogs shot through the pet flap on the porch for their final sortie. An almighty roar and their joyous barks heralded Tip's return from visiting some track team friends from his Cedar Hill Middle School days. Refusing an offer of tea, he went right upstairs to bed. I detected the faint odor of beer in his wake, but his walk was steady enough. The dogs, of course, followed him, their favorite guest.

"You can shut the boys out, if you want," I called after him.

"Naw, they're all right. Good night, you guys. Gotta start that fire by six, latest."

"Patty. That's a good idea," I said, picking up the thread of our conversation after Tip had disappeared. Suddenly I felt that Patty would be just the person to solve my music mystery. "I believe there's a Loaves and Fishes church picnic somewhere in Miles Standish Park."

Feeling much less enervated, I took the tray from him and headed for the bedroom. I still hadn't abandoned the idea of a revelatory dream. The heady scent of phlox drifted in the open bedroom window, a sweet summer sea of pink and purple. Mint, too. The robust fragrance of mint, planted around the porch where its predatory ways could do no harm, wafted into the room. How good it was to be home!

Summer nights on the South Shore were so seductive. Even the occasional blast of a tardy *rocket's bright glare* and the resulting clamor of dogs upstairs barely disturbed our lazy love-making. Afterwards, when we'd drifted off to sleep, smoke from bonfires all along the shore seemed to slip into my dreams. Suddenly that fire-breathing dragon (and this was clearly Joe's fault!) entered my dream theater with a fearsome roar, and when I looked, I saw with horror that it was carrying Molly Larsson in its slavering jaws. Scruffy was in the dream, too, growling bravely but backing away from the dragon. I screamed. But when I tried to reach up and pull the girl into my arms, a wall began erecting itself between the dragon and us. Jagged stones piled on each other as if they were alive. There was no way to rescue Molly, unless...

I never got to the next thought. I woke up and found Joe holding me in his arms, Scruffy and Raffles barking outside the door. "Wow, that was a nightmare and a half," I said. "The Serenity blend is not as effective as it used to be."

"Do you want to talk about it?"

"Not yet." I got up and padded into the kitchen, pacifying my loyal protectors with dog biscuits and helping myself to a glass of iced tea. It was only three o'clock. Joe came out and stood in back of me, his hug solid and comforting. "It was your dragon, I think," I complained.

"It was those idiots setting off left-over rockets and cherry bombs in the middle of the night," he said. "Let's go back to bed for a little while."

But I knew there was a deeper meaning in that dream. I would just have to find it within myself.

CHAPTER NINETEEN

This was a real nice clambake,
And we all had a real good time.

– *Carousel*, Rogers & Hammerstein

The day began with a little cloud cover but that soon burned off and the sun blazed forth as we had been promised. Preparation for the clambake would take several hours, of course. After the heap of logs had burned down, the coals were raked away, exposing the red-hot stones. Next, a layer of rockweed was shoveled across, steaming mightily. Then the cheesecloth bags filled with potatoes, onions, and sausages were tossed onto the seaweed, followed by the corn. Next, the lobsters (writhing still, alas. Deidre distracted Heather so that we wouldn't have to endure her Be-Kind-to-Crustaceans lecture). Last the bags of steamers. Then more seaweed, the whole mound covered with a sturdy canvas tarpaulin.

Heather's efficient butler and housekeeper, Maxwell and Elsa, had brought tubs of iced beer and wine and an array of cheeses, pâtes, and other savories to keep us from starving. Heather insisted that they stay for the banquet and relax. Dick took over serving the drinks and handed them each a glass of wine.

Despite having missed the right date, Phillipa was keeping her traditional Fourth of July dessert chilled in a cooler: a whipped-cream-frosted sheet cake with fresh strawberries and blueberries creating the stars and stripes of an American flag. There were also watermelon "baskets" filled with cut fruits, one drenched in crème de noya and one not.

Conor took a photo of those, and practically everything else. Cheery and charming as always, he seemed just as interested in recording a family picnic as he had been in shooting newly discovered Coliseum mosaics in Italy and séances in Salem. Perhaps because it was not the subject as much getting his own unique take on it that was his passion. And his work was extraordinary, with a brilliance that kept him in demand, even for portraits, which he despised. I couldn't help but wonder if a touch of genius made for good husband material. Deidre continued to wear the jade parrot ring he had given her on a chain around her neck, the hand on which to display it still not chosen.

Adam and Freddie had joined us with my two little grand-cutenesses, Jackie and Joanie, who had Deidre's crew of four for noisy company and Fiona's grandniece Laura Belle for enchanted silence. (Becky had gone off on a day-cruise with Johnny Marino's family. This looked downright promising! The maternal instinct is ever on the side of love and marriage, or at least love and commitment.)

Jordan appeared out of a roaring cloud with Rafe on his Harley. She was wearing a sun-blazoned Aztec peasant blouse over white shorts, her legs long and bronze, dark hair wild-blown and glorious. Tip blushed and brushed a hand over his forehead, embarrassed at his sweaty, dusty appearance. The ocean in Plymouth is always cold even at the height of the summer, sometimes too freezing for anyone to swim but the youngest children, who would be having too much fun to notice the chill. The icy water didn't seem to daunt Tip either, as he dove through the waves, coming out all shining and clean with a broad smile.

Joe and Tip had set up an armada of beach chairs and improvised a long table from old doors, with intermittent shade from big beach umbrellas. I sat next to Fiona under one of the umbrellas and told her about my latest aborted vision and the dream. "It's just what I feared," she said. "The wall in your dream is a symbol of the spiritual wall that surrounds the girl's disappearance. Or, let's call it as we second-sight it: *the girl's abduction.* How long has she been missing now?"

"Two days or a little more. There's still a chance they'll find her lost in the woods or something like that." Even I didn't believe my own wishful thinking.

"Lost in the woods would have been an easy take for us. No blinding lights, no slammed doors, no magic wall. Besides, this is a teen-age Girl Scout. Spending the night lost in the woods in summer would have hardly been a challenge," Fiona said, and then with an abrupt change of subject, "Should we do a little love spell for poor Tip, do you think?"

"Absolutely not. That's the worst sort of magical meddling," I said firmly.

"Oh, all right. And what about Maxwell and Elsa? Wouldn't it be nice if they were freed of those assault charges and could go back on the stage? Surely they must miss their real life." Fiona studied her be-ringed hands and hummed thoughtfully. "I could do a little thing."

"Ceres save us. I suppose so, but it would be such a cruel blow to Heather. She keeps saying that Maxwell and Elsa are too good to be true," I protested. Still, I knew that freeing the couple, if we could do it, would be a blessing...for them.

"If Heather says her perfect couple are too good to be true—were those her exact words?—that means she already knows, subconsciously. Wait, you'll see. Pretty soon she'll be asking questions." Fiona drained her wine glass and sat up brightly. "Oh, look, I think they're removing the tarpaulin. Isn't that salty, fishy smell divine?"

"Maybe what we should do is to have a talk with Stone about the predicament of the Kitcheners," I said. "He might be able to do something through, you know, *regular channels*. Even though it was a cop they assaulted, that cop was beating up their friend at the time."

"It's a possibility," Fiona admitted. "If you don't mind going for a mundane solution. Personally, I always find that it takes longer and is less satisfactory than working a little good old-fashioned magic."

"Yes, but magic has a way of turning out in unexpected ways, collateral stuff you never imagined might happen."

Fiona laughed merrily, silver bangles tinkling. "Yes. And isn't that fun!"

"Sometimes," I said, a typical Cassandra.

Joe and Tip pulled out the bags of steamers that had been layered on top, followed by lobsters, corn, potatoes, onions, and sausages, all redolent with the aroma of seaweed. Dishes of coleslaw, bowls of melted butter, and a log jam of French breads were arranged by Elsa while Maxwell cracked the lobsters' claws.

"It's a feast fit for King Phillip," Tip said.

"Spanish?" Conor asked.

"Nah. Wampanoag. My people," Tip said.

"King Phillip was a name given to Chief Metacomet who waged the first Indian war, 1675, against Puritan New England" Fiona added. "They hunted him down and killed him a year later."

"Every circle of friends should have its own librarian," Phillipa said.

We ate and drank through the long hot afternoon, the bravest of us (not me!) making an occasional run at the waves. Despite the occasional startle of cherry bombs, the canine revelers were out and about. Scruffy, Raffles, Deidre's two miniature poodles, Salty and Peppy, and Heather's so-called therapy dog Honeycomb raced every moving thing up and down the beach, taking special delight in absconding with one of the Frisbees being tossed between Joe, Adam, and Dick Devlin, until they were all exhausted. Honeycomb, being a Golden Retriever, dashed off to capture the one Frisbee that sailed out on the ebbing tide, impervious to water temperature. The other canines were content with cooling only their paws.

Rafe had brought his "boom box," and he, Jordan, and Tip were listening to some so-called music that sounded like noise to me, but thankfully, they made their own party at a distance away from us. Stone relaxed on a beach chair with a hot mug of Earl Grey tea, his favorite, brewed especially for him by Elsa.

It seemed just the right moment to probe for the latest details. "How are things in Salem," I asked him.

"Everyone is greatly relieved to have those two snipers in custody. The aborted Fourth celebration was held after all, although not quite as mobbed as usual. Tourists are creeping back warily. Gallant is a hero, and Jordan has had her share of the limelight, too, escaping from that big idiot Ward Creech." Stone swept his fine brown hair back off his forehead and cleaned the sand off his oval, metal-rimmed glasses with a paper napkin. "From what I hear, the two perpetrators have not yet ratted out each other. In fact, they lawyered up immediately and got decent court-appointed attorneys because of it being such a high profile case. They haven't admitted anything about their shooting spree. Entered *Not Guilty* pleas at their arraignment, but that's not unusual. An ugly business, those random murders and maimings. From what Gallant has been able to find out, Gregor Sokol is a champion marksman, trophies and all. Belongs to some kind of a private shooting club, The James Younger Gang it's called. After that bunch of Confederate bushwhackers, Jesse James et al. Very bad boys. But it appears that Creech was the instigator. I hardly want to call him 'the brains'. He probably talked Sokol, who's only 23, into his warped scheme to disrupt the archeology project at the Morse place. More fun for Sokol than shooting rats at the dump. "

Fiona, Heather, and even Phillipa (who had certainly heard all this before) gathered around Stone to listen. (Obviously it wasn't the moment to mention the plight of Heather's perfect couple being fugitives.) Deidre and Freddie were busy elsewhere, keeping a close eye on the youngsters bouncing and screaming in the waves.

"Was Creech a member of the James-Younger Gang?" I asked.

"As far as I know, he was not. Apparently he and Sokol met at some bar in Gloucester, and Creech may have sold Sokol on the cause that obsessed him."

"So the motive was the American Indian thing?" Heather asked. "Is that crazy, or what?"

"And he isn't even a real Indian. Tip was right all along about that," Phillipa said. "Greta agrees. I did call Greta again, did the promised Tarot reading on Skype. Also, I wanted to touch base and pick her brains. She said that the FBI was not best pleased to have their pet theory of a new Indian uprising go up in smoke signals. They were already calling their unsubs the *Ghost Dancers*. Ha ha."

"*Wovoka*," Fiona said. "A spiritual movement that grew out of desperate times among the native people. The military were panicked by what they perceived as the threat of Ghost Dancers, which was what led to the massacre of innocent Lakota people at Wounded Knee." She sighed sadly.

"See what I mean? Who needs Google when we have Fiona?" Phillipa said.

With all the children out of the water and wrapped in gritty beach towels, Deidre appeared at Stone's elbow. "That's old news. What are you doing about Molly?" she demanded.

Stone frowned. "It doesn't look good, does it? Usually if we don't find the missing youngster in the first 48 hours…" His voice trailed off. "We're doing all we can. Canvassing for leads at Camp Pocahontas where she was last seen. One of the other campers thought she'd seen Molly slip out of their sleep tent heading for the bathroom facility around two in the morning. But the camper fell back to sleep and didn't know whether Molly returned or not. We're all on the case, Dee. With many, many volunteer searchers."

"What about an Amber Alert?" Deidre was insistent.

"Certain criteria have to be met before we can issue that alert," Stone said. "We have to be pretty sure it's an abduction, not a lost or run-away situation, and that the child is at risk. And we have to have some details about the abductor, his description, or a description of his car."

Deidre frowned with frustration. "Haven't the FBI been notified, at least?"

"I think the same criteria apply, Dee. And Goddess forbid the FBI gets into this one, too," Phillipa said. "I have much more faith in our own Plymouth County detectives any day. Anyone for another piece of cake?"

We groaned at the thought of more food. But after the dog pack had been over-fed and were settled all cozy in a friendly heap (with Scruffy insisting on alpha dog status), and after a few latent fireworks vied with falling stars and a rising half moon to amaze and delight us, we would be hungry again for the Lucullan leftovers of the banquet.

Over late cold lobster and toasted baguettes, Heather invited Jordan to come for a visit soon. Surely Dickstein would give her a few vacation days. Heather (with her status as a big donor) would call him if a word would be needed. She was eager to learn more about her great-great-grandmother Alyce Morgan's diary that Jordan had seen when she tripped out of time in the Morgan widows-walk turret. Jordan doubted she could travel to the same place twice but promised she would try, and she looked pleased. A few days in one of Heather's Victorian guest suites would surely have its charms for a time-traveling girl like Jordan. She was still living with cousin Rafe; I imagined the home décor of a biker's apartment might not be all that appealing. Now that Salem was no longer dangerous, perhaps Jordan would move. Maybe Arnie Dickstein would find his plucky photographer a nicer place.

While I was still musing on Jordan's future, Tip and Rafe raced off with her to a late party organized by friends who worked at Plimoth Plantation. I thought about Tip's flute, native music that spoke directly to the heart. I wondered if Jordan had heard Tip's soulful playing. In earlier times young men had probably lured maidens to their arms with sensuous reed music. Would Tip himself realize the magic of music-making? I was tempted to hint but didn't have the opportunity that night. Perhaps when Jordan visited Heather. If Tip just happened to visit me at the same time. (*Oh, cut that out*, said my observer self. *Remember how you warned Fiona to keep wands off?*)

That observer self is my direct connection to the Divine Female, whose voice I ignore at my peril. This does not stop me, however, from turning a deaf ear on my inner Wise Woman at times of wayward impulses and hot pursuits.

Adam and Freddie strolled off down the beach, holding hands, while the twins slept curled up near me. If I could see auras, I imagined that I'd have seen a rosy light surrounding their parents, with a little of Freddie's scarlet sizzle.

After the last cherry bomb had startled the quiet night, Joe and Max began to rake up the clambake debris, while Dick and Elsa packed up drinks and food. Deidre got me aside for a few moments to say that she wanted us all to get together at Fiona's the next day, to consider what might be done to find Molly *our way*. Fiona had some ideas, Deidre told me.

"I bet she does," I said. "We're all worried about Molly, and Fiona is also mighty challenged by what she calls the 'psychic wall' she's been running into. I saw it myself in a dream. Nightmare, I should say."

"All right then," Deidre said. "I just need to know we're doing *something!*" And she hurried off to help Jenny peel off wet suits and dress the younger Ryans in warmer clothes.

Exhausted children fell asleep in laps and beach chairs. Fiona cradled Laura Belle, whose cornflower blue eyes had finally closed. I held Joanie in one arm and Jackie in the other, dreaming of future faery expeditions we would make in a part of Jenkins Park where strange things happened and sparkling creatures had been seen, even by Scruffy. I may not be a faery godmother, but I'm certainly Not-Your-Typical grandmother. Between my clairvoyance and Freddie's psychokinesis, I felt sure that my grandchildren would be talented in astonishing ways. I could feel their humming energy as they lay against me, warm and sweet.

So much to look forward to!

CHAPTER TWENTY

One equal temper of heroic hearts,
Made weak by time and fate, but strong in will—
To strive, to seek, to find, and not to yield.

– Alfred, Lord Tennyson

We straggled into Fiona's little fishnet-draped cottage in Plymouth center around eleven the next morning. Phillipa had brought a large cafetiere French press for those of us to whom Fiona's Lapsang souchong tea would not deliver a sufficient jolt of caffeine. Deidre carried a giant box of Dunkin' Donuts which we all adored and deplored, especially Phillipa. "Ugh! The odor of that fat!" she complained, selecting an apple-filled doughnut. "I wouldn't trust that cream filling, if I were you, Dee."

After we'd fortified ourselves and cleared the scarred cherry coffee table, Fiona unwrapped the protective tissue around our oldest, grimiest grimoire, a large moldering tome with no title she'd found in a box of books donated to the library sale. "It must have come from some great-grandmother's attic," she'd always said. "The heirs didn't have the faintest. I bless and thank the author, whomever she may have been. A wise and cunning soul. A bit darker than Hazel, but I think that's what we need to breach that wall. Here, Dee, you take over this time and choose something for us."

That was surprising! Fiona always took on this role herself. Maybe she was still flummoxed by her failure to dowse Molly's location. A failed "finder" might feel that she'd lost her mojo.

Deidre was looking a little wan this morning, but (in a pink blouse tied at the waist and navy short shorts) more like a sleep-deprived sixteen-year-old than a multi-tasking mother. She put aside her workbag and began to page through the fragile book, her crafty hands careful and sure in handling the antique pages.

We stood around her and peered at each page, Phillipa reading aloud the names of various spells in awed tones. "Holy Hecate! *Unburying the Dead.* Now that's one I'd never want to fool with. A good way to raise a golem!"

Deidre ignored all comments (and there were many sharp intakes of breath and murmurs of disbelief) as she turned the pages with single-minded intent. Finally she gave a little sigh and nodded her head affirmatively, blonde curls bobbing. I thought how that cuteness of hers was so deceptive and wondered if Conor knew.

"This one will do it, I think," she said. *"Breaks all Locks and Rocks.* Because if Fiona is right. and I'd put my chips on her any day of the week, there's a powerful spell we have to break through before we can find Molly. I just hope and pray she's still all right."

Heather leaned over to read, her shining bronze hair falling forward. It was getting long. I wondered if she wouldn't soon braid it again. "What will we need this time? I'll make an appropriate candle, of course. Blue, I think. Blue is such an *opening* color. Jumping Juno! Look at this! We're going to need a *door*, a whole door!"

"We have some old ones we used at the clambake," I said. "Moving one of those might be a bit of a problem. Probably better if we work the spell on my beach."

"At the dark of the moon," Phillipa read aloud.

"Holy Mother of God, we can't wait that long," Deidre exclaimed. "We'll work on the first cloudy night. That will be dark-of-the-moon enough."

"Herbs? Incense?" I took a small notebook and pen out of my handbag.

Deidre read, I wrote: *"Stinging Nettle, to remove the cursed spell and send it back whence it came."*

"Right. *Urtica dioica.* I have some dried leaves, so non-stinging now, but I wonder... Probably okay. What else?

"Earth Smoke. What in Hades is that? *To confuse and exorcise evil spirits."*

"That's Fumitory. *Fumaria officinalis.* Country folk believe it rises like a mist to obscure everything around it. Our cunning lady may have brought it with her from Britain, although it has naturalized here in a few places. I spotted some once in back of the Finch Farm Stand. I'll try to gather a bunch."

"Oh, good luck," Phillipa said dryly. "Only watch out for Wanda Finch and her rifle."

"And for incense, just our regular frankincense and myrrh," Deidre continued.

"Knock 'em, sock 'em exorcism," Fiona said, punching the air with bangles jingling. "And peaceful vibrations to those who bring peace, of course. That'd be us."

"And there are runes for the door. *An open door*, at that. How are we going to erect an open door on the beach?" Heather asked.

"We'll fake it," Phillipa said. "What runes?"

"Nyd and Haegl," Deidre said. "We're supposed to burn them into the wood. The kids have a wood-burning kit, so no problem. And nothing here says it has to be a full-size door. So before you go hauling a heavy slab of wood onto the beach, let me have a go at making something *representative*, which after all is what magic is."

"Nyd to resolve conflict and lies. Haegl for hail, powerful action," Phillipa said. "I studied up on runes before I learned tarot. On the whole, I prefer tarot, but there's an undeniable power in runic inscriptions."

"And you'll compose a rhyme, Phil? Heather will bring the candles," Fiona said. "Sounds like a plan. All we need now is a cloudy night."

"Meanwhile, I have a phrase of song running through my head. From that nightmare," I said. "I'm going over to Patty's after lunch and ask her to play it for me on their piano. Anyone want to come with me?"

"Ye, gods and goddesses," Phillipa said. "A parsonage piano!"

"I'll go," Deidre said. "We can catch a Big Mac on the way."

Heather groaned. "If you don't mind risking Mad Cow disease."

"They have perfectly healthy salads, too, now," Deidre said.

"With delicious chemical dressing," Phillipa added.

"And Twinkies for dessert," I said. "Come on, Dee. Let's get out of this den of food snobs."

❦

In the parsonage parlor, a big somber room filled with discarded Victorian furniture including an ancient upright piano, Patty Peacedale served iced Fair-Trade Blossoms of Health tea given to her by a parishioner, and a basket of Hospitality Hour leftovers, rather tasty homemade goodies, although I still avoided any chocolate stuff prepared by the Presbyterian Ladies League. Patty's rescued (by us) Maine coon cat, Loki of Valhalla, a hefty, regal fellow with a ruff of silky brown hair, a mean expression, and a very good opinion of himself, sidled into the room and was rewarded with a crumb of crumb cake. He jumped nimbly onto the back of the chair on which Patty was sitting and glared at us suspiciously, in obvious contrast to his human companion's anxious-to-please smile.

"How very, very nice to see you, dears," Patty said. "Dee, I want you to have a look at this new pattern I'm using for our prayer-shawls project." She hauled out a mess of citron wool in a zigzag stitch. I'm not a crafty person myself and barely know a knit from a purl, but it looked rather bunchy to me. And yet, Patty herself looked joyful in her work, if not confident in her abilities. She was wearing a light blue vintage Ship N Shore blouse with a navy blue cotton skirt. At her buttoned-up collar, a silver circle pin confirmed her modesty. I wondered if she was still wearing the Celtic cross under her top. We had taught her to dowse food with it during a poisoning season.

"An interesting pattern, indeed, Patty. I've never seen anything quite like it," Deidre said diplomatically, fingering the erratic stitches. "And your good intentions are clearly in evidence." She took the shawl she was working out of her workbag. It was a rich green into which she'd been knitting prosperity spells for her mother-in-law in hopes of stemming her frequent gambling losses at The Mohegan Sun. If Mother Ryan continued to bankrupt her savings on these repeated

Connecticut trips with her blue-haired cronies, she might have to give up her apartment, and she had an eye on moving in with Deidre "to be more of a help with the children." Deidre's needles clicked on feverishly. "This is something like your prayer shawl," she told Patty. "I'm using a Celtic knot pattern and concentrating on good fortune for the person the shawl's intended for."

"Oh, lovely, dear! I'm sure your good prayers for the lady in need will be answered." Patty enthused. "This one's a brighter color than I usually choose, but it's for one of Wyn's parishioners who's in need of a bit of cheer. Her husband went out to buy a lottery ticket at the corner convenience store two years ago and never returned. I've always wondered if he won some walking money. But that's neither here nor there. The problem is, we think she may be pregnant. That's why I'm making this extra big. Maybe no one else will notice her condition. For a while anyway. Wyn is wringing his conscience over it, but I say every conception is a miracle to be rejoiced, no matter how long since her husband's been home. But never mind our little problems. Cass. You've brought a tune you think I might recognize?"

"Something like that, Patty. I have the notion it's a hymn or some kind of sacred song. I heard a few phrases in a dream, and I think if I could identify the music, I might find the answer to a puzzle we're working on. The circle, that is."

"You're trying to find little Molly Larsson, aren't you, dear?" Patty said, with a quick shrewd glance at me over the horn-rimmed half-tracks she wore for knitting. Her heart-shaped face wore a grave expression. Patty may have seemed a bit vague at times, but she didn't miss much. "I pray for that child night and day. Wyn is talking about a candlelight vigil, too. Can you hum a few bars, dear?"

I did that. I can't really carry a tune, but I tried my best.

Deidre laughed unkindly. "Speaking of miracles, if Patty can do anything with that…"

Loki leaped off Patty's chair and bounded over to the piano, prancing up and down on the keys. Patty laughed in sheer delight. "Wyn doesn't believe that Loki understands everything we say, but I'm convinced of it."

I'd had conversations with Loki before we found him this forever home (practically over the Reverend Peacedale's dead body), so I knew he was as savvy as my Scruffy.

Patty sat at the old piano and tapped out the melody for *The Old Rugged Cross*, which served to point out that the instrument was indeed out of tune, but not so badly that we couldn't recognize a familiar hymn. With a baleful backward glance, Loki stalked out of the room, his lavish tail swishing, as Patty's fingers wandered off into an abstraction and then tried to play the wordless phrase I had sung. She did this several times, each rendition a bit less tentative than the last. Finally she banged out a hallelujah chord and cried out, "I know this hymn…It's *Holy Maidens in the Garden*."

"Never heard of that one," Deidre said. "But then I was brought up on Catholic music."

"Oh yes, dear Dee, of course you wouldn't know that one," Patty consoled her guest. "It's one of those obscure Lutheran hymns that most choir masters would rather forget."

"But you remember it?" I wondered how.

"Well, dear, I heard it once at an ecumenical craft fair held on the grounds of the Resurrection Lutheran Church down on the Cape. A band called the Heavenly Swingers were keeping our spirits up with music. Banjo, guitar, and zither, as I recall. Their rendition of *Holy Maidens* was accompanied by some girls in sheer white dresses cavorting about on stage.

Wyn was not amused. He called it an 'unseemly exhibition,' and I had a difficult time persuading him not to complain." Patty sighed. "So naturally the whole darned day sticks in my memory. Including the hymn."

"Naturally," I agreed. The role of perpetual peace-maker is not an easy one. But I still didn't see how a rather obscure hymn that Patty had recalled was going to be any help in our search for Molly Larsson. I would just have to let it lurk in the depths of my mind until something clicked. Oh well, maybe that spell we were going to work on the first cloudy night would bring my vague intuitions into focus. Spell-work does have a wonderful way of concentrating the mind.

We thanked Patty for her hospitality, and I said she'd been a big help.

"Dear Cass, if there's anything I can do, anything at all, please don't hesitate to ask me. My heart doesn't have a good feeling about this little girl," Patty said, laying her hand against her chest. "Remember that I'm always available to accompany you on one of your prayer jaunts. It wouldn't bother me a bit to skip one of those interminable committee meetings Mrs. Pynchon is so fond of."

I bet it wouldn't. Mrs Pynchon was the sharpest thorn in Patty's crown of martyrdom. Selwyn Peacedale, pastor of the Gethsemane church-around-the-corner-from-me, came closest to the sainthood when dealing with the church board treasurer. I wondered how he would fare when Mrs. Pynchon found out about Patty's pregnant protégé, not that single parenthood carried any stigma these days, except with the narrowest of minds. Oh well, I should just be content that Patty hadn't dragged me into her parish drama. I didn't even know the deserted wife's name, which was good, because just knowing a name is somehow involving.

"Her name is Fanny Fearley," Patty said.

"Whose name?" Was she reading my mind? I grabbed my handbag and made for the door while Deidre was still packing up her knitting.

"The young woman who is with child but without a husband. I thought you would like to know, Cass. Sometimes you have such creative ideas for rescue," Patty said.

"But Fanny doesn't need rescue. She's just pregnant. Period," I said.

"I never put a period where the Lord has put a comma," Patty said.

❧

Molly Larsson had been missing for six days when the first cloudy night happened and we five gathered for the definitive *Breaks all Locks and Rocks* spell from the ancient book of shadows. I cast the circle, no place better for it than this beach, which in itself always seems to be a sacred space. The air was hot, humid, and still, which meant that the incense and candles stayed lit. I noted the sharp smell of citronella in one of Heather's candles, a practical touch. The tide was rolling in very quietly. I thought I saw the quick dark flashes of bat wings not far away, but I didn't share my panic with the others. Traditionally, bats have a bad press. At this time, in this place, they reminded me of a swarm of evil purposes which I hoped we hadn't called among us. I shook my hands to rid them of this negative image and got a quick, sharp glance from Phillipa.

"It's so humid," I said.

Perhaps I would chance a nice cool swim after the work. The others must have had the same idea, because it turned out that every one of us was wearing a swim suit under her jeans and t-shirts. Except Fiona, who was perfectly happy to skinny dip, shades of her misspent hippy youth.

Clever Deidre had brought a little doll's-house door, with the two runes Nyd and Haegl wood-burned into it, and a picture of Molly, obviously her school photo. I felt a jolt of recognition, followed by a hot flash of fear. Molly looked enough like my daughter Becky at that age to have been her sister. (More like Becky, in fact, than her actual sister, Cathy.) The same sweet round face, bobbed chestnut hair, and some indefinable similarity of spirit looking out from those serious blue eyes. Suddenly the not-unfamiliar news story of a child's disappearance became highly personal to me. *What if that had been Becky?*

"Okay, let's put our hearts into it, then," I said. "For Molly's sake."

So we did the spell, which was powerful indeed, opened the circle, and ran into the ocean afterward. The water was frigid, of course, as it always is in Plymouth, but on that night we needed its bracing cleanliness. Heather passed around a flagon of Vizcaya dark rum from the Dominican Republic, and Phillipa sang "Yo, ho, ho," in a properly deep piratical tone.

"Say, Cass, what did you ever find out about that song fragment?" Fiona asked, wrapping her plump nakedness in a beach towel.

"Patty knew it," I said. "It's an obscure Lutheran hymn called *Holy Maidens in the Garden.* I'm still trying to figure out what it means."

"Think of your dream as your own personal theater," Fiona said. "You created the play script, the actors, and the costumes. You are the only one who can figure it out, Cass.

Dr. Freud himself could not analyze your dream better than you."

"That's very sage, Fiona, even for a super-sage like you," Phillipa said.

"*I am, therefore I think,*" Fiona said.

Shortly afterward we went up to the house for hot coffee, which Joe had brewed for us before retiring to my office to check on upcoming Greenpeace brouhahas. Possibly he was getting restless. *One foot in sea and one on shore,* that was my Joe. Scruffy and Raffles had crowded into the old borning room with him and flopped at his feet, but they sprang out into the kitchen when I brought out a sizable wedge of Vermont cheddar cheese, along with Phillipa's loaf of Anadama bread and my own homemade gingerbread with Chantilly cream.

At last a breeze had stirred itself over the Atlantic and was wafting away the oppressive humidity. We had our "cakes and ale" on the screened back porch, without any talk of what had transpired on the beach. It takes a little time to let spells settle into one's consciousness. What would this one bring?

Cheese is good for canines. Builds strong bones. Scruffy sniffed around the wicker coffee table and had to be warned not to take advantage of his height.

Strong bones! Strong bones!

I rewarded them for enforced good manners with morsels of cheese. Heather sighed with disapproval. Sensing that no more tidbits would be handed out, the dogs bounded out of the pet door to chase around the gardens. I sincerely hoped they would not run into a skunk.

"*Merry meet, and merry part, and merry meet again.*" And indeed, the swim and the food had lifted our spirits.

"I sure hope this works." Deidre was the last to leave and stood on the stairs right outside the screen door. "Now that we've made a swipe at whatever has been blocking us, why don't you have another go at your vision pillow? Fiona's going to try map dowsing again. Holy Mother, I hope whoever has taken that little girl hasn't transported her out of this area."

"No. I feel she's still close by." Suddenly I knew that was true. Molly was not so far away. That's why it was so frustrating.

"So you'll try?"

"Of course," I promised ruefully.

"Call me! I don't care what time it is. Conor's spending the night at his own apartment anyway. It's his sacred space with a workroom, a dark room, and his photo library, which he likes to keep inviolable. In other words, no kids."

Would this romance ever evolve into a real lifetime thing, I wondered. But then, I thought, sure, why not? Love makes everything possible, even in two domiciles.

Joe was coming out of the office, yawning and stretching, just as I returned to the kitchen. "The game is afoot in Eemshaven, where the biggest and most polluting coal-fired power plant in the Netherlands is about to be built." he said happily. "I expect there will be an assignment for me on the *Rainbow Warrior III.* This is probably a good time, isn't it, sweetheart? Snipers locked away, we hope for good. No crime waves brewing on the South Shore."

"Yeah, smooth sailing. You don't have a choice anyway, do you?" I countered.

"Yes and no. I'm expected to work as assigned all year, except for holidays, vacation days, sick leave. The usual. But I can also take personal days or even Sabbatical weeks. All of which options I've had to juggle whenever you got yourself into danger."

"I wouldn't say that *I got myself* into anything, honey. Sometimes danger just comes knocking on the door. But you're right. Things are calm right now. Except, of course, for Molly Larsson's being missing."

"So…you're not mounting some kind of campaign against a kidnapper, are you? Especially since all the law enforcement agencies on the South Shore are on the case night and day."

"Campaign? No," I lied, continuing to clean up the remnants of our "cakes and ale" party as we sparred "We're just praying and saying good words for the poor little girl. May she come home to her parents alive and well."

"Hmmm," Joe said suspiciously. "Much too glib. Listen, this new ship has very sophisticated communications. We can talk often. On video even. You can catch me up on Molly and anything else that's going on."

"Oh, great. Now I'll have to worry about how I look. Did you try the rum, honey?"

"You always look beautiful to me. Yes, I certainly did try the rum. It's not your usual 'rum-and-coca-cola' stuff, is it ?" He yawned again. "Aren't you tired, sweetheart? Let's go to bed."

"Heather brought the rum, so that figures. I'm not all that tired, but let's go to bed anyway."

"Even better," Joe said, with that familiar sexy smile that goes right to my second chakra.

CHAPTER TWENTY-ONE

If I had the wings of an angel
Over these prison walls I would fly...

– Guy and Robert Massey

Joe got the expected assignment the next morning, and by afternoon he'd packed his duffle and departed for a late flight to Amsterdam. The *Rainbow Warrior III* would sail to the site of the power plant and hoist a huge banner, the size of a sail, calling for clean energy, and that's all, so he claimed. (But I was not surprised later when the Greenpeace confrontation escalated to physically blocking the site.) As usual, he insisted on transporting himself to Logan in a rent-a-wreck. Judging by the jaunty angle of his Greek cap, he was rather too cheerful for a man leaving his beloved.

I, too, faked being serenely resigned to a quiet interlude of puttering around my herbal workshop. But as soon as his rental got around the corner of the pines into the main road, I sped up the stairs like a shot to retrieve the visions pillow from its hiding place under the eaves. Scruffy and Raffles, always energized by action, raced up the stairs after me and got their enthusiastic noses shut out of the rose bedroom. They slumped onto the hall floor, grumping.

*Sometimes the magic works...*and today was one of those times. As soon as I closed my eyes and lay my head down on the pungent vision pillow (a prototype never duplicated once I realized its fearful potency), I heard again the hymn that had haunted me earlier. Not just a phrase this time, the whole melody that Patty had played for me, one of those undistinguished and difficult melodies that soon faded into hymnal obscurity. At the same time, I saw a few wispy white images that might have been girls weaving about or might just as well have been smoke signals. And flowers. I saw many flowers arranged in baskets and sprays. *Holy Maidens in the Garden*; perhaps it was the words themselves that were the clue. *Gardens...gardens...*what could that mean? There must be thousands of gardens on the South Shore, public and private.

Fighting off a wave of nausea, I held onto the banister and Scuffy's collar and went downstairs.

Sure, sure. Now that you need a sturdy, loyal companion, who you gonna call?

Gonna call! Gonna call!

I passed out conciliatory dog biscuits and looked around for the cell. Not on the kitchen counters, not in my office. I punched in the number on my kitchen phone. My pocket rang.

I poured a glass of iced tea, put in plenty of crushed mint for the nausea, and went out onto the porch. Immediately, the two dogs dashed through the pet door and ran around the herb beds barking at nothing much. After I'd rested for a few minutes on the wicker loveseat, I called Fiona.

"Did you dowse for Molly? Get anything?" was my greeting.

"Cass! Yes, I did dowse all my maps of the South Shore, and at least this time the crystal wasn't totally distracted. Not exactly accurate, but not as erratic as last time. It seemed to be targeting the Samoset Crematorium and Cemetery.

"Ceres save us, that does not sound good." But it did fit right in with the flower arrangements in my vision.

"I was just going to mosey over there and take a look around. Want to go with me? Of course you do! I'll pick you up in fifteen minutes."

Before I could say, *no, no, no, I'll drive*, Fiona had hung up. We mostly tried to avoid jaunts around Plymouth with Fiona at the wheel of her venerable baby blue Lincoln Town Car which she had once run into an antique store on Court Street. Sometimes she was sharp and attentive to the road, but at other times she seemed to be operating in a vague personal fog.

Ten minutes later, Fiona drove into my driveway. I didn't know if shaving five minutes off the ETA was a hopeful sign or worrisome. I grabbed the handbag off my office doorknob and hopped into the front seat. "Want me to drive?" I asked brightly.

"No, thank you, dear. When you're following a hunch, it's best if you keep your own hands on the throttle."

"It's not an airplane, Fiona."

"So to speak. As a matter of fact, I do know how to fly an airplane. A small one, of course, not a jet passenger thing. I wonder where I left my pilot's license?"

I reassured myself there was little chance that Fiona, a small airplane, and I would ever be thrown together. I had to admit, though, I felt no reason for anxiety as Fiona drove us at a sedate senior pace to the Samoset burial ground, although we did find ourselves followed by a line of impatient drivers on a two-lane stretch of Route 3A.

The air conditioning no longer worked in the old Town Car, but it was one of those perfect summer days when it was more enjoyable to drive with the windows open anyway. Fiona turned into the access road between tall granite columns and parked near the crematorium, a pleasant brick building that could have passed for a town library, white shutters and all. Older gravesites with worn monuments were situated near Samoset Street, newer ones at the back. Small American flags signified the final resting place for veterans of our many wars. Avenues bore names like "Cypress" and "Magnolia," shaded by big comforting trees. Here and there, fresh flowers indicated recent visits, but no visitors were visible right now. Two cars were parked behind the crematorium. Personnel, I imagined. Who knows what they were doing? Otherwise, the cemetery was as quiet as a you-know-what.

"Are you sure this is the place you dowsed?" I asked.

"Positive," she said. "And I simply don't know why. Let's look around anyway." Fiona opened the driver's side door and got out, leaning heavily on her coyote walking stick. I got out, too, and we walked up and down several of the avenues, admiring the more elaborate monuments, the plantings, and the flowers decorating graves. Eventually, we had enough of this and returned to the car. It was nearly six and the evening shadows were deepening. It was hard to believe that the days were actually getting shorter, but we were weeks past the summer solstice.

"That marble angel on the Whittaker monument was quite lovely," Fiona said.

"I really wonder what we're doing here," I said.

"Keeping faith with our intuitions," she said. "*Faith is the thing with feathers that perches on the soul.*"

"That's *hope*," I said. "Emily Dickinson."

"Hope, faith, charity…same difference."

After Fiona drove me home, she took off immediately to pick up Laura Belle at her neighbor's house. "All will be revealed in the Goddess's good time," was her parting shot.

After the usual raucous canine greeting, I shunted my dogs outside for a good run before dinner. Meanwhile, I poured myself a glass of cold chardonnay, turned the local news on the little kitchen TV, and relaxed in my rocking chair.

Ten minutes later, I sat bolt upright as if electrified, grabbed for my cell phone, and called Fiona. "Turn on the news! The news!" I cried urgently.

"I know," she said. "I just saw it. A military burial took place this morning at Samoset, and that fanatic Willie Hogben was there picketing with his idiot followers, the Church of the Christian Sword. A good thing that some local veterans turned out to block their disruptive nonsense and allow the family some peace and privacy. And did you see those signs? *God Hates the Army* and *Burn in Hell All Gays*. I wonder if these people have any idea what bad karma they are making for themselves."

"Oh, never mind the karma, Fiona. Don't you think this *means* something? Because this is the same cemetery that turned up when you dowsed for Molly Larsson," I said urgently. "And I've been haunted by that hymn, *Holy Maidens in the Garden*. That just might refer to Hogben's chorus of so-called nieces. You remember, the blonde wigs and bonnets?"

"Yes, I got that. It does sound as if there's a connection. Listen, I'm just giving Laura Belle her dinner. I'll have to call you back."

"Okay. Talk to you later." My finger was already scrolling through my speed dial for Phillipa's number.

"Listen, Phil," I said as soon as she answered. "Something's come up about Willie Hogben. I don't know quite to make of it."

"Well, hello, Cass. How are you today?"

"Hello, Phil. I'm fine. And you? *Now*... any chance of your getting Stone to run a more extensive background check on Willie Hogben?" I told her about my perception of the hymn (which was actually clairaudience as well as clairvoyance) and how Fiona's dowsing had pinpointed the Samoset Cemetery, where we had found nothing. Then the news item about Hogben's picketing the funeral put him in the cemetery that very day. "I just think we ought to have a look at him."

"Sure, Stone will be glad to use the extensive resources of Massachusetts law enforcement to check out one of your psychic hunches *again. You think?*"

"What I think is that you will talk him into it with your sultry charms no matter how you protest now. Because it's important to rule Hogben out, or in."

"Yeah. Right. *Sultry charms*, is it? I'll be in touch...maybe."

Next I called Heather with the same long story. "Good Goddess, a genuine lead!" she cried. "You know, that compound of his is like a fortress, but I know how to get into it."

"Down, girl. That would be an action of last resort. Why don't you go burn a candle, or something?"

"You see, what we have to do is, back a pick-up truck up to the fence and use a wooden pallet to make a bridge over the top, and it won't matter what he's got to prevent climbing over. Just say the word."

"What about the scary guard dogs running loose?"

"Drugs, dear. Dick has perfectly harmless knock-out drugs for restless doggies. You know I wouldn't do anything to hurt an animal. And I do have a nice amber candle with amber inserts that I can burn for protection and strength."

"The candle sounds fine. The pick-up truck, not so much," I said. "Besides, isn't there a wife who guards the compound, too?"

"Ah, yes. The lovely Eureka Hogbin," Heather said. "I saw her once at Finch's Feed & Grain hefting 40-pound bags of dog chow. Ferris Finch pointed her out to me. Hair like a Brillo pad. Muscular little lady. But sometimes Eureka does drive the bus when Hogben and his crazy followers are out staging a protest. We'd have to wait for a clear field. Dogs I can handle, but I wouldn't want to tangle with Eureka."

"Phil's going to see what else Stone can find out about Willie Hogben. Maybe Fiona will come up with an idea. She's got us into places before. Heather, did you ever know that Fiona has a pilot's license?" I asked.

"*Brilliant!* That's another way we could get in!"

"And land where? It's not a helicopter license. At least, I hope not," I said.

"Okay, but we *could* do a fly-over. Take a few pictures. Do you realize that no one has seen the inside of that compound except maybe his crazy parishioners? The Hogben property covers several acres. Rumor has it that Hogben's got a bunch of ramshackle outbuildings attached to the house."

I couldn't help considering a fly-over. If push came to shove, that is. *No*, I decided. *That's totally nuts.*

I threw my bucket of cold water on the idea. "Never say never," Heather said. "A cousin of mine has a private airstrip on the Cape. Richie Rector. Owns a Cessna 210. I seem to remember that it's a six-seater."

"Your family tree is quite extensive," I said. "You seem to have no end of cousins in important places."

"Well, he's really a cousin-in-law, twice divorced. Married to Brooke Morgan, twice. The guy must have a death wish. But, yes, the Morgan family tree has many branches, Cass. Those sea captains had a lot of pent up sexual energy. Always left the lady wives with a little something under their aprons to keep them occupied when the ships sailed away. Which reminds me. Jordan's got some vacation time, and she's coming for a week's visit. I'm eager to see what she might be able to dig up about my great-great-grandmother."

"I hope it's a quiet week. The poor girl has had enough excitement this summer."

"Peaceful and pleasant, I promise. You ought to give Tip a head's up."

"Maybe. *If it harm none…*".

"*…do as you will,*" Heather finished the Wiccan golden rule.

I saved the last call for Deidre, because I knew she would be hysterical. I was right about that.

"*Willie Hogben, that sanctimonious creep! I wouldn't put it past him.*" Deidre lowered her voice from an anxious screech to a whisper. I heard a door open and close. She'd gone out into the backyard for privacy. "The cops ought to break into that place and have a look around. Goddess only knows what skeletons he has in those outbuildings. Have you talked to Phil? Can't she send Stone right in there today?"

"Same old story, Dee. We have nothing to go on, nothing that would allow Stone to get a warrant. But Phil will get

Stone to check Hogben more thoroughly. Then we'll just have to get more information on that compound."

"I bet Heather will have some ideas. Didn't she used to break into animal testing facilities to free the puppies and monkeys before she promised Dick to swear off?"

"Out of the question. Do you want to be seen on local TV being hauled off to jail, charged with breaking and entering? Neither do I."

"What other ideas did Heather have? Come on, Cass. I can ask her myself, you know."

"We talked about flying over the place and taking photos," I said reluctantly.

"Oh, goodie. Can she rent a plane? Does she have a pilot's license."

"Her cousin-in-law who lives on the Cape has a private plane. Heather doesn't have a license, but..."

"But what?"

"Fiona claims that *she* has one."

"*Fiona!*"

"Yes. I don't know if there are enough amulets in the world to keep us safe in a plane with Fiona at the controls," I said. "Heather's cousin is a possibility, though."

"I could borrow one of Conor's cameras," Deidre said thoughtfully. "We need the scenic details to be clear and sharp. This isn't something we can do with a cell phone camera. "Does Heather's cousin's plane have room for five of us?"

"It's a six-seater. But how would I be able to face Joe and confess that kind of folly? If I survived, that is?"

Deidre laughed merrily. "Is that the same Joe Ulysses of Greenpeace whose shipmates are this very day hanging off cranes at the coal-fired power plant in the Netherlands. 'Sleeping tents,' I believe the newsman called them."

"Yeah, he did tell me about that last night when we talked. But he swore on his gold cross that he was not one of the hangers-on. That's a job for the young activist volunteers, he assured me. His assignment is to help keep the boat in running order. Especially since they sometimes have to make a run for it."

"I'll call Heather and tell her to bring on her cousin," Deidre said. "I'm sure Fiona will be game for anything."

"Yeah? What about Phil? Don't want to let her in on your brainstorm?"

"I'll leave that to you, Cass. You can take the heat." Deidre laughed again and rang off.

While I made dinner for me and the dogs (a nice chicken stew) I considered the plane surveillance idea. But only with Heather's cousin Richie piloting the plane. Safer, for sure. Heather would go, of course. And Deidre with Conor's camera. And Fiona in case a finder was needed. And what about me? Would I feel like the cowardly lion if I didn't go along? Or the brainless tin man if I did?

Later I talked to Joe again and all thoughts of a crazy plane ride over Hogben's place fled from my mind. Live pictures of the activists in their hanging sleeping tents were being sent back to Greenpeace headquarters in Amsterdam. With so much going on around the ship's communications center, our conversation was rather guarded. *He was fine. He was being very careful. I was fine. I was not getting into mischief. What was going on at home? Nothing much. Looking forward to Jordan's visit. Should I call Tip?*

Even if I couldn't see him, I could feel Joe's grin. "Sure. Let Tip decide if he wants to get his feathers singed. Tell him to bring his flute."

"Funny you should say that, honey. You must be reading my mind."

"Did I? Guess I caught that from you," Joe said.

I hoped not!

CHAPTER TWENTY-TWO

Touch us gently, Time!
Let us glide adown thy stream
Gently,—as we sometimes glide
Through a quiet dream.

– Barry Cornwall

Jordan Rivers caught a ride to Plymouth with her cousin Rafe, who was on his way to a motorcycle gathering in Hyannis. With Jordan seated behind him, he roared into Heather's circular driveway amid a cacophony of barking dogs around noon the next day, and they were met by Heather's perfect couple, Max and Elsa Kissinger. Heather had gone off to button-hole her cousin Richie Rector about giving us a ride in his Cessna over the Hogben compound in Carver. Jordan was to make herself at home in the delightful Wedgewood green room with creamy leaf-and-vine cornices, bird's-eye maple furniture, a marble bathroom, and a balcony overlooking the "orchard" of three apple trees. Elsa reported later that "the young lady declared it was totally *awesome* and she would take an immediate hot bath in that *wicked* old tub" while waiting for her hostess to arrive. She'd borrowed a pack of matches from Elsa to light Heather's homemade scented candles.

Meanwhile, I had called Tip to see how he was faring in Bangor and to mention Jordan's visit. "Perhaps you'd like to come down to see us over the weekend," I suggested. "So she'll have someone besides us old ladies to talk to. You can stay with me. Keep me company while Joe is in the Netherlands."

"Hey, I saw that on the news," Tip said. "He's not one of the guys hanging off the cranes, is he?"

"He says not. I don't know if I totally believe him, however. So you'll come?"

"Sure. I don't know if Jordan will be pleased or pissed. But, whatever…"

"Bring your flute," I said.

"If I didn't know you better, Aunt Cass, I'd think you were up to something."

"Don't be silly. I haven't heard you play in quite a while."

"And what's Heather Devlin got on her mind? She's not going to hassle Jordan, is she?"

"No hassling. But maybe Jordan can help Heather to find her great-great-grandmother Alyce's diary, if it exists. The last time she was here, Jordan had one of those visions of hers that Alyce Morgan hid a little book in the turret room. Behind the wall."

"Uh oh. Call the wreckers in!" Tip laughed, that dry deep chuckle that ended in a slight cough.

"At least Jordan might save them from breaking down *every* wall," I said. "And the other thing is, I might have a line on that missing girl, Molly Larsson." I told him about my suspicions of Willie Hogben.

"You medicine women got plans, have you?" Tip said.

"I'll fill you in this weekend, dear. You'll come?"

"Sure. Have flute, will charm."

Obviously, Tip was wise to me. But I promised myself this was *the absolute last time* I was going to interfere in the young man's romantic hopes. Wise women like me ought not to mess about in other people's love lives. Sometimes unintended consequences gallop out of control. Magic is like "the butterfly effect" in chaos theory. The flutter of wings in one place in a nonlinear system may result in a chain of effects that culminates in a hurricane elsewhere.

∽

"It's all set for Wednesday! Richie promised to take us for a ride over Hogben's on Wednesday. You *are* going with us, aren't you?" Heather had invited me over for dinner with Jordan and, incidentally, to prime me for her newest scheme. We were in her Victorian red parlor (Maxwell's austere correctness always inspired us to formality) where he served us some exquisite sherry and chèvre gougères. I wondered if, despite Maxwell's air of detachment, he wasn't really taking in this entire conversation, and thinking... *what?* From past events, I knew that if a "situation" developed, he would be capable of taking on whatever role was needed.

Heather continued just as if Maxwell wasn't there. "Fiona's on board, 'with bells on' as she puts it, and Dee, of course, is purloining a decent camera from Conor. She does not want him to know, by the way, what she's up to. He's getting to be a little bossy, isn't he? Oh well, she'll sort him out. Have you spoken to Phil?"

"Phil says she'll keep her two feet right on terra firma, thank you very much. But she'll be with us in spirit."

Maxwell wafted off to the dining room. The aroma of cassoulet drifted our way. *Pork? Heather was serving pork? I couldn't believe that.*

"Probably just as well. A detective's wife engaging in extra-curricular surveillance. That might cause Stone some grief," Heather said.

"At least there will be someone who knows where we are in case we disappear off the radar or anything." I didn't much like my own negative tone.

"Thoughts are things," Heather echoed our credo, and she was right. I would visualize a safe and successful sortie with a rewarding outcome. "Elsa's making us a French country dinner. Zucchini galettes and vegetarian cassoulet. Isn't she amazing?"

"Amazing indeed," I murmured.

Jordan floated down the curved staircase in white short shorts and a crimson peasant blouse. Her dark hair was tied up with a bright blue scarf. She greeted us both with hugs and thanked Heather for the *"awesome* digs." I imagined it was a far cry from a biker apartment. The only drawback would be the Devlin dog pack barking at dawn.

Jordan passed on the sherry and asked Maxwell for a beer. "Heather wants me to, like, *psyche out* the turret room tomorrow," she said to me. "I can't promise anything, though, you know what I mean? I'm so *totally* far from controlling the action."

"I do know. But I promise, you *can* learn some control over your astral travels. Are you practicing your mindful breathing?" I certainly hadn't achieved perfect control myself, but I knew it was the ultimate goal for all of us *adepts.* "All you can do for Heather is to leave yourself open to impressions. In your case, though, you'll have to let go of chronological time, isn't that it?"

"Hold it a minute, ladies," Heather said. Her husband Dick came in from the back door. His bushy hair was tied back into a pony tail and he was still in his scrubs. Dick was a massive guy, and Heather, although tall herself, almost disappeared in his hug. "Hi, Honey! It's dinner in the dining room," she warned him. "You know what a tyrant Max is. So you'd best get cleaned up."

"Sure. Get me a beer, too, okay?" He waved at Jordan and me, then jogged upstairs.

"Does Dick know why Jordan is here?" I asked.

"I'll tell him. I'll tell him. I just have to wait for the right moment. This genealogy project may involve some deconstructive carpentry, you know."

But neither the subject of astral travel nor airplane travel was brought up at dinner. And Jordan was tactful enough not to rehash the dangers and follies of our Salem adventure, not all of which were known to Dick. Even the bullet-shattered windshield of the Mercedes had been replaced before Heather brought it home. It was enough to know that Creech and Sokol had been arraigned, still pleading *Not Guilty*, and a trial date set for September.

Elsa's meatless cassoulet proved to be amazingly rich and delicious, and Heather's semi-vegetarian principles had not been compromised.

Knowing that Elsa was partial to corgis, a few weeks ago Dick had delighted her by bringing home an abandoned fellow named Albert from Animal Lovers shelter to join their resident dog pack. Albert was not in top dog shape (in fact, he was a cowering bundle of nerves) but with Elsa to give him the royal treatment, Dick was sure that the corgi would soon be perking up. Talking of their rescues, Dick and Heather beamed at each other. Talk about *the marriage of two minds...* If I could see auras, which I can't, except in an extremely hazy way, they should have been surrounded by a glow of vibrant green, the color of healing.

"Tip will be visiting me this weekend," I told Jordan. "We must all get together. Maybe you'll come over for dinner Saturday night, if your project here is progressing okay. He'd love to see you."

Jordan raised one expressive eyebrow. "Cool. Don't think I've forgotten how he nearly got shot trying to rescue me from that badass Creech. Some cojones on that kid. "

I thought Tip would be pleased with that description, except for the *kid* part.

Dick said he hadn't heard about that, and Heather had to explain. Our own role in that encounter had been minimal, after all, if you don't count the spell-work. As a rule, it's not a good idea, anyway, to take credit for a near-hex that may have actually worked.

✦

Later I heard from Heather about the turret tour with Jordan. She called me from the Morgan mansion's small private study, and we talked a long while. Jordan was resting, Heather said. Apparently this time travel thing was quite an ordeal.

"Ceres save us, I can relate to that," I said. "Tell me everything."

From that height, with the windows open, the Atlantic could be seen and heard, unlike in the rest of the mansion. Jordan had insisted upon going out onto the narrow balcony with a wrought iron railing that encircled the turret, the wind streaming her wild dark hair like a proper gothic heroine as she leaned over, exulting in the view. This made

Heather rather nervous, but she reasoned that perhaps it was necessary to Jordan's process. Once Heather had cajoled her guest inside, however, it had seemed as if the young woman was still firmly fixed in the present time.

Heather keeps a small electric kettle up there and had prepared one of my special visionary tea blends (kava-kava, cinnamon, and some other, lesser known herbs).which she served to Jordan as they sat on velvet cushions (practically the only furniture in the turret room.) But Jordan said the brew tasted "weird," and didn't finish hers. Next, Heather lit a candle spiced with angelica root, also to promote visions. But the out-of-time trip that Jordan had experienced during her Litha visit did not re-occur.

Finally, Heather took pity on her guest, and they went downstairs to the conservatory. Maxwell brought a silver pot of coffee and served it in Limoges cups. The previous houseman, a retired sea captain, had favored boiled coffee in thick white mugs. Heather took it all in her stride and was happy to accommodate each new regime, as long as she herself didn't have to cook.

Jordan opened the "dog yard" door to let the resident pack mill around them affectionately. Watching the dogs vying for Jordan's attention, Heather, an inveterate dog-matchmaker, was already wondering if she could talk Jordan into adopting one of her sanctuary dogs. She had just fixed her mind on a recently rescued female with the silver-gray eyes of a wolfish strain known as American Indian Dogs, a species not recognized by the American Kennel Club. This one's name was Gray Smoke. *Yes*, Heather had thought, *Smoke would get all the exercise she needs running around after this young woman.* But before she could broach the idea, something weird happened to Jordan.

"It was like she was mesmerized," Heather described the scene to me. I could hear Heather taking a sip of something with ice cubes. "She stood stock still, her eyes went blank like a zombie, and her gaze seemed to have fixed somewhere beyond the conservatory doors. The dogs began sniffing her body and crying, as if she'd been injured in some way. Possibly she was 'out of it' no more than a couple of minutes, but it seemed much longer because I was so anxious. Do you suppose it was something in the coffee that did it? I don't think she generally drinks anything but Coke and beer. Imagine, a whole generation that doesn't dig coffee. It staggers my mind!"

"Yes, yes. But what was going on with Jordan?"

"Well, she *came to*, so to speak, in a couple of minutes, and sank onto the conservatory loveseat as if someone had hit her over the head. I sure wished I was carrying smelling salts as Fiona always does. After a while she said, 'Holy shit, what a trip!'"

"Did she connect with your great-great grandmother?"

"Yes, but not in the way I was hoping. She found herself, not as Alyce herself this time, but as one the crowd outside the church. From the description, I'd say it was that old Plymouth Church that was established by the separatist Pilgrims and later became Unitarian."

"What was going on?"

"It was Alyce's wedding day. She came out of the church on the arm of her new husband, Captain Nathaniel Morgan. Can you imagine? Jordan saw my ancestor as a living man. How I envy her! He had a scar, she said, that ran from his eye to his mouth. The scar didn't show in the portrait that hangs in my parlor. Perhaps the turn of the captain's head disguised it, or the artist chose to brush it away. Alyce was a delicate girl but there was a resolute strength shining in her eyes, Jordan said. Well, she didn't exactly word it that way. You know Jordan. But the thing is, the bride was holding a bouquet of flowers and that same book, or what looked like the same book, that Jordan had seen in her first time-trip. Apparently it was a prayer book not a diary. So then, why do you suppose Alyce stashed it in the turret room?"

"I don't know. But my guess is, something was hidden in the book. But here's the thing: with visions, time is always in question. We have no way of knowing what happened when. If she was married at the time at the time of Jordan's first vision, and she must have been if she was living in the Morgan mansion, possibly a letter she didn't want her husband to see. When did they get married, exactly?"

"My great-great grandfather's first voyage to China took well over a year. As soon as Captain Morgan returned home, he courted Alyce, married her, and got her pregnant. Then he left her again three months later, so she was alone when my great grandfather was born. Why, what are you thinking?"

I really didn't want to say. "Since it's probably just a prayer book and not a diary, do you still want to find it?" I asked.

"Damn straight," Heather said. "I just wish I knew which panel to remove."

"You're overlooking the obvious. Fiona is our finder. Get her up there with her dowsing pendant. Do you think she can manage that ladder?"

"I'll give her a boost," Heather said.

CHAPTER TWENTY-THREE

If music be the food of love, play on.

– William Shakespeare

Tip took his Harley over to the Devlins' on Saturday night and brought Jordan back to our place. Heather and Dick had tickets for Pilgrim Playhouse, where a New York repertoire company was giving a performance of Arthur Miller's *The Crucible*, even though Heather complained that the play always ended the same tragic way.

Since there were only the three of us for dinner, we grilled marinated chicken and ate it with potato salad and glorious sliced summer tomatoes at a wicker table on the porch while Scruffy and Raffles lay nearby, drooling for handouts. Jordan, always an easy mark, dropped a few bites of chicken into waiting mouths.

Chicken! It's chicken! You only gave us that dog food stuff for our dinner. This girl smells good, and she knows we canines need real meat to bulk up our muscles. You can keep her.

Keep her! Keep her!

"Pipe down, you two. That was gourmet dog food with real turkey and vegetables."

Ha ha. Pressed gristle with a lot of nasty green sludge. Do we look like a couple of rabbits?

Rabbits? Rabbits?

"She's all right, Jordan," Tip explained. "Cass and her dogs have a very special relationship. Like a running conversation. I bet right now they're complaining about getting canned dog food for dinner."

Tip was not mentioning that he, too, could hear Animalspeak, something I could sense but that he kept quiet. I'd never called him on it, though. Generally I tried not to embarrass people by revealing the little quirks they were concealing.

"If Cass can put up with my weird spells, I guess I'm not going to flip out over her Dr. Doolittle stuff, if you know what I mean." Jordan smiled at me and dazzled Tip at the same time. She was brilliant with her own special electric energy in a sunshine-yellow crop-top and faded skin-tight jeans. I hoped that Tip wouldn't be bowled over and retreat into shyness.

"I'm going to clean up now, and I don't need any help," I announced. "Why don't you two kids check out Joe's totem pole. I believe there's going to be an almost-full moon pretty soon."

"Your husband has a totem pole? A real one?" Jordan, the would-be anthropologist, was enthralled.

"Yes, but not an artifact like the discoveries at the Salem dig that you've been photographing," I said, stacking the dishes on a tray, prepared to disappear the way we matchmakers do when the evening looks promising. "A gift to him from a grateful, very-much-alive West Coast nation. Some dispute with the lumber barons in which Greenpeace took a saving hand."

I banged around in the kitchen and was satisfied to see that Tip took Jordan out to the beach stairs, where they admired the Eagle-Bear-Salmon totem. Also, that he slipped his flute case over his shoulder before they left.

"No, you two stay here with me this time," I admonished Scruffy and Raffles, hanging onto their collars so they couldn't follow. I closed off the porch before they could zoom out the pet door. But the window was open, and by and by I could hear the plaintive notes of the Indian flute. I thought it was a song Tip had played for me called "Raven Dreams", piercing notes at first, but then becoming fainter. Good! They were going down to the beach. I caught sight of my face in the little mirror by the back door. What a self-satisfied smirk!

◦◦

Rather than waiting up, I took the dogs for a walk (on leash!) and went to bed around ten. It was much later when I heard the motorcycle revving its noisy motor. Tip was taking Jordan back to the Devlins'. I glanced at the clock. Twelve-fifteen! Drifting back to sleep, I planned to closely question Tip in the morning. My young friend was extremely private and close-mouthed, but I am devious and persistent.

But, imagine that! Tip was off again before the dogs got me up in the morning. In fact, the bike woke the dogs. O, frustration! For Scruffy and Raffles, too, who had been looking forward to playing ball with their favorite boy. They raced out the pet door on the porch, barking their displeasure.

There was a note on the table. "Hi, Aunt Cass. Didn't want to wake you up so early. I'm going to show Jordan around town, all the touristy stuff. We'll probably end up at Plimoth Plantation, meet some friends there for lunch.

See you later! Love, Tip. P.S. I played my flute. She liked
it."

I called Heather for her report. "Elsa said they had
breakfast in the kitchen here at the crack of dawn. Looking
pretty cozy. They were headed for White Horse Beach, I
believe, and then Plimoth Plantation. Listen, I've got Fiona
coming over here for lunch. With her pendant. Why don't
you come, too?"

"Sure. You may need me to help haul her up into the
turret room." Lunch at Heather's was always accompanied
by some incredibly delicious wine, and plenty of it, so
while my head was still clear, I busied myself all morning
filling herbal orders. My Love Potion XXX was flying off
the shelves. I wondered if I should have tried it out on Tip
and Jordan. Slipped a little into the marinade. But no, I
thought, in how many myths and stories had the potion
gone wrong! Tristan and Isolde, Romeo and Juliet, Titania
Queen of the Faeries who'd ended up making a fool of
herself over a jackass. It was a miracle I'd never been sued
over some misapplied XXX. Should I look into malpractice
insurance for herbalists? I shook my hands and feet to rid
myself of the negative image. Scruffy and Raffles are always
energized by this little dance and immediately whined for
a walk on the beach. I obliged.

Down by the big rocks I found an abandoned bed of
beach towels, the striped ones I keep in a basket by the porch
door. Yes!

∽

It was a good thing there were two of us to hoist Fiona,
her reticule, and her walking stick into the turret room. Once

up there, she sank down on a purple velvet pillow with a sigh of relief. Heather lit her visions candle, and we breathed in its evocative incense. To my continuing envy, lithe Heather can sit cross-legged like a yoga without any perceptible agony. I am far less graceful. Half an hour sitting on my legs leaves me crippled.

After a while, Fiona got herself up again with the aid of her coyote stick and took a few moments to exult in the view. Plymouth Bay was cerulean-blue today, sparkling with crisp little white-tops, punctuated by lifting and gliding gulls, a regular post card. "It's worth the trip up here to your meditation room," Fiona said. "Imagine watching for a ship's return in this eagle's eyrie! What excitement! Oh well, to work then."

She took out the crystal pendant on its silver chain from beneath her tie-dyed smock, where it had been nicely warmed between her bra-less breasts. It swung in the sunshine, throwing sparkling beams of light onto the wainscoted walls below the eight small windows. Fiona walked around the octagonal room humming to herself or to the pendant, one couldn't tell which. After a while, the crystal seemed to become more agitated at one side of the room than the others, and then, after more humming, closing in on one particular panel.

Fiona smiled and caught the pendant in her hand, returning it to its snug hiding-place. "If something is hidden in the walls of this room, it's probably right here. But before you go breaking down that beautiful wood, why don't we try to see how the lady got into that secret cache herself. Perhaps there's a trick to it."

"I never thought of that," Heather said. She crouched down and began to feel around the edges of the panel. Nothing budged.

When one watches someone else trying to open anything, one is seized with the desire to take over. Eagerly, I pushed Heather aside and tried my own hand. *No joy.*

"Probably painted shut," Heather complained.

Fiona reached into her reticule and took out what Tip would call "a lady knife" in a beaded sheath. "Navaho," she explained. "Blessed by the shaman." She handed it to Heather.

We took turns poking and prying around the panel with Fiona's knife, hacking off flakes of paint. Again, nothing jiggled loose.

"I'm going down to the cellar and get a hatchet," Heather said. She opened the trap door, climbed down the ladder, and hurried through the third floor hallway, lined with small bedrooms that had once housed maids.

Fiona studied the panel over the half-tracks on her nose. The bottom half of the room was wainscoted, with a broad, thick ledge above it that served as a windowsill for the eight windows in the turret, painted the same creamy white. "Give me the knife," she said. I handed it to her. She felt the edges of the wainscoting with her many-ringed fingers as softly and intently as a safecracker. "Slight bump here." Fiona stuck the point of the knife below the ledge, piercing the paint. Then she scraped off a bit more, revealing what looked like a small tarnished lock. It had been inset flush with the wood and painted over, but time had pushed the metal out of its perfect alignment. "This is the Morgan mansion, built by Captain Nathaniel Morgan, so Alyce must have had this cubbyhole put in here while her husband was at sea," Fiona said. "Her secret hiding place, in a room that was hers alone. At least, I think the Captain had no wish to enjoy the view while he was at home, or he would have situated his mansion closer to the shore."

Heather pushed up the trap door and appeared, flushed with exertion, throwing a small hatchet in a leather case in front of her before she climbed up. "Oh, what's that?"

"Fiona found an old lock between the windowsill and the panel below it," I said. "It was painted over so we couldn't see it."

"Put away that hatchet, girl. This lock is old but I think maybe I can get it open," Fiona said. She reached into her reticule, apparently without looking, and pulled out a little plastic bottle of some oily substance and a set of lock picks. She worked away at the lock for a while and presently it clicked open. Fiona felt above the lock some more and with the point of her knife, outlined a pull-out portion of the windowsill. More probing cut through the paint that had made the secret cache invisible. Sealed with age, it refused to pull forward. Fiona oiled and hummed, and hummed and oiled. She slowly eased the thin drawer open barely enough to stick a hand inside.

"Ah!" Heather said.

"You have the honor of reaching into that thing," I said. *Goddess only knew how many generations of vermin had run through those walls.*

I was right about that. The little prayer book that had been tucked away in the drawer was moldy and nibbled. Heather brought it out reverently and laid it on one of the pillows. Then she felt around some more but nothing else was forthcoming.

From the pocket of her striped skirt, Fiona took out a man's handkerchief embroidered with her late husband's initials R.A. R. and handed it to Heather. We hovered over her as she used the white linen to brush away webs and dust from the book's cover. The faded lettering had once been

painted in gold on a blue silk background: My Prayers, Alyce
May Alden.

The binding was sewn together with a ribbon that
disintegrated upon touch when Heather opened the cover.
The pages inside were foxed, ragged, and unreadable except
for a word here and there. No letter was enclosed.

Heather kept going through the pages; they had to be
lifted now since the binding had fallen apart. At the last,
there was a small loose oval silhouette of a man's profile that
didn't seem to be part of a book of prayers.

"Turn it over," I suggested, because I was seeing something
on the back, as I do occasionally.

In fading ink, the lines read "my love, my darling Billy,
lost at sea."

"Might have been her brother," I said.

"Yeah, sure," Heather said.

"Do you really want to know more?" Fiona asked.

"There are things about the past that we will never know,"
I said. "A clue here, a clue there, and a web of guesswork
stretched between."

"What about the Ouija board?" Heather said.

"Or a séance? Do you know where Alyce is buried?" Fiona
asked.

"Yes. There's a Morgan family vault at Burial Hill
Cemetery," Heather said.

"Wow. Good company," I said. "The Bradfords, The
Brewsters, and Squanto."

"We Morgans go way back," Heather said. "Why do you
ask?"

"Because Fiona is saying we could have a séance right
there," I said.

"Not on your life," Heather said. "How do I know which Morgan ghosts would come trooping out of that vault? It might not be sweet Alyce."

"And if Jordan is willing, we'd ask her to participate," Fiona said. "Full moon, preferably."

"I'd love to have the girl visit us again, but I draw the line at a séance. Not all my forebears were reputable sea captains. I've heard tell of a pirate in Barbados…"

Fiona took a small book out of her reticule and consulted it. "Eight days to the next full moon," she said.

"What part of *no séance* don't you gals understand?" Heather demanded nervously.

"Let's just hold the idea in reserve, then. Maybe at Samhain," I said. "Who would have suspected that the Morgans, those pillars of Plymouth's sea-faring history, harbored so many skeletons in their closet. Horse thieves, did you say?"

"No, I said *pirate. P-I-R-A-T-E.* A much nobler trade in those days. Captain Benedict Morgan. There's a family legend that, after Benedict was hanged in Boston, his son, Horatio, brought his body back to bury in the family vault. A year later, Horatio made a voyage to an unnamed island off the coast of Britain and somehow came into a fortune in French gold coins, Napoleons, which he used to finance his brother Nathaniel's expeditions to the Far East. Fine export china with a sideline in the opium trade. No, I don't think I want to conjure up those Morgan rascals. *Rest in peace*, I say."

"How lovely to have such a colorful family history!" Fiona enthused. "So much more interesting than the Cabots and the Lodges."

୬

Tip roared back in the afternoon, alone. I glanced at him covertly. That flush on his cheeks, his gray eyes gone soft and luminous. If there's one thing that can never be hid from a clairvoyant, it's the glow of sexual love. Not unless the clairvoyant deliberately puts up magician's screens to hide the news from herself, as one might with an erring husband. And indeed, with my young friend, I felt embarrassed by my intrusive talent.

Always it was my fate to be the woman who knew too much. With that thought, I found myself humming *Que Sera, Sera*, which made me giggle while I fixed us some supper, a dish which I privately called *Greek American Chop Suey*. Talk about fusion food!

"I'd better start back to Bangor tonight," Tip said. "Uncle John's expecting me at the shipyard tomorrow morning, bright and early."

"The pups will be desolate. You'd better give them a good ball game after supper. Anyway, I'm glad you came," I said. "Jordan needed someone her own age to have fun with, and also to shake off that time thing. I imagine the flute music helped, therapy without words."

Tip grinned. "You're up to something, medicine woman. You don't fool me."

"*Moi?* Not at all. I just think it's grand that you two hit it off.

✺

"A séance? Burial Hill at the full moon does sound like fun!" Deidre brightened, but immediately the sparkle faded. "But I vote for holding off until Samhain. It just seems wrong, somehow to be doing fun things when we're all so worried about Molly. I simply don't understand why the cops haven't found even a trace or a clue." She glanced at Phil darkly, as if it were all her fault.

"I think they're doing everything possible, Dee," Phil said. "So, cut the officers of the law some slack, will you? And besides…remember that *we're* on the case."

"Listen up, everyone! *There will be no séance at my family crypt. Ever,*" Heather said. "Deidre's got the right idea. We ought to just concentrate on Molly."

We'd met for tea at Fiona's, to make plans for our forthcoming flight over the Hogben compound.

Heather said. "Richie says it's a go for Wednesday. Too bad you're not coming with us, Phil. You're going to miss all the excitement."

"That's okay. You ladies go ahead and have fun," Phil said drily.

Fiona poured steaming Lapsang souchong tea into thistle mugs and passed a plate of her miniature cream scones. Omar Khayyám, her resident Persian aristocrat, walked across the back of the sofa, arching his back and complaining. Fiona gave him a crumb of scone, and he flounced off to the broad windowsill to keep watch on the bird feeder.

Fiona said, "I, too, have a pilot's license, let's not forget. If only I could find it. Even finders lose things. Especially dowsers, who travel in so many dimensions at once. How can one be expected to keep track of car keys and reading glasses when one is absorbed in detecting underground veins of water?"

"Always put them in the same place," Deidre suggested. "And *be present* when you do. Really, at the risk of being an atypical witch, I believe in mindfulness and order."

"Personally, I like to think it's my mission to create a little creative chaos out of order," Fiona said.

Phil and I glanced at each other. "I have to start writing this stuff down," she said.

"Are you absolutely sure you need me?" I said. I didn't have a good feeling about this escapade, but I suppose it would be cowardly of me to desert my friends because of a niggling premonition. Self-preservation is a pretty strong motivation, though. "But maybe *you* should reconsider, Phil. Possibly you could report whatever you see to Stone."

"Not on your life," Phillipa said. "Didn't I hear Heather say that her cousin Richie has a death wish?"

Heather laughed gaily. "Only because he married my cousin Brooke *twice*. Cass, you've met Brooke. You were on a jury together."

"She's a formidable woman of passionate energy, as I recall. An ace real estate agent," I said, prettying up my personal estimate, *a man-crazy, ball-breaker*.

"And man-chaser," Heather said. "Brooke believes in betting on love against all odds. A real string of losers. Except for Richie. I have a sneaking fondness for Richie. He's something of a bon vivant with Lucullan appetites. But always a gentleman, even if his head is in the clouds."

❧

Joe called that night around seven. I was relieved on two counts. He wasn't in jail or the hospital, and he wasn't coming home for a few days yet. Meaning, he wouldn't be here for the airplane excursion.

"Oh, too bad, honey. I miss you something fierce," I said. "What's going on? Haven't you finished your assignment with dangling off the smoke stacks and so forth?"

"We've made our point. The searchlight of public opinion has been trained on the problem, and we got plenty of press coverage with our young guys in the hanging sleep tents, poor bastards. We were, in fact, on our way home, when the Amsterdam director decided we ought to take on another mission."

"Like what? Not the Pategonian toothfish again!"

"That one really captured your imagination, didn't it, sweetheart? No, nothing that glamorous. This is merely a summer training cruise for student activists. Show them a few of the sights, a whale sanctuary, a trash vortex. Easy stuff."

"Lots of good-looking, athletic young women, I presume?"

"About equally divided, but not much opportunity for romance. We run a tight ship here. And besides, I only have eyes for you. You're a beautiful woman, and I love you. I'm missing you every moment I'm away. You want to know what I miss the most?"

He went on to enumerate, *let me count the ways*. Joe always says the right thing. That's what worries me. All those years he had to practice reassuring love-talk before we met.

CHAPTER TWENTY-FOUR

I know that I shall meet my fate
Somewhere in the clouds above...

– W. B. Yeats

Wednesday was one of those misty, rainy days of summer, which didn't seem to me the greatest flying weather, although not exactly dangerous. Leaving Phillipa to fuss and fume and warn us to keep in close contact with her by cell phone, Heather drove us to Rector's private airstrip on Old Tower Road near the Cape Cod National Seashore. The tarmac runway was adjacent to a sprawling gray-shingled home with a swimming pool, a three-car garage, and of course, an airplane hangar, on substantial acreage well-screened by a surround of scrub pines.

Richie Rector was a round-faced cherubic man with receding blond curly hair and a comfortable paunch. I couldn't put him together in my mind with sleek, fashionable Brooke, but then, even for a clairvoyant, it's difficult to predict another person's taste in lovers or literature. That's why it's such a tricky business to arrange blind dates or give books as gifts. (Famous last words: *I know you're going to love this one.*)

Of course, this pricey layout might be reason enough to brand Richie as good husband material. Heather had said Richie was heavily invested in Boston real estate, which would have been another attraction for Brooke.

Wearing a sporty Red Sox jacket, he greeted Heather like the proverbial prodigal cousin, and she introduced us all around. "Heather tells me you gals want to fly over this property on Herring Brook Road in Carver and take pictures? She's given me coordinates and I've submitted the flight plan, just a sightseeing joyride around the South Shore and back here again, so everything's good to go." He paused to light a cigarette (an unfiltered Camel, I noted) which dangled from his mouth as he continued with eyes squinted against the smoke. "I'm supposing you already tried satellite photos, and that didn't do it for you. Is this, like, a spy mission?" He seemed to be looking directly at me, but it was Fiona who answered.

"Too gray and grainy. We need more detail," she said. In her brown leather jacket, helmet, goggles, and silk scarf, she put me in mind of a plump Amelia Earhart. Silver aviator's wings were pinned to her green reticule. "We're hoping you can fly low over the compound. Dee will take the pictures."

Dee grinned and waved Conor's camera. "It *is* a sort of spy mission," she said. "There's this crazy preacher. Willie Hogben. Maybe you've heard of him? Rumor has it that his so-called compound has a series of linked outbuildings, but no one's been able to get inside to check it out."

Rector frowned thoughtfully. "The name does ring a bell. Nasty protests and picketers?"

"Yes, that's him," I said, hoping Deidre wouldn't go into any more detail.

"We think he may be hiding..." Deidre started to say.

Heather interrupted. "Well, let's get going, then. I think we'll have Fiona sit up in front with you. Dee wants to get shots from directly above the target, and that might be better from in back, don't you think?"

"What about this rain?" I asked nervously. I'm not fond of small planes. I prefer my aircraft to be so big and substantial that I can pretend I'm on a bus and not suspended high above land in a metal crate with many points of possible failure.

"Don't worry about the weather. This is nothing," Rector waved his hand dismissively at the murky skies. "And besides it's going to burn off. But before we get going, we ought to have a 'stirrup cup', don't you think? " He grinned broadly and stamped out his cigarette on the driveway.

He graciously motioned us inside his home, which was furnished in early Kennedy- Bouvier style, upscale comfortable furniture, Brunschwig & Fils fabrics, and family photographs in sterling silver frames, some faces being familiar, as belonging to the rich and famous. Rector lit another cigarette and propped it in a spacious crystal ashtray where there were already several butts.

Fiona and I took the opportunity to use the facilities before being crammed into the little Cessna. The bathroom was lavish in marble, linen, and lavender. When I joined the others, Rector was passing around a tray of several small glasses filled with some liquid too dark to be wine. I sipped mine cautiously. A very strong brandy, I thought.

A notion that was confirmed when Heather cried, "Cognac! And an excellent one." She and Rector had refills. A smiling, middle-aged Latino woman appeared from the back of the house.

"This is Rosa, my housekeeper," Rector said. "*Gracias*, Rosa. Hold the fort. I'm taking these gals for a ride."

"*Sí, señor. Buena suerte. Vaya con Dios.*" Still smiling, Rosa took away the empty glasses and the ashtray.

It was time at last to board the aircraft and take our assigned seats, which were club-style chairs upholstered in rich tan leather.

Heather and I sat in the first row of passenger seats, Deidre in the second row with the empty seat beside her, giving her room to maneuver. Fiona sat up front in the cockpit with Rector, who was now sporting goggles and a Red Sox baseball cap to match his jacket. "My my," Fiona said mildly, looking over the complicated control panel.

"Sweet, isn't it, Miss Fiona? As you see, this buggy used to be a trainer, so it's a bit fancy," Rector said. "Care to be my navigator today? There's the map in that side-pocket. Oh, don't worry. It's only an honorary title. I know the route by heart."

"That's a comfort," I said. At least we wouldn't have Fiona dowsing the map for directions.

"There's a refreshment stand to your right, Heather, in case you gals get thirsty," Rector cried merrily as he taxied out on the landing strip.

Personally, I thought we had all had quite enough alcohol, but Heather was checking out the cabinet beside her with obvious interest. "This is a fine Bordeaux," she said. "Saint-Julien."

"We need to keep clear heads today," I said.

Rector continued to be in jolly spirits, humming some thirties song, *Come, Josephine, in my flying machine...* as we rose from the runway into the gray, drizzly sky and made a lazy half-circle over the Cape Cod National Seashore below. *Only mildly scary*, I thought, relaxing a little.

In an incredibly short time we were flying over Plymouth and then Carver. Deidre got her camera ready, poised at the window.

"It's there! It's right there," Heather cried.

"I know," her cousin said. "I've got it all plotted. Now what I'm going to do is to swoop down closer. Are you ready, camera gal? You need to be on the left side, then when I turn around and come back over, move to the right side."

"Got it," Deidre said.

The Cessna descended gracefully over the Hogben place, perhaps a bit lower than was comfortable for me. I could see the tall board fence with a suggestion of wire on top, the outbuildings, which appeared to be ramshackle affairs. Two or three dogs were running around. I couldn't hear them, of course, but they were surely barking their heads off. Deidre kept taking photos of everything below in a very professional manner. She must have been learning from Conor.

We were still low over the property when a big woman appeared in the yard.

"That must be the lovely Eureka Hogben," Heather said, leaning over to peer out my window. "What's she shaking at us?"

"A rake, I think," I said. "Possibly she's not too pleased to be buzzed by some crazy small plane that's exciting her animals into a frenzy." The clouds were beginning to break up at last, and the sun shone through with quite brilliant, artistic rays. I had to admit the view was superb.

"I'm changing sides now," Deidre said as Rector, having turned the plane around, began to swoop back over the compound a second time. She continued to snap photos without pause. "I don't see anyone except the wife, do you?"

"No, nothing," I said. This time I was leaning over Heather. A ray of sunlight hit me directly in the eyes, and I sat down in my seat with a thump. The plane in which we were traveling vanished from my perception. In its place, in my mind's eye, I was in a small wooden room constructed of mismatched boards. There was a cot, and a little girl lying on the cot, who seemed to be asleep. Or drugged.

The vision faded in what was probably only an instant.

"Uh oh," I heard Heather say. "You'd better pass those smelling salts back here, Fiona."

I heard the tinkle of Fiona's silver bangles. Then I was treated to a whiff of that noxious stuff, and the episode passed. I found myself back in my seat on the aircraft, with Heather hovering over me anxiously. "She's okay now," Heather said.

"I feel sick," I said.

"There's a barf bag in the seat's side-pocket," Rector said. He was busy guiding the plane back to its cruising level. "Did you get everything you wanted, Dee?"

"Plenty of views but I'm not sure they'll be all we hoped for," she said.

I found the barf bag and kept it clutched in my hands, but the nausea was already beginning to recede. "There's a little girl inside one of those outbuildings," I said. "I saw her lying on a cot, maybe sleeping."

"What's she talking about?" Rector asked.

"Cass is a clairvoyant," Heather said. "Apparently, she's just experienced a vision."

"No shit! Does she do, like, horse races and football games and things?" Rector said. "What about the World Series?"

"No, Richie. My second sight is not *on call*," I said.

"Jesus!" Rector exclaimed. "I need a drink. Okay, we'll head back now."

As the little plane soared over the Cape, I gazed out the window, determined to enjoy a view I might never have again. A few moments later, though, a nameless uneasiness began to bother me. I struggled to bring it up to my consciousness.

"Are you feeling quite all right, Richie?" The words came out of my mouth, without any idea of where the thought came from.

Rector made a low groaning sound. "Bit of a pain in my arm," he said.

It seemed to me that we weren't gliding through the air as smoothly as we had been earlier. Suddenly, Rector slumped over sideways, resting his head against the window, with his cap askew. "God damn," he muttered. "Must be indigestion." The plane wiggled alarmingly as one of his hands clutched his chest.

"Mother of God," Deidre cried. "What's wrong with Richie?"

"Oh, dearie me, I think he's having a heart attack," Fiona said.

"*We're all going to die!*" Deidre screamed, quite a piercing sound in our cramped quarters. "Do something! Do something!"

"Ceres, save us, I didn't see this one coming *in time*," I said. Now the plane seemed to be wobbling in midair.

Rector's head fell forward on his chest. His seatbelt prevented him from collapsing onto the controls.

"Put a sock in it, Dee. We're not going to die!" Heather said urgently. "Fiona, you'll have to take over for Richie. You know how to fly the plane, right?"

"Goddess help me," Fiona moaned. "This panel is awfully complicated. Dual controls, but Richie still has a death grip on his yoke. Dearie me, he's really out of it. I wish I could reach my corn pollen."

"Forget the friggin' corn pollen, Fiona! For Goddess's sake, rev up your glamour thing," I was speaking from my inner self, which tends to radiate absurd authority. "Take on the persona of that West-with-the-Night babe. Beryl Markham. *You can do this.*"

The plane began to descend. Deidre mumbled words I recognized as the Hail Mary. Heather clutched my arm.

But all at once, Fiona seemed to sit up taller. "Wait! Wait! I think I've got it," she caroled with delight. "The yoke is responding. I'm taking her up!"After another heart-stopping wobble or two, the plane began to right itself into a smoother flight, at least not as terrifying. "Now where did we put that landing strip?" she mused.

"What about the radio?" I said. "Can you call for help? I think you're supposed to say May Day, May Day."

"What's Beltane got to do with it?" Deidre stopped praying long enough to ask.

"Can't reach the earphones. Richie's leaning on them," Fiona said. "What I really want to know is, where in Hades are we?"

"Look at the map. Richie put the map right there in your side-pocket." Heather reached over Fiona and pulled the map out herself. She opened it up between the two of them.

"This is right," Fiona said, glancing over and pointing. "I think."

But I was steeling myself to peer out the window. "Heather, we're already over the Cape Cod Seashore. Let's look for actual landmarks below. Remember that deserted tower we flew over as we ascended from the landing strip this morning? Gray stone, it looked like. We drove to Richie's place on Old Tower Road.

Deidre seemed calmer after her prayers. "Does she really know how to land this thing?" she asked in a trembling voice.

"We're about to find out." I was still studying the ground below. At last, I thought I got my bearings. Unbuckling my seatbelt so that I could lean over Fiona's shoulder, I said, "Hey, Fiona. See over there! The tower, the road. Follow that road to Richie's place. You'll see the landing strip."

"Roger!" Fiona cried. *"The owl is landing..."* She adjusted her goggles and gripped the yoke with surprising authority. Fiddling with levers and switches on the control panel, she hummed to herself, that tuneless hum that brings her into magical focus.

"Cass, how's Richie doing?" Heather asked.

Rector was still slumped over his seatbelt, but I could see the slight movement of his chest rising and falling. I felt the pulse in his neck. "He's breathing, he's alive, but apparently unconscious, poor baby. We need to get him to a hospital."

"Is it okay to use a cell phone?" Heather asked while she craned her neck to observe Fiona fearfully, but Fiona seemed to be fully in charge, still humming.

"I have no idea," I said. Sitting back down, I punched in 911.

A young woman answered, "What is the nature of your emergency?"

I explained that we were about to land a Cessna on the private airstrip in Plymouth on Old Tower Road, but the pilot had apparently suffered a heart attack. We needed an ambulance to meet us at his address immediately. I gave the address.

"Is there someone else there who can fly the plane? Who's manning the controls right now?" the operator asked in a measured tone calculated not to excite panic. Are they always that unflappable? Rather than attempt to explain that Fiona had taken over, I thought the best thing to do was to end the call. Which I did.

"I hope one ambulance will be enough," Heather said. "Let's say a group blessing,"

But before we could decide on which blessing to recite (*We are one with the Earth, Mother Earth* didn't seem just right) Rector's place came into view below us and Fiona began her descent.

"Buckle up your seatbelts," she ordered us in a surprisingly calm voice. "It's been a while, but I believe I remember. Here we go.... *Coming in on a wing and a prayer.*"

Deidre returned to her Hail Marys, and Heather and I gripped hands.

The plane began to glide downward. "I'm not going to do the flaps thing. The throttle is controlling my airspeed just fine," Fiona declared with satisfaction. "Now I've got to let the gear down. Oops, it seems to be stuck."

"What gear? *What's the gear?*" Deidre wailed. Neither Heather nor I wanted to tell her that Fiona was fiddling with the wheels, without which we would be landing on the plane's belly. Also, we were holding our breaths, which made it difficult to speak. A few seconds that seemed like an hour passed while Fiona wrestled with the controls.

"There it goes. I've got it!" Fiona exclaimed with delight. There was a gratifying thump.

Fiona began humming again as the plane descended to the landing strip.

The plane touched wheels to tarmac.

It swerved and bumped and skidded and jolted and screeched and bumped again, heading straight for the hangar.

"*Stop!* Holy Mother of God, will you stop this damned thing," Deidre cried.

"Seventy miles an hour is just about right," Fiona said. "It's important not to brake too sharply. It might blow the tires."

But Fiona did stop the plane, finally. Practically in the hangar but not quite. I felt like applauding, but there wasn't time. We had to see what we could do for Rector.

In the distance, we could hear the wail of an ambulance.

Somehow we got ourselves out of the plane. Heather and I pulled Rector out of his seat onto the ground, as gently as possible.

With siren blasting, the ambulance raced onto the airstrip. Hearing the commotion, Rosa ran out the door, crying and wailing in Spanish.

Two paramedics, both of them as hefty as Sumo wrestlers, lumbered to our side. How thankful I was that my uncertain CPR skills would not been needed! I vowed silently to take a refresher course as soon as possible. The men hoisted Rector onto the stretcher, and began to administer oxygen. They checked his pulse rate, then gave him nitroglycerin and aspirin. We hovered around helplessly, trying not to get in the paramedic's way. "How's he doing?" Heather asked anxiously.

I thought I saw Rector's eyelids fluttering, which I took to be a good sign.

"How're you doing, Sir?" one of the paramedics yelled at the patient in a loud tone.

Rector groaned. "What happened to my plane? Did we crash?"

"Appears to be a cardiac event," the other paramedic said to us. "He's coming around, seems alert. These are good signs. We're transporting him to Cape Cod Hospital. You can follow, if you like."

The first paramedic, still yelling at Rector said, "You're going to be all right, Sir. Just hang in there. We're bringing you to the hospital now."

"Your plane is in the hangar." Heather, too, raised her voice to shout at her cousin-in-law. "Fiona brought it down okay. And we're all safe, too."

"No shit…" Rector said as they took him away. "Tell Rosa…bring cigarettes…"

Fumbling with her reticule, Fiona managed to toss a sprinkle of corn pollen over Rector before he was whisked into the ambulance, which raced away with the siren screaming again. Then Fiona administered smelling salts to Rosa while reassuring her that her employer was going to make a full recovery. Lulled by Fiona's reassuring voice and manner, Rosa calmed down enough to offer to make us a pot of coffee.

"Oh, good idea," Heather said. "And bring the brandy, too, please."

"*No way*," Deidre said firmly. "You're driving, and I want to get home to my children in one piece."

The coffee was welcome indeed. While we sipped it, I called Phillipa.

"Well, it's about time!" she complained. "How was your flight? Uneventful, I hope?"

"Not exactly" I said, and launched into my story, punctuated by exclamations of horror from Phillipa.

"*Fiona landed the plane! Blessed Brigit!* And everyone is all right, then?" she asked anxiously.

"Everyone except Richie. But it seemed to me he was stabilizing by the time the paramedics took him away to Cape Cod Hospital. Heather's going to bring us home, then double back to visit Richie and speak to his doctor. She's also going to get in touch with ex-wife Brooke, too, for all the good that will do. Brooke is too busy chasing men to care deeply about any one of them."

"Remember Heather joked that Richie had a death wish? Too true," Phillipa said. "And your disastrous flight was all for nothing, as well."

"Well, there *was* one more thing that happened. I had this vision while we were flying over the Hogben place. There's no way to know for sure, though, if what I saw in my mind's eye was in the compound or somewhere else entirely."

"What! What?" Phillipa demanded.

"I saw a girl, sleeping or drugged, lying on a cot in a room that seemed to be constructed of boards. I don't suppose you want to impart this to Stone?"

Phillipa was silent for a few seconds. Finally she said, "I guess I will, but there'll be absolutely nothing he can do about it. Keep Hogben under closer scrutiny, I guess."

"If it's true, and Molly Larsson is being kept prisoner in that compound, we can't *not* do anything. We have to find out the truth," I said.

"Damn straight!" Deidre exclaimed. Everyone was hanging over my conversation with Phillipa.

"What if Hogben panics," Heather said. "He might feel forced to harm the girl. Unless...wait! I have an idea."

"I was afraid of that." Phillipa was still listening.

"Listen, Phil, we're going to talk this over on our way home, then I'll give you another call. Bye-bye." I clicked off before she could lecture me further.

CHAPTER TWENTY-FIVE

There's fennel for you, and columbines;
there's rue for you; and here's some for me;
we may call it herb grace 'o Sundays.

– William Shakespeare

Heather spoke soothingly to Rosa before we left, promising to check on Richie's condition and speak with his doctors as soon as she had brought us home. She would call with a quick update, to let Rosa know if it was okay yet to contact Richie on his cell and how soon he might have visitors. "But *do not* bring Richie any cigarettes or brandy, Rosa," Heather warned, "no matter what he says."

We got in the Mercedes and were rather sober and silent for the first few miles.

Then Fiona said, "Maybe I should take up flying again. A refresher course, you know. Life is uncertain, and it's important to keep one's skills honed."

"O, take that out of the law, dear Goddess," I murmured.

"You have an idea for getting into that compound, don't you, Heather?" Deidre was not to be digressed from the crusade at hand.

"Dogs," Heather said. "If there were to be reports of, say, severe dog abuse, the Animal Control Officer can demand entry. I'm going to report that we were flying over the compound and saw Eureka Hogben beating a dog with a stick."

"Will the Dog Officer believe that?" Deidre asked wonderingly. "Won't you need, like, some real evidence?"

"You have photos of the dogs, right? So we know there are dogs on the premises, and we can prove it. And the Plymouth Animal Control Officer is my cousin."

"How many cousins do you have!" I exclaimed.

Heather laughed. The first time any of us had laughed since we set foot in the Cessna this morning. "We're an old family in these parts. Historic and prolific. I have a cousin in Parks and Recreation, a cousin in School Administration, but he's only a third cousin, another cousin in the Tax Assessor's office—lucky break that!—and, yes, in Animal Control as well. Gray Morgan. Graham, actually."

Fiona said, "You and Gray are going into the compound with banners flying, I presume?"

"Of course, and I'm going to take Cass as well," Heather said, just as if there was no need to consult me.

"Oh, no fair! *I* want to go," Deidre declared.

"Sorry, Dee. Too large a posse might definitely look suspicious. I wouldn't take Cass, but I need her third eye."

"Lucky me," I said dryly. But the truth was, wildebeests wouldn't keep me away.

"Wait up, Heather. I believe some good old-fashioned magic is what we need here," Fiona said. "You may get into the compound with a phony abuse complaint, but what are you going to see? You'll have no excuse to search all those connected shacks. Let's do the magic first, then follow it up with your official raid."

"Fiona has a point there," Deidre agreed. "Best would be if we do some serious spell-work to bring Molly home safely, plus Fiona dowses my photographic layouts. If one of those outbuildings appears to be 'hot,' Cass can break inside that one while you and Gray keep Eureka busy."

"Completely crazy," I said.

"Sounds like a plan," Heather said, "a better plan, actually. Sometimes I do tend to go off half-cocked."

"*You think?*" I said. But the others ignored me. Fiona, Heather, and Deidre chattered on about the best kind of magic to find Molly, if Molly was indeed being held by the Hogbens. Fiona remembered a likely spell in *Hazel's Book of Household Remedies*. "If memory serves, it's called 'Finding the Lost Darling.'"

"That sounds just right," Deidre declared. "The poor little thing. Let's everyone meet at Phillipa's to cast the spell. I'm sure she must be aching to get in on the action, after she missed our surveillance expedition and all."

Mortal fear fades fast, I thought. "Phil wasn't exactly hot to go," I reminded them. "And I think we should check with her first, before we all show up there with wands and brooms, or whatever—don't you?"

I punched in her number again. "Okay if we meet at your place this afternoon for a confab?" I said. "I'm just going home to gather a few herbs and things. Dee needs her stuff, too. And Fiona will have to collect Hazel's book."

"Sprigs of baby's breath and a Molly poppet," Deidre said.

"But I have to go back to the hospital," Heather said. "Will you be able to manage without me and my candles?"

"Heather's got to return to the Cape to check on Richie," I said to Phillipa. "Got any candles?"

"Sure. Cape Cod bayberry, which we can anoint with your essential oils."

"I'm thinking vervain, rue, and fennel to surround Molly with love and keep her safe," I said. "Sandlewood incense. All purpose against negativity. Let me know if there's anything else, Fiona. Call me before I leave home for Phil's."

Fiona hummed a noncommittal reply. She was gazing out of the car window in a creative coma, but nonetheless was probably hearing every word, even those unsaid.

"Oh, crap! I hate to miss all the spell-work!" Heather said, loud enough for Phillipa to hear.

"Come for dinner afterward," Phillipa said. "All of you. If there's no major crime wave on the South Shore before six, Stone will be home and you can regale him with your suspicions. And I'll throw something together with chicken."

And so it was agreed. We'd meet at Phillipa's in an hour or so, zap Hogben, save Molly with one of Hazel's magical recipes, and have dinner together. *The perfect ending of an imperfect day.*

☙

It was only just past two in the afternoon, but I felt as if I'd lived a whole lifetime in one morning. In dog-time, too, I'd been gone for an unacceptable number of hours, as Scruffy and Raffles were quick to remind me.

How long are we supposed to keep our paws crossed, Toots? I have to pee so bad I'm floating.

Floating! Floating!

As soon as I stepped out of the way, Scruffy and Raffles shot out of the porch pet door and relieved themselves on the nearest pines. Then they raced around the yard in the sheer exuberance of canine freedom, occasionally nipping each other's ears and bouncing against sturdy bodies. Scruffy still had a slight edge of robust weight, but he was a little stiffer with age now. Watching his bravado performance of growls and shoves, I sighed. Why couldn't I be as feisty about advancing age as my senior dog was?

While they were larking about in the yard, I went downstairs to my cellar workroom to gather the ingredients we would need. My herbal "office" had once been as cozy and primitive as a mountain cave before my beloved handyman had been inspired to modernize it with sturdy new shelves, track lighting, and a pine worktable. I had only just managed to hang on to my ancient rocker, the old green-shaded, single-bulb, shadow-swinging light hanging over it, and a distressed gate-leg table of which I was very fond. I turned the lamp on now and roved through the jars and bottles to choose dried sprigs of herbs, sticks of incense, and essential oils to scent the candles.

While I was packing my basket, Fiona called me on my cell. "This is a very simple spell," she said, "and everything you mentioned is fine. But here's my worry. I've suspected all along that this creep Hogben is a natural sorcerer. I believe he prevented me from finding Molly when I first dowsed for her. Oh well, at least your vision kicked in. Anyway, dried rue is especially fine for hex-breaking, and maybe you should add rosemary oil as well. Those two may work against Hogben's mojo better than anything. Oh, and bring some lavender oil for purification. And sage tea for a ritual cup."

Not surprisingly, I'd already packed rosemary, lavender, and sage with the other supplies. Someone like me is always operating on two wave lengths at once, one full of conscious purpose and the other flying blind on unconscious impulses, which experience has taught me to trust.

As I brought the basket upstairs, I suddenly realized that I hadn't had any lunch. That empty feeling in my stomach was hunger. For the sake of cheering us all up, I made a fast frittata with peppers and onions, which I shared with my salivating friends, all of us intent on the joy of *food, glorious food*. After any previous plane ride, I'd always felt how good it was to be alive, but never more than I did this afternoon. *Close call!*

After our late lunch, I took Scruffy and Raffles for a consolation walk on the beach so I wouldn't feel guilty when I took off without them again. The ocean in July was nearly the blue-aqua of the Caribbean rather than its usual gray-green, and the hot salt smell of the shoreline was familiar and refreshing to my recovering sense of security. The waters off the Plymouth coastline, even in deep summer, would be icy, but the sand "under paw" was so baking-hot that my companions were not unwilling to return to the house and belly-flop on the cool kitchen tile.

I drove to Phillipa's house, just on the other side of Jenkins Park, deep in uncertainty. Was Molly Larsson truly a prisoner in the Hogben compound? No one doubts my visions as much as I do myself. But I'd had enough direct hits to pay careful attention to each new revelation. Fiona kept maintaining that Hogben was a sorcerer. I had no experience with sorcerers, but this didn't sound promising. Actually, I thought the man was brainless. How could he hope to kidnap a local girl and keep secret her presence in his property?

"Most criminals are stupid. That's how they get caught," Phillipa declared later when we'd gathered at her place and I'd posed this same question. "When they get away with a crime, it's usually dumb luck. Or dumb investigators. There have been incidents of law enforcement searches that missed the evidence of a kidnapped victim right on the property. Local cops are sometimes reluctant to believe that one of their townspeople maybe a pedophile or BTK sicko. But don't tell Stone I said that. And he, of course, is not to be so easily deceived by good old boys. "

"I wonder, now, about that nubile girl chorus that travels with Hogben, his so-called nieces," I said. "Between their blonde wigs, dark glasses, and cover-up prairie dresses, it's as if they're in disguise. Who are they, really? Where do you suppose they came from? And how come Eureka Hogben puts up with this female entourage?"

"I can't believe those girls are with him against their will," Phillipa said. "Right out in public like that. There must be some back-story we're not aware of."

"Has Stone ever looked into Hogben's past?" I asked. "Where he comes from and all that? The mad preacher hasn't been wreaking the Lord's vengeance on the South Shore for more than a couple of years, right?"

"Yes, of course Stone has checked, and no criminal record came to light. That is, if Hogben is the preacher's real name," Phillipa promised. "Now, let's get wreaking our own vengeance!"

∽

Deidre cast our circle, and we worked our spell with a lovely little Molly poppet surrounded by a nest of baby's breath and small pink roses. We followed Hazel's simple ceremony to "find the lost darling." Then, on our own, without benefit of Hazel's guidance, we zapped Hogben with our own brand of *shake 'n bake*. If he'd taken Molly, sorcerer or no, he was going down.

"This is the second time we've tip-toed on the dark side," I said. "I hope we're not going to make it a habit. I mean, this stuff could really crack open a pothole in one's spiritual path."

"Yes, best not to fly around dispensing vigilante magic," Phillipa agreed. "Tempting though it may be."

"Oh, for mercy's sake, ladies," Deidre exclaimed. "Enough with the Goody Two-shoes."

"Ah, the story of Goody Two-shoes," Fiona said. "The reward for virtuous behavior after many grievous trials. A poor orphan named Margery Meanwell..."

"I don't believe any of us could be accused of being a Goody Two-shoes," Phillipa interrupted. "And I can cite many an anecdote about you guys that proves my point."

"That's what friends are for," I said. "To bring up your guilty secrets at inconvenient moments."

The evocative scents of herbs, oils, and candles still filled our senses and possibly prevented any further soul-searching as we sipped sage tea in Phillipa's exotic living room. For summer, the fireplace wall had been filled with multiple varieties of shiny green ivy in pots, and there were blossoming plants—hibiscus, gardenia, jasmine, begonia—basking in the light from the long windows facing the backyard. I was surprised to find that a derelict old boxer, Boadicea, rescued by Heather and foisted onto Phillipa as a guard dog when there had been dangers lurking, lying in the midst of Moroccan rugs and slate floor tiles, smiling and drooling in her sleep.

"So, you decided to give dear Boadicea a forever home, after all," I commented *sotto voce.*

Phillipa shot me a dark look. "Have you ever tried to return a sanctuary dog to Heather? She who is mistress of shame, guilt, and recrimination? Well, anyway, Boadicea keeps me company, you know, when Stone is working nights, and she and Zelda have reached a kind of détente."

Zelda was at that very moment sunning her sleek self on a silk pillow.

Fiona laid a photo of the Hogben place on one of the circular brass tables arranged near cushioned chairs in the spacious room. Deidre had enlarged the best shot of the entire compound for Fiona to dowse.

Phillipa slipped away to start "the chicken thing" in the kitchen, ordering me to call her the moment there as a "hit." Boadicea stood up with a groan and pattered after her new mistress. *She'll dine like the queen she's named for*, I thought.

Fiona had drawn the crystal pendant from underneath her tie-dyed shirt and was "warming" it up over the photos. Deidre and I hung over her shoulder.

The crystal circled, and circled, and circled. Finally, it shot clear off one side of the photo. "What in Hades does that mean?" Deidre asked crossly.

"I believe there's another building somewhere over there. One that didn't appear in your photo," Fiona said. She herself looked perplexed and uncertain.

"Or it's underneath," I said suddenly. I never know in advance what's going to come out of my mouth, but as I said the words aloud, I "saw" a room made of boards underneath another. Could it be the same room in which I envisioned Molly? "Perhaps the pendant is confused. Like the rest of us."

Fiona took a small silver-rimmed magnifying glass out of her reticule and studied the photograph more closely. "The pendant jumped off right here. See this outbuilding with two broken boards, like a rough window, at this edge of the picture." She tapped the place with a silver-ringed finger.

"If Heather and Cass get into the compound, and Heather's cousin provides enough official distraction, perhaps you, Cass, can have a look beside or underneath this spot."

Phillipa came back into the room and had to be filled in on every detail. "This is a pretty risky expedition," she said. "*Illegal search* comes to mind. *Harassment.*"

Fortunately, the harangue was interrupted by Heather's arrival. She was carrying a large basket of various wines. "Myocardial infarction," she announced to us all. "Richie's in ICU, but he's awake and fairly comfortable. His cardiologist says the attack was not as serious as it could have been, and Richie is expected to make a full recovery. But Dr. Farah says Richie will have to make some serious changes in his unhealthy life style, *ha ha.* I certainly do hope Richie does reform, but I have my doubts. Before I left, he managed to whisper to me that I should bring some brandy in a thermos on my next visit. Something I warned Rosa not to do, either. So...what's going on here?"

Heather examined the photo we'd been hanging over, and we filled her in on our thoughts, imaginings, and afternoon of spell-work.

"Eureka's going to be fit to be tied, but we can do this," she declared. "If Cass finds any evidence, any suggestion at all of Molly's presence, we'll immediately call for the cops. I trust that Eureka won't actually sic those guard dogs on an official Animal Control posse. "

"Are you sure you're going to need me?" I asked nervously.

"Don't be a wimp," Heather said. "We'll carry air horns and citronella spray. And Gray will have Ketch-all poles. It will be fine."

"You have to realize that Heather is fearless when it comes to canines," Phillipa said.

Just then we heard Stone walk in the kitchen door, so talk of our proposed intrusion into the Hogben compound was instantly tabled. Phillipa and Boadicea welcomed him warmly, and vice versa. Deidre and I packed up our gear pretty fast. Fiona tucked the photos in her reticule. Heather removed the sage tea and replaced it with a wine opener and glasses. It was amazing how quickly and efficiently the atmosphere of a Wiccan commando bunker was whisked away.

Later, over Phillipa's *Bistro Chicken with Artichokes* and Heather's *Pouilly Fuisse*, Deidre asked Stone about his search into Willie Hogben's background.

Stone ran his long fingers through his fine brown hair with a worried air. "After that jumped-up preacher picketed your shop and Phil got herself involved, I did a thorough background check on the man. He really doesn't have any criminal priors, just a bunch of citations for disturbing the peace and harassment, which generally came to nothing because of First Amendment issues."

"He's only been in this area for a few years," Deidre said. "Is he a legitimate pastor? Where did he come from originally?"

"Yes, he has some specious papers ordaining him to an evangelical ministry in West Virginia," Stone said. "There's not much we can do about Hogben except to block his worst tirades at funerals and so forth. But that picketing incident is over and done with, Dee. What's your present interest? Phil has recently asked me a few questions about Hogben as well. I smell a conspiracy." He tapped the side of his nose, looking like a veritable Sherlock Holmes, whom he actually resembled as the "consulting detective" had been portrayed in *The Strand magazine*. Tall, thin, teacherly, ascetic. Not a pipe smoker, though.

"What about those girls who travel with him?" I asked, hoping to add more fuel to Stone's curiosity. I figured he might as well follow our train of thought, since, sooner or later, we were going to need him

"What about them?" he parried.

"Are they really his nieces? Did they come with him from West Virginia? Do they all live together in that fortress of theirs?"

"He doesn't exactly hide them. What are you thinking, Cass?" Stone asked.

"Cass has had the notion that the little girl you're all looking for, Molly Larsson, might have been taken by Willie Hogben," Phil answered for me.

Stone flushed, possibly with annoyance, and I wouldn't blame him. "Really, Phil, that's rather a stretch, isn't it? I don't like the man any more than you do. He's a troublemaker, no doubt about it. But it's a long way from picketing to pedophilia and kidnapping."

"Okay, honey," Phillipa said. "But you know Cass. She sees things that no one else sees, and often she's right. So we think you should take her seriously."

"You realize, don't you, Phil, that I can't investigate this off-the-wall suspicion without probable cause?" Stone said.

"Of course we do, dear Stone," Fiona jumped in. "But just on the off-chance that something turns up...well, you'll want to pursue it."

"We're talking about a little girl's life here, not some stuffy regulation," Deidre declared hotly.

This was not going well. "All right, ladies," I said. "Let's not ruin Phil's lovely dessert with wrangling.'

They got the hint, and we turned to other subjects while Phillipa cut slices of fresh peach pie, the glory of summer.

But Stone remained quiet and thoughtful. Never mind, Heather and I would soon be on the track of some real "probable cause." I just hoped that wouldn't make him out of patience with us. But no, we'd been through many trying times together, and Stone had hardly ever been really cross with us unless we put Phillipa and ourselves in grave danger. But surely a little "drop in" on Eureka Hogben would not be hazardous to our health.

How fortunate that Phillipa had married this intelligent, sympathetic man, who despite being a detective did not dismiss our several talents out of hand. Quite amazing. The smiles they shared over Deidre's impatience and Fiona's vague predictions revealed just how unruffled he was by our shenanigans. Joe was like that, too. Seeing Stone and Phillipa together, in that particular aura of wordless understanding that surrounds well-married couples, I felt quite lonesome.

And that was another thing about Stone; he wasn't wandering the seven seas in search of environmental dragons to slay. He was right here where he was needed.

CHAPTER TWENTY-SIX

Endurance, foresight, strength, and skill,
A perfect woman, nobly planned,
To warm, to comfort, and command...

— William Wordsworth

Heather called me as soon as I got home. There was a military funeral scheduled for Saturday; a young soldier killed in Afghanistan would be buried in the St. Joseph Cemetery. Rumors had been going around that Hogben was planning a demonstration, probably leaked by him to assure plenty of press coverage. With Willie Hogben and his entourage off on one of his offensive crusades, it would be the ideal time to bull our way onto his home turf.

Meanwhile, Fiona had a visit from her Wiccan friend and Salem celebrity, Circe La Femme. She had been impelled to deliver in person a dire warning to Fiona and her "coven." Circe had received a communication from her spirit guide, a deceased Indian princess named Pauwau. Fiona called to invite us all to have tea with her and Circe and hear the message. It took some convincing, but Fiona assured us that Circe was an authentic psychic, if a bit theatrical in her presentations.

"Don't be fooled by way she markets herself. Every witch has to make a living," Fiona said. "It's just a little color for the Wicked Good Gift Shoppe. But Circe herself is in touch with cosmic energies, of that I have no doubt."

It was my ill luck to catch a ride to Fiona's with Phillipa, whose skepticism was loud and clear. "Princess Pauwau, indeed," she scoffed.

"Fiona says it's an Algonquin name meaning witch," I said.

"You don't say! I can hardly wait to see Circe floating about in diaphanous black clothing." she said.

I noted that Phillipa herself was wearing black linen pants and and a black silk shirt.

"Many Wiccan shopkeepers like to dress the part, or at least, what the public expects a witch to look like. I hear that Tabitha Wisen wears the full mythical garb, not to mention carrying Scabies, her pet rat, in a glass cage," I said. "It's just show biz, Phil. And Circe's come all this way because she's Fiona's friend and she's worried about us."

"Yeah, yeah. I bet she'll be wearing enough silver to sink a battleship. In case the ordinary tourist in the street should miss the fact that she's a witch, the multiple pentagrams hanging around her neck would be a clue." And more in that vein. I was relieved when we arrived at the little fishnet-draped cottage and were welcomed by a beaming Fiona. Heather and Deidre were already there, chatting amiably with Circe about the efficacious use of candles and amulets. Fiona bustled about making a pot of Lapsang souchong tea.

Circe, ensconced in Fiona's chair, was not exactly what Phillipa was expecting. She was what the bra ads call "a full-figured gal," wearing a crinkly lavender muumuu. No silver jewelry, not even multiple rings such as bedecked Fiona's hands. She held a purple book in her hands, the size of a prayer book but inscribed with a silver pentagram instead of a cross. A small purple silk bag hung over her wrist, attached by a gray silk cord. It bulged in a knobby fashion, filled with Goddess-knows-what. Her sixtyish face was bare of make-up, her eyebrows rather sparse and unruly, but she had a sweet, youthful smile. Her long gray hair was carelessly held in place by a purple headband. Even so, she exuded a remarkable aura of regal amplitude, like a Pagan Queen Victoria. What a treat for the neighbors, who were frequently seen spying on Fiona's doings from behind their tweaking curtains. Plymouth center did not afford Fiona the privacy that the rest of us enjoyed. Good thing it didn't seem to bother her a fig.

After we were all settled with our thistle mugs of steaming tea, Circe held forth in a deep dramatic voice. "As she often does, Pauwau came to me two days ago while I was channeling for a few guests in my parlor. After the usual messages from dear ones who had passed on to Summerland, Pauwau became unusually agitated and knocked over our little round table. My guests were quite startled and left soon after. But Pauwau did not leave. Instead, she became was quite insistent that I bring you a warning."

"That Cass is giving witches a bad name with her crazed criminal crusades?" Phillipa asked.

Circe continued, undisturbed: "That you five are being stalked by some dark young person intent upon revenge."

Phillipa snorted. I stepped lightly on her foot. This was no time to change the subject.

"But the Salem snipers are locked up in the Essex County Jail awaiting trial," Heather protested. "And investigators are convinced that those two madmen were working alone on some beef about the American Indian artifacts being dug up at the Morse homestead. Really, I think that was just their silly excuse to go psycho."

"All true," Circe declared, "but Pauwau says that is not the end of your danger. Even now there are evil forces skulking around you here in Plymouth, my dear sisters. The princess said you would not believe her unless I came here myself and delivered a spirit crystal to draw the evil into the open." She removed the silk bag from her wrist and rummaged around in it, withdrawing a jagged quartz crystal, transparent lavender. "Pauwau herself has infused this crystal with her intention to reveal the malefactors. She says that she and Fiona knew each other in an earlier time." Circe put the crystal into Fiona's hand. "Wrap this in silk and keep it by you always. Evil will be revealed."

It's rare to see Fiona struck speechless, but clearly she was temporarily over-matched in the oracle department. Omar sensed it, too, and leaped up into her lap, glaring at us all defensively.

"Fiona has always felt a closeness to the American Indians," I filled in for her.

"And I've brought these, too." Circe's hand went back into her silk purse and brought out a handful of polished onyx stones. "We need to place a white candle where it will be reflected in a mirror. Then we arrange these stones in a half-circle between the candle and you ladies. As we light the candle, we imagine all wickedness and negative happenings going into the mirror. I will blow out the candle toward the mirror and give each of you one of these stones to carry for protection." Circe leaned back in her hostess's chair with a profound sigh "Got anything stronger than tea, Fiona?"

Fiona unearthed her bottle of Drambuie, dusted it off with the end of her tie-dyed t-shirt and set it out on the scarred coffee table. Deidre found liqueur glasses. I nipped into Fiona's bedroom where I had seen a mirror on a mahogany stand that would serve quite nicely. Heather found that she had a white candle in her faux-alligator handbag. "I like to carry this for emergency banishings," she explained. "It's scented with cinnamon."

I really couldn't imagine what in Hades Circe and Princess Pauwau were babbling about, "lurking dangers" indeed, but she was Fiona's friend, so I went through the ritual with as good grace as I could muster, and I was gratified that Phillipa did, too.

Heather and Deidre, however, seemed suitably impressed, although Deidre muttered, "And here I thought we had enough on our altars already with our search for Molly."

Soon after, we left Fiona and Circe in cozy cahoots. I drove home with a slight headache, feeling burdened with this new worry. Scruffy and Raffles were eager to stretch their paws, but my head couldn't stand the thoughts of brilliant sunshine on the beach, so I took them instead to the welcoming cool shade of Jenkins Park.

I sat on a favorite fallen log and vegetated while the dogs ran around in joyous pursuit of every moving thing. *Carpe diem* is the basic canine philosophy. After a while, Scruffy came back and threw himself down beside me, while Raffles continued to nose about in the scent-rich underbrush.

"This is a fine mess we've got ourselves in," I said. "Not only do we have to break into Hogben's place under guise of an animal cruelty complaint, now along comes Circe with the spectral voice of doom. Who needs it?"

Scruffy put his head on my knee in quiet sympathy.

"I'm worried about so many things," I sighed.

We canines like to keep life simple. One thing at a time. Eat, play, pee. If trouble creeps in on little cat feet, our keen senses will warn us soon enough. Nothing on the wind right now, so how about we trot home, refresh ourselves with a cool bowl of water and a nap, Toots?

"Good idea, Scruff. Let's go home and rest a while. Maybe everything will look better after a little shut eye. Maybe Joe will tear himself away from those nubile activists and call me. That would be nice."

A person could do worse than learn from her dog. There's no multi-tasking and worry overload in the animal world. Sufficient unto the day is the crisis thereof.

We ambled home. After slobbering water with great gusto, the dogs flopped on the tile floor; I turned on the radio, "Cape Classical," and rested my head against the back of the rocker. Tchaikovsky's Violin Concerto in D soared through the kitchen. Normally I would have soared with it, but it seemed somehow that my usual energy had sunk into a morass of criminal concerns.

Maybe I was hungry. I couldn't actually remember having breakfast.

Maybe you're hungry, Toots. I could use a few biscuits, some of those nice crunchy ones that keep my teeth bright and sharp.

Do dogs actually read our minds? *Coffee*, I thought, and dragged myself over to the coffeemaker. *Grilled cheese and tomato sandwiches.*

Hold the red stuff on mine, Toots.

My cell phone rang. It was Joe sounding breathless and sexy. "Got a reprieve from the orientation cruise! I'm at Logan, sweetheart, and I'll see you in about an hour."

"Oh, honey, how wonderful!" Now what would I do about our foray into the Hogben compound? This was going to be tricky. "I can hardly wait, but drive carefully. You know what Cape traffic is like in summer."

At once, I shook off all my fatigue as fast as a dog shakes off rain. Coffee would wait until Joe arrived. Also lunch. Grilled ham and cheese? A lovely tomato salad? and…? I ran around the house, making food plans, straightening up this and that small muddle, then upstairs for a quick reviving shower. No time now to immerse myself in a restorative thyme and jasmine bath, alas.

Maybe this unexpected homecoming would be problematic to our plans, but so what? Joe's arrival was always a heart-lifting event, even when a total surprise. I thought of Penelope hearing that beloved voice and throwing down her weaving shuttle at once. Worrying how to get rid of all those suitors loitering in the courtyard. Opening an amphora of the best wine.

Love is always worth all the trouble it causes.

CHAPTER TWENTY-SEVEN

Earth's the right place for love:
I don't know where it's likely to go better.

– Robert Frost

Joe arrived in a little red rental car and jumped out looking tanned and fit from the peaceful orientation cruise, rather than battered and bruised by some spirited confrontation with the evil forces of pollution. His smile was all I needed to lift my heart above all the worries and troubles that had sprouted up since our sojourn in Salem. When he put his arms around me, I had the distinct feeling that I had come home, although he was the one who'd been away and returned.

This was a much pleasanter and more leisurely greeting than last time, when he'd arrived amid a hail of sniper bullets. It was enough to make a gal rethink her whole *modus operandi*. Ought I to be putting our loving lives in danger by chasing after justice time after time? I resolved to give this notion a good think-through as soon as we solved the disappearance of little Molly. I hoped and prayed that she was still alive. Although every day that passed made this statistically more unlikely, in fact, in my innermost being, my center of truth, I believed Molly was alive and would be rescued.

But now was not the time for soul-searching. Joe and I were together again! We had lunch. We went to bed. Well, actually in reverse order, after shutting the bedroom door on the grumping dogs.

"My beautiful Cassandra, how I've missed you," Joe murmured. "This orientation thing with the college crew had me feeling like an old man. Your touch makes me feel young again."

"I noticed that," I said, inhaling the deliciously familiar scent of him. Love in the afternoon, when all the world is about its ordinary daytime pursuits, has a whiff of sinfulness that's particularly sweet. But eventually, we have to get up and go on with life. And lunch. At such times, a bottle of cold white wine is a good decompressor.

Later, Joe asked, "So, what have you ladies been up to while I've been away?" *The dreaded question!*

We'd finished the wine and sandwiches; I was putting on a pot of coffee (hot, black, and strong, just the thing to bring us back to the real world.) Now that Joe was here in the midst of everything that was going on, it was definitely time to *tell all*, before someone else did. As for instance, the story of our ill-fated "sight-seeing" trip over the Cape had already been the subject of one of those feisty-old-woman stories in the *Pilgrim Times*. So I described our flight over Hogben's place, making as light of it as one could when a pilot has a heart attack in mid-flight. I presented Fiona as a regular Amelia Earhart, expertly saving the day (and our necks) rather than being her usual scattered self and scaring the rest of us into fits. I even told Joe about Circe's visit to warn us of a stalker, which personally I didn't believe.

He accepted a mug of coffee and shook his head sadly.

"It doesn't seem right to have evidence of the little girl's whereabouts, so close, too! and the law not be able to follow up," he said. Not the lecture on MYOB that I'd been expecting. Well, he'd get to that later, I felt certain.

"We have *evidence*, all right, but it might be called *spectral evidence*, which hasn't been legally acceptable since the Salem witch trials," I said.

"So what are you planning to do now?" Joe looked out the window where the bird feeder hosted a pair of rosy house finches. *Feigning indifference*, I thought.

"Don't know, yet. Heather might pay a call on Eureka Hogben Saturday morning," I said casually.

"Why Saturday?"

"Because the mad preacher is going to be raising hell at St. Joseph's Cemetery where there's to be a military funeral that morning."

"And you know this, how?" The finches were long gone, but Joe's gaze was still averted.

"Because Hogben always leaks his plans to the press. Apparently he doesn't care how much trouble he gets as long as his ugly mug appears on the six o'clock news."

"Heather's 'paying a call' all by herself? Surely not."

"I believe her cousin is going with her," I said. Now it was my turn to look away.

"*And who else?*" Joe whirled around and put his hands on my arms, turning me gently but firmly to face him. It's really difficult to out-and-out lie to someone you love when you are looking into his eyes, practically nose to nose.

"I've been asked to go along. It's nothing really," I said. "You know, I have the second sight, as Conor calls it, and I might be able to 'see' where they're hiding Molly. Always supposing she's there in the Hogben compound. I'm afraid I'm responsible for that idea, too."

"Do you even think*, for one minute,* that I'm going to hang around the house here while you're getting yourself in harm's way?" he roared.

"Hogben himself will be busy elsewhere. And Heather feels that, if too many of us show up, it's going to look suspicious. Her cousin, Gray Morgan, who 's the dog officer, will lead the way, ostensibly investigating a report of animal cruelty."

"*Jesu Christos!* Dogs, too? Salivating pit bulls, I suppose?"

"American Stratford Terriers," I corrected him automatically, having been well brain-washed by Heather. "Yes, I guess there must be dogs, honey," I giggled nervously.

"Okay, then."

"How do you mean, *okay then?*" I asked.

"Okay, then, I'm going with you. The freaking cousin can deputize me into the Animal Control SWAT team," Joe said, in his brook-no-opposition voice, which was not loud but effectively chilling.

Now how was I going to explain this to Heather? "Heather may not agree," I said.

"If she wants you, she'll have to take me, too," Joe said. "We're a package deal."

"Oh, well. Gray can probably use another hand with the dog control stuff," I said.

"You do expect trouble with the dogs, then?"

"Hmmm," I said. "*Semper Paratus* and all that. The real worry-and-a-half is Molly. The compound is cluttered with a bunch of ramshackle outbuildings as well as the main house. I've *seen* Molly in one of those huts, maybe an underground room. That's what I'll be looking for."

"Good of you to share that," Joe said. "Guess I'd better bring some break-in tools, then."

"Oh, *would you*, honey?" I smiled for maybe the first time since he'd begun this third degree.

So with one thing and another, the dispute ended in kisses.

CHAPTER TWENTY-EIGHT

If it were done when 'tis done, then 'twere well
It were done quickly: if the assassination
Could trammel up the consequence, and catch
With his surcease success; that but this blow
Might be the be-all and the end-all here..

– William Shakespeare, *Macbeth*

I thought it best not to give Heather any advance warning, so I just showed up with Joe at her place on Saturday morning. She looked less than pleased about this.

"All for one, and one for all," he told her pleasantly, with his killer smile, which personally I find irresistible. She did seem mollified after he turned back his jacket to reveal a tool belt that would have done credit to a house-breaker.

"All right, then. This is Gray Morgan, the Animal Control Officer. He has a warrant to investigate a complaint of animal abuse at the Hogben compound. That's how we're going to get in."

Her cousin was younger than I'd expected, fair and sunburned, with the Morgans' patrician profile. He wore a yachting cap and Ray-Ban sunglasses, but at least his regulation gray shirt bore an Animal Control Officer embroidered shoulder patch along with a metal badge and gold nameplate.

"This is all Heather's idea," Morgan said by way of greeting. Not much family loyalty there! "As long as you're going in to serve this warrant with us, Joe, why don't you carry the air horn and citronella? I need a free hand with the Ketch-alls." Apparently, Morgan was referring to the two long rods with loops at the end that he was carrying over his shoulder like fishing poles.

Joe took the two cans and put one in each of his jacket pockets. "You're really expecting trouble with the dogs, then?" His sidelong glance at me suggested that I'd hear about this later. Another lecture!

"Never can tell about dogs. I could tell you stories...," Morgan said. "But forget that for now. Let's go and get this wild goose chase over with. Heather, you're going to owe me big time for this. And I still don't know what in hell you're really after."

My heart echoed Morgan's *let's go and get it over with*. We got back in our cars; Joe drove my RAV4, following the Mercedes. It was always a treat to be a passenger, I thought, although that pre-feminist notion was based on the assumption that driving is *a man's job*.

"It seems as if Heather didn't enlighten her cousin on the real reason for our visit to the Hogbens," Joe remarked.

"Guess not. Guess he wouldn't have agreed to be part of an illegal search, or whatever this is," I said. Truth to tell, I was beginning to feel those gremlins in my stomach.

An ill-maintained, rutty road led to the Hogben place, which was located in one of those end-of-the-world pine-woodsy areas of North Carver. The compound was completely surrounded by a stockade fence that looked illegally high, but there were no neighbors to complain. The gate, wide enough for a truck, was part of the stockade. We parked next to one another, got out of the cars, and fell back behind Morgan as he marched up to the fortress and banged on the gate with all the intrepid boldness one expects of an officer of the law and a Morgan.

Immediately there was a cacophony of barking and growling in the low register that suggested the dogs inside were big bruisers. Joe pushed a little ahead of me, which meant that I was now bringing up the rear.

A harsh voice was heard ordering the pack to "shut up, you bastards," and the gate opened a crack, still held together by a thick chain. The woman who peered out at us with mean, beady eyes was squat and broad, as muscular as a gladiator. Her wasp nest of gray hair put me in mind of Marjorie Main.

"What in hell do you lot want?" she snarled. I looked again and saw that she was holding a baseball bat down by the side of her overalls. "If you're selling something, we're not buying it, so shove off."

Morgan held out his warrant where Eureka Hogben could read it.

She did read it. "What the fuck? *Animal abuse, my ass!* Don't you know that this place here is church property, and you sonsobitches are trespassing on a sanctuary? So you take this piece of crap and shove it where the sun don't shine, Sonny."

Having had her say, Eureka began to push the gate closed again. Morgan pushed against her, but she was stronger. Seeing the impasse, Joe stepped around Heather to give Morgan a hand. Between them, they managed to thrust back the gate until the chain pulled free of the wooden post.

When we'd succeeded in bulling our way into the compound, I expecting Eureka to take a swing at us, but instead she stepped back with a Madame Defarge smile and opened the door to a giant kennel crate that faced into the dirt-floor courtyard of the compound. Three barking, growling. salivating dogs surged forward.

It could have been a scene from the Coliseum. Only dogs not lions, and Wiccans not Christians. All three animals appeared to be mixed-breeds, possibly some combination of hounds, huskies, and shepherds, with the aggressive characteristics of each.

Joe had taken out the air horn and citronella spray, and he now proceeded to use both alternatively. The intense noise of the air horn only served to excite the dogs more, but the citronella spray, when it hit a target, caused that startled dog to back up and shake his head momentarily.

I stood behind Joe and glanced Heather's way to see how she was fending off the onslaught. She'd moved over next to Eureka and was simply standing her ground, eyes averted so as not to challenge the attackers, or maybe she was praying. Meanwhile Morgan danced around trying to catch one of the dogs in a Ketch-all, sort of like trying to catch a giant butterfly in a net. When he succeeded in snaring one dog, he handed the pole to Heather and went after a second.

Eureka stood with her arms folded, smirking at the mayhem. "Any one of my dogs look abused to you, Deputy Dipshit?" In truth, they were lean and mean, possibly hungry, but not emaciated, and appeared unmarked and unfazed.

One of Fiona's proverbs sprang to mind...*It's never or now, my dears*. In the midst of the melee, I made myself look around at the veritable shanty town of outbuildings. I was searching for the shed I'd seen in my vision, built above another room, one that was hidden below ground level. When I spotted it on the left side of the main house, I took advantage of the noise and confusion to sidle in that direction. I thought no one would notice me.

But the third dog, dancing around still free, came after me full tilt, snarling.

There was a barrel standing by the shed, and I leaped up on it, pretty surprised that I had a jump like that in me. But it appeared that the attack dog could jump even higher. He leaped for my ankle. Hastily, I pulled that foot away from his sharp teeth. He went for the other ankle. I lifted that one out of his reach. One foot, other foot: a dance of desperation.

"What the fuck do you think you're doing?" Eureka yelled at me, as if springing onto a rickety barrel to twirl the light fantastic was my intention.

"Call off that damned hound," Joe demanded, "or I'm calling the cops." He strode in my direction with a hammer in one hand and his cell phone in the other. "Stay right where you are, Cass. I'm coming."

Eureka laughed and slapped her side with the hand that wasn't holding a baseball bat.

Heather let go of her Ketch-all pole, and her prisoner ran off dragging the thing. Then she blew a piercing note on a whistle hanging around her neck. All the dogs swiveled around in her direction, including the one with whom Morgan was still struggling. She reached into the pocket of her safari jacket and pulled out a handful of mini frankfurters which she threw widely over the ground between us.

"Don't you dare strike that poor creature, Joe!" she ordered. But she could have saved her breath. All three dogs had dropped their attack mode and were rooting about in the dirt for the delectable hot dogs. Heather had a second handful at the ready. "Better the carrot than the stick," she said. "Dogs are noble creatures, you know."

The noble creatures were actively competing with each other for the fast-disappearing treats. The growling and snapping began to have a vicious ring to it. Joe swooped me down off the barrel and stood in front of me, still holding the hammer at the ready.

Heather tossed out the second handful of hot dogs, buying us some time.

"Just a minute, honey," I whispered. "I need to duck in here and see..." I slunk into the interior of the shed, feeling around the walls and the floor for a door. I could find nothing, but there was another barrel standing in the corner. I tried to shove it aside but it was too heavy for me.

"Help me move this thing, Joe," I urged. "Hurry, honey."

Between the two of us, we were able to slide it to one side. Underneath was a trap door, padlocked. "Open it! Can you open it?" I cried. Then I banged on the door itself. "Molly, are you in there?"

There was no answer, but it didn't matter. I *knew* Molly had been in that underground room. *But she was not there now.* She'd been moved to another hidey-hole in the compound, because Hogben the sorcerer was too smart for us. The trouble was, I didn't know if all these impressions I was receiving were wild ideas or had actually happened. The veil between the real and the imagined is thinner for me than for most people.

But Joe had learned to believe in me even when I appeared to be acting crazy. Without a second thought, he took a wrench out of his tool belt and attempted to break the padlock. At least I would be able to see if the room had been occupied. It was not happening, though. Maybe he didn't have the right tools for a lock this heavy-duty.

As Joe banged and cursed, I became aware of a commotion in the yard where we had left Heather, Morgan, and the indefatigable Eureka. And I heard a voice that didn't belong to any of them.

"Uh-oh, Joe. I think Willie Hogben has returned."

"Okay, I'm not having much joy with this padlock anyway, and I don't want us to get arrested." With one mighty heave, Joe pushed the barrel back in place, grabbed my hand, and pulled me back toward the others, where a vociferous argument was in progress, accompanied by a chorus of barking canines.

Hogben stood at the open gate, waving his Bible and his staff. "Out, out, you unholy minions of Lucifer! I know your faces! The Witches of Plymouth! Fornicators and lesbians! *Thou shalt not suffer a witch to live.*" And more rabid invective of that nature. At one point, the madman seemed actually to be frothing at the mouth. Flecks of foam appeared on his beard.

The three "nieces" who had accompanied him to the cemetery protest at St. Joseph's scurried into the main house, heads down, their faces obscured by those prairie bonnets. The waves of fear emanating from the girls were palpable. What *was* with them? I wondered. They didn't seem to be prisoners of the Hogbens or in any way unwilling to be here, unlike my vision of Molly.

Then it came to me. *Runaways.* Those girls were in hiding here! I would get to Stone with that notion later.

"We've been executing a legal warrant, sir," Morgan said, holding the paper up in front of the raving preacher. "A complaint of animal abuse. We've checked it out, everything seems to be in order, so we'll be on our way. If you'll just step aside, sir."

The raving preacher grabbed the warrant from Morgan's hands, tore it across and across again, threw the pieces onto the dirt, and banged it repeatedly with the end of his staff. "You don't fool me, you imp of Satan. These wicked, ugly women are consorts of the devil, and you are his spawn," he screeched into Morgan's face. He waved the staff in front of his chest horizontally, as if to bar us from leaving.

"Hey, who are you calling ugly, you creep!" Heather's cool demeanor was deserting her, finally. "Have you had a good look at your helpmeet lately?"

We were on even more dangerous territory now! Eureka raised her baseball bat and headed for Heather with a nasty gleam in her mean little eyes. Heather pulled a can of something out of her safari jacket. It was pepper spray! Something she would never have used on a dog but she did not hesitate to brandish in front of Eureka.

I jumped behind Eureka and grabbed for the baseball bat. Although several inches shorter than me, she was, however, stronger, so I sort of hung on it and was dragged forward. "No, no, Heather," I yelled around Eureka's broad flannel-shirted back. "Let's just get out of here before someone calls the cops!"

"That would be me, Cass." Joe stepped up to Morgan's side, holding up his cell phone. "Move aside, you pious jerk, or I'm calling for back-up. You don't want the Carver cops swarming in here, do you?"

For a moment, I considered that possibility. But, no, the officers still couldn't legally search this place as it needed to be searched. We'd have to find another way to get to Molly.

So we left the Hogben compound in some disorder and totally frustrated.

"Tails between our legs," Heather muttered. "How I would have loved to spray that Ma Barker with a shot of eye-weeper! Oh well, better part of wisdom and all that. Come to my place later and we'll talk."

Back in our car, Joe said, "That damned preacher is a menace and a pervert. It wouldn't surprise me at all if he was keeping the little girl hidden under that trapdoor. If the cops can't do it, we've got to find a way to get her out."

"We were too late, Joe. As soon as you started banging on that padlock, I knew Molly was gone. Not only because my sixth sense told me, but also because if she'd been there, she would have cried out. Hogben has moved Molly elsewhere.. If he hadn't returned right then, we might have…"

"Hogben hasn't seen the last of us," Joe muttered. "We'll find a way…"

Clearly, Joe was getting the same vibes as I, finally. And he was angry! This was getting as serious to him as an ocean-polluter or rain-forest destroyer. *Good!*

CHAPTER TWENTY-NINE

Stone walls do not a prison make,
Nor iron bars a cage:
Minds innocent and quiet take
That for a hermitage.

– Richard Lovelace

We arrived home to the usual aggrieved canine chorus, but I was too depressed to care and left Joe to dispense comfort and Milkbones. I could hardly wait to take a lovely soothing chamomile and lavender bath to get the smell of the Hogben compound off my skin and the evil vibrations of the place off my mind. More than ever, I was convinced that the Hogbens were hiding Molly, and I was despondent over our failure to bring off a legal search. In grave need of that emergency immersion, I was literally throwing off my clothes all the way to the bathtub (a procedure that Joe eyed with interest.)

"Oh, never mind that," I told him sharply. "Just bring me a medicinal whiskey, will you? Whatever you have in that parson's cabinet will be fine."

"Certainly. And will you be wanting company in the tub, madam?" I shot him a dark look, and he hastened to fill the drink order. But just as I sank into the heavenly scented hot water, my cell phone rang. Isn't that always the way?

"Oh, hi, Dee. I'm so tired and rattled at the moment. I'll call back in a little while, okay? Sorry to say, we didn't find Molly."

"I'm not calling for that!" she said with a sob in her voice. "Turn on the TV this minute. Molly's parents are about to make a plea for her return, the poor things. Oh, my heart is broken! I already assumed you didn't manage to get the place searched and find Molly, or that would have been on the news instead."

"You assume right, despite our best efforts. We're all meeting at Heather's this afternoon around three. "

"Okay, then. Later." She punched me out immediately, so as not to miss the Larssons, I assumed.

Joe came in with my drink, a generous one, and said, "I just turned on the news, and Molly's parents are about to give a statement. I'm recording it."

"Oh, good. Thanks, honey. Give me fifteen minutes and I'll be just like new. Maybe."

When I watched the recorded broadcast, wrapped in a bath towel, still sipping whiskey, I thought how right Deidre was. It was a heartbreaker. Bert and Jean Larsson leaned together, mingling their tears, and were nearly inarticulate in their grief and worry. The search had broadened far beyond the camp grounds without finding any trace of the girl; police were now treating the case as a possible abduction and were consulting the FBI. The Larssons pleaded with the abductor to return their daughter to her loving home. The reporter oozed sympathy, while wringing the last possible sob out of Jean Larsson. The Plymouth County Prosecutor Paul Kowalski and Chief of Police Walter Standeven each said a few words about law enforcement's continued efforts to find Molly and the need for anyone with information about the girl's whereabouts to call the police tipline. Its phone number ran across in a continual loop at the bottom of the screen.

My cell rang. It was Deidre again. "Why can't I call in an anonymous tip?" she demanded.

"Last resort, Dee" I said firmly. "How will you explain yourself if the call is traced? Let's see if we can come up with something better this afternoon. I have some ideas..."

"No offense, Cass, but so far your ideas have led us down the up staircase."

"A witch is not without honor except in her own circle," I said. "See you at Heather's."

Over BLATs (which are BLTs with sliced avocado), I asked Joe if he wanted to join our war council, and was grateful that he declined. "But I definitely need to be informed of your next wild escapade, sweetheart. No more going it alone."

An easy promise, when I had only a few vague notions of what we could do next.

೧൭

We met in Heather's conservatory among the potted palms, hibiscus, and abandoned chew toys. The French doors were open to the Cape breezes and Heather's pack of rescues snuffling on the other side of the screens or lolling under shade trees. Maxwell glided in silently with a tray of mimosas and a pitcher of iced tea.

Heather rattled on about the morning's adventure just as if Maxwell weren't there, a tribute to his perfect butler's invisibility. Phillipa and I rather hung back on commenting until he had wafted back to the kitchen.

"Here's what I think about those Hogben girls," I interrupted as soon as Maxwell had departed. "That trio of so-called nieces, who don't seem to be at all anxious to escape the Hogben clutches, it came to me that they might be runaways. And I also think, Phil, that we should ask Stone to run a check on Eureka's past history, just as he did on the preacher. I have a feeling that she may be a link to the girls' histories. Maybe he'll uncover something we can work with. If, for instance, one of those girls is a missing person in West Virginia, that could call for a new investigation of the compound." Conscious of having imbibed a healthy slug of whiskey before lunch, I waved away the mimosa and poured myself a glass of iced tea.

Phillipa sighed. "Okay, I'll ask him. That's something I think he could do without coming to grief over his psychic friends."

"I have another plan," Deidre said. "What if we phone in a fire alarm!"

Phillipa sighed again. "Dee, the penalty for a false fire report is one year in jail or a $500 fine. And besides, what kind of scandal would that be for a firefighter's widow?"

"I didn't mean I would call *personally*." Deidre lowered her gaze to the embroidery on her lap, a green pillow into which she was stitching the motto: *Leprechauns Are Our Friends*. "I thought Cass or Heather…"

Meanwhile, Fiona was busy browsing with the smart phone she'd pulled out of her reticule. "I think I can run a prelim on Eureka Hogben right now," she said. "And nix on the false alarm, Dee. Our whole karma this summer has been beset by the issue of false versus true, and we don't want to mess with karma. *This above all: to thine own karma pay heed …*"

Phillipa glanced at me and raised an eyebrow. "The fractured bard..."she murmured.

"Here's why I have hope that Molly is alive," Deidre said, still busily stitching. "Recently, you may remember, the victims who've caught our attention have appeared to me as ghosts. Ugh!" The sharp little needle missed the pillow and drew a bright drop of blood from Deidre's finger.

Almost without looking, Fiona took a band-aid out of her reticule. "Here, dearie. You don't want to stain that pretty creation."

"And Molly has not," Deidre continued as she applied the band-aid to her finger. "I don't enjoy seeing dead people, but I suppose if some waif trailing wisps in ectoplasm isn't peering in my window, we can take that as a good sign."

"I, too, don't believe Molly has been harmed, except psychically. The trauma of being held prisoner by that Bible-thumping..."

"...sorcerer," Fiona finished my sentence for me. "Whatever we do, we have to get past his protective wall. Well, we did do that spell...maybe it's crumbling at last. The wall, I mean."

"I wonder if we should bring Patty Peacedale into this," I said.

"Are you crazy, or what?" Phillipa protested. "Her husband, the very reverend, will have us in stocks."

"Here's something," Fiona said, still busily scrolling through options. "A preacher named William Hogg was involved in a scandal at the Epiphany Evangelical church in a West Virginia town also called Epiphany. Funds for a new roof disappeared and so did Hogg and his wife, Shirley."

"Ha ha! Imagine that lady wrestler with a name like *Shirley!*" Heather scoffed. "I suppose it's possible for a couple to reinvent themselves and make a complete new start in another state."

Just as Heather made that pronouncement, Elsa had come into the conservatory with a tray of miniature cream puffs. She looked up with a startled expression, tripped over a well-chewed shin bone, and upset the tray. The cream puffs slid to the floor amid a confusion of apologies.

"You're talking about the Hoggs, of course," Phillipa said loudly. "From West Virginia."

"Yes," I agreed, "the preacher and his wife Shirley."

"Oh please don't trouble about that mess," Heather told Elsa. "I'll just open the door and let the doggies in."

"There are more in the kitchen, madam," Elsa said. "I'll fetch another tray."

She skittered out while Heather was still telling her "not for Goddess' sake to call her *madam*. It sounds like we're all in a Noel Coward play." She opened the French doors, and a pack of seven or eight dogs flooded into the conservatory and made short work of the mess on the floor.

"Oh, do be quiet, Cass," Heather said, although I hadn't said a word. "Normally, I would never feed people crap to healthy, well-maintained canines, but this is an emergency. We don't want my excellent housekeeper to lose face."

"It's so hard to find good help these days," Phillipa said softly. I gave her a look, meaning, *this is no time to kid around.* Actually, I was proud of her quick-witted save. I thought we'd both made it clear enough that the Maxwells were not on the griddle here.

"So where were we?" Deidre got back to the search at hand.

"Well, there's no photo of the couple, alas," Fiona said. "But this is interesting. According to this report in the

Wheeling News-Register, Shirley Hogg ran a shelter for homeless teen-age girls whom she and Pastor Hogg had rescued from the streets of Wheeling, a cause to which several businesses were donating. The Shelter was called the Mary Magdalene. Its bank account also went missing, along with several of the homeless girls. Okay, ladies, I think we have something here."

"You're always and ever our best finder," Heather crowed. "No offense to Stone."

Maxwell came in quietly and laid another tray of cream puffs on the coffee table, and then shooed the dogs back out, since they had cleaned up all evidence of the cream puffs and were now polishing the floor.

We were silent for awhile, mentally reviewing our options.

"I'll tell Stone what Fiona has found," Phillipa said. "But…"

"…chasing down these runaways through Missing Persons isn't going to get us to Molly," Deidre finished the sentence.

"But…as I was going to say…" Phillipa resumed. "if Stone can compare a news photo of Willie Hogben picketing a local funeral with a photo of William Hogg in West Virginia, if such a photo exists, and there's a good resemblance, there must also be a West Virginia warrant for Hogg's embezzlement. The Plymouth police can go in there and arrest the lot of them. Poor girls, though. I wonder what will become of them."

"Oh, good," I said. "Much better to have the police handle this. I don't relish another encounter with the formidable Hogbens."

"I'll be in touch as soon as Stone has some news for us." Phillipa was already on her way out the door. "Fiona, send that link to my computer. I do want to dazzle him with your prowess. This time he won't be able to throw his hands up in the air over our psychic whim-whams."

Driving home, I thought how pleased Joe would be if the police took over our crazed investigation. And I wondered about those girls. Why had they stayed with the depraved preacher?

ᚖ

It was all true, what Fiona had unearthed. When Stone sent a photo of Willie Hogben to the West Virginia police, they identified him as William Hogg, but that was the end of the good news. The preacher was no longer wanted for embezzlement in his home town of Epiphany. The missing funds had been returned, and the Epiphany Evangelical Church had dropped all charges. In fact, Hogben's identity had come as no surprise. He'd been on the national news once or twice, picketing military funerals, and some of his former parishioners had recognized him. Applauded him, in fact. Accepted the return of their roof money, with interest, in good faith. Offered Hogg a.k.a. Hogben the ministry of their church if he cared to return. Admired the way he had achieved a reputation and donations from some ultra-conservatives who shared his anti-gay, pro-gun sentiments.

Impasse!

As far as the Mary Magdalene girls were concerned, no one knew what had happened to them, and, apparently, no one cared. Possibly the girls had absconded with the funds and gone back to the streets of Wheeling.

"Holy Mother!" Deidre exclaimed when we gathered at Phillipa's long marble kitchen table to commiserate…and eat, course. "That Hogben pervert has foiled us at every turn. What in Hades are we going to do now?"

"*Nothing illegal*," Phillipa said firmly, bringing forth a huge platter of Cocque Monsieur and Monte Cristo sandwiches along with a delectable tossed herb salad. "I don't care if it's immoral or fattening."

"I have an idea that's none of those." Fiona helped herself to a sizzling sandwich. "Much as I am loathe to admit it, this Hogben is too powerful for me. So far. *Time wounds all heels.* Meanwhile, here's another thought. Let's dodge around the Hogbens and do a calling to the girls. Maybe we can lure one of them to split from the compound."

"Oh, champion!" Deidre crowed. "Just the thing. Let's try that, whatever it is. Today, Now. I mean, right after lunch."

"What exactly is a calling, Fiona?" I asked. "Do we need anything?"

"Not this time," Fiona said. "This will be a visualizing, chanting, and humming spell."

"I never heard of that one," Heather said, pouring Kendall-Jackson chardonnay all around. "But I'm feeling inspired all ready."

"Neither did I," Fiona said. "I just made it up. *Where there's a witch, there's a way.* Phil, do you think you could improvise a chant?"

Phillipa gazed toward her kitchen "picture" window and the perfect herb planters underneath it, and thought for few moments. We honored her creative coma with silence while we demolished her savory sandwiches. Except for Fiona who was already humming.

"What we need is a weak link, a likely target, the girl who most dreams of running away from that horrid place," Deidre said. "Cass, turn on that inner eye and see if you can get a glimpse of our easiest subject."

"You know I don't like to do this kind of thing *on demand*. And I have no idea what the girls look like under those wigs and bonnets," I said uncertainly. "Oh, well. I guess I'd rather try this than risk another confrontation."

Now it was my turn to court a trance, which I did by fixing my attention on the shining copper pans hanging on an oval wrought-iron ring above the table. I allowed their light to reflect into my eyes. Soon that familiar floating feeling began to loosen me from the here and now, like an escaped helium balloon.

Still...nothing.

Except maybe one of the girls, the oldest one...

I began to sense her dream of getting away from her indenture to the Hogbens. Underneath those opaque sunglasses, her eyes were a luminous brown, her skin golden. Her hair under the blonde wig was cut as short as a boy's. Then I saw the scars on her arms and back. She'd had trouble all her life. It was her stepfather she ran away from. Got picked up by Shirley Hogg on the streets of Wheeling. *Out of the frying pan*, into the clutches of the preacher. Lately she'd begun to feel hopeless and depressed. Sometimes she despaired of finding a way out of her holy prison.

I shook myself free of that disturbing vision. *Enough already!*

"Okay, there's someone." I described the girl in my vision. "I'll keep her in my mind's eye. It's the best I can do," I said.

Fiona passed me her smelling salts, but I waved them away. This time, I'd pulled back from the vision before I was actually faint. "Just give me a cup of black coffee."

Deidre investigated Phillipa's complicated coffee machine, then looked around helplessly. Heather strode over, eyed the thing, and punched a few buttons.

Phillipa was still deep into her poetic mode. *"In your heart, a yearning to be free once more...Let the Goddess guide you through her moonlit door,"* she recited.

"All right!" Deidre said.

"Why do you think those girls followed the Hoggs when they absconded with the church funds?" Heather wondered.

"It's what I said, sorcery," Fiona said. "Maybe even sexual sorcery. If one girl's freeing herself, that's a miracle."

"I'll bet they're all underage, too," Phillipa muttered darkly. "Oh, this is going to be so satisfying!" She took over the coffee-making and soon brought a fresh pot to the table. I drank a scalding cup thankfully.

"Let's hold hands around the table," Fiona said, and we did.

Heather brought forth a "midnight moonlight" candle (darkest purple chased with silver) she just happened to have in her Susan Nichole vegan handbag. As she lit it, she invoked Hecate, in her incarnation as keeper of crossroads and entrance-ways, as formidable a goddess as one could wish to organize an escape. We chanted Phillipa's rhyme the usual thirteen times, then Fiona began humming and we joined her, for Goddess knows how long.

Finally, Deidre said, "How will we know when our target has hopped the fence?"

"Lurking," Heather said. "One of us will have to lurk around the place until she bolts. I'll take the first watch."

I groaned. "Okay, what time shall I spell you?"

CHAPTER THIRTY

The best laid schemes o' mice and men
Gang aft agley.

– Robert Burns

"Listen, Joe, here's the thing," I confessed at dinner. "I've got to drive over to Carver about midnight."

He looked up at me with a chilly gleam in his Aegean blue eyes that were normally so warm and approving. "Okay, lay it on me. You're going to the Hogben compound, aren't you? This is something Heather has organized, right? Tell me it isn't a break-in! I remember you said that she used to organize break-ins to animal testing labs."

"It isn't a break-in," I said. It occurred to me then that a married woman is not exactly free to pursue her own devices and desires without tedious explanations. *Bummer.* Then I had to shake my hands under the table to rid myself of that negative disloyal thought.

Hey, Toots, how about shaking a little lamb my way. Scruffy nosed my knee affectionately.

My way! My way!

I tore off two shreds of meat from the chop on my plate and handed them out to the two dogs nested around my feet.

"Now be quiet," I admonished.

Joe raised his eyebrows and assumed a hurt expression.

"I'm talking to the dogs, as you well know," I said. "It's not what you think, over at Hogbens'. Heather's only keeping watch to rescue an escaped girl. One of those so-called nieces. And I promised to take over the next shift. You don't even have to go with me. In fact, it might be better if…"

"Out of the question! *Wither thou goest, I go*, sweetheart. But what makes you think that one of the Hogben nieces is going to fly the coop tonight?"

"I *feel* that one of the girls is ready to run."

"You mean you *see* her?"

I sighed. It was so difficult to explain. "What happens when you close your eyes, Joe?"

"It's dark."

"Right. But sometimes, for me, a kind of window opens in that darkness, and I see a picture, or more likely, a film. Often it only lasts for a moment, sometimes in silhouette, or limited color. I have to think about what I see *in words* that very instant, or it's lost to me. But, over time, I've learned never to discount those visions. Imagine, honey, if you could see an accident happen in time to swerve or whatever you have to do to avoid it. That's something you don't mess with."

"Has that happened to you? You saved yourself or others?"

"Yup. If the Captain of the Titanic had seen that iceberg…"

"It takes a cruise ship at least one nautical mile to turn to another direction, sweetheart. Still, a handy talent. But you're saying that you believe the future isn't fixed?"

"Nothing is fixed, past or present, as you know very well from reading all those books about the new physics. 'Reality is merely an illusion,' according to your hero, Einstein."

He grinned sheepishly. "True. Fascinating stuff, but I don't always apply it to everyday life. Maybe I should. Anyway, back to the madness at hand. How do you know the girl is making a break for it *tonight?*"

"We can't be sure. But we did a little *thing* when I was over to Phil's for lunch today. *We called her.*"

I saw that Joe wanted to ask more questions but decided against it. *For now.* Instead, he got up and cleared the table, while I stacked dishes in the dishwasher. And he put on a second pot of coffee.

He said, "This escapade of Heather's reminds me of the night we met. Do you remember that she'd staged an all-night vigil to save those nesting eagles? Some of the local trigger-happy Neanderthals wanted to shoot them before they could carry away small children. So stupid. I'm sure the eagles would find ducks or bluefish much tastier."

"What a comfort. Of course, I remember. Heather had contacted every conceivable environmental vigilante to help us, including Greenpeace, since your ship was conveniently moored in Plymouth Harbor. And there you were! We met. We talked only for a few minutes. And then you were assigned to drive around Jenkins' woods all night."

"Yes. But I decided to stop at your house. For coffee. And also because you're a beautiful woman who obviously had bewitched me."

I smiled. *He'd never really know.* "And the rest, as they say, is…not history…*legend* is a better word."

Well, of course this conversation ended in kisses, but we did manage to get ourselves to Carver and relieve Heather.

"Not a creature is stirring…" she said. "Dee promised to come by at about four. She said Conor's been getting up *early-early* to set up for a series of dawnscapes on Cape Cod so it

would be no problem. Actually, she sounded a little down
in the dumps. I wonder how the romance is going with the
fey Traveler? A tad unreliable for a practical gal like Dee,
I fear. *Anyway*, Phil will take over from Dee in the late
morning. We're thinking we won't ask Fiona to take a shift,
considering the erratic way she zooms around in that ancient
blue bomber. And she doesn't have a regular nanny like Dee."

Thus worried and briefed, we took up our watch, parked
off the road under overhanging tree branches, barely within
sight of the compound. We opened the car windows to allow
the caressing night breeze to take over for the air conditioning
system. The sliver of new moon did not give enough light
to betray our hiding place. From time to time, I may have
dozed a little, my head on Joe's shoulder. Not him, however.
Joe stayed alert, sipping black coffee from the thermos we'd
brought with us. Probably some part of his mariner training
where they keel-haul the sluggard who nods off when he's
supposed to be watching for icebergs.

Sure enough, Deidre pulled up behind us at four-fifteen.
We gave her our report, which was "nothing to report," and
drove home to collapse thankfully on our bed.

Although Scruffy's at the age where he enjoys sleeping in,
Raffles is always up with the birds, rejoicing the way dogs do
in the thrill of another glorious day. I pretended not to hear
when Joe let the two of them out for a run, then staggered
back to bed.

So it went, taking turns for three days, until our
changing-of-the-guard schedule was beginning to seem like
some sleep-deprivation torture. Bettikins, Deidre's nanny,
was starting to rebel at the odd hours, and her shop assistant
Hal wanted to go on the vacation he'd been promised.
Phillipa blamed our weird routine for the repeated failure of

her sour dough starter. Even good-natured Dick Devlin was grumbling, although well looked after by the Kitcheners. So with one thing and another, we finally did ask Fiona to take one evening's watch, we were that desperate.

And that, of course, was the escape window when Aretha Jones, the Jamaican girl who'd been in Hogben's custody, got a chance to slip out of the compound just after dusk turned to dark. Without her blonde wig, bonnet, and pastel prairie dress, in a hooded sweatshirt and jeans, Aretha was nearly invisible as she tried to quietly close the compound gate. But the gate was big and old; it squeaked, rattled, and bumped. One of the Hogben dogs barked a warning, and soon all of them were raising a ruckus.

Aretha almost ran past Fiona's Lincoln town car. Baby blue is not the most discreet of colors for a getaway vehicle, but maybe Fiona had cast her invisibility glamour around the car as well as herself, because Aretha didn't seem to notice her. Hastily, Fiona opened the door and reached out, speaking quietly to the fleeing girl.

"Whatever did you say to her?" Phillipa had to know.

"I said, *Come with me, child. I'm here to help you and take care of you.* And I took her hand. Because touch conveys so much more than words, don't you think? If I were merely some social services person on the prowl, Aretha would have known…and run."

"What happened when the dogs gave the alarm?" Deidre asked.

We had gathered at Fiona's house to hear all about the night's adventures. Phillipa was waiting for Aretha to wake up, so that she could question her about what was really going on in that compound, and, of course, if Molly was a prisoner there. We needed something substantial to bring to

Stone. But Fiona wanted to give the girl a chance to sleep and recoup.

"One glimpse of a badge and Aretha will just run away again," Fiona had said. "She's lost trust in everyone. Social workers, religious do-gooders, runaway services, helpful strangers, even the police...that girl has been betrayed by everyone."

"What about St. Rita's?" I suggested. My friend ex-nun Serena Dove ran a sanctuary for abused women in an abandoned convent.

"Maybe later. Right now, I fear the religious trappings would panic the girl. So anyway, after the dogs got all riled up, the compound's floodlight came on in a blaze like daylight. Lit up the surroundings, too. That place is guarded like a prison. Then, before I could even get the car turned around, Hogben was standing in front of it! Looking like a wild man, Jehovah ready to smite the sinners!"

"So...what did you do? Drove over him, I hope!" Heather demanded.

"He banged on my windshield with that staff of his. Cracked it, too. Aretha screamed and tried to get out of the car. I had to hold onto her with one hand. Jumping Juno! There was only one thing to do..."

"What? What?" we chorused.

"I reasoned with him."

"Oh come on, Fiona! Reasoned?" I protested.

"Well, I did take out my new Glock 19, which I just happened to have in my reticule and got him in my sights. And I'm happy to report that the pastor seemed to see the light. At any rate, he jumped into the shadows, and I took the opportunity to race out of there. We got away."

"*Your new Glock 19!*" Philliipa screamed.

"Now don't get yourself excited, Phil. It's perfectly legal, dear. Class A registration. Not so difficult to procure, after all. I gave Stone as a reference, by the way," Fiona said. "It's a 9 millimeter. Simple design. Easy to hold. One of the 10 top handguns preferred by ladies. Perhaps you should all…"

"But you're required to keep a handgun in a lock box," Phillipa interrupted.

"And so I do, usually. Anyway, I brought the girl back here, gave her a cup of Cass's Calm Child Tea with a few milk lunch crackers, and tucked her into my guest bedroom."

"The one with the magical animals painted on the wall?" Deidre asked, keeping her attention (and her smirk) directed to the pillow she was embroidering, *I believe in faeries*.

"Yes, of course. The same as Laura Belle's room. I thought it best to let Aretha rest and gain back her strength before asking her any questions. But she did let me know that she'd had a troubled time. So I simply assured her that she would be safe here, and that no one would take her away. And I plan to see that no one does, Phil."

Phillipa had her cell phone in hand and was already calling Stone. She took it into the entry and had an earnest conversation, not entirely audible. Then she came back into the living room. "Stone will be here in a few minutes. Alone," she said.

Before Fiona could make a fuss, the girl herself came bounding down the stairs, stopped short, and looked startled to find a circle of concerned faces.

"Holy shit! I woke up, and there were spiders crawling on the bedroom wall. But it was only some freaking painted border," she exclaimed.

"It's all right, dear. Spiders are comforting and inspiring spirits, especially to us Scots." Fiona said. "These are my friends, and we're only interested in your welfare. And there's a very kind gentleman on his way here to talk to you. I want you to tell him what's been going on with you and the other girls at the compound."

"Yeah? Well, thanks a lot for the bed, but I'm splitting from this nuthouse *right now*," Aretha said. "I'm not about to be dumped in some fucking foster home again. And I've had enough already of 'kind gentlemen' jumping on my bones."

Fiona talked soothingly to the girl, promising that she personally would deal with social services, and Phillipa more or less barred the front door by standing in it, arms akimbo.

Aretha took in her situation with a sharp glance and backed into the kitchen. Then, before we could stop her, she jumped out the back door and was gone in a flash. Deidre and Heather ran out after her.

Fiona's cottage, although located on a side street, with a tiny back yard and a glimpse of the ocean, is still part of Plymouth center. Aretha soon disappeared from view among the shops and restaurants of the town's main street. Deidre returned a few minutes later with exclamations of frustration. "Heather's going to keep searching," she said. "But I want to talk to Stone myself."

"Oh dear, I'm afraid we frightened the girl. Where in the world will she go now?" Fiona moaned.

"I guess we're back to square one," I said.

"Now what am I going to tell Stone!" Phillipa exclaimed. "We got our hands on the perfect witness, and we lost her."

"She won't have any money for a bus," Fiona said. "Whatever will she do?"

"She'll thumb a ride to Goddess-knows-where, of course. She must have assimilated some street savvy before the

Hogbens grabbed her," I said. "Now what's our best next move?"

That burning question remained unanswered, because Stone arrived soon after. We graciously allowed Phillipa to explain matters to him, and, to his credit, he remained calm, merely sighing heavily and running his fingers through the fine brown hair that never stayed in place. "Did she tell you anything at all, Fiona?" he asked.

"Yes, last night, when she'd had her tea and calmed down a bit." With this, Fiona had all our attention. What else had she learned from the girl?

"Tell me everything she said," Stone said quietly.

"The girl told me that she and the others were all required to be the pastor's 'brides,' and his wife encouraged this. Aretha found Hogben and his Bible-babble disgusting, so she's been just waiting for a chance to run away. Last night was her first opportunity. Apparently Hogben forgot to padlock the gate for once. Aretha thought that was because he and Eureka had been hitting the whiskey bottle pretty hard all afternoon."

"What's the girl's last name, and how old is she, if you know?" Stone began making a few notes on his phone.

"Jones. Aretha Jones. She said she's sixteen, but she looked more like fourteen to me. She ran away from home three years ago, so there may be a missing persons report," Fiona said.

"Holy Mother!" Deidre exclaimed. "Now, Stone, I don't care how you do it, but you've just got to get in there and look for Molly. And get the other girls out of there, too."

"Yes," Stone said, to our infinite relief. "I have an idea, but I want you ladies to stay clear of the Hogben place. Do you promise?"

We promised, as we had done so many times before. Stone gave us a long, skeptical look, moving from face to face, but he seemed mollified when his gaze reached his wife, whose dazzling smile was the clincher. "Okay," he said. "I'm trusting you to keep your word. Wiccan honor!"

I wished he hadn't put it like that.

"As long as you really pull it off," Heather muttered. She'd come back toward the end of our conversation, breathless, and was lying prone on the floor in recovery mode. Now she jumped up, her strength apparently restored in her usual vigorous way. "Otherwise, I'm going get myself a truck and *batter down that wall.*"

"What's that?" Stone's head snapped around toward Heather.

"Heather just wants to *leave the matter to you after all,*" Phillipa explained. "What's your plan, darling?"

"It's called exigent circumstances." Stone was already on his way out when he offered this tidbit.

Phillipa smiled. "Of course. *Phone me* as soon as you know anything." She had to holler after him as he was already racing to his car, calling his partner Billy Mann to meet him at Hogbens'.

"What in Hades are exigent circumstances?" Deidre asked after Stone had run out the door.

"You'll be glad to know that Stone doesn't want to wait long enough to wring a warrant out of some judge on evidence from a girl who can no longer be questioned" Phil said. "The only other way to penetrate that fortress is if he has good reason to believe that someone inside is in imminent danger. That makes it okay to break in. The law does allow for such situations. And I believe he and his partner will hear a scream or see some damsel in distress hanging out the window, something of that nature."

"Super!" Heather said.

"It's about time," Deidre added.

"We might as well go home, then, and await developments," I said, and they all agreed. Phillipa would call us if and when there was news.

∾

"The Hogbens flew the coop last night, and there's no sign of Molly." Phillipa's report was the ultimate frustration, but there was at least a glimmer of good news. "The other two girls were still on the premises, though, scrounging up some lunch for themselves, if you can believe it. They looked fairly emaciated, Stone said. I doubt that they were being fed right, or even fed."

"Never mind the nutrition report, Phil. What did the girls *say*."

"At least Stone was able to question them and establish that what Aretha told Fiona was true, damn him. *Brides of Jehovah*. They're both under age, too. But they seem to know nothing about Molly. They did say, however, that Hogben was keeping someone hidden in the 'bunker' and talking about taking on another bride 'when the time was right.' Stone and Billy searched the place thoroughly, of course, and they found that shed you told him about, the one with the cellar room underneath. It appeared to have been recently occupied, too. At any rate, the Hogbens are now wanted criminals, so the search is on. Oh, and they abandoned the dogs, who also seemed to be scrounging for scraps. Heather is going to be fussed about that."

"She'll take them over to Animal Lovers, I don't doubt," I said. "For dogs, that's like winning the lottery."

There was much more to hash over, but we ended the call so that Phillipa could pass on the latest news to the others.

Right after she'd heard from Phillipa, Deidre called me "Never mind the damn dogs, what's to become of Molly?" she wailed.

"She's alive. She'll all right. And we're going to find her," I said, with more assurance than I felt.

CHAPTER THIRTY-ONE

But the fact is, I was napping, and so gently you came rapping,
And so faintly you came tapping, tapping at my chamber door
That I scarce was sure I heard you. Here I opened wide the door.
Darkness there, and nothing more.

– Edgar Allan Poe

"Where will he have gone?" I asked.

"Home, or some version of it," Fiona replied. "The hunted animal returns to his safe hole."

"West Virginia?"

"That's my guess, but I haven't dowsed on it yet. I get the feeling that Stone is becoming mighty tired of our intuitions. Still, I feel we have to do something. *You* should do something."

I groaned. Of course I would have to call on all my clairvoyant skills to find Hogben. Especially where I was certain in my heart that to find the mad preacher was to find the missing child Molly.

Fiona and I were in my living room compulsively switching between CNN and the New England news channel in hopes of a break-through. Joe had taken the RAV4 to Home Warehouse to scout out supplies for his do-it-yourself project, a greenhouse beside the garage. Laura Belle, Fiona's grand-niece, was perched on the window-seat with Scruffy and Raffles. She sat quietly as always, simply being where she was, a hand on each dog's shoulder, watching with her morning glory eyes each trembling leaf and stirring grass blade outdoors. It was not her habit to talk much, a matter that had once been of much concern.

Hey, Toots, for a little person, this one is better than most. She doesn't pinch, wiggle, or holler in our ears, and she smells like cookies.

Cookies! Cookies! Raffles took a rapturous sniff of Laura Belle's hair.

"*This one's* name is Laura Belle. Not all children are little animals, if you will excuse the expression," I said.

You must mean disagreeable, disgusting feline animals, Toots. Canines have better sense, and better manners, than most human kids. Heel, Sit, Stay, No Bark. Those little slobs don't even know the basics.

"You have a point there," I said.

"Talking to Scruffy?" Fiona was used to my cross-conversations.

"Yes. They prefer Laura Belle to children who fidget and gab."

"Very discriminating of them," Fiona said. She took a map of West Virginia out of her reticule and laid it out on the old sea chest that serves as my coffee table. "If you want to go lay your head on that vision pillow for a few moments, I'll hold the fort here."

There was no help for it. Being a clairvoyant is like being a nurse. When it's a matter of life and death, we just have to step up. Putting the kettle on low for the nice cup of ginger tea I would need for the predictable nausea, I ducked into our bedroom and found the dreaded item where I had stashed it in Joe's closet under his duffle bag. I trusted that its potent vibes wouldn't turn him into a clairvoyant, too.

I shut the bedroom door and lay down with my cheek on the strongly scented linen. The aroma of that potent mix of divining herbs went right to my inner vision as always, the nose being the most direct route to the brain. It took a little while, but gradually a picture formed in the darkness of my closed eyes.

Mountains. I glided in misty blue air over mountains, moving softly downward toward a forest of towering pines. Rustic cabins. From a distance, they sprouted among the trees like brown mushrooms. As my feet touched ground, a sign became visible, but the lettering blurred as the scene rapidly faded from my sight. I stayed still, hoping that I would see more, but the vision would not return.

I opened my eyes, feeling decidedly hung over and woozy. I wished I had left the bedroom door open so that I could lean on Scruffy when I got back onto my feet.

There was a tap on the door. Fiona. "Are you all right, dear?" She opened the door a crack. "May I come in now? You were gone such a long time, we were beginning to worry."

Scruffy nosed past her, insinuating himself through the slit in that supple ways of dogs. *My superior senses tell me you need a loyal supporter, Toots.* He padded over to the bed and offered me his broad back. Just the ticket! Together we moved back into the living room, where I collapsed on the sofa. Fiona had already made the pot of ginger tea and a dainty cup of cambric tea for her grand-niece. A tray was waiting on a side table, the sea chest being entirely covered with Fiona's map. Scruffy and Raffles resumed their snuggle with Laura Belle on the window seat.

"What a trip!" I murmured. "Fiona, you'll want to dowse the mountainous regions. Although I suppose that's most of West Virginia. Anyway, what I saw was a remote cabin. I couldn't read the sign, but it occurs to me, since there *was* a sign, it *might* have been a state park. No trailers, just cabins, not too close together. I'm thinking maybe Hogben has rented a place under an alias, maybe even changed his appearance now that he's a wanted man."

"He'd have needed to alter his bombastic style as well. And get rid of that Moses staff." She poured me a cup of tea. "Here, drink this, dear. You look like something Omar dragged in."

"Oh, thanks for the compliment. Visioning is always such an enervating experience. Do you think we could get jobs as psychic profilers?"

"I prefer our amateur status." Fiona drew the crystal pendant from the warm place where it had rested between her breasts and studied the map, which was a large one that sprawled off the sides of the sea chest. Adjusting it to the north western part of the state, she held the pendant quite still over the mountainous regions. It began to swing in large lazy circles. "Tell me where that Hogben is hiding, O spirit of the crystal," she crooned.

The circles became narrower and smaller over one particular spot. I leaned forward to read the small red lettering. "Devil's Nose State Park. How appropriate. I'll call Phillipa but I don't know how Stone can possibly inspire the West Virginia police to check out that particular place."

I sipped my tea and let my stomach settle. Then I punched in Phillipa's number. "Hi, Phil. Fiona and I have been working on Hogben's trail."

"Well, that's just great. And I assume you're calling me with the latitude and longitude ?"

"We can't let this go, you know that."

"Yes, I do. I've just watched the Larssons making another heartbreaking TV appeal. Did you happen to catch that?"

"No. But I watched the first one, and that was wrenching enough. I did the vision pillow thing and Fiona dowsed. We're zeroing in on Hampshire, West Virginia where there are cabins for rent. Devil's Nose State Park."

"I'm not surprised that the devil had a nose in it," Phillipa said. "I don't know if there's any way that Stone can make use of this, but I do know he'll want to. He's beginning to get really fussed about Molly. It bugs him to think he may have lost the chance to rescue her from the compound. He does credit your visions, you know."

"Let me know what he's going to do, okay?"

"Absolutely. Back to you soon."

Fiona and Laura Belle left right after I talked to Phillipa. This turned out to be a good thing.

Still resting on the living room couch, I heard a weird kind of thump on the front door, the one that no New Englander ever uses, always preferring the kitchen entry.

Wake up, Toots! Stranger, danger, hurry, let me out there! Out there! Out there!

"No bark, no bark, you two! Scruffy, I am *not* getting up to let you guys out right now. What do you think I am, your personal doorperson? It's only some tree branch. You know how those old pines out there like to keep us on our toes with the odd falling limb. Nothing to worry about." I drowsed on while Scruffy paced and fumed, uttering the odd growl from time to time.

Joe rushed in a half hour later, looking quite agitated. The dogs used his arrival as an opportunity to race out of the pet door on the porch, barking all the way. "What's that thing stuck in the front door," he demanded.

"I don't know…what?" Alarmed by his anxious expression, I jumped up from the couch.

He dropped his handful of greenhouse brochures in the nearest chair and began to struggle with the wrought iron latch. My front door is the original one, wide-planked, heavy, and cranky. Getting it open is always something of a project. Joe tugged and wiggled the thing until it suddenly gave up and swung free.

Stuck there in the cranberry-painted planks was a wicked-looking arrow!

"Ceres save us," I exclaimed. "This old door hasn't had an arrow stuck in it since the 1600's," I said. "Do you suppose some hunter…? Oh, thank the Goddess the dogs weren't outdoors!"

"Damn thing is steel-tipped!" Joe said. "This is not hunting season, sweetheart. I'm calling the police. Do you suppose this has anything to do with Hogben?" He pushed the door shut and shot the big black bolt.

"No, they're gone. West Virginia, we think. This is someone else entirely." My second sight was kicking in again.

Joe was already dialing 911, explaining the incident to the dispatch person, assuring her that, although no one was hurt or, he thought, in imminent danger, we needed a couple of officers to survey the situation immediately. "Tell them to approach with caution. *The shooter may still be out there,*" he warned.

The realization made me scream, "The dogs! The dogs! Get Scruffy and Raffles in the house this instant." I could hear them frantically barking, as they had been ever since they ran outdoors. I dashed for the kitchen door, but Joe was quicker, shoving me behind his sturdy body.

"You stay here. Let me see what's up. Who knows... maybe they've treed the bastard."

"Never mind that! Just get them in here before he shoots again."

I tried to push past Joe, but he pushed back harder, stepped out the door, and shut it in my face. "Leave this to me, Cass."

He was using his commanding Captain Bligh voice. Might be useful in quelling mutinous Greenpeace recruits but not with me. I thrust the door open. Joe was standing just inside the porch, his hand on the door knob, surveying the yard. The dogs were at the edge of the pines where our driveway meets the main road, still barking but in a distracted, frustrated way. Obviously, the quarry had vamoosed!

"Whoever it was must have driven off," Joe said. "Didn't I tell you to stay indoors?"

I ignored him. "Scruffy! Raffles! Come at once!"

"At once" wasn't in their canine vocabulary, but they did slink back finally. I was reminded that there was something lacking in my dog-training regime. Heather had explained to me more than once that for a dog to come instantly when called was a life-saving imperative. She had a special whistle that brought her pack racing back to sit at her feet in perfect obedience.

Our growls are fierce and our teeth are sharp! We chased him away, Toots, but you'd better leave us outside in case he comes back. Comes back! Comes back!

"Not on your lives." I shooed us all inside and shut the door firmly. I could already hear a siren in the distance. It sounded as if the dispatcher had sent only one cruiser. "We're going to let the cops handle this one."

"That will be a refreshing change," Joe said. "Any chance this was a random act of violence, do you think?"

"That will depend."

"On what?"

"If it happens again. Or to anyone else in the circle."

I was already calling Heather on my cell phone. "Get your animals inside at once," I said. "We've just had an incident here. Someone shot an arrow into our front door. Oops! The cops are here. Gotta go. *Call the others!*"

"Yes. Go. Talk later," she said. The Goddess loves a friend who gets the message without endless chatter.

The cruiser sped into our driveway with its lights still flashing, the siren silenced, but not soon enough to keep the dogs from barking like crazy. We shut Scruffy and Raffles in the kitchen, complaining mightily, and went outside to meet the cruiser.

Two officers, a man and a woman, jumped out. Youngsters, by the look of them, but everyone in a position of authority was looking juvenile to me these days. A moment later, recognition clicked in; it was the same couple who had responded before to some weird situations we'd got into. "Barbie and Ken," as we privately called them. Barbie was fresh-faced with a mousy pony tail. Ken was a head taller and carried his thin frame awkwardly.

"Officer Mattel. My partner Officer Barb Roberts," he announced. "What's the trouble *this time?*" Obviously he remembered us as well. There'd been that snowy afternoon at Phillipa's with the Molotov cocktail, and before, when I'd given a couple of poisoners a taste of their own medicine. Almost got me arrested, as I recalled.

This time I had Joe to run interference. "Some bastard shot a steel-tipped arrow into our front door," he said angrily. "We think the guy must have driven up to the main road and walked in quietly. He wouldn't have had to come very near. Those hunting bows have a good range, maybe thirty yards. I'd been out on errands and the minute I drove into our driveway, I saw the arrow sticking in our front door. My wife was resting at the time and only heard a thump. Come on around to the front of the house, and I'll show you. Mind if I let my dogs out? They won't bother you."

The dogs galloped out with anxious barks, and Joe herded us all around to the front door. A sorry sight. I'd have to have it repaired. *Again.* Someone had put a bullet in it a few years ago. Joe had run outside that night, wearing only my big pink shirt. Thinking of that night, I giggled. Joe gave me a sharp look, and I stifled myself.

Ken and Barbie surveyed the murderous thing, and Barbie wrote a few words in her notebook. "See if there's any marker on it, would you, Ken?"

Her partner peered at the arrow and detected nothing. What did he expect? A name and address? Meanwhile, Scruffy and Raffles ran up to the road, scenting the footsteps of the intruder from where he had stood to where his car had been parked.

"The dogs are showing you right where he stood," I said. But Ken and Barbie hardly glanced their way.

"Do you know anyone who might be wishing you harm, Ms. Shipton?" Ken asked. I thought I detected a smirk on Barbie's face.

"Could just be a random act of violence," Joe said, bristling a little at the officer's tone.

"We did run into a little trouble in Salem over the Fourth," I admitted. "But those people are in jail now. The Salem Snipers, you know. No chance of their getting out on bail."

Barbie made another note. "And wasn't there some kind of fracas at the Hogben place in Carver recently?" she asked.

"I don't think it was Hogben. I can't see him shooting a bow and arrow, can you? Hurling a bolt of lightning, perhaps," I said. "And besides, they've fled the state, I believe. You might talk to Detective Stone Stern about that. Some runaway girls were involved."

My cell phone sang out, and I took the call. It was Fiona. "Phil just called me! *Trouble, Cass. Trouble!* This is just the sort of incident that my friend Circe tried to warn us about!" She sounded a bit hysterical.

"Stay calm, Fiona. The police are here and have the matter in hand."

"Ha ha. Well, *woe betide* that shooter if he shows up here."

Uh oh. I pictured Fiona loading her ladylike Glock. "Okay, Fiona. Don't you go off half-cocked. Goddess will get the shooter. And I'm going to send Phil over to stay with you," I said.

CHAPTER THIRTY-TWO

I shot an arrow into the air,
it fell to earth I know not where...

– Henry Wadsworth Longfellow

Right after Fiona clicked off, I punched in the number for Phillipa on my speed dial. Conscious of Barbie listening, I tried to be circumspect. "Ah, Phil...I just talked to Fiona and she sounded a bit addled. *'Woe betide'* and all that. I'm still tied up here with the responding officers. It's Mattel and Roberts, by the way."

I could hear Phillipa chuckle. "Them again? Poor dears."

"Yes, you might very well say that. So, anyway, I wondered if you'd pop over to Fiona's and check up on her. You know how antsy she can be when there's danger. But first, do take care to shut Boadicea and Zelda indoors where no one can take a pot shot."

"You want me to find out if Fiona is waving that handgun around, is that it? Okay. But that's not our only tizzy. I just had a second call from Heather. She's got all her little ones inside except Houdini, her newest rescue. She can't find that poor old greyhound. I told her to stay indoors, but I doubt she listened. So I rang Dick at the hospital, and he's going home to keep an eye."

"Fiona?" I reminded her.

"*Right, then*. I'm on my way."

A few minutes later, after having done absolutely nothing but look around aimlessly, except to remark that *the perp probably used regulation tackle, not a cross-bow*, Ken and Barbie wrapped up their "investigation" and took off to make their report. We were advised to call 911 immediately if there was any recurrence.

"My guess is, this was an isolated incident," Ken said. "Some vandal with new archery tackle and no brains."

"Maybe trying it out for deer-hunting season," Barbie added.

"That's not until October," Joe protested.

"Never mind, honey," I said. "The officers have done all they can, and the shooter is gone. For now, anyway. Phil says that one of Heather's dogs is missing. A greyhound. I'm going over there to give her a hand with the search. Keep Scruffy and Raffles in the house as much as possible."

"You're kidding, right?" Joe said.

"Well, if they have to go out, keep it short. And watch out for yourself, too."

"I don't think the shooter will be back here," Joe said. "He's made his statement, the coward."

❧

By the time I got to the Devlins', Maxwell had found Houdini in the apple orchard. Unconscious, with an arrow in his flank. Heather was fit to be tied, muttering Goddess-knows-what dire maledictions.

How fortunate that Heather had married a vet, who at least could take on any kind of trauma that afflicted her canine crew. The hazardous life we'd been leading since our karma had led us onto this vigilante path had sometimes spilled over to threaten our nearest and dearest. Other Wiccan circles were simply "Merry meet and merry part and merry meet again," with a little incense and chanting, and maybe the odd sky-clad dance in the woods.

Simple and bucolic, I thought enviously. *"And it harm none, do as you will." Where did we go wrong?*

Predictably, Heather glared at me and said, "This is all your fault, Cass!"

"Not this time, dearie," I protested. "I'm thinking this guy is linked to Salem, and you're the gal that got us into that nightmare."

"Salem? Holy Hecate! Oh, all right. Let's not quarrel. Dick seems to think Houdini will make it, but he may be left with a limp. As if being practically emaciated and traumatized and unsocialized isn't enough of a drag, poor little thing! He's the only one of the pack who knows how to sneak out of the dog yard for a romp. The squirrels get themselves drunk on fermenting fallen apples, and Houdini likes to race after them while they're weak and inebriated. Bit of nostalgia there for the old days of chasing the fake rabbit, I guess."

Dick, with Maxwell's help, took Houdini to his animal hospital in the Wee Angels ambulance. While we waited on the patio for the police to respond to this new assault, Elsa, wearing a little white apron, brought Heather and me a pot of French roast coffee with lemon peel, which she poured into Lenox demitasse.

After she had disappeared into the kitchen, Heather said, "I've begged Elsa not to wear that ruffled thing. Sometime I think I'm living in the second act of *Lady's Windermere's Fan*, if you know what I mean."

I knew more than I could say right then. Time enough for Heather to learn that her perfect couple were actors on the lam when Stone Stern had succeeded in getting the charges against them dropped. So I said, instead, "Heard from Jordan lately?"

Heather brightened. "Oh, yes. She's coming to visit this weekend with...you'll never guess!...your Tip. I think he's planning to stay with you, though."

"I haven't heard from him yet. But that's okay. I'll always have room for Tip. But do you think that's wise? Aren't you afraid they'll be targets for this guy who's running amok here?"

"Well, the thing is, Jordan has actually been working on control, as we advised. So now she believes she can initiate one more time trip, or whatever it is she does, and find out the rest of the story on Great-great-grandmama Alyce. And what about this 'darling Billy' of hers, tucked into her prayer-book and hidden in a secret lock-box? Wouldn't it be a hoot if it turned out that all us Morgans weren't the progeny of Captain Morgan after all?"

"Has it ever occurred to you, Heather, that there are some chapters in a family's history that are better left unread?"

"It's not in my nature," Heather said. "Nor yours, either, Cass."

Soon after, it was Ken and Barbie following up on the crazed archer for the second time today. It seemed as if they were taking our shooter a little more seriously now. Possibly because they'd consulted Detective Stern, and he'd connected the dots for them, making it clear at the same time that he was appalled by their casual handling of the first incident.

Heather took advantage of their presence to allow her pack a quick run in the dog yard.

No wonder Stone was pissed off! The detective was on his way to West Virginia to liaison with the Hampshire police force and the FBI in hopes of apprehending Hogben, and the whole operation was on Stone's head. He'd had to claim an anonymous tip led to the fugitive possibly holed up in Devil's Nose State Park with the missing girl, Molly Larsson, in order to hide the fact that the tip actually came from a couple of his wife's loony Wiccan friends. Added to this, Stone was worried about Phillipa's safety, with a sociopathic targeting members of our circle in his absence.

Phillipa, of course, had urged Stone to follow through on our psychic hits. She would be very careful and stay home with the doors locked, she'd assured him, because finding Molly alive was the real imperative. She'd agreed to check in with her husband on his personal cell phone several times a day. *Fingers crossed.*

Ignoring her promise, she immediately hurried to Fiona's, trying to avert an unfortunate incident, such as the discharge of a weapon in a residential area.

Ken and Barbie were diligent this time about taking notes and searching the Morgan estate, which was, of course, another exercise in futility. As soon as the cops left, Heather brought all her dogs inside again. Leaving them in Elsa's care, she headed over to the Wee Angels Animal Hospital to see how Houdini was recovering from surgery. I breathed a sigh of relief and went home.

Joe was at the kitchen table drawing plans for the greenhouse, with two disgruntled dogs at his feet. It had not been a fun morning. I told him about finding Houdini and our subsequent second interview with Ken and Barbie.

"I cleaned and loaded your Grandma's 22," he said. That was the rifle I kept for sentimental reasons where Grandma always had, hanging over the living room mantel.

"It's like being under siege," I said.

"We are," he said. "And I won't hesitate to defend us if I see so much as the glimmer of an arrow through the pines."

My hero! Not only was he ready to protect us against all intruders, judging by the delicious fragrance wafting through the kitchen, he was also roasting a chicken with garlic, lemon, and herbs. I opened the oven door. Ah! Roasted potatoes, too!

"Maybe we can have a little supper before the next crisis," I said.

Meanwhile, at Fiona's insistence, Phillipa had called Circe La Femme with an update on our situation. Circe said she wasn't surprised and she'd get back to them. Phil made a nice pot of kava-kava tea for Fiona and herself, and by the time they'd taken the last calming sip, Circe called back. She'd checked with a Wiccan friend in Bruce Gallant's task force, asking about some known associates of the Salem Snipers. The James Younger Gang, a private shooting club, had been mentioned (Gregor Sokol, one of the snipers, had been a member), and that rang a psychic bell with Circe. The boys had a reputation in Salem as a bad lot, and Circe knew most of them. So she called another pal at the Salem Town Hall to find out if any of those guys had obtained a license to hunt deer with a bow and arrow. *Bingo!*

"Circe's a witch after my own heart. It's like she's Miss Marple and Morgan Le Fey all rolled into one," Phillipa said when she called me later "Not just scrying in a crystal ball, but also making good use of contacts in high places. Circe's as well-fixed with friends and relatives in Salem as Heather is in Plymouth."

"Your opinion of Circe has improved? Good. And we're looking for who?"

"Paul Seed and Skene Moody of the James Younger Gang each applied for a bow-and-arrow hunting license this year. But I doubt it's both of them, don't you? Probably on some kind of vendetta inspired by friend Greg Sokol. I know I shouldn't, but I'm going to tell Mattel and Roberts to look into that angle. It's not, like, some wild allegation. After all, I am Detective Stern's wife and have a certain amount of credibility. Ken and Barbie will be anxious to get back into Stone's good graces. I wonder if they've actually ever solved a crime?"

"Why don't you ask them?" I said.

"No, but I will tell them who we're looking for."

I called Deidre at her shop to pass on Circe's news, but her assistant Hal said she'd gone home for dinner and left the evening hours to him.

"I'd better drive over there and update Dee," I said, stacking dishes after supper. "So much has happened today."

Joe was already heading out for his workroom in the garage. "I'll keep the dogs with me, don't worry," he said.

I found Deidre alone with the children. Mother Ryan had gone home, and Conor was at the pied à terre where he kept his books, slides, and photographic equipment safe from curious little hands. We sat outside at the redwood picnic table to watch the full moon, deeply yellow, rising over the Ryan jungle gym, while Jenny entertained her siblings with *Finding Nemo* in the living room.

"Circe's our hero, then," Deidre said. "Will the Plymouth police pull in those Seed and Moody characters, do you think?"

"Phil's working on it."

Those words were hardly out of my mouth before we saw the glint and heard the *thwack* of a steel arrow hitting the maple tree where the kids had a tree house. Instantly, Deidre and I slid off the bench and crouched down under the table.

"Mother of God! He's here!" Deidre whispered. "Jesus, I don't have my cell phone in my pocket. Give me yours."

"It's in my handbag. In your kitchen," I whispered back. "Maybe he didn't see us."

"Yeah. Or maybe he'll go away now that he's made his point."

As if in answer to that notion, a second arrow zoomed through the backyard and quivered in the top of the picnic table.

Jenny opened the back door and hollered, "What's that noise, Mom? Is it okay if I make popcorn?" By the time Jenny got to the word "popcorn," Deidre was already racing to the back door, where she blocked her daughter's body with her own and pushed her inside.

Before she could slam the door shut, I heard Deidre cry out.

She's hit, I screamed silently, still crouched under the table. There was nothing for it but that I would have to make a run for the house, too. I waited for three heartbeats. *No sound* except crickets, lazy summer breezes in the maple trees, and two manic poodles barking inside the house.

Who would believe a lady of my middle years could cover that distance in record time? I grabbed for the door, but...*it was locked.* Quick-thinking Jenny, I supposed.

Rolling myself into the smallest target I could muster, I banged on the door with both fists, conscious that my back was exposed to a steel arrow that could kill me instantly. *Or not.* I imagined feeling the pain of being split in two. My heart was beating a crazy staccato, and I felt chilled and feverish by turns. I could hear crying and barking on the other side of the door, but it did not open to my repeated assaults. *What in the Goddess's name was going on in there?*

It occurred to me right then that panic was not the best use of my emotions. Pulling on the shreds of my inner resources, my magical strength, I tried to wrap myself in that damned elusive blue-white light of protection. Next, I tried to conjure up a confounding mist. Then I visualized the phantom archer falling out of a tree and breaking his head. After that, I thought, *this fucking door is not going to open no matter how hard I beat on it!* But maybe it was safer for the Ryan kids to keep the door shut, even if it did leave me in a precarious target position. I could only hope that Deidre or *someone,* probably Jenny, was calling 911.

Finally, I thought, *I'd better get the hell out of here.*

You don't know how truly difficult it is to crawl any distance until you actually try it. My elbows and knees seemed to hit every rock, pebble, and twig in the Ryan's yard while I made my way to the front door. But somehow I felt safer when I had finally crawled around to the other side of the house. Even though there was a streetlight a short distance away, the demented archer would surely want to stay in the shadow of trees. In which case, the house would shield me from him. I stood up and rang the bell. Very insistently.

Willy, Jr., opened it a crack with the chain lock still in place. "Are you the police?"

"No, Willy, it's Aunt Cass. Let me in right away."

"Mommy's hurt. Jenny said not to let anyone in the house."

"Jenny will want me to help Mommy. *Jenny!*" I called into the slit in the door.

No answer from Jenny. But, after studying my face for a good while, Willy finally decided to unhook the chain lock so that I could wedge myself inside. Immediately he slammed the door shut again and locked it. *Good boy!*

Safe at last! It was good to have four walls around me. But more than that, I was conscious of an unreasonable relief, the sudden sure knowledge that the siege was over now. The mystery attacker would be hearing the same thing I was, sirens coming closer at full speed. He'd be feeling pretty macho, having avenged his pal Sokol, and he'd want to save his own hide. It was time for him to *get out of Dodge.*

I hurried after Willy into the kitchen where Jenny was holding a dish towel to her mom's arm, and there was plenty of blood. Bobby and Annie, their faces white, were under the table, not crying, just hugging the poodles, Salty and Peppy, who were struggling to get free and whimpering. Willy, who'd already been brave enough, joined them.

Goddess only knows how deranged, disheveled and hysterical I must have looked to Deidre. One glimpse of my face and she said, in her best motherly voice, "Let's calm down now, Cass. *It's all right.* The arrow just nicked me and went right through. But I fainted, can you imagine that? "

"Sure I can. Your arm is a mess, and it must hurt like crazy. Where's the arrow?"

"It does hurt, but I'm being brave so the rest of you won't fall apart. Willie put the arrow in the sink while Jenny was calling 911. Do you think there will be fingerprints on it?"

"Probably not. But I think the guy is gone, maybe for good. It feels to me as if this was his last hurrah, like the final display of fireworks at the Fourth of July. Why he tried to target you is a mystery to me. Where's the hydrogen peroxide?"

"In the lav. And look in the cabinet for a big gauze thingie. What makes you think he's gone?"

I was already in the downstairs lav gathering wound supplies. "Oh, you know...I just do," I said, as much to myself as to Deidre.

Two cruisers and a rescue wagon screeched up to the front door. "Open the door, Jenny, before they break it in," I said, beginning to unwind the dish towel from Deidre's arm.

I was glad enough a few moments later to turn the clean-up job over to the paramedics who hurried in the front door after two uniformed officers, both of whom had drawn guns. They holstered the weapons quickly when they saw that the room was full of children.

While the cops were clattering around through the house and one of the medics was trying to check Deidre's vital signs, she leaned around him and said, "Maybe he wasn't targeting me, Cass. Maybe he was following you. I think Sokol sicced him onto you and Heather. The Salem snipers probably think they'd still be enjoying their killing spree if it weren't for you two amateur sleuths."

Sadly, it made sense. I felt like Typhoid Mary, bringing death and destruction while remaining untouched by harm myself.

"Oh, don't beat yourself up," Deidre said. "We signed up to get the Salem Snipers, and *we did it*. That was the important thing. As long as the children are okay. Say, maybe you should call Conor." She scowled at the medic but winked in my direction. "Better you than me."

"Is Mrs. Ryan going to need stitches," I asked the medic.

"For sure. And antibiotics. We're taking her to Jordan Hospital right now. I assume you're a neighbor who can stay with the children?"

"Of course."

After the rescue wagon sped away with Deidre, I called Conor and got quite an earful of abuse, only cut short by his need to race over to the hospital to meet Deidre and bring her home.

Meanwhile I explained matters to the officers, who were not Ken and Barbie this time. "If you'll check with Detective Stern's wife, Phillipa, I believe she'll tell you the names of two young men who may have committed this assault and were responsible for two more incidents that happened today, one at my house and one at Heather Devlin's place. Or it might be only one of them. Salem boys, we believe."

This was the gist of my fairly garbled report. Since I kept repeating the part about Detective Stern's wife, Officers Novick and Norris finally checked with Phillipa. But I still had to answer many more questions about *why us* and how we came up with these names. Soon after, detectives replaced the uniformed men, and I had to go through the whole scenario again. Fortunately, one of the detectives was Billy Mann, Stone's partner. His familiar red-cheeked, beefy presence was reassuring.

In the course of their association, Billy Mann had got the word from his partner that it was a good idea to pay attention to our assertions, however wild they might sound. Mann assured me that Paul Seed and Skene Moody would be considered "persons of interest" and picked up for questioning, whether in Plymouth or Salem. Also that a Plymouth officer would be "keeping an eye out" until our assailants were off the streets.

It was getting late. Reluctantly, I called Joe and confessed that there'd been a "spot of trouble" at Dee's place, and I wouldn't be home for a while. He knew me too well, however, to be satisfied by that minimalist report and soon managed to get the entire scary story out of me. Like Conor, Joe was not a happy camper about this latest escapade, even though it was hardly our fault.

Joe insisted on joining me at the Ryans' while Deidre was getting patched up. Once he had me at arms' length, he fixed me with a steely gaze and said it was time for me and my friends to give up these dangerous *cops-and-murderers* games of ours.

Conor brought Deidre home about midnight and said just about the same thing.

We agreed. We promised. We kept our fingers crossed behind out backs. That was a little more difficult for Deidre, who had her arm in a sling.

CHAPTER THIRTY-THREE

See the conquering hero comes!
Sound the trumpet, beat the drums!

– Thomas Morell, from *Judas Maccabaeus* (Handel)

Although he was not a man who ever sought the limelight, Detective Stone Stern came back from West Virginia to a hero's welcome in Massachusetts, front-paged in newspapers and extolled on TV news, national as well as local. The classic photo, the one that was repeatedly pictured every time the incident was mentioned, showed Stone supporting a wan, pale Molly Larsson between himself and a female officer from the FBI as they brought the girl home. Her parents were incoherent with joy, and Mrs. Larsson cried enough tears to satisfy the rapacious press.

Reporters were not allowed, of course, to get anywhere near the traumatized little girl, or her parents after that first glimpse, but Stone was fair game, besieged at every turn. He scowled, ran his long fingers through his fine brown hair, and ducked for cover. He got away with this because he was not, by a long shot, the official spokesperson; that was the Massachusetts Attorney General and the FBI's Special Agent in Charge. But while the DA and the SAC trumpeted this gratifying success for the forces of law and order, their interviews didn't include any specifics about how the girl had been rescued.

In private talks, however, Detective Stern was having a hard time trying to explain to the FBI from whence came the anonymous tip that led the SWAT team to that cabin in Devil's Nose State Park where Pastor Hogben and his wife Eureka had been holding Molly in a closet. It hadn't come through the tip line that had been set up when Molly was first judged to be the victim of an abduction. Tip line calls had been taped. The FBI looked but did not find any record of a call from West Virginia to the detective's cell phone.

Stone "remembered" that someone had contacted him on the land line at work, a man who claimed to be a groundskeeper at Devil's Nose. The detective couldn't explain why he'd followed up. Just a hunch. Something every law enforcer learns to trust. When Stone faxed a news photo of the Reverend Hogben to the state park's office, a park ranger had recognized the preacher, although he no longer wore a beard and a clerical collar. Hogben had showed a picture ID card that gave his name as "Abraham Hobbs," and he'd introduced his wife as "Sarah." They'd rented the most remote cabin in the park and paid cash in advance.

No employee of the state park would take credit for the initial tip call to Stone, however, even though there was a substantial reward involved.

◦◦

"Grooming her to be his next handmaiden." Phillipa spat out when she filled us in on all the details that didn't get into the news accounts. We met at her house the morning after Molly's safe return to be filled in on all the details *not* fit to print. Gathered around the long marble table in Phillipa's kitchen, we fortified ourselves with strong coffee and fresh scones.

"I hope Stone manages to explain his way out of that suspicious 'tip'," Heather said.

"He's still under a cloud there," Phillipa sighed. "And he's had a few sharp words about it to me. '*Never again*,' and like that."

"He doesn't mean it," Fiona said. "He's the hero of the day, in the public's eye anyway, which never hurts a guy's ego, but his true satisfaction has to be in having found Molly. A real triumph. And that's what will be remembered about Stone when all this other nonsense fades."

"She's all right, then? Hogben didn't...did he?" Deidre shuddered. She was no longer wearing a sling, but her arm was still bandaged.

"She'll never be all right again, if you ask me." Phillipa whacked the life out of a few cloves of garlic with the flat of a chef's knife. "Snatched from that girl's camp, interred in some earthen hut at the Hogben compound for weeks, '*purified*' for goddess' sake with vegetable juices so as to be fit for her handmaiden '*duties.*' Then hauled off in the middle of the night to another state and imprisoned in a closet. But no, she wasn't raped. *That* would have come later."

"The Smith girl seems to have recovered," I said. "Remember that case two years ago, grabbed out of her own bedroom? Several months later she was spotted walking on the street with the abductor's other 'wives.' She's given interviews since and appears to be quite normal."

"On the surface, perhaps," Phillipa said, turned away to her Viking range, as she continued putting together a marinara sauce. When Phillipa's upset, she's like the sorcerer's apprentice in the kitchen.

"We ought to do a purification ceremony for Molly," Fiona said. "Today. *Strike while the trauma is hot,* I say."

"Can't hurt, might help," Heather said. "Blue candles. Blue flowers."

"The larkspur are still in blossom, and Stone has a photo of Molly in his study," Phillipa said, vigorously chopping fresh parsley and basil. "Let's do it now, and then you must all stay for lunch."

Our impromptu purification blessing was probably as healing for us as for Molly. Her abduction had been like an open wound to our souls all through these summer months.

I hoped with all my heart that our loving thoughts would touch her spirit.

Fiona had to go home for Laura Belle, but the rest of us stayed on gladly for penne with marinara sauce —who could resist that delicious aroma? And a bottle of Chianti Classico, which cheered us all considerably.

∽

Skene Moody had an alibi; he'd been in the company of other guys from his shooting club, The James Younger Gang, dodging grizzly bears in Canada while arrows were flying in Plymouth. That focused the investigation, conducted by both Plymouth and Salem detectives, on Paul Seed, who was proficient enough in archery to plan on hunting deer with bow and arrow. Seed had visited Greg Sokol more than once; the Salem Snipers were being held in Essex County Correctional Facility while awaiting trial. But all of this was circumstantial, and Seed would not confess. He claimed to have been at home with the summer flu, and his mother backed him up, swore she had been nursing him back to health at the relevant times.

Fiona and Circe la Femme were in communication over this inconclusive conclusion to Seed's alleged assaults. Circe said she would see what she could do. Seed had a very able attorney, but Circe had friends in the Salem Wiccan community with whom she would confer.

"I hate loose ends," I said when Phillipa stopped in with her usual basket of goodies, like a veritable *little black riding hood.* "And there have been too many of them. We haven't even resolved the matter of Maxwell and Elsa yet."

"Welcome to real life." Phillipa unpacked Cornish pasties and British rock cakes. "Stone said he'd look into it, but the matter will take time. I don't look forward to consoling Heather when her perfect couple returns to the stage, do you? Goddess only knows who her next housekeepers will be."

"You're right, Phil. Real life is never neat and tidy," I said. "That hemlock poisoner we thought we'd put away, for instance, got into some drama program at McLean Hospital and is practically free to roam at will, a case in point."

"My money's on the witches of Salem," Phillipa said. "Care to make a small wager?"

"What did you have in mind?"

"How about dinner for four at Chez Reynard in Chatham?"

"Speaking of loose ends. Francis Reynard probably has a beef against us for that business with his brother."

Let's face it," Phillipa said. "The South Shore is littered with folks who bear us a grudge for one reason or another. Is it a bet, then?"

"Oh, all right. You really think that Circe and her friends will catch up with Seed?"

Phillipa laughed, her wicked witch's chuckle that's so infectious; I couldn't help but join in the moment. The air crackled with our energy.

Joe came in the kitchen just then from setting the sprinklers in the herb gardens, bringing me a heady bouquet of blossoming lavender. "What are you two chortling about?" he asked, laughing with us at he-knew-not-what. "Bodes ill for someone." Not in the least nonplussed. One of the reasons I love him so much

CHAPTER THIRTY-FOUR

It seems we stood and talked like this before,
We looked at each other in the same way then,
But I can't remember where or when...

– Lorenz Hart

"Sometimes, when everything is right, you know, I can slip through *this* present into *another* present," Jordan explained. She sat on a purple cushion in Heather's turret room and gazed into a distance of time and place. "I never imagined I could just take off *whenever*, until I met you witch-ladies and started actually *working* with the all that *stuff* you taught me. Breath control, meditation, visualization, chakra alignment, grounding, balance. Easier said than done. Better than the alternative, though. I can do without those *wicked* surprise trips I used to take when something just *shoved* me through the portal, or whatever it is, you know what I mean?"

Heather, Fiona, and I were leaning against the paneling trying to be perfectly silent. *Surely my heartbeat is too loud,* I thought. Three white candles with tiny clocks embedded in the wax were alight in their chalices. The aroma of frankincense and sandalwood circled around us. I felt slightly giddy at the vibrations of flickering light, the visioning scent, and something else that I couldn't identify. Affected by the time slippage, I guessed. Clairvoyants are born with too thin a skin.

Jordan's dark hair was loose and flowing. She wore cut-off jeans and a woven tunic top in sunset colors that seemed to waver in ribbons. Her breathing was slow and even, and her expression was calm and meditative. I guessed she was invoking an alpha state, or even theta, 4 to 7 cycles per second, which would trigger ESP experiences. We waited, holding our collective breath.

The octagonal room's high windows were open, but the only sound was a slight breeze in the tallest pines. We were too high and away for street noises to intrude. If something didn't happen pretty soon, I might drop into the even deeper delta state and probably snore.

Jordan moaned once. Then it was quiet again for who-knew-how-long.

Suddenly she emitted a piercing keening sound that woke us all from our dreaminess with a jolt of alarm.

"Something going on there," Heather murmured to me.

"Shhhh," Fiona whispered. "Nothing must disturb the girl now or she'll rush back too soon, and we'll learn nothing."

Minutes passed but none of us could have told how many. Slowly Jordan stretched her neck, loosened her shoulders, shook her head, then her hands. She opened her eyes.

"Wow. That was, like, *too intense*, you know?" she said. "Alyce. Alyce May Alden. I wasn't *being* her. I was, like, *watching* her, but I could read her thoughts, feel her feelings. *Desperately* in love with a young man named William Conrad, her cousin. They are secretly planning to be married when he returns from the China Seas. No one must know because they are cousins. First or second—I don't know. Alyce can't imagine why this is forbidden. Only that such a union would never be allowed, and besides, he is very poor. That's why he's gone to sea, to make his fortune in China. Every day she waits for his ship to sail into the harbor, so joyful, so excited. Captain Morgan's ship."

"My great-great grandfather," Heather said. "Did she know him, were they married?"

"No. The captain is a stranger, and Alyce is immediately frightened when she opens the door of the parsonage, and he is standing there, tall and bearded, a stern man with a scar. It is he who comes to tell her and her family that her cousin has perished, swept overboard in a terrible storm. The captain has no knowledge of her secret betrothal, but he has found a silhouette of Alyce in Billy's kit, with her name written on the back, nothing more, and he knows Alyce's parents. Her father is pastor at the Plymouth Church. When he calls to condole, he finds Alyce alone, so he gently explains the reason for his visit. She cries out and faints."

Jordan paused. Tears were running down her cheeks. Fiona said, "Jordan, you must be more careful. You're absorbing too much."

Jordan wiped her face with the end of her tunic and continued. "The captain is very solicitous of Alyce's sorrowful state. Brings her a glass of sherry and tries to hold her hand, but she is clutching her prayer book. All she has left is Billy's silhouette that is hidden there. It matches the one he had of her. They had drawn them on a night long ago, the night they first kissed. I sense that the captain is thinking, 'All this for a cousin?' but he is also thinking, 'How lovely she is, this tender-hearted maiden.' She is wishing him gone, gone, *gone*, but she knows she must be very careful not to betray her unseemly grief. There will be time enough later, when she's alone."

Heather said, "I'm feeling a little guilty, dear, to have put you through all this. But I did learn something that's important to me."

Jordan said. "Good. I don't have to go back then?"

Fiona said, "Not on your life."

"At least I know now that we Morgans are really Morgans," Heather said. "Although if Billy had got Alyce pregnant, it might have explained some of my present-day idiot cousins. But apparently that's not the case. Poor Alyce. I do hope she learned to love Captain Nathaniel. Eventually."

Jordan said, "I can see scenes, feel some things, even *be* someone else, but we can never know what the heart will do, can we?"

"No, thank the Goddess. Let's go downstairs and have some really strong coffee," Heather said. "And a shot of sambuca wouldn't go amiss.

∽

Tip was waiting for us in the kitchen, talking to Elsa. He took one look at Jordan's face, which was noticeably pale and drawn, and scowled at the lot of us. He put his arm around her waist and eased her into a chair; *most tenderly*, I thought. Then he jumped back, pushed a chair against the wall, and sat there, with his brown arms folded against his chest, glowering. Elsa poured a glass of iced tea, squeezed in a lemon slice, and handed it to the girl. Then she put on the kettle and spooned out superfine coffee into the French Press.

Jordan smiled faintly and winked at me. "I call him by his real name when he gets like that," she said. "*Thunder* Pony." I looked at her, looked at Tip. Sometimes it's just too easy to read people, especially young people who haven't learned to guard their eyes.

Tip was in a fair way to get his heart broken, but when I got home later and related the day's adventures to Joe, he said, "That's called first love, and it's supposed to end in heartbreak. She is older, and bolder; he is young and vulnerable. It's a learning experience. She'll teach him how to make love." He sighed. I didn't like that much. *What's he remembering with that little smirk?* "Later, when he grows up and finds the true love of his life, he'll have some experience. It's the way of the world."

᠂᠂᠂

"It's the Wiccan way, not the way of the world," Fiona said to me later that day, meaning something entirely different, when she called with a report from Circe. *The way of the world.* My life resounds with echoes like that: serendipity?

"Paul Seed?" I inquired.

"Too slick by far for the cops, you know. And frankly, I don't know how hard they are pursuing the matter. After all, they have only our suspicions that Sokol has been targeting us from behind bars."

"Yes. I've decided I'm willing to let the matter go. Or rather, leave it to divine justice. As long as he never tries harassing us again."

"Not with archery tackle, he won't," Fiona said. "At least, not for a while. The poor lad got himself into a brawl at the White Shark Pub in Gloucester."

"I remember it well," I murmured

"Some big bruiser broke Paul's arm in two places," Fiona continued.

"I hope that wasn't Circe and her sisters," I said. "Three-fold bad karma and all that."

"Circe says no. She says she'd only begun to think on it when she got the news."

Maybe. But Phillipa wasn't going to believe that. She was still going to insist on my paying up on our wager. And who knows, really?

CHAPTER THIRTY-FIVE

'Twas I that led you through the painted meads,
Where the light fairies dance upon the flowers,
Hanging on every leaf an orient pearl.

– Thomas Stevens

We had much to celebrate on Lammas. The Salem snipers
were awaiting trial. Molly Larsson was home safe, and, we were
told, recovering from her ordeal. The Hogbens had been taken
into Federal custody, for kidnapping and various other related
charges. With deep breaths of relief, we gathered at Heather's
stone circle on the evening of August 1. It was a time to revel
in the peace, beauty, and bounty of late summer, even while
we prepared for the dark season to come. The South Shore
was rich in the colors of ripe apples and cranberries, plums,
blueberries, grapes, corn, squash, and pumpkins. Phillipa
had baked loaf after loaf of Lammas bread to serve with local
organic honey. No guests were invited to this very private
ceremony which we dedicated to our own recovery from the
turbulence of the past months. Healing and purification were
our themes, and gratitude for the blessings of survival in
danger. The scent of sage, lavender, and rosemary perfumed
our quiet rituals.

Near the end of August, we celebrated Laura Belle's birthday. A perfect Virgo child, gentle and sweet, but not as compliant as her serene demeanor would suggest, and of course, honest to a fault. Fiona suggested we organized a woodland picnic with the children rather than an official (noisy!) birthday party, which wouldn't have suited the quiet little girl at all.

I remembered a clearing where the sun shone more brightly than elsewhere among thick overhead branches in Jenkins Park. A bed of yellow-pinkish grass took advantage of the available light; a stand of asters would be blooming right about now, and goldenrod, inviting monarch butterflies. The Jenkins brook ran nearby, shallow at that end, cascading over wet-bright rounded rocks, edged in late summer by tall spikes of white turtleheads (*chelone glabrai*). Perhaps there would be dragonflies or jumping toads! A lovely place for a picnic party, provided that we were all well-protected with my herbal bug-off.

I arranged to wrest my grandchildren, Jackie and Joanie, away from the clutches of their English nanny, the impeccable Miss Sparks, and Deidre brought her two youngest, Bobby and Baby Anne. Well, we couldn't really call her *Baby* Anne any longer, now that she was about to begin nursery school. *Annie* she would be from now on. The vivacious little girl was the spittin' image of Deidre, the same blonde curls and mischievous sparkle in her eyes. My Joanie, although fair and apparently fragile, had her mother Freddie's cat-like strength. Jackie was the inheritor of his dad's tall muscular frame and uncommon green eyes (*my* eyes!) The twins had mostly outgrown their tendency to jabber away at each other in a language only they understood, and had advanced to imperative sentences such as "*More* ice cream!" or "I want to ride *now*."

We packed a simple lunch of little people's favorites, a selection that would only have met with scorn from Phillipa, but it suited our party just fine. After some soul-searching, I decided to invite Scruffy and Raffles to come along, first delivering a stern lecture on good manners for canines in the company of children. (Scruffy thought I should be lecturing the *nasty, grimy shorties*, not him.)

We assembled at my house and set out at eleven. Just walking the way of least resistance, avoiding roots and rocks, on our many foraging expeditions, had created our own special paths. Naturally Scruffy insisted on leading the procession. "No, no, not the eagle tree," I told him when we came to a fork in our personal map. "We're going to the soft, sunny place today, over by the brook. You can watch the fish, like you did last time."

"You're talking to your doggies now, aren't you," Deidre said. "Do you actually hear them answer?"

Humph. Those two meddling poodles at her house are too busy making trouble to understand anything but din-din *and* cookie.

Cookie! Cookie!

Muzzle it, pup. We're busy guarding here.

"Yeah, sort of," I said. "But they're on guard duty now, very important stuff. No time for chit-chat."

Damn straight, Toots.

I dropped back in case Fiona needed an arm, but she seemed to be a little spryer than usual today. She carried a tartan blanket and her reticule with apparent ease. Deidre hauled the cooler, and I hoisted the picnic basket. By the time we got to the clearing, we were quite ready to give up our burdens and rest in the sun. We were lucky. It was warm but not sweltering, and the sky was a mass of puffy white clouds that kept it that way.

We ate our peanut butter and marshmallow triangles, fingers of cream cheese and jelly, and mini-hot dogs with swigs of real lemonade. A pink cake with candles was brought forth, and we sang the birthday song softly to Laura Belle, whose rosebud mouth curved into a delicate smile. Her princess presence seemed to quiet the impulse to holler and romp in the other children, although at one point I did have to yank Jackie out of the brook when he leaned over to observe the fish.

The dogs crunched Milkbones and took long drinks from the tumbling brook, then settled down for a post-snack nap, as indeed, we did ourselves. Fiona leaned her back on a sturdy maple. Deidre and I propped ourselves against a fallen pine trunk of ample proportions. The children lay on the blanket between us and "read" the linen picture books that Fiona had dredged out of her reticule.

I was just drifting off blissfully when Deidre nudged me and whispered, "Cass! Look over there at the asters. What's that? A dragonfly or just a sunbeam?"

I looked. I saw a wavering light, like the shimmer of heat, roving from flower to flower.

"*Faeries*," Laura Belle announced in her high, clear voice, pointing at the sparkle, her morning glory eyes wide and wondrous. "See the faeries, Aunt Fifi?"

Fiona turned with infinite care and followed her grandnieces dimpled finger. Bobby, Annie, and Joanie looked up from their books. Jackie, who was beside me, started to jump but I clamped my hand on his arm. "Don't scare them away," I said quietly.

"I want one. Get me one, Grandma!" Jackie whispered urgently.

"*No!* You stay put *or else.*" Seeing my expression, Jackie gave up his antics and leaned against my arm docilely enough.

"Laura Belle says they're faeries," I whispered to Deidre. "And she can only speak what's true, according to Fiona. She says her grandniece has been blessed by Ma'at, the Egyptian goddess of truth."

"Oh, dear! Speaking of blessings, we'll need to leave gifts for the fairies as we did at Litha." Deidre, who had created hundreds of faery dolls, did not doubt what her eyes were seeing, so closely did it match her imaginings. Only I felt a note of uncertainty. Were we all deluding ourselves, dazzled with sunshine and duped with August heat? I looked at Scruffy and Raffles, thinking that dogs are not deceived by illusions. They had both lifted up their heads in attitudes of alertness, but otherwise they remained still as statues, sniffing the air and eyeing the woods, but without alarm. Strange! If the unseen presence had been anything else but faeries...a ghost, for instance...the dogs would have "run for the hills."

"Listen," Fiona murmured softly.

What was that? A breeze? A swarm of something? I wondered.

At once, we were surrounded by a humming music that seemed to be coming from all sides. The clearing shone with an opalescent radiance. Starry pinpoints of light danced around the tips of asters and goldenrod. A frisson of eeriness flowed from the top of my head to the tips of my fingers; exciting but not unpleasant.

Why is it that children are hardly surprised when imaginary creatures come to life? Maybe because they're immersed in stories of faeries and elves and magical kingdoms where dreams come true? Not that Miss Sparks ever read anything of that sort to the twins, but I did, often. And at this moment, the five youngsters were as enraptured as if they were watching a puppet theater, heads swiveling in wonder at the luminous, singing circle of *something* all around us.

Laura Belle clapped her hands with no sound at all, just as I thought I saw a tiny silver pixie flying from flower to flower.

"See him!" Deidre sighed. "I've never made a silver one. I should try that!"

Slowly, achingly, the vision, or whatever it was, faded and hummed to a close, leaving only the ordinary woodland whispers and brook murmurs.

Laura Belle removed a pink candle from her cake, licked off the icing, and handing it to Fiona. "For the faeries, Aunt Fifi."

Surprisingly, my Jackie immediately fished a tiny model car, a red convertible, out of his pocket, and handed that to Fiona as well. We arranged these miniature treasures on the stump of the log we'd been resting on.

"It needs something else," Deidre said thoughtfully. "Bobby? Annie?"

Bobby brought forth a tiny action figure, like Conan the Barbarian. Annie had a scrap of embroidered hankie, looking as if it were meant for a doll. Fiona added butterscotch candies from her reticule.

"Let's all hold hands before we leave," Fiona suggested, and we did. I think we could all feel the blessings that fell on our circle, softly as snowflakes or stardust, weightless but tingling with energy.

It seemed the right time to pack up and leave, so we did that. Deidre had a high, sweet soprano, and she sang as we walked back to the house.

Forever I'll be glad and good,
And blessed I will be,
For I have seen the faeries dance,
And they have sung to me...

The children chimed in, even Laura Belle, and we made quite a lighthearted party trudging home. On the way, I spotted a maple branch on which every leaf had turned scarlet, the first I'd seen this year. Signal of summer's end.

Autumn was on its way, brisk and energizing, bringing Goddess-knows-what unknown challenges. I felt the chill of presentment. There would be a rich harvest of blessings, and something unexpected (something wicked?) coming our way.

But not yet, not yet. We were still enthralled in deep summer, and alive in the moment, as we should be. Tomorrow would take care of itself. Best not to rush the river to go faster.

Just listen to the children singing. I wondered if they would remember this day when they were all grown up and sensible.

Well, we wise women would be there to remind them. Believe in magic and it is everywhere around you, invisible and real, like love.

THE CIRCLE

Cassandra Shipton , an herbalist and reluctant clairvoyant. The bane of evil-doers who cross her path.

Phillipa Stern (nee Gold), a cookbook author and poet. Reads the tarot with unnerving accuracy.

Heather Devlin (nee Morgan), an heiress and animal rescuer. Creates magical candles with occasionally weird results. Benefactor of Animal Lovers Pet Sanctuary in Plymouth.

Deidre Ryan, recent widow, prolific doll and amulet maker, energetic young mother of four.

Fiona MacDonald Ritchie, a librarian and wise woman who can find almost anything by dowsing with her crystal pendulum. Envied mistress of The Glamour.

The Circle's Family, Extended Family, and Pets

Cass's husband **Joe Ulysses**, a Greenpeace engineer and Greek hunk.

Phillipa's husband **Stone Stern**, Plymouth County detective, handy to have in the family.

Heather's husband **Dick Devlin**, a holistic veterinarian and a real teddy bear.

Deidre's new love, **Conor O'Donnell**, a world-class photographer and Irish charmer.

Cass's grown children

Rebecca "Becky" Lowell, the sensible older child, a family lawyer, divorced.

Adam Hauser, a computer genius, vice president at Iconomics, Inc.,

married to

Winifred "Freddie" McGarrity an irrepressible gal with light-fingered psychokinetic abilities,

and they are the new parents of twins, **Jack and Joan Hauser**.

Cathy Hauser, who lives with her partner **Irene Adler**, both actresses, mostly unemployed.

Thunder Pony "Tip" Thomas, Cass's Native American teen-age friend, almost family, whose tracking skills are often in demand.

Fiona's family

Fiona is the guardian of her grandniece **Laura Belle MacDonald**, a.k.a. **Tinker-Belle**.

Deidre's family

Jenny, Willy Jr., Bobby, and **Annie**

Mary Margaret Ryan, a.k.a. **M & Ms**, mother-in-law and devoted gamer.

Betty Kinsey, a diminutive au pair, a.k.a **Bettikins**.

The Circle's Animal Companions

Cass's family includes two irrepressible canines who often make their opinions known, **Scruffy,** part French Briard and part mutt, and **Raffles,** his offspring from an unsanctioned union .

Fiona's supercilious cat is **Omar Khayyám,** a Persian aristocrat.

Phillipa's **Zelda**, a plump black cat, was once a waif rescued from a dumpster by Fiona. Recently, Phil has added a rescued boxer, **Boadicea** to her family.

Heather's family of rescued canines is constantly changing, and far too numerous to mention, except for **Honeycomb,** a golden retriever and so-called Therapy Dog who is Raffles' mother. Deidre's two miniature poodles are **Salty** and **Peppy**.

ELSA'S VEGETARIAN CASSOULET

Homemade cornbread makes a good accompaniment. Beans and corn together make a complete protein, which is a vegetarian bonus.

2 leeks
6 ounces "Baby Bella" mushrooms
¼ cup olive oil
3 stalks of celery, sliced
2 carrots, sliced
1 large tomato, diced
2 cloves garlic, minced
2 (14-ounce) cans white beans (cannellini) drained and rinsed
2 peperoncini (Italian pickled peppers, slightly hot)
2 teaspoons Herbs de Provence (or pinches of dried basil, rosemary, and thyme)
½ teaspoon salt
¼ teaspoon pepper
1/8 teaspoon ground cloves
1 cup water (add more if casserole appears dry)

Trim off the green leaves of the leeks and cut the white part in half lengthwise. Wash between layers and pat dry. Chop the leeks. Clean the mushrooms and cut them in half.

Heat the oil in a heavy pan that can be transferred to the oven. Sauté the leek, celery, and carrots until they have begun to change color and some pieces are lightly browned. Add the mushrooms, tomatoes, and garlic, continuing to sauté for about 3 minutes. Stir often.

Add the beans, peperoncini, Herbs de Provence, salt, pepper, ground cloves, and water. Bring to a simmer and transfer to a preheated 300 degree F. oven. Cook for about 40 minutes. Check a couple of times to be sure the casserole has not become too dry. Add a little water if needed.

Taste to correct seasoning, adding more salt and pepper if needed.

4 servings.

CASS'S GREEK AMERICAN
CHOP SUEY

3 tablespoons olive oil
1 pound ground lamb (ground turkey can be substituted)
½ cup chopped onion
1 sweet bell pepper, chopped
2 cloves garlic, minced
1 (14-ounce) can chopped tomatoes with juice
¼ cup chopped fresh flat-leaf parsley
1 teaspoon dried oregano
Crushed red pepper to taste
½ teaspoon salt
Black pepper to taste
¼ cup pitted, halved Kalamata olives
½ pound medium shell pasta, cooked according to package directions
½ cup or more crumbled feta cheese

In a large skillet, heat about a tablespoon of the oil, and brown the lamb, breaking it up with a spatula, until there is no pink left. Drain the lamb to remove the extra fat.

Heat the remaining oil and sauté onion, sweet pepper, and garlic until slightly softened and fragrant, about 3 minutes.

Add the browned ground meat, and sauté together 3 more minutes.

Add tomatoes, parsley, oregano, crushed red pepper, salt, and pepper Simmer the mixture with cover ajar until thickened and reduced, about 20 minutes. Stir often. If the mixture seems too dry (depends on the tomatoes), add a little broth or wine.

When the sauce is finished, add the olives and continue to cook about 1 minute.

Combine meat sauce with cooked pasta in a serving dish. Sprinkle with feta cheese and serve.

Note: If ground turkey is used in place of lamb, the first step can be skipped as there will not be extra fat. Simply brown the meat with the vegetables, again until there is no pink.

PHILLIPA'S BISTRO CHICKEN WITH
ARTICHOKE HEARTS

2 tablespoons olive oil
2 tablespoons butter
3-pounds boneless, skinless chicken breasts, each cut in half
2 shallots chopped small or 1 small yellow onion
1 ½ teaspoon dried tarragon
Salt and pepper to taste
2/3 cup dry vermouth or dry white wine
1 cup chicken broth plus more if needed
2 tablespoons lemon juice
2 cans Pastene quartered artichoke hearts, drained (or whole artichoke hearts cut into quarters)
2 tablespoons flour, optional

Heat the oil and butter in a large skillet, and sauté the breasts until they are golden on both sides. Add the shallots when you turn over the chicken. Season the chicken with tarragon, salt, and pepper. Be sparing with the salt; the broth will add more.

Add the vermouth, 1 cup broth, and lemon juice. Cover and cook the breasts through on low heat, about 20 minutes, until the largest piece is shows no pink juices when cut in the middle. Do not overcook.

Meanwhile, drain the artichoke hearts and, if necessary, cut them in halves or quarters.

Remove the chicken Over high heat, reduce the pan juices by half Watch carefully that the juices don't boil down to nothing.

Cut the chicken into chunks and return it to the pan along with the artichoke hearts.

The dish can be prepared a day or a few hours ahead to this point; refrigerate.

When ready to serve, heat the chicken through over medium-low heat.

This step is optional: If you want to thicken the pan juices, pour 1 cup of additional cold broth into a jar, add the flour, and shake until no lumps remain. Heat in a small heavy saucepan , whisking constantly, until thickened. Simmer for 3 minutes (to cook the flour), stirring often, then pour the sauce into the chicken and stir gently.

Makes 6 or more servings.

Note: A (14-ounce) can of drained, rinsed chickpeas can be added to this dish.